THE FOREVER MARRIAGE

THE FOREVER MARRIAGE

A NOVEL

ANN BAUER

THE OVERLOOK PRESS
NEW YORK, NY

This edition first published in paperback in the United States in 2013 by

The Overlook Press, Peter Mayer Publishers, Inc.
141 Wooster Street
New York, NY 10012
www.overlookpress.com
For bulk and special sales, please contact sales@overlookny.com

The Library of Congress has catalogued the hardcover edition as follows:

Bauer, Ann.
  The forever marriage : a novel / Ann Bauer.
    p. cm.
  ISBN 978-1-59020-721-5
1. Widows--Fiction. 2. Marriage--Fiction. 3. Self-realization in
women--Fiction. I. Title.
  PS3602.A933F67 2012
  813'.6--dc23

                                    2012008053

Book design and type formatting by Bernard Schleifer
Manufactured in the United States of America
ISBN 978-1-4683-0632-3

10 9 8 7 6 5 4 3 2 1

For John, my Riemann

April 2007

Jobe died on a cool April morning that smelled of wet earth and cherry blossoms.

It was just after nine o'clock and Carmen stood in the kitchen, about a dozen feet away, holding a dish towel in one hand and her second cup of coffee in the other. She had been looking in his general direction, out the window above his daybed and into the backyard, thinking about the many things she might be doing if her husband were not dying: walking the dog; sitting on a riverbank with a sketchpad and a pencil; lying naked in a bed at the Days Inn next to her librarian, watching *The Wire* on HBO.

On the sun porch where he lay, Jobe took a long, weak, wet breath and then simply stopped. It was as when a mosquito quit buzzing, or a jackhammer was turned off. His silence caused a still, nearly prayerful relief. So much so that it took a full minute for Carmen to compute what it meant, that this thing she'd been waiting for had finally happened. And once she did—realizing that she was, for the first time in more than twenty-one years, uncoupled and alone—she walked toward her husband's body, excitement mixing inside her with horror and a snaking sense of dread.

It was not as if she'd killed him, Carmen told herself. And simply craving someone's death was not the same thing. Yet when her steps echoed on the oak floor, she tried to quiet them, setting her feet down carefully, one after the other, toe and then heel.

There was a pre-Christmas sense of the possible. If Jobe was gone, it would mean everything was over: her marriage, their family, this whole false happy life. She touched his neck while watching a rabbit cross the backyard, its haunches unfolding loosely as it hopped. Her husband was still warm and she doubted for a moment that he was actually dead. Perhaps he was just holding his breath and waiting, curious to see how she'd react. But that wasn't like him—it was, actually, more like *her*—and when she put her fingers in front of his mouth, she felt nothing where there should have been an exhalation. She washed her hands anyway and leaned against the lip of the sink, staring at his body. A wave of something unexpected moved through her, loneliness like a dark thundercloud. What now?

His mother, Olive, had gone home to sleep just an hour before; she'd been up with Jobe all night, waiting, and was exhausted and cold. Carmen had tried to make her comfortable, bringing her a sweater and a thick quilt around 2:00 a.m. The house was drafty, Carmen whispered, the night cooler than she'd anticipated. Olive put on the sweater but draped the comforter mostly over her son. In the morning, Carmen found her mother-in-law pale and icy and offered to make tea, but the old woman only waved her liver-spotted hand and spent several minutes fussing with Jobe's blankets as if he were a baby in a crib. Carmen put the coffee on instead and stood drinking her first cup and watching from the doorway, aching for Olive, thinking about how Jobe was, in fact, her baby. She would be forever crippled by his death.

So would the three children that Carmen had then gotten off to school. This included Luca, their eldest, who should have graduated two years ago but went instead to a day program at the high school on a small blue bus. He carried his lunch in a cloth bag, holding it against his body and swaying as he waited on the curb. Every morning Carmen peered through the front window, watching the vehicle stop and swing its door open, fascinated by the way her son climbed up the steps intently, tilting his egg-shaped body forward as if walking against a strong wind. In order for her to be released from this marriage, a mother had to lose a son and this boy had to lose his father. An undeniably good man. It wasn't fair.

Carmen walked in a half-circle around Jobe's still body. Something like a sob threatened to open in her throat but she swallowed it. She wouldn't give up the house, she thought instead. The boys loved it, especially Luca, who had for ten summers stumped around the yard after his father, a foot shorter with a rectangular head set deep into his shoulders, learning one weekend to plant ground cover and prune rose bushes then forgetting it all by the next. The architecture was vintage Baltimore: a three-story A-frame with a peaked attic and an old-fashioned weathervane, built in 1900—their dream home back when Jobe was well and able to repair whatever went wrong. High ceilings, floors of slanted oak, windows that hung on ropes and rattled in winter. The sink was original: thick, cream-colored porcelain made into a deep bowl and a drain board, jutting straight out from the wall.

Carmen paced through a slant of sunshine from the south, feeling its contradiction on her back, draining her cup. Suddenly, she was full of questions. Jobe was the one who'd always known about form and process. There were procedures you were supposed to follow in this situation. But she could not recall in this moment precisely what they were. Was she supposed to phone 911, though he was already dead? Should she call the police nonemergency number? Or could she go directly to the funeral home where Jobe had told her he wanted his service?

Someone—at the very least—had to call Olive. Then, perhaps, the rest would follow. A proper funeral, a burial. But Carmen was not certain what would happen if she picked up the phone. She wished now for tears, if only for Olive's sake. "I'm finally free!" she imagined herself blurting out to the old woman. "Who would have thought after all these years of waiting, he would disappear easily as that?"

The person she really wanted to talk to was Danny—he would make this alright, put it in the proper perspective, understand her point of view—but he was probably sitting behind the information desk where he'd been the day she met him. Enoch Pratt had opened its wide doors half an hour ago and by now Danny would be giving out information about Greek myths and Milton Friedman and the sex lives of animals. She couldn't call him at work; she couldn't call him at home, either. For the past year, they'd conducted their relationship mostly through a series of text messages, but Carmen was puzzled over how, exactly, to key this one in: *Jobe died 2day. Meet me @ 5?*

So instead, she watched her husband not breathing. His body seemed an affront without life in it: huge and wasteful, like an empty container that would have to be disposed of at great difficulty and cost. She envisioned herself telling their children, the two—Siena and Michael—who would not be surprised because they had been expecting this, coming in from school and peering around doorways every day for weeks as if they were asking the question. And Luca, who probably would not understand no matter how many times she explained.

"But when will he come home?" she imagined their older son asking in his thick voice. And in that moment, looking at Jobe's still body, she felt a clear stab of pain. This, though she knew it came too late to redeem her, was a relief.

Outside, birds sang. The smell of dewy grass came through the window screen, along with pale sunlight and a sudden gust of warm air. Carmen crossed the room again and reached out more gently. She took Jobe's hands—which were large and sickly orange with prominent veins—and placed them neatly at his sides. He was her husband and she had loved him, though never well enough. Her resentment dissipated quickly and she ran two fingers over the skin of his cheek, drawn taut above the line of his beard, up and over the curve of the bone. She'd taken good care of Jobe these last months, never once forgetting his medication, getting up in the middle of the night to sit with him while he breathed through the pain. There had been plenty of chances to end his misery and her own—for months, thanks to the bag full of morphine in the refrigerator, his life had been literally within her control—but she had never seriously considered it. Even those few times when Jobe himself, with eyes like an animal, had proposed the idea. She could see he was more frightened than hopeless, hoping she'd say no, and so she had.

There was only that one time on their honeymoon, many years ago, when he had almost died and she'd realized with a bolt of clarity: *This* was the only way she would ever be free.

The conditions had been right that night: darkness, a sharp drop-off into the Mediterranean, not a soul around to witness. But it hadn't happened. In fact, it was she who caught his arm and reeled him back from the edge, but whether out of conscience or affection Carmen couldn't say. She considered, as she always did when she thought of this, whether she would have been happier living the other way, as the brave young widow who was her secret twin.

If Jobe had died back then, she probably would have moved from Baltimore to New York or San Francisco. She might have gone on to find someone for whom she felt real passion, and with Olive's blessing. She almost certainly would not have had Luca whose defect, the doctor had told them—given her young age—was an anomaly, one inexplicably blighted sperm or egg, a mistimed collision. Had she let the unwanted husband fall to his death, all this could have been prevented. These children, this house, two decades of life steered in the wrong direction, as if she'd veered off a highway accidentally and couldn't get back on.

Carmen shivered and glanced around at the sparkling, silent room. Was it possible that Jobe could hear the things she was thinking, now that he was dead? Perhaps he had discovered in just the last five minutes her infidelities and frustration. The fact that she had played this game in her head hundreds of times over the years: If she could go back in time, would she change things? Unmarry the man she had never wholeheartedly loved and prevent the damaged child from being born? She answered herself differently on different days. Today she could not think clearly enough to decide. So instead, she took a breath and lifted her hand to pick up the phone.

"Olive," she said, when the old lady answered. "He's gone."

The funeral went off without a hitch. Bewildered by the details, that's how Carmen had come to think of it, like a stage production they'd managed to put together without anyone falling down or forgetting his lines. The children, dressed in black, were model mourners. Siena wore her hair on top of her head and cried quietly during the entire service. Michael looked startled, as if he had seen something that frightened him, his legs still for once as if there were weights strapped to his feet.

It was Luca who surprised her. Not only had he understood when she told him about his father, but he had appeared already to know. He'd nodded his large head in the way he did—without much of a neck to flex, it was more a bobbling gesture—and looked at her with an oddly wise expression in his small, wide-set eyes. Now, sober and stolid and wearing one of Jobe's striped ties though it was at least five inches too long, he kept one wide hand on the casket as he stood beside it, stroking lightly as if his father inside would feel this and be soothed.

Someone waved at Carmen from across the chapel. It was Danny, who looked like a puppet among this crowd of tall men. Jobe's two brothers—Will and Nate—her sister Esme's banker husband, the professors from Hopkins wearing their uniform of unruly beards and open-necked shirts, black jackets, and long, pipe-leg pants. Even Michael, who had grown several inches in the six months since turning twelve.

Only Luca, who was built more like a platypus than a man, was similar in stature to her lover. Historically Carmen had preferred tall, broad-shouldered men, but she also had a weakness for paradox: Danny had Cherokee skin and hip-length dark hair combined with pale Irish eyes. He drove a Jeep and listened to rap music, but he also wore reading glasses on a chain around his neck and sat at an information desk each day.

She waved back, discreetly, with two fingers. Danny had said he would come but she didn't know whether to believe him—*Who was filling in at the library? How had he explained his relationship to Jobe?*—and now that he was here, she wasn't sure she was glad. It felt unnatural for the two men to be together in one room, now that her husband was dead. Whereas, she recalled, she'd found it strangely stimulating the one time they met before.

It had happened entirely by accident, about a year ago. Jobe and Carmen had been at a Federal Hill restaurant with people from his department and she had leaned back during a long conversation about the mathematical constants of bridge building, letting her ears relax so that she stopped processing syllables and heard only the various notes and sounds. When she saw Danny walking behind the maître d' with a blonde at least ten years younger than he, she was numbly unsurprised. Carmen tracked them as if they were characters on a movie screen: the woman especially, who looked like a superhero cartoon character, constructed in perfect proportion for a form-fitting zip-up rubber suit.

Danny was in a soft blue shirt that night and his long black hair hung in a braid down his back. The very same back that she, Carmen, had dug her nails into just that morning as she strained against him and came. It was surreal to see him now, devotedly living his other life. But there was also power in watching—in his being unaware of it—and Carmen basked for several seconds in an unfamiliar sense of control.

Then Danny turned his head, as if he'd felt her eyes on him. He registered her with two blinks and accommodated quickly. Carmen saw him lean toward the blonde and whisper something into her ear; she imagined his breath, laced with American Spirit cigarettes and the vapor of hazelnut-flavored coffee, which he drank at his desk all day. Then they were walking over. It was an interesting move—ballsy and unnecessary—that felt to her like the opening play in some sort of high-stakes competition. It turned her on, not just to him but in a general way.

"Carmen, hi! I thought that was you." Danny seemed proud, standing close enough that she could smell his cologne, which was leathery and sweet. "I'd like you to meet my wife, Mega."

Danny and the superhero shook hands all around: Carmen, Jobe, plus the various other mathematicians who were sitting at the table, nodding and pushing their glasses up, ogling Mega's tiny waist and perfect melon breasts.

"Jobe," she said, as her lover's hand reached out to meet her husband's, "this is Danny. He works at Enoch Pratt."

"Ah, the library," Jobe said, nodding. And there was that interminable pause that always followed his pronouncements of the obvious, while everyone at the table struggled for a way to continue. Carmen breathed through the space, the way she'd learned to do.

"So what do you do, Jobe?" Danny finally asked, though he knew not only *what* but also the specifics of the Riemann hypothesis and had gone so far as to research "nontrivial zeros" one day when the library was slow. "I can usually wrap my head around any topic well enough to give you the high points, at least," he'd told Carmen afterward. "But I've read about a dozen articles on this Riemann thing and whatever it is just evades me. Something about prime numbers, quantum mechanics, the meaning of life." Danny had shrugged. "Your husband must be freakishly smart. Some kind of modern-day Gauss."

Yet now Jobe answered, as he typically did, "I teach," and let it go at that. Sometimes his modesty struck her as false, this two-word response somehow more pompous than the longer one: *I'm the Dwight Enright endowed professor of higher mathematics at Johns Hopkins.* On this night in the restaurant, however, she saw that it was in his view simply the most accurate and economical answer. Warmed by the combination of soft candlelight and wine—as well as the weirdly satisfying sense of being, literally, between these two men—she reached out and took Jobe's hand.

"You make it sound as if you have a third-grade class some-where," she said, stroking his knuckles with her thumb. "Like you're teaching simple division."

Jobe looked startled. It was, possibly, the first time she'd touched him in weeks. He'd glanced at Carmen with gratitude—she remem-bered this now, at his funeral, how his eyes had suddenly been alight—before one of the other math guys broke in. "Might as well be," he said gruffly. "Teaching the undergrads. All they care about is getting drunk and getting laid."

"Sounds just like every third grader I know." Danny flashed a quick "no-offense" grin and waved. "We'll let you get back to your meal then," he said, though there was no food left, all the plates had been cleared, and only Jobe was still drinking coffee.

This had happened during his remission: after the checkup where Jobe's original cancer was pronounced "cured" but a few weeks before he would begin running a low fever, and bruises spread like ghostly crabgrass across his back and legs. That night when he was supposedly healthy they had made love, for the last time ever, even though she'd been slightly too full from the meal at the restau-rant: fat homemade pasta, oily salad, and tiramisu for dessert.

If it had been Danny, she would have avoided sex because she felt flabby and possibly flatulent. But this was her husband. He had pulled at her nightgown, tugging at the hem like a child, the way he had for more than twenty years. And she had lifted it over her head without embarrassment. They hardly kissed any more; she couldn't remember the last time she'd encountered his tongue. But that night she'd tried, a drunken experiment, and his beard felt stiff and foreign against her cheeks. Within minutes, Jobe was inside her and his long, bony body was against hers, like a pencil indenting a soft eraser. He moved in and out, pistons working. She couldn't have reached his mouth again if she had wanted to—he was rigid and had drawn back for thrusting, so his face was too far above her head—but this only added to the alchemy. Alone beneath Jobe, Carmen entered a dreamy place where divisions disappeared.

Nearing orgasm, she pictured the moment when Danny and Jobe shook hands: palms pressed together, the two men had mingled. Minute dustings of each one left on the other. And this—having each of them inside her within the space of less than a day—felt not like a betrayal but like a gift: She was bringing together two completely disparate men to make a whole. The next morning, she'd been mortified by all this mental blather, even though only she knew how ridiculous she'd been.

Now she watched the priest drape Jobe's coffin with an embroidered, white cloth and imagined his gaunt, still body inside. His cells, finally, had stopped reproducing their mutant selves. The factory of ducts and tubes that had produced his half of their children was silent. The hand that had once touched Danny's was beginning already to decay.

The man who'd been present at the births of their children. The one she'd once promised to love until they were parted by death. The boy who had saved her twice when she was broke and offered her shelter and given her a family and to whom she owed a lifelong debt. So much for all that.

Carmen shivered. All morning she'd been numb, but now there was a big, empty space opening inside her, like a pool filled with ice into which she might fall. When Luca returned to the pew, she reached out and pulled him toward her, standing behind him, placing her chin on top of his squarish blond head. He patted her arm with stubby fingers and radiated a rosy glow that she could feel like sunlight warming her skin. Throughout the rest of the service he propped her up. But also, he was the only thing holding her firmly to the ground.

Their house was quiet in the days that followed. Carmen was expected to stay home.

The owner of the ad agency where she worked had come to the funeral and the luncheon afterward. Fred Lang was a tall, silver-haired man who did things the way they were supposed to be done: His tie was charcoal gray, his shoes polished but not shiny as befitted the occasion. He kissed Carmen, Olive's mustardy potato salad on his breath, and told her to take as much time as she needed.

"Such a tragedy. Jobe gone at forty-seven, his children still so young." Fred shook his handsome head gravely. "Please. Call if there's anything I can do. . . ." So many people said that. But what needed doing, Carmen thought, had finally been done.

Danny attended for only a few minutes, long enough to eat a few cookies and hug Carmen. No one noticed; everyone who came through the door was reaching for her. She clung to him for a good minute and breathed in his scent, then watched a little lost as he walked back out through the door. Olive, too, left early, supported on either side by her remaining two sons.

Her friend, Jana, had provided most of the food but had to leave midafternoon to attend to some refrigeration crisis at the café she owned. So a number of other people stayed on to clean up, chattering cheerfully and prolonging the task, it seemed, much longer than was necessary. Oddly, they were the ones Carmen knew least well—friends of friends or secretaries from the math department whom she'd never had the chance to meet—and none of them seemed to know the others. Yet they moved like a team and appeared to be having great fun.

Loudly, they devised an assembly line for washing the serving dishes and stowed them all over Carmen's kitchen so she knew that she would be opening cupboards for months to find stray platters and creamers and big, metal spoons. But it was easier to let this happen, simpler than figuring out a way to say, "Please get out, I've been waiting for twenty years to have this home to myself. Just go."

Finally, they did—all in a group that Carmen imagined would stay intact for years: They would start meeting for coffee once a month to discuss the sad event that brought them together, move on to trading book suggestions, form a club. And then, suddenly, she was alone in a house that felt as if it were breathing. She was in the living room, having just ushered the last of the do-gooders out onto the porch where she could hear them cluster and trade phone numbers and talk on. When she turned, she saw the outline of Jobe as if he'd been drawn in white chalk against the empty air, ducking his head so as not to hit it on the ceiling as he came down the front stairs.

The children were watching TV in the den with the volume turned down so low they couldn't possibly hear it. Siena was talking as if she couldn't stop and the boys would answer her, Michael's voice high and Luca's thick and low. Carmen knew she should go in and say something to them but she simply didn't know what that thing was. While she tried to figure it out, she walked through the rooms of the house, touching items. It seemed odd to her that Jobe was gone but his clunky black watch still lay on the kitchen counter, casually, as if it were something he'd meant to take with him but had accidentally left behind.

Around nine o'clock, she stood in the doorway looking at her three children on the couch. The program was changing, going from flashy half-hour comedies to an hour-long drama, something with lawyers.

"I just wanted to check. . ." Carmen began. The children turned to her, Michael and Siena with faces not frightened but flat and lifeless. Carmen's heart beat fast. Could the death of a father be communicable, she wondered? Maybe his children were in danger of tripping off the earth after him. She would have to keep watch.

"You seem glad that he's dead," Siena said abruptly, and Carmen caught her breath. Her mind raced: Siena knew! She'd been living with the fact that her mother did not really love her father. That when she, Carmen, grabbed her gym bag at 6:00 a.m. and claimed to be taking an early morning spinning class, she actually was leaving to fuck a long-haired librarian at a hotel with a low, last-minute Priceline rate. In that moment, Carmen's carefully constructed world seemed to be made of wet paper.

She thought about turning and leaving. Then she looked at Siena and saw there was none of this: no sneering or disapproval. This wasn't about her or Danny, their infidelity; it was about Jobe. "I'm happy for *him*," she said, at least half honest. "For your father. I'm very glad he's no longer in pain."

Siena nodded and Carmen breathed. This was the right answer. "And none of us has to worry about him anymore. You included. It'll get easier. You'll go to school and it will feel better, not having to think about your father here, lying in bed so miserable, wondering if he's"— she swallowed only slightly before saying what came next—"died yet. Now, you know."

"But I *don't* know. At least, before, I could picture where he was. Now, he's just . . . gone." Something washed across Siena's face and Carmen recognized it immediately as nausea. Years of mothering kicked in. She considered, briefly, grabbing Siena's arm and whisking her into the bathroom rather than let her make a mess on the rug. Then the moment passed.

"Dad's fine. He's happy now." Luca would have sounded matter-of-fact except that he couldn't, the way his teeth hugged his fat tongue and the words came out like they were wrapped in cloth.

"You don't know that," Siena hissed, turning. And Carmen watched as she always did, the way these two wavered and danced, taking turns being the older child. Luca's placidity and three extra years of life meant the title was his. But he couldn't add a column of numbers or summarize a newspaper article. Siena, who was taking AP pre-calc this year and had her first boyfriend—an eerily polite kid named Troy who'd attended the funeral with his mother and held Siena's hand when they stood beside the grave—enjoyed every advantage. Sometimes, like now, Carmen resented her daughter for this.

"Yes, I do." *Yeth, ah doo.* "Dad told me."

"When?" Carmen asked. "When did he tell you?"

"The night he died." *Daahd.*

Carmen leaned her head against the doorway. "How did he tell you?"

Michael's gaze switched back and forth between his mother and his brother, like someone monitoring a debate.

"This is bullshit! I'm not listening to this." Siena stood, her face even whiter than before. Carmen put two fingers on her daughter's arm as she flew by. It wasn't much, but enough to make contact, to say: *I'm here. I'm staying. I'm not as good a person as your father, maybe, but I'm going to stick around.*

"You probably had a dream, honey." Michael's frightened face floated in the periphery and Carmen was aware that she had two parenting jobs to do at once. It came as a sharp surprise that what she needed—what she wanted in that moment—was Jobe. He could talk to Luca while she took Michael into the kitchen and comforted him. She pictured them with their heads together: Jobe would be grave, serious about Luca's claims. There were infinities too small to calculate, she could imagine him saying to their older son. Particles that couldn't be seen even under the most powerful microscope. Who's to say there weren't also spirits made up of all the tiny, incalculable bits that humans left behind?

Carmen closed her eyes and felt a shift in her head, a gear locking into place. "Or," she said, opening them, looking at her two sons at once, "it could be you and your dad had a way of communicating that none of the rest of us understand. Maybe that's your, you know, gift, the way Michael . . ."—she shifted, the word *gift* still lingering, precious and too sweet on her tongue—"the way your brother has a talent for making people laugh."

The boys actually seemed satisfied with this, which surprised her. And above them, for a fleeting moment, Carmen saw something glimmer: a leaf-shaped luminescence twirling in the air. Then she blinked and it was gone. Fatigue, she decided. This was far more difficult than she'd anticipated.

In fact, it was not at all what she'd imagined. Having Jobe gone.

The next day was Saturday and it rained, a cold, continuous sheet of steel. Spring had gone into hiding.

Siena had returned that noon to her job as a waitress at the Pizza Pub. Michael had a baseball game that got called off but he immediately found a friend's house to go to. Carmen drove him the five blocks so he wouldn't get wet. And in between looking at the road she glanced at her son whose expression eased in tiny shutter jerks—like a time-release series of photographs—as they moved away from the house, the site of his father's death.

"Have a good time," she said as he put his hand on the latch.

But instead of throwing the car door open and calling back, "Okay!" as he always had, her younger son turned to her and said, "You, too," in a perfect mortician's voice. She stared as he unfolded himself from the car and walked—Jobe's walk, with a slight swing to his left foot—hurriedly up the drive.

On the way home, Carmen thought about how nice it would be if Danny came over. They could make love with hands and mouths like octopus suckers, attaching to each other in a hundred different ways under the water, then when they were finished they would lie and listen to the rain. She squinted, trying to recall if she and Jobe had ever done that. Before she had begun to chafe at their marriage in earnest she hadn't been attracted to him, exactly, but she found him warm and comforting and it was pleasant enough to be touched by him when her body was ripe.

There was a time, while she was pregnant with Siena and sexed-up all the time, that she recalled straddling him one night and riding him, looking down to see his horsey Abraham Lincoln face contorted as he concentrated on the task at hand, ignoring that and putting it out of her head and imagining instead that he was a woman with long, dark hair. How to account for the penis, she didn't know or care. It was rare enough that she and Jobe succeeded in getting this far, Carmen was determined to take advantage; in her fantasy, there had been a group of rapt men watching from the corner of the room.

Suddenly, something darted in front of her car and she braked hard. A raccoon or a small dog, she couldn't be sure. Or maybe there was never anything at all. Carmen breathed for a moment and drove on slowly. The thought came to her that she was her children's only parent now. There was an extra burden of responsibility to stay alive.

She pulled into the old garage and turned the key. There was silence, and she missed the way her previous car used to tick after she switched it off. They had meant to replace this garage. It was the next project that Jobe and Luca were going to tackle, once spring came. At least that had been the thought last winter, when Jobe was still planning to live, before myeloid leukemia came to fill the vacuum where lymphoma had been.

Carmen got out of the car and ran out the wide open door of the garage—which required manual closing, something she would not stop to do today—thirty feet to the house. By the time she got inside, her hair was streaming with rain.

She climbed the creaky wooden stairs and went into the bathroom to towel off. She was lucky she wasn't as short as her sister, Jobe had commented when they bought the house, because the medicine cabinet, set permanently into the wall, was so high. But even at five-foot-seven, in bare feet, Carmen's chin was cut off by the mirror's bottom edge. Taking her towel into the bedroom, she stood in front of the full-length mirror that Jobe had affixed to the back of the door. Faded jeans and a black shirt, no makeup, silver rings on the long, slender fingers that had just recently begun to wrinkle. It was the uniform of the domesticated bohemian, only now there was no one around to tame her. Carmen had the option to become the sort of middle-aged woman who ricocheted through town in long, brightly striped scarves and caftans and earrings made of tiny bells.

But of course—it was like a voice intruding, neither male nor female, speaking directly into one of the synapses of her brain—*you always could.*

Down in the kitchen, she made a second pot of coffee. She'd always consumed too much when Jobe wasn't there to drink his share and now he would never again oblige her by taking his cup and a half. Again, the strange rudeness of this thrust itself at her. She had yearned to be unyoked from him for years but had never computed all the small inconveniences Jobe's absence would cause, or the flashes of loneliness: that first morning after it happened, waking before dawn in bed and sobbing until she could hardly catch her breath. Carmen

shook off the memory and washed the metal apparatus of the coffeemaker, picking the silt off with a paper towel, calling for Luca to
come down.

"Hey, honey?" Her voice was raised and artificially bright, like
in a horror movie when the heroine is trying to deny that she is
scared and alone inside a big empty house. "How about some chocolate coffee?"

This was something Jobe had dreamed up for Luca, who tended
to be sleepy in the morning and difficult to awaken for school. He
would heat half a cup of milk in the microwave, then fill the rest with
coffee and squirt in a spoonful of chocolate sauce. When Carmen objected, saying this was like having dessert for breakfast, Jobe showed
her the ingredient list on the flavored non-dairy creamer she used. She
could still see her husband's hairy, many-jointed finger, pointing to
the sugar content—5 grams—and tapping the side of the carton. She'd
been furious then but had taught herself in the weeks that followed to
drink her coffee black.

Luca came down the back stairs now, a narrow wooden passage
that led directly into the kitchen. He stood with his head cocked to
one side, watching from his small eyes as she measured the chocolate
carefully with a large metal spoon. Outside, the rain had picked up
and was making the sound of hundreds of corks tapping on the tile
roof. The coffeemaker sent off clouds of steam.

"It might not be as good as Dad's," she said, setting Luca's mug
down on the table.

He shrugged and shuffled forward, pulling out a chair and sitting tentatively the way he did, like a traveler who'd stopped to rest
on a rock. Carmen took the chair opposite him and held her cup in
both hands.

"How are you doing?" It sounded as if she were reading from a
script. *What to say after your son's father dies.*

"Okay." Luca took a sip of the drink and looked worried.

"More chocolate?" she asked, pushing against the long wooden
table in preparation to stand.

"No. It's too much."

"Oh, I'm sorry."

"T's okay. Dad told me. . ." Luca got up then, tipping his ovoid body out of the chair and walking over to take the pot of coffee from the warmer. He poured about two ounces into his cup then waved his hand over the top. Carmen watched, fascinated. Was it possible her son could perform incantations using nothing but coffee, chocolate, and milk? "Want some?" He held the pot forward and Carmen let him refill her cup, even though she was starting to feel the buzz inside her bones.

Luca sat again and Carmen reached for something to say. Jobe never seemed to have this problem and could sit with Luca for hours, communicating in single words and small random gestures. Jobe had never, she thought with furtive affection, displayed the slightest frustration with Luca's disability. Sadness, certainly. But even that only at the very beginning, and then he was done.

"It used to rain like this when I was in London," Carmen said. "All the time. I remember feeling like my hair would never not be wet." *I was your age*, she almost said. But then she was struck by the quick bolt of pain that always came when she compared her firstborn to other twenty-year-olds, even herself back then. For her the sadness had never quite disappeared.

Luca said nothing and she went on. "But the day I met your dad was sunny and warm. It was like . . . being born, you know? Coming out of this wet cave into the light."

She knew it was ridiculous, talking to him like this. Luca didn't understand metaphor; he barely knew the facts about childbirth. Yet he nodded gravely, as if he understood everything.

Carmen, aching, wondered what she could do for her son. "How about goulash tonight?" she suggested. This was the meal he requested each year for his birthday. It was his favorite, and Jobe's, though she could never get it quite spicy enough for the two of them no matter how much paprika she put in.

"Good," he said, nodding so dramatically his chin kept hitting his chest.

"We'll invite Troy," Carmen said, and again Luca nodded, but more gently this time. Then they sat silently, drinking their coffee, listening to the sound the rain made on the roof.

It was a raucous evening. Not only did Troy show up, but also Michael's friend, Jeffrey—an undersize boy who adored Luca genuinely and followed him through the house, imitating the way he walked not out of meanness but awe.

There was a crowd of kids around Carmen as she poured oil into a cast-iron pan and set the meat in to sizzle. She distributed cutting boards and they chopped onions and garlic and red and green peppers while she opened a bottle of wine and poured herself a sturdy glass. Once, the house shook with wind, and this was followed by a loud pause and a crack of thunder, then torrents of rain. Jeffrey retreated to the couch in the den—trying to look casual through his terror—and had to be coaxed back into the group by Luca. As Carmen spooned tomato paste into the pan, Troy turned on the kitchen radio and she heard a familiar beat and synthesizer chords, then the sweet, high voice that had threaded through her high school years: *Now the mist across the window hides the lines / But nothing hides the color of the lights that shine.*

"Oh, my God, turn that up!"

"This?" Troy turned, looking perplexed. "But it's . . ."

"Old people music. She knows." Siena shrugged. "Just indulge her and it'll be over soon."

"Indulge *me*? You used to love this album." Carmen took a swig of wine and closed her eyes, catching a glimpse of the jaunty, young Jobe dancing in his metronomic way with a blanket-swaddled baby girl in his arms. "We used it to put you to sleep when you were a baby. I always thought I'd play it at your wedding."

Troy shot Siena a winsome look and Carmen stopped, a box of elbow macaroni poised midair above the bubbling water, to watch. Jobe's death had done something to her relationship with her seventeen-year-old daughter; it had gone from sweet to fiery in only a matter of days. Carmen pictured Troy and Siena plotting like a pair of Shakespearean characters, texting back and forth, meeting furtively at night, growing their little high school romance into a dramatic life-altering event. *Don't do it!* She felt like shaking her daughter. *Look at me. I married your father when I was too young to understand the consequences and got stuck for more than two decades.* But of course, she couldn't do that.

"Jeez, making a baby listen to this, that's like . . . child abuse," Troy said. And right in front of Carmen's eyes, he and her daughter turned back into impertinent teenagers. This thought made her sigh with relief.

They sat in the kitchen, all six of them, almost like a family. Carmen passed the bowls of salad and steaming meat and noodles and got up twice—once for butter and once for more bread. As often happened while she was watching the children, she barely ate herself. They dazzled her with their unexpected opinions and differences. Of course she wouldn't repudiate these three people for the chance to have had a real life all to herself! The idea of never having them seemed horrific right now: even Luca, *especially* Luca, who ate neatly and seriously, the way his father had, as if it were a job to be done.

Near the end of the meal, she felt her phone's text message alert vibrating through the pocket of her sweater. And later, when she checked—while the older children cleaned up together and Michael and Jeffrey played a game of Risk—there was a message from Danny. "Miss U. Call me."

Typically, she would have taken the phone outside, but the rain continued to pelt down. Carmen looked for a private place on the main floor, wandering from room to room. Siena and Troy were in the kitchen, lingering over the last few dishes. Michael and Jeffrey were sprawled on the rug in the living room. Luca was, by this point, in the den solemnly watching TV. She took the back stairs up but stopped when she got to the threshold of her bedroom. She and Jobe had shared this room—this bed—up until the last few weeks when he could no longer make it up the stairs. Carmen had dreaded night-time throughout their marriage: They'd become alien to each other, exquisitely careful, lying sealed off, each occupying a separate half of the bed.

But there had been other nights—random, scattered, occurring for small reasons—when the space between them had briefly disap-peared. Seven years ago she'd had the stomach flu, for example, and was recovering: weak from a day of throwing up and another of leav-ing her body empty so she wouldn't. Jobe had come into the room after tending to the children, then still young, and groaned slightly as he took off his shoes. He lay on top of the covers while she was underneath, anchoring her in a pleasant way. And when he'd reached out that evening to put his hand on her forehead—checking for fever—she had turned toward him and curled like a possum into the space under his chin. If he was surprised after months of feeling only her back in bed, he didn't let on.

He had reached over her with one long arm to turn off the lamp at her side, but stopped as he was retracting his hand, hesitated, and began stroking back her long hair. He'd made no move to take off his clothes or get under the covers. And somehow being swathed and touched by him in this way felt different, almost as if she were a child and he were anointing her. A holy man.

Standing in the doorway, staring at the flat, empty bed, Carmen considered the memory of that night. The next day, she'd chalked it all up to post-illness euphoria: Her body was healing, her brain swim-ming from lack of calories and hydration. Within a week, she'd returned to being uncomfortable in Jobe's presence, bristling at the way he chewed his food rhythmically, or blew his nose three times in a row then looked in the tissue to see what he'd produced. But now, she recalled the way she'd slid into the crevice his body made by pinning down the blankets and sheets. It was snowing that night, tiny, icy flakes that fell at a slant, ticking sharply against the windowpanes. She'd fallen asleep to this sound and to the glowing sensation of Jobe running his fingers along the tops of her ears, her brain empty of everything else.

It felt wrong to sit in that room and talk to her lover about the easy life now that her husband was dead, the children were hers alone, and she didn't have to explain to anyone where she was going on Tuesday or why she sometimes came back damp with her hair smelling of hotel shampoo. Carmen took one last look at the bed, a flat plane without even the faint impression of Jobe's body. It was, she thought, as if he'd never been.

Something about this made her angry as she climbed the stairs to the attic. Her husband had left with so little fanfare, just as he'd lived, quietly writing his papers and talking to students, trying to solve the Riemann hypothesis though he and everyone else knew it was impossible to do in one lifetime—especially Jobe's, short as it was.

Carmen had to duck when she emerged from the narrow stairwell, the way Jobe had once needed to downstairs. But after she had crawled up the last few steps and walked to the center of the peaked room, she could stand and reach her hands all the way up without touching the ceiling. In some ways, the attic was typical, with dancing dust motes and small windows and a faint, ghostly, gingerbread smell.

Carmen knew from the previous owner's daughter that the family that had lived there for half a century before them used to keep their Christmas cookies on the attic stairs. *It was dry and cool there*, the woman had explained. She was a portly little peanut of a person with snow-white hair and soft, latticed cheeks. She told Carmen that none of the seven children in their family would touch the cookie tins once they were stacked on the wooden steps. *I don't know why*, she had said and laughed. *It wasn't that we couldn't, of course. But there was something special about the attic. It somehow wasn't a real part of the house.*

Carmen knew what she meant. Coming up here felt like ascending through a tunnel and entering a different world. This was an attic with eaves, which went completely against type. The way it was furnished added to this feeling. It was the furniture from their first five years of marriage, which had been Carmen's—and Jobe's, because he tended back then to go along with what she wanted—modern phase. There were teak tables, blond and sleek and low to the ground; geometrically patterned rugs; and a sectional couch made up of twelve different pieces that could be combined in a nearly infinite number of ways, like children's blocks. They were the exact opposite of the hinged trunks and rocking chairs one might expect to find in an attic, and Carmen had arranged the set as if for company. But she was the only person who ever went up there—mostly to be alone during the period before Jobe's diagnosis when he seemed always to be in her way, expecting some pseudo-wifely act.

She sat and stared at the phone in her hand. But at the edge of her mind, crouching, was the memory of Jobe lying against her, his hand in her hair, chin grazing the top of her head. It had been years since she'd thought about the way he took care of her that night. The moments she tended to recall from their marriage were the ones in which she'd felt nothing except that void between two people that was worse than being alone. Reading in a chair and feeling the air change, his presence intruding on its molecules, when he sat on a hassock that he'd pulled to within a few inches of her feet; trying to come up with a trip for their twentieth anniversary, which she was afraid would be a week of painful small talk and the question every night about whether or not they would make love.

They didn't throughout the whole trip, which turned out to be to Bermuda. And Carmen was relieved but also hurt. She'd spent her days in a low-cut, black bathing suit, with a gauzy skirt pulled over it and a pair of sandals for when they walked into town. Yet her husband no longer even tried to put his hands on her. He got into bed each night like a brother, sometimes patting her hip before turning to face the wall. Sex between them had never been quite natural, but now it seemed like something hopelessly complicated that required physical contortions they'd both forgotten—a gymnastics move, which had been difficult yet possible when younger but now was completely out of reach.

There was sex with Danny, of course. But that was easy. Anyone could have sex with Danny, she often thought. In fact, anyone had.

When she met him, he'd admitted to her that theirs was his fourth affair; he was good at this. And he had a reasonable excuse, because his wife was far less interested in sex than she was in food, which she sometimes wouldn't eat at all and other times consumed in huge quantities then purged from her body in various ways. They had an entire plastic bin full of different kinds of laxatives, Danny told Carmen, because she had to switch brands whenever her body became used to one and refused to budge. She vomited only once or twice a week— as a last resort.

Danny couldn't touch Mega's body without her shuddering and moving his hand, complaining about the roll of fat on her thighs or her stomach or wherever else he happened to land. This decimated his erection every time, he told Carmen, who had tried to smile as if it were perfectly normal to think about him getting hard with someone else, even his wife. Carmen had never come right out and told Danny how infrequently she and Jobe had sex, but as her husband grew more skeletal it seemed obvious. While Danny's wife wanted to waste away but couldn't, Jobe's skin was becoming pulled tight around his bones, like Saran Wrap.

Raindrops danced just a couple of feet over her head as she dialed Danny's number. "Hey," he answered immediately. She could tell that he was smoking from the wet, rubbly quality of his voice.

"Where are you?" she asked.

"Shed," he answered. "I'm going to burn this thing down some day."

"That would be hard to do in this rain." She watched drops ooze like tears down the small, pointed windows. "It looks like it might never stop."

"Carmen's Ark?" Danny laughed. "Do you think God is angry, wiping the world free of sinners?"

"If he were, we'd hardly be the ones he'd save," she said, and Danny laughed again, though she hadn't meant to be funny.

"I'd ask if you want to meet me, but I don't know where we'd go in this storm." He seemed suddenly to crouch closer to the phone.

"It would be nice to touch you. I'd lick you and make you come, then leave right away. Run away through the rain."

Carmen slid one hand up along her thigh. Danny electrified her with his dirty talk, and his habit of sometimes doing exactly as he said: working her up quickly, bringing her to climax, and disappearing before she'd even had time to open her eyes. The first time they were together she'd felt as if he were an incubus or a spirit, something she'd conjured up for the purposes of satisfying her the way her husband did not and allowed to dematerialize as soon as she'd gotten what she wanted. But that only made her want him more.

"Speaking of places to go." Danny cleared his throat. "I'm a little short this week. Mega's been on another spending spree. I know it's my turn, but do you think you can cover the hotel on Tuesday?"

"Oh, we can just . . ." Carmen paused. She'd been about to say *come here*, but now she was trying to imagine the two of them in her house, Jobe's absence looming over them, a tangle of bodies but where? On the kitchen table? The couch in the den where Luca sat to watch TV? In the bed she had shared with her husband for nearly twenty-one years? "Yeah, I guess I can cover it. I'm expecting a big insurance payment."

"Really?" She heard the flare of his lighter and the indrawn breath of another cigarette. "How big?"

The answer was $5 million. She saw the numbers flash in her head, all the zeros lined up. Jobe had insisted on buying the policy back when Luca was three or four. Their son would always need care, Jobe reasoned, and if he were to die before his parents—before coming into his inheritance—Carmen would need money. From the beginning, it seemed, Jobe had been planning for this.

When he was first diagnosed, Carmen had thought about the life insurance and wondered how much Jobe had known about what was to come. Lymphoma was a cancer of the entire body. It may have been starting, cells mutating in small, random corners: his left shoulder, lower abdomen, big toe. Perhaps he had even felt it taking hold. Then, when it looked as if Jobe had survived both the disease and its treatment, getting to within two months of the five-year cure mark, she'd decided this was nonsense. Not only had her husband been making payments on a useless policy—one that would pay off only about one-tenth of his net worth once both his parents were dead—he was going to battle his way through the surgeries, chemo, and radiation, only to end up thin and tired but healthy after all. Then the leukemia set in.

"Um, you know, the standard University payout," she said, before even realizing she'd decided not to tell Danny the truth. "Five hundred thousand."

"Mmm." The sound came from low in his throat. "That's not so much. You'll need it."

"Yeah, I suppose." Carmen squirmed; now she was lying to her lover about her husband. Would this never stop? "But I could spring for a whole night somewhere nice. That wouldn't cost much and it would be nice to sleep in. You can tell Mega you're going to a conference or something."

"I'd love that, babe, but the only conferences I've ever gone to happen in fall. Modern Library and the Poe Association. I think she might catch on."

"So?" Carmen knew she was being petulant but for the first time since that eerie spring in London when she was still nearly a child, she was afraid to be alone at night. Getting away and pretending there was something normal between her and Danny was the only way that she could think of to make the strange, random memories from her life stop. "You've told me a hundred times she knows you have relationships with other women. What does it matter if she knows?"

"My going to some cheap, hourly-rate hotel with someone while she's having a pedicure, that's one thing," Danny said. "She's probably glad, it takes the pressure off her. But going somewhere she might like . . . you know, taking a real trip . . . that crosses her lines. Believe me. I've tried it before."

He'd tried it before. Carmen forced herself to think about this: Danny with other women, in other cities, other hotels. Muttering his hot, dirty talk.

"Besides, I don't want you spending your insurance money on something for us." His voice became suddenly the one from the library: reliable, grave, concerned. "Half a million isn't going to go that far. Especially with the kids and . . . everything."

"You're right." Heat swept through Carmen as it occurred to her that she had a habit of misjudging every man in her life, dead and alive. Now was not the time to remind her lover—who seemed, unbelievably, to have forgotten—that in addition to the insurance, Jobe's family was rich. "So I'll see you Tuesday."

After they set a time and Carmen promised to text him with the name of the hotel when she booked something, Danny said good-bye and Carmen flipped her phone closed, letting it fall to the smooth surface of the cushion where it lay looking out of place, like an artifact from a different time. Back when they bought this furniture, cell phones were enormous flesh-colored appliances carried only by real estate agents and brokers—successful ones whose need to get in touch with their clients was so urgent, they were willing to haul around the clunky dumbbell-shaped objects that got reception only on the tops of buildings and hills.

She'd read a book once about a man who lived in an ancient Central Park apartment looking out onto a stretch of New York that was left untouched by the previous century. He wore clothes from the 1880s, used an icebox, and shaved with a straight razor. Eventually the man in the book had faded back in time, an initially hazy process, she remembered, that began as a dreamlike state but became over the course of weeks so concrete that he was able to walk out his own front door into a New York of horses pulling wagons and ladies in long skirts carrying parasols.

The rain continued its steady tattoo on the roof. Carmen was drifting pleasantly on the sound but also growing chilly; the warmth from sparring with Danny had drained from her abruptly, leaving her with a pale sensation inside her skin. She reached for a blanket and pulled it over her, stretching out on the sectional whose length would have accommodated her twice, at least. Light from the wine, atop a house filled with children who were going about their individual lives, Carmen relaxed. She wondered what, in addition to this sectional, it would take to go back to the 1980s. Leggings and off-the-shoulder T-shirts? Joe Jackson albums? Microwaves with big, round rocket ship dials and digital watches that glowed bright green?

She must have fallen asleep at some point, because she failed to notice when the bulb in the ceiling light socket sputtered or snapped and burned out. It was much later—at least it felt that way, as if she had been asleep for hours and surfaced in one of those dream cycles— that Carmen had the sensation of lifting her head and seeing Jobe sitting at the end of the couch, just inches from her draped feet.

He didn't look the way he had just before he died, skinny and sick and bruised, but neither did he appear like the younger version of himself. This was a Jobe she hadn't ever seen before: straight and strong, with the outlines of a man one and a half times the size he had been in real life. Yet there was something soft, almost smudgy, about him. His beard was like a forest, his eyes large and dark, focused but as gentle as a camel's.

What an odd thought, Carmen recalled telling herself as she sank back down into sleep. She had never seen a camel, not even in a zoo. Her only experience, really, was those Christmas cards that showed the three wise men riding animals whose golden eyes shone through the night sky. Placid, yet as brilliant as stars.

JUNE 1985

The sky was glossy and blue, like a polished bowl turned upside down. Carmen walked along a path in Kensington Gardens, imagining that she'd dwindled to the size of a cereal-box figure and entered some perfect storybook landscape—a diorama with a punk rock theme.

She wore black leggings, a long, hot pink T-shirt tied in a knot at one hip, and black ballet shoes. There were ten earrings in her left ear and seven in her right, a long feather hanging from one lobe. Her dark hair was streaked with a neon two shades lighter than the color of her shirt, and spiked. Close shaved on the sides of her head, long on top and in back.

Carmen stopped at a cart near a stand of brilliant red flowers to buy some potato wedges and a cup of jasmine tea. The sun shone hard. The potato man smiled at her with gold and missing teeth and said, "G'day, miss," when he held out the paper cone and her tea with two sugars and a small paper cup of red vinegar. Still holding her string bag in one hand, Carmen took the potatoes, the tea, the sugars, the cup of vinegar; she accepted the ten pence change in one sweaty palm. Then turning, juggling these items, she looked for a clear place on the grass to sit.

The whole world sparkled, blinding her momentarily. There were clusters of people dotting the grass in every direction. She blinked and saw a small patch of green bordered by two long, blue bars. Heading toward it, she stepped high over the threshold, which suddenly shifted. Startled, Carmen dropped the smaller cup—containing the vinegar—and lost a third of the tea as well, when it sloshed as she lurched. A distinctly American yelp came from the area around her feet. She looked down, eyes watering from the light and smelled a waft of jasmine rising from warm denim. Below her, there was an impossibly long skinny boy, on his back, looking up. A dark stain bloomed directly over his crotch.

"Oh, God, I'm so sorry!" Her feet fidgeted as if dancing and she juggled the things in her hands, dropping the coin as well. "Did I burn you? I did! Oh, shit. Here." She handed him the potatoes and her purse and ran to a cart that sold Coca-Cola in short, thick bottles. "I need a cup of ice, fast!" she told the Indian boy manning the cart. And when he scowled, she added, "I promise, I'll come back and buy something from you. But I think I just castrated some guy with my tea."

When she got back, however, the boy was sitting up looking not maimed but disapproving.

"Here." Panting, Carmen handed him the paper cup of ice. "Just pour this down your pants. Don't worry, no one's looking. And that would be better than going through the next week with a blister on your. . ."

"I'm a total stranger," he cut her off, placing the cup of ice neatly on the ground. "What are the chances you'll leave your money and your. . ." He had opened the bag and was fingering through it cautiously, "your passport and your *bank card* with some guy in a park and he won't take off with them?"

Carmen kicked off her shoes and ran her toes through the warm grass. "Pretty good, I guess. 'Cause you didn't, did you?" She peered up into Jobe's scowling face.

"No, I didn't," he said. "But that's hardly the point."

"Oops, I almost forgot!" She snatched her bag from Jobe and took off, running toward the boy's cart in bare feet this time, her soles tickled by the blades as they lit. She returned moments later with two Cokes and handed one to Jobe. "I promised him I'd buy something," she said. "You see? I always keep my promises."

"That's an admirable trait." He sounded suspicious, as if he required more proof.

"Yes, it is." Carmen dropped to the ground now and rolled onto her stomach; looking back over her shoulder, she could see her dirty feet waving in the air. Jobe lowered himself carefully, leaving a shoe box worth of distance between them. "Another one is that I'm just a very good judge of people—which is why I trusted you with my things. Besides, I thought I'd, like, *emasculated* you forever. Can you really blame me for valuing your future children over my stupid purse?"

He grinned, a slash of perfect, white teeth appearing on his horsey face, and for the first time since she'd tripped over him, Carmen thought Jobe might actually be cute. Sporadically, at least.

She reached to pluck a potato wedge from the cone that lay on the grass by Jobe's left knee and broke it open. "Ooohh, good, they're still hot!" she said as it steamed furiously in her hand. He watched silently as she peeled a chunk of crisp skin from the flesh and placed it on her tongue. "Have one," she said.

Jobe took a wedge and ate it whole, opening his mouth to breathe out steam like a dragon. The stain in his pants had grown tendrils that ran down his long legs.

"Okay, you're probably right." Carmen stared at her hands, picking at a chip in the black polish. "I shouldn't have left my bag with you. But you do seem more trustworthy than most people."

Jobe leaned back then, assuming the position he'd been in when she tripped across him. He sighed. "Yeah, I suppose I am. That and my parents are loaded, so I don't have a big incentive to steal."

Carmen got up on her elbows. Not only was this an odd thing to blurt out to a stranger in a park, but back in Detroit, rich people tended to be beautiful. Not just their faces and their bodies and clothes, but the air around them. It seemed to glow. Yet this was the most ordinary-looking person she'd ever encountered, remarkable only because he was so skinny but otherwise completely unmemorable. Worn, as if he might fade into the background. Come to think of it, he had.

There was a long, awkward pause and Carmen considered getting up and moving on. He might get the wrong idea if she stayed there. The problem was she had no place to go. She had another week in London and roughly fifty American dollars to make it through. Sitting in a park was about all she could afford.

"So what are you doing here?" she asked, leaning back with her eyes closed. The sun made black things blossom on the inside of her lids.

"You mean in London, or here with you, or in a bigger sense?"

"Yeah, I'm asking for your theory of the universe." Still sightless, she grinned. "No, wise guy . . ." She opened her eyes and he met them with a sober face. "What I meant was," she went on, her voice softer, "what are you doing here in this park?"

"Just reading." He tilted his head toward an old book, now tea-splattered, lying face down.

She picked it up. "*Riemann's Zeta Function*. Hmmm, sounds fascinating."

"It is, actually. This guy claims there's an infinite sum of complex numbers that will prove—"

"What are you, some kind of math prodigy?" Carmen cut in. "I've heard about guys like you."

Jobe sat silently for a couple of seconds and she wondered if she'd embarrassed him. She was about to apologize, though she didn't know for what: She alone among her high school friends had always looked up to—secretly envied—the brainy few who set the curve. *I didn't mean* . . . she opened her mouth to say. But before she could form the first word, he answered matter-of-factly, seeming not offended at all.

"I don't know if you could use the word *prodigy* for someone who's twenty-five. And I'm not even that good with numbers, except the imaginary ones and the ones that don't exist."

"There are numbers that don't exist?" She sat up, genuinely interested.

Jobe grinned again and flashed that nearly handsome look. He shrugged. "Maybe. That's what I came here to try to prove."

"But if you prove it, doesn't that mean they *do* exist?"

Jobe leaned back on his hands and seemed for the first time not to know how to answer. "You're smarter than most of the girls like you," he finally said, as if he'd been debating the whole time whether or not he should.

Carmen flushed with a combination of pleasure and indignation. "What do you mean 'girls like you'?"

But snatching up his book, Jobe rose without answering. "I'll be here again tomorrow, if you want to have lunch." He spoke quickly, as if he were giving dictation. "Same spot. One o'clock. See you then . . . maybe." And he left her sitting alone in the grass.

Carmen hadn't been planning to go. He was a funny boy—nice-seeming, too, in his rather priggish way—but definitely not her type.

Then, the following morning, her purse was snatched off her shoulder while she stood in the Oxford Circus station studying the Tube map. All she had left was her TravelCard, because she'd already taken it out in preparation to board the train and was holding it in her hand. She showed up at the park at a quarter after one, fuming, to find him in the exact same spot, reading with a grim expression on his furry, ugly face.

"Hey," she barked, and he looked up to flash that startling, bright smile, as incongruous as a full moon over a junkyard.

"Did you put some sort of hex on me?" she asked while they waited in line for vegetarian masala, for which Jobe had insisted he would pay. "I've been through three other countries so far. Holland, Belgium, France." She counted them off on her fingers, which were long and delicate, decked with half a dozen silver rings. "Nothing. *No* problem at all. Then I meet you, Mr. You're Not Careful Enough, and wham! Everything on me is stolen. My *identity* was stolen. And I'm just some poor, dumb American wandering around London with no money and nowhere to sleep at night."

"Is that true? You're going to get kicked out of your place?" Jobe looked suddenly even more serious than usual. Carmen nodded, truly frightened for the first time since landing in Amsterdam five weeks earlier. "Tell you what," he said. "We'll go to the embassy this afternoon and they'll help you out with your passport. I don't know about the money, though. Maybe . . . you could . . ." He stared at the ground for a few beats. "You might have to stay with me."

"I can't do that." She patted his arm and felt the fur overlaying his hard bones, like something you might touch in a museum. "Look, I'll call my father and he'll be furious, but he'll wire me some money. It'll be here by . . ." She looked into the distance. There was a hot air balloon, a fat green thing like a floating bug, hovering over the park. "Monday, I should think."

She liked the way that sounded. She'd picked up a number of small Britishisms in the eight days she'd been on the island. *Rather, brilliant, arse.* She would go home carrying these with her like souvenirs.

"What happens 'til Monday?" Jobe asked.

Carmen shrugged. She was getting hungry, and the scent of curry mixing with the sunshine was making her feel nearly drunk. "I don't know. I'll crash with friends, or something. It's not a big deal."

"It's my fault, as you said. So you'll stay with me." He made this pronouncement as they reached the front of the line. "Two veg, with naan," he said to the shiny-faced man behind the counter. Then he turned back to Carmen. "I'm not going back to Oxford until Wednesday. It'll work out just fine."

Carmen snorted. "Yeah, right." But she reached out—tentative, as he faced the other way—and briefly touched the narrow band of his side. "Thanks."

They sat on the grass again to eat their masala and it tasted better to Carmen than she was expecting—the way something does when you've been hungry for a very long time. Then they got up together and threw their paper cartons in the trash bin and began to walk. Jobe was a good eight inches taller than her and gangly as a marionette; he kept placing one hand on her shoulder, in the manner of a school monitor. She liked this. No one had touched her since the man in the Red Light District, who had been trying to steer her into a dark corner of the alley after they'd smoked too much hash. Jobe's hold on her was light and nonthreatening, so they went together to the youth hostel where he was staying with another student from his hall.

"This is weird," she said, wandering through the barren room— nothing but two nearly identical American-made backpacks, a low, scuffed wooden table with chairs, and a couple of beds. "Where am I going to sleep?"

Jobe looked around, as if seeing the hostel's ugly linoleum and pale blue walls for the first time. Then he shrugged. "You can have my bed. I'll put a sleeping bag on the floor."

"But there's another *guy* staying here, right?" Carmen said, her eyes darting toward the other bed. "It won't work."

Jobe grinned but cleared his throat nervously. "Sorry. It's just that you seem like the kind of girl who would be . . ."

"What?" She glared up at him.

"Um, you know, okay no matter what happens. Like pouring hot tea on a total stranger or getting your purse stolen. I mean, you seem like you just . . . accommodate." He looked at the floor. "I've always wanted to be more that way."

Carmen studied him and felt a slow melting. There was something about this odd person that got to her, made her want to be nicer. "Alright," she said. And this one word, thankfully, gave them plenty of things to do. Jobe rode with Carmen on the subway to the room-ing house where she'd been staying. It was dank: a tiny mouse hole of a room. She'd convinced herself it was daringly Bohemian when she'd agreed to rent it, by the day, from the bushy-browed Irishman with the scar who'd leered and asked, "Will ye be needing linens, miss?" while he ran one finger down her left breast.

Now, looking at the place alongside Jobe, whose cell-like hostel was at least clean, Carmen was embarrassed by the cracked walls and mouse droppings in the corners.

"My dad said he'd already paid a fortune for me to go to Amsterdam and Paris, he wasn't going to shell out more for London." She shrugged. "This is what I could afford on my own."

"So why'd you come?" Jobe was stuffing rolled-up jeans and T-shirts into a knapsack he'd found on the floor. He'd already explained to her that he was from Baltimore, studying at Oxford—earning his doctorate at the Mathematical Institute—but it was spring break so he'd taken the train down to London with her. "Was there something in particular you wanted to do?"

Carmen tilted her head so the feather she wore brushed her shoulder. "I couldn't stand the thought of coming all this way, over an ocean and everything, and not seeing more. It seemed so . . . boxed in. I don't know. I'm not explaining this very well. It just. I wanted to feel like things were *possible*, you know?"

"I know exactly what you mean," Jobe said. And he looked directly into her eyes, holding himself steady, skinny chest barely mov-ing. It was as if he were calculating, she thought. He was figuring her out, adding her up. Despite his wiry hair and bony, gawky body, this drew her in.

She considered moving toward him, but the attraction wasn't exactly sexual. There was no part of her that wanted to touch him; he was fascinating the way a live lobster was. All those disparate body parts—claws and tail and antennae—moving in ways that looked mechanical and surreal. "What's up?" she said finally.

But instead of answering, he dropped his gaze and went back to folding her clothes.

Back at Jobe's hostel, his friend from school had arrived: a brawny boy named Tim who wore a flannel shirt open over a white tank top. His jeans were soft and work-worn, his feet in unlaced, oversized boots. He was sitting wide-legged in a chair, drinking a beer, reading from a book that lay open on his lap. Immediately, Carmen forgot her mild interest in Jobe. This was more like it: broad shoulders and big hands. She could see herself with Tim.

The three ordered a pizza for dinner. A mistake. The Brits did many things well, Carmen had learned—tea, scones, meat pies—but pizza was not one of them. It was undercooked and dripped with a tasteless tomato sauce. She gnawed on a slice but felt increasingly queasy about the flop of soft, bready crust on her tongue. When she put it down, half eaten, Jobe stared and looked fretful. "You okay?" he asked.

She itched with irritation, the way she had when her mother used to hover over her. Carmen's mother, dead nearly a year now, had been fretful and easily hurt. It was, Carmen often told herself, a relief to be on her own. But then, as sometimes happened, darkness spread through her like ink and she felt simply small and sad. "I'm tired," she said to Jobe. "And cold."

The once-sunny day had collapsed into a stormy evening with extravagantly frothy brown clouds. Rain spattered the dirty windowpanes. Everything seemed unfamiliar, and Carmen tensed her cheek muscles so she wouldn't cry. It was probably hormonal; her period was due in a couple of days. She really needed to get a grip.

As if he'd heard her thoughts, Tim rolled his eyes. He was from South Dakota, a boy with bizarre, savantlike mathematical skills, Jobe had told her while Tim was out in the hall, using the bathroom. His buffalo-ranching parents had thought he might be insane when he was growing up. Now, Tim turned to Jobe and yawned. "How long are we going to be babysitting?" he asked.

Carmen flushed and the room around her pitched. Fixing her glassy eyes to the floor, she stood. "I'm going to leave so I don't throw up all over your table, okay?"

But, of course, there was no place to go. They were all in one room, with the all-purpose table wedged in a corner. Jobe had made a bit of ceremony out of unrolling a camp-style sleeping bag for himself on the floor.

Carmen pulled a book from her bag and tried sitting on Jobe's bed, but the mattress was thin and lumpy, so after a few minutes she sank to the floor and into the sleeping bag, which was covered in flannel and filled with soft down. Exhausted, craving a sort of nest, she burrowed down inside, not even caring that the men were still watching. Once inside, she wriggled out of her jeans and tossed them out of the opening, onto the floor. Then she closed her eyes but didn't sleep. Instead, she floated dreamily on the low murmur of their voices—once Tim and Jobe had resumed their conversation—the way she had when she was a child and her parents were talking in the front seat of the car.

She must have fallen asleep at some point, because she awoke in the middle of the night, abruptly, unable to figure out for a couple of minutes where she was. There were bodies above her, two large forms like shadowy specters. Still struggling to place herself, frantically trying to remember the night before, she wondered whether they were good or evil. She thought for a flash that she might have died somewhere along the way and was just becoming aware of it. Or perhaps she was underground in a cave, buried alive among foreign things.

She moved—it was excruciating, like stepping into a scary, dark chasm—and then became aware of a stickiness between her legs; the hazy, moonlit night beyond the windows; and the eyes of Tim, either awake or sleeping with them open. Maybe he *was* insane. She untangled herself from the sleeping bag, feeling with one bare foot the streak of blood that she'd oozed like slime.

Emerging like a trapped bug tearing its way out of a spider's web, she gathered her shirttail and tried to cover herself, wrapping it around the upper part of her legs where she imagined there were probably bright stains.

Lurching a little as she walked toward the door, Carmen rubbed her abdomen and moaned. How could it be that she'd never asked Jobe where the bathroom was? It had to be close; Tim had been gone only a few minutes when he used it. But was it for men only? Was it locked? And if so, where was the key? Carmen looked around the room, which became more real by degrees. The fuzzy illumination of a streetlamp came through the window. Tim blinked, his eyes yellow slits in the soupy light.

"Hey, where's the bathroom?" She tried to sound tough, but she was beginning to panic. There was a heaviness in her gut, thick liquid on her legs, and she had to pee, urgently.

"What's wrong, little girl? Not feeling well? Need some love?" Tim's voice was low and sinister, and he pulled back the covers to show her that he was naked underneath. "Come on in. I'll make everything better."

Just then a cloud covered the moon and the door's outline vanished into the murk. The room seemed to have sealed itself, like some sort of pod in a science fiction movie. She stood clenching like a kindergartener about to wet her pants. And she was furious, but for some reason this made her feel like crying. Tears and urine threatened to let down together. Then she heard a voice from above, low and as mean as a six-year-old's and wrecked with sleep.

"Leave her alone, Tim." There was a rustling of covers and now Jobe was standing beside her, his skinny chest bare and brushing her arm. Carmen clenched and managed to contain the liquid that threatened to spill out of her. "Here." He grabbed her arm almost roughly. "I'll take you."

Jobe's hand found a doorknob that materialized for Carmen the moment he reached for it. He pulled the door open and led her down the hallway to a tiny WC where he tugged a cord and an overbright light flooded the room. Carmen covered her eyes and whispered, "I need my knapsack, from back in the room."

"Okay, I'll be back in a minute. You . . ." Jobe gestured, then seemed at a loss for words. He backed out and Carmen slammed the door, then peeled her sticky underpants away and sank down onto the chipped toilet.

A couple of minutes later, there was a knock. She stood and slid herself back into her squishy clothes. "Here." Jobe shoved the knapsack through the wide crack she made in the door, along with the longest white T-shirt she'd ever seen. "Here's something to change into. I'm going to wait out here to make sure you get back."

There was blood on Carmen's fingers and a few drops on the floor. The little WC was beginning to look like a crime scene, and her panties were completely ruined, the elastic bands around the leg holes soaked a rusty red. She looked around, but the room had no wastebasket. Just a toilet with a tank on the wall and a sink with one faucet—undoubtedly cold—and no soap.

She washed herself off as best as she could, using the water (which was, indeed, ice cold) and a wad of scratchy toilet tissue. Then she fanned herself, one foot up on the toilet rim. Someone had left a towel on the sink. Carmen picked it up, found a rough edge, and ripped it, folding the square she made, praying it was mostly clean, using it to line a fresh pair of underwear, then putting them on. Finally, she pulled on Jobe's T-shirt, which fell to her knees. By the time she'd washed her hands, stuffed her bloodied panties into the space behind the toilet, and opened the door, fifteen minutes must have passed. But he was still there, leaning against the wall at a tilt, eyes closed, half sleeping.

"Everything okay?" He moved carefully, detaching from the wall as if he were protecting his sharp bones. He was wearing scrubs, like a doctor, the pants tied tightly around his narrow hips.

She nodded and said quietly, "I'm fine," and felt an abrupt wave of affection for him. Alone, in the dark, his awkwardness was touching.

They walked silently back to the room. Jobe reached down with one hand to work the knob and pushed the door open with the other above her head. For a few seconds, she was inside the span of his arms. And surprisingly—like when, many years ago, her grandmother had taken her out for lunch and Carmen had ended up enjoying the prim meal of Cobb salad and Earl Grey tea—she experienced a flicker of pleasure. Jobe reminded her of a tree, the kind you take shelter under. It wasn't sexy, but maybe it could be nice for a change.

She had been with plenty of men: four just since arriving in Europe, and six in her lifetime before that. All but three of them had been dark-haired and handsome. One was black. There'd also been a Scot—her first redhead—just a few days before. Ten was a risky but not an unreasonable number, on the far edge of normal (most of her girlfriends claimed between five and eight) but nowhere near the territory of a true slut. Many of her friends were skirting the rules anyway, by going out with men and doing only "uncountable" acts: jerking them off, giving them blow jobs, or sleeping in the nude—this was the oddest one, as far as Carmen was concerned—pressed up against each other but utterly chaste.

She knew she didn't want to suck this guy off, and tonight there was no chance of her sleeping without clothes to hold her diaper on. But Carmen decided on the spot she would be willing to trade a quick hand job for a spot next to Jobe in his clean bed.

"I'm sorry it's, um, kind of a mess . . . ." Carmen said, gesturing at the sleeping bag. "Look, I'll find a laundry and wash it tomorrow. Can I just get in next to you? I promise I won't kick or anything."

"Sure." Jobe's voice was so low she could barely hear it. "Come on." He flattened and inserted himself into the bed like a sheet of paper in an envelope. She followed, feeling round and extravagantly three-dimensional next to his plank of a body, lying in the space he'd created by backing all the way up against the wall. They lay for a minute not touching, though this must have required Jobe to practically not breathe. Finally, he relaxed and his body contoured against hers, all ridges and planes, long angled bones, and the distinct shape of his erection.

She moved her hips slightly, and it grew. Carmen was caught between disgust and a sense of power. It required so little effort for her to control a man's body—this man in particular, it seemed, who wanted her despite the fact that she'd soaked his sleeping bag with blood. She reached down with one hand and touched the hard, curled lump that was straining against his cotton scrub pants, causing Jobe to jump back a half inch or so.

"Does it hurt?" she whispered. "It's like a rock. I can't imagine having a part of me just . . . change like that."

"Uh, no, not hurt, exactly." Jobe was still edging back in the bed, but he couldn't get quite far enough away from her for his penis not to be touching. "I'm sorry, it's just something that happens sometimes. Maybe if I lie on my back."

"Oh." Carmen had been preparing to close her hand on his cock, but it looked now like she didn't have to do anything in order to stay.

Outside there were drops falling like coins on the roof and Carmen relaxed into Jobe's side. The arm he'd stretched out under her neck—because where else was there to put it?—tightened and curled a little, drawing her in. And she sighed and drifted as if she were being carried on a raft toward sleep, nose against Jobe's upper arm, the faint, spicy deodorant smell of him mixing with the steel scent of the rain.

May 2007

Tuesday afternoon, flopped on a bed at the airport Holiday Inn, Carmen looked out the smeared window at planes lifting, showing her their bellies as they rose through the air.

"It'll be strange going back to work." She reached for her glass. There was no longer any concern about Jobe's smelling the wine on her breath when she got home at five, having to come up with some invented client meeting that involved marinated olives and a bottle of Chardonnay.

"Afraid you'll have to play the part of a devastated widow?" Danny, lying beside her, reached for her free hand.

"Sort of." She sighed. The truth was that Carmen was confused. The house felt large and lonely, she was perpetually turning corners expecting Jobe to be there. But how did she explain this? *I didn't expect to be sad about my husband's death, but in fact, I am.* Instead, she had to pretend that there had been no such gap—that she was slowly ascending from dark horror rather than just now going into it. "People will be whispering about me, asking constantly how I'm holding up. Even if Jobe *had* been the great love of my life, I doubt I'd have known how to grieve."

"Don't worry, I'll get you a copy of Joan Didion's book. You can study up." Danny ran his hand up Carmen's torso, tobogganing it roughly over her nipples and sending sparks through her chest and up into her throat. "Just wear dark clothes, buttoned all the way up to your neck. You'll have to hide these beautiful breasts for at least a year." He grew serious then, wearing his library face. "Or you could tell them the truth: that you're exhausted from the last year and relieved that Jobe's not in pain anymore. People will give you space."

Carmen took the last swallow and lay back as Danny used both hands to massage her breasts then moved his mouth slowly down her body, finding the place he wanted between her legs. She couldn't even talk to her lover, revealing that she wasn't simply relieved; she was, to her surprise, constantly wistful, thinking about Jobe. His death had released memories that puzzled more than distressed her, but he was always present in her thoughts—even now. She closed her eyes and floated on the sensation of Danny's gentle licking and it became like a series of warm rings that kept expanding out. Infinite golden zeros. At the same time, something was happening to the part of her body farthest from Danny, who was crouched inside her knees. It felt like two oversized palms—one on her forehead and the other at the nape of her neck—supporting her head.

After she came, he plunged into her like a javelin, practically making an arc with his small body as he leaped up from the foot of the bed. They were almost exactly the same size, Carmen often thought: like two matching toys designed to be locked together. No wonder this had always worked so well.

Little had changed since Jobe's death, at least on the surface of their meetings. Danny still held to the same schedule: every other week, on Tuesday, from one to four. How he'd worked this out with the library, she never knew, though he had a relationship with the director that led Carmen to believe they'd slept together at least once. She imagined the woman with her proper suits and tight hair getting a little tipsy after a party—something to celebrate the digital conversion of the card catalog perhaps—making out with Danny in some dark corner, tomes about botany sitting dustily on the shelves around them, taking him back to her office where there likely was a comfortable couch. The woman was married, and an indiscretion would have given Danny leverage, leeway. It was a small price to pay for freedom. This, Carmen understood.

One thing did feel different, however. It was something that Carmen had trouble naming. The sex was just as good, and Danny's manner with her was, if anything, even more accommodating. That could be because she had insisted on paying all three times for the hotel, putting a stop to that odd moment at the front desk where they usually negotiated quickly whose turn it was, feeling guilty about the $5 million insurance check, which had arrived and sat in her bank account like a phantom that had taken up residence. Despite Jobe's parents' wealth, they'd never lived like anything but a professor's family: comfortable and scruffy. Now, her return to work had become a choice, a diversion. And this affair somehow no longer was.

It reminded Carmen vaguely of unloading the dishwasher, taking bundles of forks out and setting them in a drawer. Not unpleasant, by any means, and satisfying in its way. Her relationship with Danny still seemed necessary, but more in the way of an everyday task. The daring otherness of it had evaporated. No longer was this the secret that gave dimension to her unfulfilling home life. These days, with Jobe gone, it felt simply like three recreational hours in a cheap hotel.

She scissored up to sit in bed, using her abdominal muscles the way she'd been taught in Pilates class. It wasn't like Carmen to beg but she was desperate to shake Jobe from her thoughts. "What I need is a change of scenery," she said to Danny, who had turned the other way and was reaching down for his boxers. "I know you can't get *away*. But let's do something, I don't know, different. Maybe a museum in D.C.? It's not like Mega has spies. We could get a room at the Monaco; have dinner somewhere really nice. I have some extra cash right . . ."

Danny made the motions of putting two legs through the holes of his shorts then turned to look at her, his face set and mournful in a way it never was.

"Carmen," he said, putting one hand on her sheeted leg and staring at her exposed breasts, rather than her face.

"Don't worry, I'm not asking you to leave your wife." She inhaled, defiantly jutting her chest out. "All I want is some room service, a little champagne. C'mon. I'm a little rattled, frankly. I don't think this is too much to ask."

"It's not that." Danny shook his head and when he raised it, his face was sad. Carmen never thought of him as Indian, but seated there with a stony expression and his broad bare chest he reminded her of the photos she'd seen of warriors, sitting atop horses, feathered headdresses blowing in the wind. "I, uh, felt something, earlier. I've been trying to think of a way to tell you. It's right . . ." He reached out and touched two fingers—so lightly that Carmen suspected he actually was hovering a single electron orbit's distance away from her surface—to the outer curve of her left breast. "Here."

She sat perfectly still. Danny withdrew his hand and revolved slowly so he was facing her, cross-legged on the bed. He took both her hands, the concerned gesture of a husband or old friend. Carmen was certain he did it to keep her from touching herself in the same spot.

"You felt something like . . . what?"

"I don't know." He shook his head. "It was smaller than a golf ball, bigger than a marble, I guess. Kind of rough and"—he took a breath—"very hard. From everything I've read, it's probably something you need to get checked out."

"You've read about this?" Even she could hear how sarcastic and frightened her tone was.

"People call the library for information. You'd be surprised. Sometimes it's the first thing they do after talking to a doctor."

Terror was licking at her now, icy against her temples and neck. "Lucky me. I can just bypass that medical part, seeing as how I have the librarian's ear." She pulled her right hand free and Danny let her but kept gripping the other. Gently, as if afraid of hurting herself, she traced the outside of her left breast, starting at the top, around one o'clock, thinking of all the self-exams she hadn't done, pressing the pads of her fingers into the skin more deeply as she went along.

There was nothing there! He was wrong. He must have been imagining it; could it be he wanted her to be sick, wanted her out of the way now that she was free of her marriage and could become a bother? A stalker. Showing up at his house late at night, slashing Mega's spandex clothes with a steak knife, boiling rabbits on his . . .

Carmen's fingers ran into the knot just at the point where she had become too confident and started digging down in earnest. Why anyone would call this a lump, she couldn't understand. The word implied a softness, like the lumps of flour in gravy that could be easily batted apart with a wooden spoon. This thing was more like something you'd encounter in the bark of a tree, heavy and coarse, with an odd, spiraling tail that seemed to trail down into the space under her arm.

"Oh," she heard herself cry, just before Danny moved in and closed his arms around her.

"It could be nothing," he said into her ear. "In most cases, that's what happens. You go in, they take a biopsy, and it's perfectly benign." He had the loamy smell of unshowered sex and Carmen knew she should warn him: He must not go home to his wife this way. Instead, she let him hold her until a few minutes before four o'clock when they both scrambled for the rest of their clothes.

"You'll make an appointment tomorrow?" Danny asked as he pulled his pants on and started fastening his belt with its complicated silver buckle in the shape of a wolf, his Cherokee clan. She was silent, and he stopped what he was doing. "Carmen?"

She looked up at him from where she was sitting on the unmade bed, holding her long dress socks in one hand, not moving. Danny sighed and sat next to her, lacing his hands together. She shifted her gaze to them, the very fingers that had detected her (she refused even to think the word *lump*) comet made of stone.

What if she'd never come here with him? Carmen played the game. What if she'd loved her husband better and grieved him right, staying home to rearrange his clothes in the closet and weep? What if, back when she'd sat in a room with Jobe and heard the doctor say non-Hodgkin's lymphoma, she had never felt even the slightest twinge of reprieve? Any one of those things might have changed what was happening right now. Perhaps thoughts have weight—enough to push the balance of events from one outcome to another—and every action alters molecules in tiny but profound ways. This cancer—because she was certain that no matter what Danny said, that that's what it was—had been shaped by everything she'd done and wished for over the past many years. It was the product of her life: an evolving enemy living in the pocket under her left arm.

"Look, if you want me to, I'll call in sick and take you. Maybe there's a clinic in Frederick where we could go."

"No." Her voice came out calm, almost ghostly. "That would be stupid." What she meant was that Baltimore had one of the best medical facilities in the civilized world—it hadn't helped Jobe, but still, one did not leave the Johns Hopkins system to be examined by country doctors with flickering, outdated X-ray machines. Danny, however, took it another way.

"Okay," he said. "I suppose you're right. There's no need to take the risk, because you're probably just fine. They'll do a little minor surgery and take out this . . . cyst." He made a hand gesture she took to mean the swipe of a knife. "I'll be careful of the stitches next time and spend a lot of time helping you relax and recover." He'd been caressing her thigh but Carmen saw Danny turn his hand so he could look at his watch, as he bit the inside of his cheek.

"Listen, I hate to do this, but I have a dinner thing . . ." he said finally.

"Go." Carmen was still holding her socks in one hand. It was possible she might go barefoot, she decided. The weather was warm. May. Things were growing; if you were very still, you could feel it in the air. "I have a couple phone calls I want to make and the room is paid for."

Danny shot her a look, but she hadn't meant anything by the comment—or if she had, it wasn't worth going into. "Okay," he said after a moment. "Call me at work tomorrow, will you? Tell me what you find out?"

"Of course." She lifted her face, prompting him to rise from the bed and kiss her. Then he took ahold of her shoulders and tipped her chin up farther, so she was looking into his eyes, where the Irish blood shone through Indian skin with two gleams of ocean green. "Carmen, I love you. Maybe not in the traditional way, but I do. And if you need something, you can call. I'll find a way to explain it to Mega."

She nodded and blinked, wishing there were tears there. Why, if she could cry for the man she'd disdained couldn't she cry for this man, whom she'd dreamed of since she saw him sitting behind his desk decorated with leather and turquoise two years before? But rather than returning his feelings, she felt only a vague, unfair anger toward Danny, who had changed everything in a single afternoon: first by diagnosing her with his busy hands and then by proclaiming his love.

"I'm sure it's nothing," Carmen lied. "But I'll let you know."

The attendant brought her tea, in a cup with a saucer and a linen napkin and a tiny spoon. This was like being at Olive's house, Carmen thought, only in an ugly pink fleece robe and jeans, waiting for her turn to have her breasts smashed between the plates of a huge machine.

"So you've had . . . one mammogram? Is that right?" The woman sitting next to her had a clipboard and a springy bracelet around her wrist with a key that she used to open the dressing room doors.

"Yes. I had a baseline at thirty-nine. My mother died of breast cancer, so I wanted to be careful."

The interviewer grimaced. "But nothing since?" Carmen turned to the woman, who had drawn on eyebrows with what must have been a felt-tip marker. They were weird and furry-looking but perfectly flat. "We recommend mammograms every year after forty, *especially* for first-degree relatives. For you it's been"—she flipped back to a previous page—"more than two."

There was a pause. No point in reviewing the fact that she'd been told something completely different when she was in last time; back then, the technician had said if the scan was clean, Carmen could wait safely until forty-five.

"Well, my husband was very ill and I seem to have forgotten," Carmen said. This was like a tactical checkmate, a move you couldn't use until the opportunity was presented directly to you, but then it worked every time. Not that Carmen was much interested in chess. But Jobe had been determined to teach Luca—even buying a set with the characters from *Alice in Wonderland* to help capture him—and sometimes after dinner she would watch them play.

"He passed away last month," Carmen said, though she was still picturing the two of them hunched over the board. "I guess I haven't been thinking clearly since."

"Oh, Lordy." The woman's face went through a montage of sad expressions; then she put her hand on Carmen's arm and squeezed. "You've been through *everything*, haven't you, dear? I don't know how people like you stay so strong."

"Are there any other options?" Carmen asked, then immediately felt bad. If she was going to use Jobe's death to elicit sympathy, she should at least be grateful when that's what came her way.

"Now, dear, I want you to show me where you found the lump." The woman sat, pen poised.

Carmen looked around the room, where half a dozen women

sat. There were also two husbands—if they were here, the X-ray probably was not routine for their wives either. She pointed with her right
finger to her left breast. "Here."

"I need an exact spot, if you can," said the woman, pulling out
a sheet with a crude outline of a female form. "Can you still feel it?
Has the lump gone away since that first time?"

Carmen shook her head, amazed that her fantasy was such an
ordinary possibility. She'd been prodding herself obsessively, hoping
the comet would simply disappear. But each time she'd checked, it
was in the exact place where Danny discovered it nine days earlier.

Now, she slipped her hand inside the robe and palpated her
breast until she homed in on the location, touching herself directly
above. "It's right here," she said, and the woman with the key made
a neat cross on the top left side of the drawing. Like a treasure map.

The procedure itself was as Carmen remembered. She was ordered
to turn, lift her arm, slant her body at a weird angle so her breasts
could be smashed between two plates. And as she had the first time,
Carmen wondered how much damage was being done. A few of these
lifesaving tests and a woman could end up with two stretched-out
teats dangling to her knees.

The technician did her right breast first, pictures from the front
and the side, then released that one and gingerly lifted the left onto the
Plexiglas platform of her machine. "Will it hurt, because of the . . ."—
Carmen forced herself to speak the way others did, using the word
they preferred—"lump?"

"It shouldn't. But if it does, you tell me the minute you feel anything and we'll stop and readjust." She was young, probably not yet
thirty. *What did she know about these things?* But the girl patted Carmen's back in a friendly way and scratched it a bit with her long fingernails, which felt good even through the fleece. Carmen relaxed and
was surprised when her left breast lay squashed below her that the
comet neither hurt nor popped from the surface of her skin. She'd
been expecting to see an outline, the way you did with a baby's foot
when it kicked from inside.

"Everything okay?" the technician asked.

"Fine," Carmen said, though it was at least in part a lie.

They had her sit in the waiting room, still in her robe, in case they needed more "films," as the technician referred to them. Carmen did nothing as she sat, neither reading a magazine nor drinking tea, but simply waiting for what she knew would come. And then it did.

A man emerged from a back room—the first one on staff that she'd seen since entering the breast center—and introduced himself with a name she immediately forgot. They needed an MRI to follow up, he told her. Then, most likely, a needle aspiration biopsy. It would be relatively painless; just a little local anesthesia. She would be able to go home and cook dinner for her family tonight.

"Only a guy would say that like it's a desirable thing," she cracked and he smiled, but she could tell he was thinking she should, indeed, be grateful. There was a family, she could feed them. These things might not always be true.

This time Carmen was given a gown that tied in front. It seemed to have been made of wax paper and was, again, pink: the color of the stuff you had to swallow when you were nauseated. The socks they gave her—thankfully, however much they clashed—were a pale blue. Then she was led down a long hallway by a wide-hipped woman who looked like a prison matron. The sweet, young technician had disappeared; Carmen was, apparently, too far gone already for her.

Inside a steel-gray room, the matron extended her hand like a knight to help Carmen up onto a wide metal table. "Are those what I think they are?" she asked, pointing to a bustier-shaped contraption that lay on the table's surface.

"Yep. That's where your bosoms will go. So let's just get you ready." The matron reached out and began untying the gown, oblivious to the intimacy of the act. Carmen leaned back, almost enjoying the play. "Chilly in here," she said.

"You'll be warm soon enough. That's something a lot of gals complain about: the heat."

"What heat?" The woman had eased the gown back from

Carmen's shoulders so that she sat bare-chested in the strange room. It was amazing how good that felt, almost like the wanton feeling of going to a topless beach, which she and Jobe had done once on their honeymoon. Now she recalled his face—her young husband—when she had wriggled out of the top half of her one-piece suit and lay back on a towel. He'd stood over her, supposedly blocking the sun but also obstructing people's view of her, until she'd had to beg, "Please sit down, Jobe. You're throwing a shadow and I'm getting really cold."

He'd sunk to the sand, cross-legged beside her, and taken her hand. For an hour they'd stayed this way, Carmen touched by Jobe's protectiveness but also shamefully titillated by the idea of men and women walking by and ogling her perfect, naked breasts.

"Okay, now, you're gonna lie this way." The woman pivoted Carmen on the shiny surface so she was facing the bustier thing. "I need you to lower yourself down into the coil and I'm going to guide you in."

It was like doing a reverse push-up: Carmen had her hands on either side of the cast and the matron, standing at the head of the table, had reached out to grab one dangling breast in each hand so she could settle them into the cups. This was not a woman who appealed to Carmen; some did, but they tended to be slim and rugged, women strangely like herself with dark, wavy hair and muscular arms. Still, she couldn't help but be turned on when anyone touched her breasts. It had happened at every gynecologic exam she'd ever had. Danny could make her come simply by standing behind her while she was fully clothed, rubbing and pinching her nipples through her shirt. Even Jobe had figured out that touching her there was a catalyst, the magic key to orgasm no matter how awkward their sex.

"Okay, now you're in. I'm going to put an IV in your arm."

Carmen closed her eyes. Her back was starting to hurt already from being propped this way and she was worried now. If surgeons had to cut the comet from her, would they also cut the nerves that made her shudder that way? It had never, in all the years of watching pink-ribbon-wearing women marching on TV, occurred to her that mastectomy was the equivalent of castration above the waist.

"Relax now," the matron said. "This won't hurt much. You're not a fainter, are you?"

"Hardly," Carmen said, her voice muffled against the pillow under her chin. "But what would it matter, anyway? I'm lying down."

There was a burning feeling on the top of her right wrist, then the rush of fluid entering her. "There," said the woman, taping the needle into Carmen's arm and patting it curtly. "Now, I need to put some ear plugs in, to keep you comfortable." Again, she was sliding something into Carmen's body: this time, a squishy little bullet in each ear. Then another pat. "You're all set. I'm going to run and get the MRI guy and we'll start."

Nothing happened for a while but Carmen didn't really care. They must have stuck some kind of sedative in the IV. She had drifted into a gauzy fog, her back forgotten, when the table she was on began to move. "Carmen?" A man's tinny, muffled voice came from nowhere and everywhere. "We're going to need you to lie perfectly quiet, okay? If something happens, if you start to feel sick or dizzy, you just say so. The machine is miked. But otherwise, I want you to hold yourself as still as possible. Ready to start?"

It was odd, speaking into this tubular cavern, trusting that her voice would be heard. But she did. "Sure, go for it," Carmen said, and within seconds the most incredible banging racket started around her, sounds like the battering of a thousand deer hooves against a huge tin can. There was nothing to do but lie propped and let this happen and Carmen was doing fine, until the reality of what this could mean flared out at her. She saw her children lined up, Luca and Siena and Michael at another funeral, watching another casket being lowered into the ground. This made her not panicked so much as angry. Not only was it wrong for her children to lose both their parents so young, but she had *earned* this part of her life. She'd stuck out twenty-one years of marriage, trying as hard as she could under the circumstances to be a good wife; surely she had a little freedom coming to her! Could it be that now—just as she was about to find her way back on to the right road—Carmen, too, was going to die?

"It will be very hard for a while," the voice coming through the speaker said. Only this time it didn't sound so echoey and metallic; also, it was a few shades lower. "But you'll be fine in the end."

She shifted to the right, craning her head to look over her shoulder. "I need you to lie still, Carmen," said the original voice. "Just a few more minutes and then we'll do your contrast."

"Sorry," she muttered, but the word was lost in the combination of deer thunder and anxiety. Then she felt the warmth the nurse had talked about, a slow turning-to-orange like the heating of a burner on an electric stove. And—as she had that day with Danny when he'd found her comet—that long, smooth hand on her forehead and another on the back of her neck.

"It will be fine," she heard again, only this time it was more like a vapor of words, neither spoken nor written on the air but something she could not pinpoint that was in between.

After the MRI, she waited again, growing cold and shivering in her wax gown and blue socks. And when the matron came back, Carmen knew immediately from her eyes that the comet had burned through all their tests. A four-year-old could look at the images and know.

"Doctor saw your results and he wants a biopsy," the nurse said.

She offered her hand as if Carmen were frail and needed help out of her chair. And to her surprise, Carmen accepted it gratefully, pressing her palm to this large woman's, feeling the sturdy workings of healthy blood and flesh under her own weak skin. She was lightheaded as she rose and wished fleetingly for Jobe to lean against, his arm reeling her in against the long, tall trunk of his chest.

"This is going to sting," the nurse admitted as they walked toward a door marked with a number 8. "My advice is to breathe through it."

"You could just give me some of that stuff you used for the MRI," Carmen said. "That worked like a dream."

"What stuff?" They pushed through the door and into yet another room of white tile and steel. "All we did was pump a little saline into you, then some contrast. There was no need for any sedative. Some women, they panic inside the tube. But other than that one time, you were perfect." She helped Carmen up onto another cold metal table and fussed over her like a nanny, untying and retying more tightly the laces on her gown. "We did hear you talking to yourself in there, but sometimes that happens. It's a little like a sensory deprivation tank. People have their visions."

Carmen lowered herself onto the paper-covered pillow though it was the last thing she really wanted to do. Suddenly, she was terrified. More than anything, she wanted to get up and go home—forget this had ever happened—the same way she'd tried when she was giving birth to Luca. Prior to this, she'd assumed there was always the option to change her mind; when, halfway through a thirty-hour labor, she'd realized this was a permanent trap that would go on without her control, she thought she might go insane.

A doctor came in and spoke to her, but she barely listened. When he unsheathed a long needle and stood aiming it at the tiny X she and the matron had together drawn on her breast with a pen, Carmen was bored. *Just let this be over*, she thought. There was a prolonged, burning sensation. A few minutes of painful probing. And then it was done.

Pathology would have to process the biopsy; he would then add these results to the others. Someone would call her within two days to schedule another appointment. Carmen nodded. She would have agreed to anything in that moment simply to be able to retrieve her clothes and leave.

Walking into the house, Carmen felt as if days, or weeks, had passed since she'd last seen it. Objects appeared bold, as if each was at the center of a still life: the ceramic bowl in the hall where she dropped her keys, the staged portrait of their family from six years ago that hung in the living room, a pair of shoes that Michael had left—one toe crossed over the other—on the dining room floor. Each nearly pulsed with presence. Overwhelmed, Carmen wanted to hide.

But when she entered the kitchen and saw Siena hunched over an enormous book, everything righted and Carmen nearly cried. "What's up?" she said, struggling to keep her voice normal.

Siena crossed her eyes and wrinkled her freckled nose. "Calculus." She spit the word out like a curse. She was wearing her hair in two long braids, which made her look wholesome and about twelve. Carmen ached hard to go back in time and fix things. Five years would give her the chance to . . . what? Exercise more? Eat more broccoli? Remain faithful to Jobe?

"Need help?" Carmen offered absently, still wondering what happened to the people that they were: to Luca, in high school, and Michael, only a small child.

"Yeah sure, Mom. Pull up a seat. Tell me everything you know about derivatives of cubic polynomials."

Carmen stiffened. "I might know more than you think."

"Really?" Siena's sarcasm cleared like a thundercloud shattered by sun. She looked at Carmen hopefully.

"No, not really." Carmen pulled out a chair anyway and sat. She stared at the paper in front of Siena and was bewildered that her daughter could make such foreign-looking hieroglyphs.

"Something wrong?" asked Siena. "You look . . . funny."

"No, I'm just missing your father. He would have known how to help you with this." She hadn't planned to say that. She hadn't even known she thought it. And the moment it was out of her mouth, Carmen was terrified that she'd made a terrible mistake. Reminding Siena of Jobe's absence—looming as it already was—seemed cruel.

But as she opened her mouth to apologize and met Siena's eyes, Carmen saw that just the opposite was true. Her daughter was teary yet luminous, her young face filled not with horror but awe. "Yeah, he would have," she said softly.

There was a moment's pause, and into it Carmen let out the breath it seemed she'd been holding all day.

The call came precisely forty-eight hours later. It was a hot Friday afternoon filled with the hazy sound of insects. Carmen was pulling weeds, which had always before been Jobe's job. She was on her knees. And as she dug into her pocket for the phone, she understood this was it. The answer had been screamed by her cancer cells into a pathologist's face, noted on a form for the doctor, conveyed to the staff. Carmen's feet, propped toe-first in the dirt, felt deadened, like stumps.

"Doctor would like you to come in for a consultation right away next week," the caller said.

Carmen's heart was shrinking, becoming—she was sure—the size and texture of an apricot pit. The cancer might be spreading there as well.

"Glenda?" she said, remembering the voice and the name tag of the woman who had helped her with her paperwork. "Is this Glenda? Do you remember me?"

"Yes, this is she. But I see so many women, you know."

"I'm the one whose husband just died." Carmen made a brief silent apology to Jobe. "Do you remember? I've got three kids, Glenda. They just lost their dad. I need to prepare them. I have to know."

Why? That was the question. Why did she have to know? Why couldn't she spend one weekend free of the truth, ignoring the problem, using some minuscule portion of her bankroll to take her family on some wacky, roller coaster tour of Memphis or St. Louis or Austin. She could bring Troy and Jeffrey along and buy everyone enormous cowboy hats. Why not just do it, forget this cancer thing and go?

But before she could reverse herself and tell the woman she'd been too hasty, knowledge was not what she wanted at all— she'd been right back in that hotel room with Danny, before the comet was even discovered; what she really wanted was escape—Glenda spoke. "I'm so sorry, Mrs. Garrett."

It was good Carmen was still kneeling because the whole world swooned brightly with these words.

"You really need to come in as soon as possible. This is not the sort of thing you let go. For the sake of your children."

After the call was done, Carmen stayed where she was for a

moment, staring at the houses in her neighborhood and then—tipping her head down—at the earth around her knees. It was dark and wet and busy. Microscopic creatures trundled over the soil. She lowered toward the ground. It was a whole world, apart from hers, filled with an infinite number of lives.

She hadn't made a decision about whom to tell first. But after watching ants and mites and spiders for a while, Carmen rose and went inside. Siena was at work, Luca at his day program, Michael at baseball practice—and it was Jeffrey's parents' turn to pick them up. The house was silent.

Carmen changed her clothes and got in the car, driving to Jana's café, the only business on a hickory-lined street near the university. It was 3:20, which was a perfect time to visit because Jana would be past the lunch rush and just pulling her second Amstel Light out of the refrigerator. Her mornings began at five, Jana always said, so her cocktail hour should rightfully start at three.

But when Carmen pushed the door open and walked under the strings of dangling chili pepper lights, she was disappointed to see that Jana had a nearly full house. There was a party of seven at a table they'd made by pushing together two four-tops, a man sitting across from a little girl, two pairs of women chatting over steaming cups, and lone people with computers and plates at all the other tables. Only one of the three high stools in front of the coffee bar was free, so Carmen wedged herself onto it, trying to quell her irrational irritation that these strangers were obstructing her access.

"Hey, bad timing," said Jana, raising her multicolored, dreadlocked head to wave a knife at Carmen. "I'm swamped and fucking Emily broke up with her boyfriend last night and couldn't stop crying, so I sent her home."

"Can I get some coffee?" Carmen asked.

"Help yourself." Jana went back to chopping cilantro. "Now that you're a wealthy widow, I figure you're good for it."

What Carmen really wanted was a beer and for Jana to drop everything and sit down and talk to her, but she sipped the tepid

French roast instead—wondering if she should let Jana know her hot pot was not doing the job even though that would only delay her friend more. "Can I help?" she finally asked as Jana put the last of seven plates on a tray and hoisted it on her shoulder.

"Honestly, yes. You could clear a few tables. That would be tremendous."

This was a change: In a year and a half of visiting Jana at the café, Carmen had never crossed the line between the front of the house and the back. But the whole world had changed, so why not? She shouldered her way into the tiny kitchen and found an apron hanging on a coat tree, tied it over her T-shirt and jeans, and picked up an ugly gray bus tub. She was headed out into the dining room with it when Jana caught her elbow. "Huh, uh, use a tray. Looks better. Okay? Thanks, sweet."

Carmen nodded and headed back into the kitchen to trade the bus tub. No one else, not even Olive, could tell her what to do; but Jana somehow was different. Perhaps it was the fact that she was the only person on earth who knew about Danny, and about Jobe.

Carmen had poured everything out one night shortly after meeting Jana, when she came into the agency to ask about having a web site done. In the end, Jana hadn't been able to afford their quote but Carmen had felt immediately compelled—almost attracted—by her and worked out a deal with the creative director to cut her a break: doing one static design for the home page and giving Jana templates she could use to program in her own information. Then Carmen had offered to go to the café a couple of times and sit with Jana, teach her how. It was like courting. She needed a friend who wasn't attached to her through Jobe or his parents or the kids. During their third meeting, the one where Jana happened to ask if she was married, Carmen told her the whole story. She was shocked when Jana disapproved.

"You're not being honest." Jana shook her head, dreads swinging. "He's an okay guy, a good dad. You yourself admit that. This just isn't right."

Carmen was piqued more than upset by what Jana said. This

was interesting. Her new friend might be a lesbian, a woman who dyed her hair Easter egg colors, and a self-identified witch, but she had a strict moral code.

"I was an impetuous kid," Carmen told her. "I *did* stuff like this: You know, I'd take off for a road trip to California with three people I'd just met. I'd drop acid then go out sailing on Lake Huron in the middle of the night. So I met this guy and he was nice to me at a time when no one else was—probably for good reason. His parents were really good to me, too; they took me in, they paid for my last year of college. My mother had just died and I was kind of screwed up. Lonely." Carmen shrugged. "So I mistook gratitude for love. It was a stupid, childish thing to do. But I married him totally on a whim, thinking I owed it to him and I could make it through. Then the reality of 'forever' kind of sank in. I mean it; I regretted it within days."

"So?" Jana was stolid and unmoved. "You could have told him you were sorry, you made a mistake, divorced him."

"I almost did, on our honeymoon." Carmen felt a flicker of guilt. She would tell Jana about the night Jobe nearly died—and her understanding of what it would take to end their marriage—another time. "But we were in Italy and I didn't speak a word of Italian. He had all the money because it came from his parents, his mother . . ."

Jana raised her eyebrows.

"Our wedding gift," Carmen said. "I mean, one of them. Anyway, by the time we came back, I was pregnant. Another, uh, sign of carelessness, I guess. Jobe was thrilled. I was terrified. Then Luca was born and he had Down's. It was just incomprehensible: I couldn't take care of this kid on my own! He'd have medical bills and besides, Jobe loved him just the same as if he'd been, ah, normal." She gazed off for a moment and when she refocused, Jana's face had softened toward her for the first time since she began.

"So you stayed."

"I stayed and I got pregnant again. Jesus, I was fertile. We hardly ever had sex and even when we did, it wasn't . . . well, anyway. I thought about leaving again when the older kids were, I don't know, five and eight. We'd been married long enough I knew Jobe would take care of them no matter what, be that weekend dad and give me enough alimony to survive. But it seemed so awful. Really, I was trying to do the right thing. And this man had done *nothing* wrong, nothing to deserve being left. He was good to me; he was great to the kids. So we started talking about how it would be unfair to Siena when we were both gone, you know, having Luca to take care of all on her own."

"Ergo, Michael?"

"Yeah." Carmen shifted, feeling a little looser, like retelling the story was helping her, again, make sense of how this could have happened. "By then, we'd been together for more than ten years. We had the house; Jobe had tenure. I was what? Thirty-three. And I had this life. This forever marriage. So I adjusted."

"How many affairs?" Jana asked bluntly. And Carmen could tell it mattered: There was a number at which sympathy would no longer be possible.

"Just two," she said truthfully. "Danny's the second. There was a guy back about three years ago. Someone from work. It seemed convenient for a while: You know, all we had to do was tell our spouses we were working late on the same project and we were covered. But he wasn't . . ." Carmen shook her head, realizing something for the first time. "Honestly, the only exciting thing about him was the circumstance. When you really came down to it, he did even less for me than my husband, and I would go home feeling crazy, like I was juggling these two men, but for what? I still didn't have what I was looking for."

"Which was?" Jana asked. "As someone who's never had a taste for men, I'm really curious. What *was* it you were looking for?"

Carmen paused. "The only thing I can come up with is freedom. I wanted someone who would make me forget about every dumb thing I'd done to tie myself down and destroy my life. The great thing about Danny is we have a great time but he doesn't expect a single thing."

"Hmmm. Sounds like marriage really isn't the best idea for you."

"No. And yet . . ." Carmen remembered now, as if she were outside of herself watching, the way she'd spread her arms as if to encompass the entire café, all of Baltimore, the world of traditional couples. "Here I am."

Jana had never approved, but she'd helped nonetheless, covering for Carmen when she wanted to leave with Danny at odd times of day, even bringing food to Jobe and the kids when Carmen was gone. "I do it for him," she told Carmen. "I like your husband. He's the only Maryland boy I've ever met who knows my name isn't spelled with a Y. He says it's because he's spent a lifetime being called Jobey. He really cracks me up. You sure you can't figure out how to love him?"

After she'd finished clearing tables, Carmen emptied out the pot of lukewarm coffee and brewed another one. Someone came up to the counter asking for honey and she found a sticky bear on the spice shelf above the griddle. An elderly man wanted coffee but she didn't know how to run the cash register so she made it and brought it to him and told him it was on the house. When Carmen glanced at the clock and saw that it was 4:30, two things ran through her mind. One was that she would have to leave soon in order to convert some leftovers into dinner for the kids. The other was that she'd actually forgotten for a whole blissful hour why she came in to talk to Jana in the first place.

As if they could hear her thoughts, the remaining three customers rose and walked out the front door with its jangling bell, leaving her alone with Jana.

"Beer, madam?" Jana walked out with two open bottles hooked between the fingers of her left hand, plucked one and held it out for Carmen with her right.

She took it and drank a tiny sip that tasted almost fruity. She was thirsty. Carmen recalled the technician's warning her she should drink plenty of water for a few days, to flush out the contrast.

"Who's coming in tonight?" Carmen asked, looking warily toward the door.

"Uh, that would be me. Candy-ass employees with their non-stop personal problems. I don't know why I do this."

"I do. That was actually fun."

Jana narrowed her eyes. "Okay, now I know something's wrong. If Gloria Vanderbilt enjoys clearing dishes, there has to be a problem."

"I keep telling you, I'm just a girl from Detroit. Why is that so hard for you to understand?"

"Yeah, so was Madonna, way back." Jana settled back, eyes glittering, and took a swig. "I assume you have something you want to talk about."

"I do." Carmen checked her watch. It was ten minutes to five. "But I should probably get home and feed the kids."

"Don't worry about it," Jana said brusquely. "Just let 'em know you'll be late and I'll send a bunch of stuff: I have a great chicken-tortilla soup and some of those fudge bars the boys love. It's the least I can do to pay you for your work. Here." Jana gathered her own empty bottle and Carmen's, which still had three inches in it that she chugged. "I'll get us more beers."

Carmen texted Siena and Michael but called Luca, whose blunt fingers were too clumsy to text. "It's okay, Mom," Luca said. "I'm watching *The Real World*."

"How dreadful," Carmen said, then laughed because she sounded exactly like her mother-in-law rather than that Detroit girl she'd once been. "Have a good time."

Jana came back with two bottles. "There's some food all ready to go for the kids." She motioned with her head at a large paper bag on the counter then settled back in her chair. "You know what? I'm kind of surprised to see you. I thought maybe you and I were done."

Carmen took a long swallow of beer and thought again about how she really should be drinking water. Slowly, she placed the bottle on the table. "Why would you think that?"

"Because now that Jobe is dead you don't need anyone to keep your secret anymore, so my usefulness is pretty much gone." Outside the window, a dirty-looking man hovered near the doorway of the café, acting as if he might come in. Both women watched until he walked away then returned their gaze to each other. Unblinking.

It made sense, Carmen had to admit. She hadn't seen or talked to Jana since the day of the funeral, hadn't even thought about her until the call from the clinic came in. "That would have been a shitty thing to do to a friend," she said, which was true yet fell short of admitting anything.

"Yeah." Jana leaned back and looked at Carmen with slitted eyes. "The whole situation was shitty. I had a job to do: I was supposed to keep your secret. But sometimes it's dangerous to know too much."

"You were worried I might have you killed?"

Jana laughed. "Nah, we've already established that's not your style. But I did think you might decide you wanted to start fresh, pretend you just lost the love of your life, just . . ." She made a gentle shooing motion with her fingers. "Fade away."

Carmen sat perfectly still—as she had been inside the MRI machine earlier—staring at the rope bracelets looped around Jana's thick wrist. She had a sudden urge to chew on one of them, feel the sinewy fibers in her mouth, taste Jana's sweat. "Well, I guess I'm not done with you. Jobe's dead. Now I have breast cancer. Maybe I need someone who'll tell me this is divine retribution."

Jana sat up swiftly. "Are you serious?"

Carmen nodded and there was a pause. When she looked up, she saw that Jana actually had tears in her eyes. This had never happened before that she could recall—not even when Jobe died.

"I mean," Carmen corrected, "it's 99 percent certain. They did the mammogram and an MRI and a biopsy. I got a call telling me to come in for a consultation. Fast. But I'm also . . . I just know. It's cancer. I've been sure of it since the day Danny and I . . ." She put her head back. The beer was starting to kick in and her eyes felt heavy.

"Danny found it?" Jana asked. "Did he run for the hills? No more good time girl, you're just a regular old mortal with an imperfect body." Her words were harsh, but her voice was low and soothing, her face creased with concern. "God knows the man never signed on for that."

"I don't know what he'll do yet, honestly." Carmen was too tired to argue. Besides, she'd been wondering the same things herself. Danny had never been tested—at least not by their relationship. That was the beauty of it: nothing serious. Cancer ruined everything. "I haven't talked to him about this. I just got the call and I haven't told anyone but you."

"So I'm the go-to woman for loveless marriages and cancer. I suppose I can deal with that." Jana gazed at the bottle in her hand and crossed her eyes. "You suppose I could have one more and still work the night shift? It's not like I have a big crowd. Sometimes I think I got that liquor license just for me."

Carmen slumped back in her chair. "Perfect. Get another beer. And bring me a glass of ice water. I'm supposed to be drinking a lot and I don't think this"—she lifted her own half-full bottle—"is what the doctor meant."

When Jana came back she had a tray with her own bottle, two glasses of ice water, and a basket of chips and homemade guacamole. "Here, try this," she said gruffly, placing everything on the table. "It's got about a tablespoon of this new hot sauce in it. I think it'll do you good."

"Thanks." Carmen wasn't hungry but she knew Jana needed to feed her, so she dipped a few chips into the bowl and ate them. She took a long drink of water, then a sip of beer. Her stomach shifted pleasantly; she'd been wrong. She needed food after all. "Okay, thanks, I feel slightly less like total crap. And I'm tired of talking about my incredibly fucked-up life. So tell me what's going on with you."

"*My* incredibly fucked-up life? Well, there's the café. And a date with this pretty little blonde lawyer who's 'experimenting.'" Jana made quote marks in the air with her fingers, work-worn and red with ragged nails. "Jesus, I hate that. Nothing worse that a straight woman who goes down on you once then says she's going back to her husband."

"She did that?" It felt wonderful to eat and talk about something other than the comet that was trying to eat her alive. Carmen dug another chip into the guac, smearing it on her fingers and licking it off.

"No." Jana shook her head, and her colored locks leaped and danced. "But she will."

Carmen sat for a moment then started to rise. The children were waiting for their dinner.

"There is one more thing," Jana said. "I took your daughter to get birth control pills."

Carmen was piqued—this was an interesting twist, normal in a way that nothing else had been today—and a little hurt. Siena had confided in Jana. But of course, this was exactly what she'd always told her children to do: Find a trustworthy adult when they needed help.

"I assume this means she's having sex, or planning to."

Jana shrugged. "Her dad died. If you believe her, and I'm inclined to, she and Troy never did it until that first night Jobe was gone. She couldn't stop crying and you were busy making funeral arrangements and talking to the boys. Not that anyone's blaming you. But Siena went to her boyfriend and he was comforting her and . . . well, he *comforted* her. Then it happened again the next couple of nights. I think they decided they'd found some amazing new cure for grief."

"Yeah, I know how that feels," Carmen said softly.

During the months after Luca's birth, when Carmen felt sore and frightened and guilty, she and Jobe had made love at least twice a week. It was the only time she could remember wanting him, leeching warmth from his body. The only time he'd acted recklessly, as if he genuinely longed for her. The only time he'd responded automatically, his body rising to meet hers.

Jana looked at Carmen sharply. "Do you know? Because I certainly don't. I mean, what good am I in a situation like this? I haven't had sex with a man in fifteen years."

Carmen shrugged. "You made sure she was alright, not doing anything stupid." Suddenly the resentment was gone and she was only grateful.

"Yeah. We went to Planned Parenthood." Jana blushed. "I hope you don't mind; I said I was her mother. They really don't care, but it seemed to make it easier for them to prescribe. Oh, and they did a pregnancy test. She's fine. They also made her promise to use condoms in the meantime. You know, 'til the pills take effect."

"Thanks for doing that. Really." Carmen sat for a moment absorbing, drinking her beer and wondering how things might have been different if she'd known this woman earlier in her marriage to Jobe. Surely Jana—three years older, Brooklyn-born, an ethical drifter—would have helped her find a way out, advising her the way she had Siena. *You're going to live like this, lying, every day for the rest of your life?* Carmen imagined the young Jana saying. But it hadn't been her whole life, and if she hadn't stayed, they wouldn't be sitting here right now, discussing Siena. Carmen and Jana would be, what: lovers themselves? Partners in a French bistro? Estranged after knowing each other only a short time? Who could say?

Just then the bell over the door jangled and a couple came in. The Corona-and-tamale crowd. In a few minutes, Harvey, the bluegrass guy, would set up in a corner of the café and the mood would be festive and a little bit New Orleans. Carmen rose quickly, dropped a twenty-dollar bill on the counter despite Jana's protests, and kissed the other woman on the lips.

"You'll be okay," Jana mouthed before dashing unsteadily behind the counter. Carmen picked up the bag holding her children's dinner and left.

At home, things were still too quiet. The main floor was dark and Carmen wandered from room to room, switching on lights, which made various items—Jobe's stereo, the cedar chest where they kept old photographs, a coat tree—leap out at her all sharp corners and cave colors and spikes.

"Hello? I have dinner," she called up the back stairs. There was a rustling, then the slow footsteps of Luca, plodding toward her voice. He appeared at the top of the stairs looking newly wakened; it was as if the house had been under a spell. "Where are your sister and brother?" she asked. But he only shrugged.

There was more movement upstairs. A few minutes later, Siena and Troy appeared, entangled in a way that Carmen couldn't even figure out. Their hands and arms were wrapped together in some sort of strange way—as in a yoga pose. She opened her mouth to say something about their having been upstairs, probably in Siena's bedroom, alone. Then she realized there was no point.

"Hey, where's Michael?" she asked, turning to the cabinet to get a pot for Jana's soup.

"He's staying at Jeffrey's tonight." Carmen had to turn to determine who had spoken; she'd never realized Siena and Troy actually *sounded* alike. And they looked more—she shivered—like brother and sister than they did like Romeo and Juliet.

"Okay, perfect!" Oh, two beers were too many, she thought. One would have given her courage, but the second was making her overly cheerful and dumb. She poured herself a glass of water and drank half of it, standing over the sink, while the three young people watched. "Jana sent dinner." She took the bowls and a fistful of soupspoons to the table and began doling them out to each of four places.

"You saw Jana today?" Siena asked.

Carmen turned. She might as well get this over with. Meeting her daughter's gaze, she locked on and said, "Yes, we talked for quite a while this afternoon."

"Oh." Siena bowed her head and reddened, and Carmen thought again of the night after the funeral when her daughter had been so wild with grief, she'd looked on the brink of throwing up. If Carmen hadn't been so busy with her own unexpected longing for Jobe, with bedding Danny, and now with doctor appointments and worry, she might have noticed how effectively Siena had calmed. Carmen stared at her daughter and wished ardently for the twelve-year-old she'd glimpsed the other day, or the imperious three-year-old with sheets of golden-red hair.

Siena was opening the bag from Jana's café, Troy's hand resting on her hip—as if he owned her!—while she leaned forward to look inside. "Mmmm." Siena inhaled in a way a little too sensual for Carmen's taste. "Smells really good."

What kind of hypocrite was she? Carmen wondered. Not long ago, she'd been distracting herself in bed with Danny, practically begging him to get out of town with her so she could stop thinking about Jobe. Siena and Troy were just as entitled to their rites of comfort even if they were still teenagers, probably even more. She sighed as she poured soup into the pot and lit the burner underneath. It was hell sometimes being a mother who'd misbehaved. Carmen wished for the clarity Olive must have felt, her past so pure she could make rules without wavering at all.

The food was ready and Carmen wished again that she hadn't drunk so much beer. It would be nice to have a glass of wine to hold right now. But every headline she'd ever seen linking alcohol and breast cancer was dancing through her head. She could picture herself drinking Merlot, the wine drizzling directly into the comet and plumping it out, encouraging it to grow.

"Can you call Luca, please?" she asked Troy through a tight, fake smile. *And take your hands off my daughter's ass*. He did so but not without patting Siena lovingly, the gesture of someone who was parting from her for days.

As on the night they'd eaten goulash, Carmen saw an image of the two of them at an altar and knew that their relationship would become, in time, what her own marriage had been. Siena was brilliant, the child whose mind was most like Jobe's; Troy was an average student and gifted baseball player. She'd grow tired of him in about five years—around the time she'd be ready for graduate school, the luster of Troy's athletic sex would begin to wear off—which was probably just long enough to get a marriage and a baby started. Was there no way to stop history from repeating itself?

Carmen shook her head and laughed to herself. She was just tipsy enough to be paranoid but too sober to shrug it off. *What the hell? The cancer was already there.* She poured herself a glass of red wine.

She sat with this while the children filled bowls and plates at the counter.

"Why aren't you eating with us?" It didn't matter how much Luca aged. His voice sounded childlike and plaintive to her. Carmen's first impulse was to jump up and get some food. But the alcohol had dulled her impulsiveness as well as her inhibitions.

"I ate earlier, with Jana," Carmen said in a dreamy voice. "We had a lot to talk about."

Siena scowled. Why did teenage girls assume everything was about them? *Sweetheart, you're not the only one with secrets*, Carmen thought wistfully. But the moment passed quickly and the practical, motherly self reclaimed her body. "I needed to talk to her about your dad—Jana is the only person who understands how I really felt about him." This was true, however misleading. So far, Carmen was negotiating the minefield well. Now the question was how to tell her children about Glenda's phone call without implying they'd soon be orphans.

"You're sick." Luca formed his words carefully this time, the way the speech therapist had taught him. And instead of sounding like a little boy he suddenly struck her as ageless and wise. She'd always loathed when other parents talked about their disabled children's "special" connection to the spiritual. Sentimental bullshit. But she couldn't deny what she'd taken from holding on to Luca during the funeral. Or from the intensity she felt facing him now.

"Yes, I am," Carmen said. "But maybe not in the way you mean."

"How then?" Strangely, it was Troy who'd asked—Troy who looked the most frightened and stricken.

Carmen cleared her throat. "I have cancer."

"Are you *serious*?" Siena sounded not concerned but indignant, as if her mother had stolen the diagnosis from her father.

"Breast cancer," Carmen said, which caused Troy to look at her chest and blush bright red. "I don't know how advanced yet. It could be very early, nothing to worry about. But I'll be going in for appointments next week instead of going back to work. I might need some help around the house. With Michael."

"I'll drive him places." Again, Troy appeared to be the only one who was responding appropriately. Siena was sparkling with fury. Luca appeared lost in thought.

"Thank you, sweetheart," Carmen said. She tipped the wine bottle and poured an inch and a half into Troy's empty water glass. He was nearly eighteen; he was sleeping with her daughter. He was, after all, acting like a man. Maybe this would bring some color back into his face.

"Thanks." Troy took a quick swallow—refined, even under these conditions. He was a young man of breeding; Olive would tell her to take solace in that. "When will you, uh, know?"

"I'm going back to the clinic on Monday. I should find out more then." Once she said it, Carmen realized what this meant. There was an entire, empty weekend to be lived before she found out how decayed her body had become. All those years, all those terrible thoughts about Jobe. They'd been cancerous. *Stop*, said a voice in her head. *Life is not a linear equation. Most events are random. This is not yours alone.* It was loud enough to startle her, and she wondered, briefly, if the children had heard.

Carmen shoved her glass away. She should be ashamed of herself, drinking to the point of hearing things. (The nurse had been able to explain it that last time: the isolation chamber effect of the MRI.) "I think, eventually, I'll be fine" she said, even though she didn't quite believe it.

She looked around the table. Luca was staring at her, no longer elsewhere, his small eyes glittering with concern. Troy had taken Siena's hand, which he held on top of the table, and her expression had softened. She was again that stubborn child, bewildered by her own immoderate emotions. Like mother like daughter, Carmen thought. Like father like son. And the room began to recede until she could make out only what existed in their small island of light.

Carmen lay in bed weary, her body faded and grateful not to be holding itself up any longer, but unable to sleep. Something had changed inside her that day, like the small pointer on a radio being turned from On to Off. What was it? Her hope, her determination, her confidence—none of these was quite right. Reaching one hand out in a sweeping, stretching gesture, trying to find her place on the wide mattress, her fingers brushed Jobe's pillow and she jackknifed up abruptly, aware in a way she hadn't been before that he was truly gone.

It wasn't *his* disappearance so much as anyone's, the fact that it could occur so quietly and completely, that she herself could vanish that way. The wrong treatment, a few radical cells that broke off and decided to travel, one opportunistic disease, and she, too, might die. But instead of leaving a gaping hole, the world would close around her absence, the way it had already started to close around Jobe's. The kids had resumed their lives, the department had figured out a replacement for his classes; Riemann might never be solved, but this was no different from the way it was before.

If she were honest, Carmen had to admit her presence would be even easier to erase than Jobe's. Thousands of people could design banner ads and flyers. Siena and Troy might marry and heroically raise Michael. Danny would find someone else to sleep with and he'd probably tell her, occasionally, the sad, true story of Carmen's early death. Thinking about this, her fists clenched. He might even woo other women this way, telling them tearfully about the one he'd seen through her husband's gruesome end only to detect—*with his own hands*—the comet that would kill her. Carmen envisioned the sweet, pitying expression of a woman barely thirty who put her arm around Danny's shoulders and drew him toward her pert, healthy breasts.

This was insane. Carmen checked the clock: a few minutes past midnight. It didn't matter, really. She had called the HR director at her agency to say she needed yet another week of leave and the man had granted it, sounding forcedly concerned and slightly irritated, as if he suspected Carmen of malingering, playing up her grief because she'd become entranced with shopping and daytime soaps.

"I have cancer now!" Carmen almost shouted but didn't. She might decide to go back to her job if the biopsy proved this was nothing: a comet-shaped hallucination they'd all palpated and shared—she, Danny, the doctor. Perhaps it was an alien chip, intended to keep track of her, that had been implanted while she was sleeping. Maybe Jobe did it before he died.

Carmen stared into the murk outside the window: a foggy sky with a sharp white scythe of moon. "Did you?" she asked silently. "Did you plant this thing to teach me a lesson? Did you know how I felt about you when you were alive?" But there was nothing out there. No answer. Certainly not Jobe.

She shook her head and got out of bed. This was ridiculous: fear had turned her into an idiot. That's what it was, she suddenly realized —that was exactly what had been lost. Her fearlessness. And she desperately wanted it back.

At least the weather had grown warm. It was the perfect temperature to be in bare feet and one of Jobe's old T-shirts, so long that it covered her underwear sufficiently for her to walk around in front of the kids. She padded down the wooden stairs and into the kitchen where the remnants of Jana's fudge bars sat wrapped on the counter. Carmen picked the plastic apart and stood, breaking off small pieces and eating them, gooey chocolate coating her teeth and the roof of her mouth.

There was a small portable CD player on the counter nearer the wall. It had been Jobe's: He used it when he worked around the house, carrying it with him from room to room. Carmen loosened the cord that had been wrapped around it, no doubt by her husband in the weeks before he died. She pressed the button to open the round compartment and found a CD of violin concertos played by Itzhak Perlman. The itchy discontented feeling returned for a few seconds: She would have preferred Blondie or Prince or even an old Beatles album. But Jobe had listened to those only as a concession to her. It was classical music he loved because it was mathematical and helped him think. He'd also enjoyed disco, Carmen recalled, grinning into the night. Sister Sledge. The Bee Gees. It made no sense unless you listened to the rhythms and counted; dance music tended to be as metrical as Beethoven or Bach. But her husband hadn't been the least bit self-conscious; he kept his Earth, Wind & Fire collection filed between Dvořák and Grieg, just where it belonged in his world.

She picked up the little boom box, stopped at the sink for a glass of water, and headed up two flights of stairs. The attic was stuffy. Carmen opened two opposing windows and stood limply between them, letting the breeze sift through her legs. She plugged in the CD player and pressed play; long, sweet, crickety notes began and she sank to the old sectional couch, pulling off her shirt, scratching her back on the nubbly fabric like a bear, finally comfortable, even pulling a fleece over her bare skin.

She raised her hand to touch the comet, feeling its jagged outline like some miniature planet. Maybe this was like *Horton Hears a Who* and an entire other world was lodged in her breast. "We are here, we are here, we are here," she heard the Whos chant. *Horton* had been Luca's favorite book when he was six years old; she probably could still quote long passages if she tried.

Lying back against the cushions, Carmen listened to the golden sounds of the violin mixing with amber cello notes. This wasn't so bad. Her hand moved in widening circles and grazed her nipple and it was suddenly hard. So her breast still worked! Even after all the prodding and squashing that day, the chemicals that had been pumped into her to light up flawed spots. "Use it," said a new voice that was more like an idea quietly floating through her head. "Why not?" And she raised her other hand to rub the right nipple as well. There was a sense of excitement so low and gathering it was almost an ache. Then the dilemma a woman always faces if she's alone: She had only two hands. Moving the right, more dexterous hand down and slipping it inside the waistband of her panties, she darted the left back and forth, fluttering against each of her breasts equally as she found her clitoris and ran her fingers over it and back, slipping them inside only long enough to get them wet and running them back out and up.

The music changed, becoming a soaring symphonic rush—an early ancestor of the Moody Blues—for which she was grateful. Carmen was breathing raggedly now, pressing down harder and arching her back to rub her nipples against the coarse blanket, which she held taut with one hand. Her eyes were closed but dots of gold light appeared behind them, larger and larger in succession. Her shoulders were opening like wings, her whole body thrashing and about to break into waves, when she felt suddenly that she was being watched.

Carmen stopped abruptly, her hands bearing down firmly on her body as if to quiet it. This was a familiar pose. Over the years, after they had quit making love regularly but before they slept apart, Carmen sometimes touched herself late at night while lying next to Jobe in their bed. She always waited until he'd given some sign of sleep: steady breathing, or a single adenoidal snore. Once in a while, though, she would have a sense that he was lying too still to be truly sleeping and was, instead, listening. With Danny, she'd learned to masturbate for a man, and to watch with leering pleasure while he stroked himself in front of her. But it felt weird and unseemly to be doing this in front of her husband, and at least half a dozen times Carmen had simply ceased and turned over, acting as if she'd only been restless, keeping her hand—as it was now—pressed between her legs.

She opened her eyes and looked around the attic, which was lit only by the sliver of moon outside. Could it be possible one of the children had awakened and wandered upstairs?

The dark was thick, almost palpable, and it hung like fabric unfurled from ceiling to floor. Nothing moved. "Hey?" Carmen called out in a brusque whisper. But there was no answer, and after a few moments she was satisfied and settled back and started the process all over again. This could be better, actually: pushing herself almost to climax and stopping just short, then starting again and feeling her body accelerate ten times as quickly as before, becoming wet and open in a matter of seconds with that near–roller coaster sensation building in her throat.

As her orgasm started to take hold, Carmen untensed the way one yoga instructor had advised her years ago. She'd been an older woman, tiny and freakishly flexible, who'd thrown out life advice at the most unlikely times. "Relax your pelvic floor for this pose," she'd told a class that included a dozen women and three men. "Breathe. Slowly. Ladies, you might try this during sex. It will make your climax much higher."

It was during this class, actually, that Carmen had realized she could not continue having sex only with her husband. Jobe was not yet sick, but the way he touched her—and avoided her for long periods of time—already had begun to make her feel wooden. While in downward-facing dog, looking between her legs at her own reflection in the mirror, Carmen decided she had to do something. She would find a lover. That was the only way to get through until the kids were grown.

Like a movie, it all played in front of her as she came. There were flashes of her home life with Jobe and the strange, old-fashioned doctor's office where he'd been told about his cancer; moments with Mike, the man from her office; and then random glimpses of the forty or so times she and Danny had been together, his blunt hand on her side, the curtains of the hotel room falling at a slant.

There were flashes of the funeral, of her black-clothed children walking neatly in a line, of the café with Jana and of the mammography equipment, of she herself sitting at the dinner table across from her son and daughter—as if Carmen had stepped outside of her body completely and could watch her own life. These images swirled but not one of them was disturbing. Calmly, even as her body kept rippling, she saw them tinged with the light from behind her eyes. She felt held, not just her forehead and neck this time but her entire being, and this sense remained even as the waves finally receded.

When it was over, her hands fell away from herself and, effortlessly, she slept.

August 1985

Carmen landed in Baltimore for the first time on a day so torrid that the city seemed to shimmer when she walked out of the airport with a bag slung over each shoulder and began immediately to sweat.

Someone honked, and she saw Jobe wave from behind the wheel of a dark green BMW. Her father would be furious if he were here; he'd order her not to get in the car. If these people wanted to go to Europe for their automobiles, they weren't loyal Americans. She should have nothing to do with them. This, more than the sight of Jobe himself—with a freshly trimmed beard that only made the angles of his face slightly more monsterish—made Carmen run to open the passenger door and jump in.

"Hey," she said, tossing the larger bag in the back seat. "Thanks for coming to pick me up."

"Sorry." Jobe turned red, as if she'd said something to embarrass him already. "I would have gotten out to help you, but I was afraid they'd ticket me or I'd lose my place in line."

"Always the rule follower, aren't we?" There, now she actually *had* said something to embarrass him. And she'd been in his car, what? Thirty-five seconds? Carmen sighed and resolved for the hundredth time to be considerate and behave herself. This was not one of her hardened high school girlfriends; Jobe never seemed to be anything but decent and nice.

She settled back and breathed. There was an odor: not a new-car smell but something better. Leathery and outdoorsy, though nothing could have been further from the truth. Inside the car, the temperature was a perfect and transparent 72 degrees; it said so in blue numbers that glowed from the dashboard. It also posted the outside temperature in red: 102.

"Jesus, is it always this hot here? I'm, like, melting." She stripped her overshirt off, leaving her in only a white tank top and bra. Luckily, she'd thought to shave under her arms that morning. She'd debated, but it had seemed the right thing to do if refined East Coast people were going to let you stay with them for a week.

Jobe darted glances at her as he drove and it was clear he was looking at her breasts. She could not figure this guy out. She'd slept in his bed for two nights (well, one and a half, technically) and he'd never even tried to have sex with her, despite the fact that he'd had an erection three-quarters of the time. Then he'd called her from Oxford once she got home, which must have cost a fortune, just to find out how things were going. Everything was terrible, Carmen told him, figuring she might as well spill her guts to this guy she probably would never see in person again.

Her father had picked up his drinking while she was away, the house had gone to hell, and the housekeeper who'd come twice a week for as long as she could remember had disappeared. It seemed her dad's job at GM was on the line: They'd given him six months slack after his wife's death, but he'd reached the end and his boss was offering alcohol treatment or a voluntary layoff.

"'I'm no fuckin' drunk,'" Carmen made her voice gruff and mimicked her father over the hollow telephone line. "'I'm an asshole, maybe, but so far as I know there's not a treatment program for that.'"

"Hmm, what do you think will happen?" Jobe asked, sounding exactly like the professor he wanted to become.

Carmen didn't mind the blandness of his question. Any one of her friends would have made a joke about how at least now she could get high in the house and no one would notice. She found herself appreciating Jobe's earnest quality, feeling for once listened to, thinking about the tent he'd made with his arms that first night when she was achy and scared.

"I don't know," she said, sighing. "I'm not even sure I'll be able to finish college. I keep asking him, but I don't think there's any money left."

What she didn't tell Jobe was how her father had changed. Once swarthy and handsome with sharp brown eyes and dark hair—a second-generation Italian who had married his European twin: a shy, beautiful Spanish girl—he had become hunched and slightly flaccid and gray looking. He no longer noticed when Carmen came or went, though he'd always taken great pride in her. She, the younger daughter who was both prettier and more clever than her sister, Esme, had been the one he doted on. He'd told everyone they knew the story of how Carmen had started kindergarten as a precocious four-year-old. The day she went to her junior prom, he'd taken about a hundred pictures; when she graduated with honors, he'd thrown a party for three hundred people with an open bar.

The only problem he'd ever had with Carmen was when she mouthed off to her mother, a sweet, timid, chronically frail woman who was easily hurt. And though he'd never finished high school, he'd risen swiftly at GM, from line worker to shift supervisor to management. He had the confidence of a working-class man who had succeeded entirely based on merit, making more money in a year at thirty-five than *his* father had ever made in a decade. They lived in a five-bedroom house with a pool in the backyard. And nothing Carmen asked for was too much: Throughout high school she'd had a credit card she could use at will that drew directly from her father's account. If he kept track of what she spent, he never said.

But things changed just before her trip to Europe. It had been planned the year before, back when doctors were still telling her mother the cancer was contained—a simple procedure to remove it and she'd live a long, healthy life. By the time Carmen was due to board the plane, her mother was freshly dead, her father stunned and angry. He was pursuing a lawsuit against the hospital because they'd assured him his wife was going home less than thirty-six hours before she expired. And he was drinking significantly more than the three or four glasses of bourbon he'd typically had when he came home in the evening. These days he just kept the bottle at his side.

Even worse was Carmen's sister, who had suddenly become their father's keeper. Married to a sturdy but boring guy who managed a bank and seven months pregnant, Esme had somehow displaced Carmen entirely while she was out of the country. She came over several times a week in her frilly maternity tops—looking more beautiful than she ever had before, her body giving in to its natural plumpness, her plain face glowing—and fussed over their father.

"You could help out a little," she said to Carmen one day as she stooped precariously to pick up the plates and glasses he'd left on the floor near his favorite chair. "Daddy's taken care of you for twenty years. Is it too much to ask for you to wash a dish?"

But then she'd marched to the kitchen with the armload and washed them herself, making the question rhetorical so far as Carmen was concerned. Sometimes, when Esme was not due to come for a couple of days—because Carmen would *not* give her sister the satisfaction—she vacuumed and straightened and tried to coax her father into setting his alarm before he went comatose in his chair at night. But he came home, one of the few times he actually made it to work in July, with a pink slip. It was the very same day that her tuition bill from the University of Michigan arrived. Because of nonpayment in spring, the letter said, she would have to settle her account and prepay for the fall semester in order to continue. She could call the number for the financial aid office if her circumstances had changed. Carmen was about to do this when Jobe phoned for the second time.

He was back home in Baltimore and said casually that it might be nice for her to come out for a visit; he had several thousand frequent flyer miles racked up and he'd be happy to use them to fly her out.

"Wouldn't your parents mind?" she asked, looking around her own kitchen and seeing that it was grease stained and filthy, which was made all the worse by the fact that it was enormous and modern with a six-burner stove she probably should clean. "I mean, technically I'd be using *their* free ticket, right?"

"My parents," Jobe said, "have no idea frequent flyer miles even exist."

"So tell me about these people," Carmen said now, sitting in the purring BMW, sucking in the icy air as if it were oxygen. "Your parents. What are they like? And how much do they know about me?"

"The young lady from Detroit?" Jobe grinned. "I think they have some vague idea you're the daughter of the chairman of Ford."

"And they got that vague idea . . . how?"

Jobe shrugged. "Most of what I told them was that I met you in London and helped you out when someone stole your purse. My mother was robbed once in Greece, so she felt an immediate bond."

"And their names?"

"George and Olive. But you should call them Mr. and Mrs. Garrett."

"Seriously? I mean, my friends' parents told me to use their first names when I was in, like, sixth grade." She thought back to summers in Elise Jacobs's house: playing jacks on the hardwood floor, making fortune-tellers out of folded paper, rifling through her dad's old *Playboy*s then having him come home and tickle them both on the couch until they nearly wet their pants.

"My parents are . . . " Jobe concentrated, furrowing only one eyebrow, and for an instant Carmen caught sight of the cute boy she'd glimpsed in Kensington Park. "They're kind of hard to describe. Do you read much Somerset Maugham?"

Carmen shook her head. "You read, too? I thought you were supposed to be some kind of genius math geek."

"Yeah, well." Jobe turned into a driveway that Carmen couldn't see the end of; it had to be a quarter-mile long. "Sometimes we read."

Carmen had her own room—an irregularly shaped space on the third floor with a double bed, a dresser, a desk, and a small easy chair with a reading lamp, all in shades of plum—and her own bathroom with a shower but no tub.

"Where's your bedroom?" she asked as he showed her around, flipping on light switches and pointing things out like a bellman.

He reddened. "It's down a level. My parents are kind of conservative when it comes to these things."

"What 'things?' " She could feel herself blushing, too, which was rare. Why did this guy have such an odd effect on her? "I didn't say I wanted to have *sex*, I was just asking where your bedroom was." She looked over her shoulder at Jobe, who was standing with his hands in his pockets, and wondered if she actually *did* want to. The truth was, she had no idea why she was here in this strange city with this boy she barely knew. It was clear he was interested in her and she didn't want to lead him on, but her feelings were—for one of the only times in her life—completely unclear.

One minute she'd be aggravated by his accommodating her moods, wishing he'd stand up to her the way her high school boyfriend had, calling her out and saying, "Stop being a bitch, Car," whenever she got snotty or demanding. The next, Jobe would tug at her with a quiet insistence; she would remember falling asleep next to him in London and feeling safe for the first time since her mother died. Also, she'd discovered that cute, brawny boyfriend from high school —her first—was secretly sleeping with other girls, and the worst part was that she later figured out it was he who had leaked the information so she'd find out and break up with him. A dirty, cowardly trick.

She'd always had high standards, dating at her "level" or sometimes even above. Few girls could pull this off, but Carmen had discovered early on that sheer moxie often bought her entry into social groups—and relationships with men—that seemed out of her league. So she became, by sixteen, the girl most likely to sing onstage or play strip poker. She painted seriously, setting up a studio in a corner of the basement at home, stretching her canvases herself. Don't do anything half-assed and forget what other people think; these rules were, she would have told anyone who asked, the secret to a successful life.

Only lately, the formula hadn't been working. The situation with her father was not her fault, but other things seemed to be directly related to the choices she'd made. Her friends from high school all had drifted out of her life. Her last relationship had been with a philosophy T.A. at Michigan, a thirty-two-year-old post-doctoral student who had a wife and a six-month-old at home. He'd been serious, with small, round, John Lennon glasses and thick, silky hair. They got together mostly in his office after hours and drank vodka from Styrofoam cups before having sex. Then one day she showed up and he announced loudly that he could no longer tutor her privately and firmly shut the door.

It was time to do something different, and Jobe certainly was that. But being pursued so diligently, the object of someone else's hopeful reaching from a lower social caste, made her cringe. She knew now exactly how her high school boyfriend had felt: looking at her from time to time, gauging whether she was quite good enough to be seen with, feeling as if he had to peel her off him like a too-tight sweater.

At least Carmen wasn't mean. She had no desire to do this to someone. The truth was she'd never before given much thought to people like Jobe, those knobby math club boys with strange faces and bodies like wire hangers who seemed to exist only at school. You never saw them at parties, or at the mall, or even in the library. Occasionally, you might help out one who was stammering through a presentation or struggling to connect with a volleyball in gym. One moment's kindness, a quick, warm smile. That was all it took.

But now she was faced, hours at a time, with a real grown-up version of those prepubescent seventeen-year-olds she'd once passed blithely in the halls. And he was doggedly helpful, making it very difficult for her to keep from taking advantage.

She wished there were someone she could talk to. But Carmen was between girlfriends and her sister was not a possibility. Her mother was dead and her father had his own problems. Finally, she was ready to listen to advice but there was no one who could tell her what to do.

"So what's our plan? We hang out here with George and Olive . . . oh, excuse me, Mr. and Mrs. Garrett . . . all week?"

Jobe scratched his beard and it made a foraging-animal sound. "Ah, tonight for dinner, yeah, that's the plan. They want us to be ready by seven, if that's okay. After that?" He shrugged. "You hungry now?"

Carmen hadn't realized until that moment that she was. "Starving. What do you have?"

Again, he shrugged. "There's always something. Want me to help you unpack and then we'll go look?"

Carmen remembered his helping her throw her things into a knapsack in that soiled London hovel she'd been renting. "Sure. You can fold my underwear."

She hadn't really meant it. Yet when she turned around, Jobe was in fact placing her panties in a neat stack in a top drawer of the dresser, and arranging her bras like octopi with arms hugging themselves, setting these alongside.

"Can I ask you a question?" She was hanging her shirts in the closet, something she rarely did at home. "Why do you still live here with your parents? Aren't you, like, twenty-five or something?"

For the third time, he shrugged. This seemed to be his major method of communication. "I don't, really. I was away at Princeton for four years and I only came back summers."

"To work?"

Jobe shook his head. "Not in the way I think you mean. I did a lot of work in mathematics but I didn't have a summer job."

"So your parents paid your way?" She tried to keep the jealousy out of her voice.

But again, he twitched his head quickly, left to right. "No. I had a Churchill fellowship. They paid my tuition and gave me more money than I could ever imagine needing for expenses. I still have a lot of it, in the bank."

Inside Carmen's head, she added this fact to the others she knew and suddenly an idea blossomed. "You didn't have any frequent flyer miles, did you?" she nearly shouted. "You paid for my ticket yourself. Oh my God!"

Jobe had his back to her. He was unloading her makeup-smeared cosmetics bag, placing the brush and black mascara and eyeshadow with sparkles on the dresser's top. "Okay, yeah, I did. So what? It was no big deal."

She sat on the bed, her stomach itching in random places, as if there were a moth trapped inside. "It *is* kind of a big deal. To me. I mean, I need to know why." He turned, looking frightened, and Carmen suddenly felt so sorry for him she almost stood and opened her arms to give him a hug. But that would have sent exactly the wrong message, so instead she stayed still.

"Like I told you in London, I like the way you just *do* stuff." He crossed his arms. "You don't think things all the way through and figure out the safest way to go."

Carmen snorted. "That's for sure. And just look where it's gotten me." She spread her arms wide and the seventeen silver bracelets she wore clattered one into the next with an appropriately calamitous sound. "I'm begging total strangers to take care of me because my own life is so fucked up."

"Or." Jobe took a few steps toward her, appearing to build confidence as he moved. "You're here for a while to make our lives more interesting." He sat on the bed next to her—here they were again, she thought—only this time he stayed a full foot away. "You know I told you about Bernard Riemann?"

She thought hard. "Sorry . . ."

"The Riemann hypothesis, it's the hardest problem in math, you know, the distribution of prime numbers, zeros, and curves over finite fields. We talked about all this in London."

"Yeah, now I sort of remember." Carmen settled back against the headboard and drew up her feet. She'd been in the top 25 percent of her class, but suddenly she understood what it felt like to be one of those struggling students in the back of the room. "I would have paid more attention, but I didn't know there was going to be a test."

"I'm not talking about the theory, which, by the way, he never finished because he had this sad, pathetic life that involved mostly studying religion and math and having nervous breakdowns. Riemann was brilliant—probably one of the smartest people who ever lived—but he was weak and scared all the time, and when he died of tuberculosis at thirty-nine, his housekeeper threw out his papers and probably destroyed the proof he'd been working on his whole life." Jobe took a breath and looked down, as if studying the quilt. "I don't want to end up like that."

There was a moment of silence. "Okay, what I can't figure out is why that even occurs to you," said Carmen. "I mean, things change. People change. You can do whatever you want; even if today sucks and it seems like there's no way out, there usually is. You just have to think of it."

"See, that's why I asked you to come." Jobe paused and his face became so grave, Carmen felt as if she were looking at a statue in a museum, a man from long ago, perhaps this Riemann guy himself. "May I tell you something?"

"Yeah." She waited. "Any minute now. You promised me food."

Jobe grimaced and swallowed, making a face as if he were tasting something bitter. "Fine. Here it is. I'm going to die young, like Riemann, and I don't want to do it like he did: live this frightened, sad life and leave nothing but an unfinished formula that gets thrown in the garbage."

Carmen stared at him, no longer thinking of food. "Are you sick?"

Jobe bowed his head. "Not that I know of. Yet."

"But you're sure you're going to die."

"Well, I mean, everyone's going to die, so yes, I'm sure. But if you mean am I sure I'm going to do it younger than most people, I don't have scientific proof but I'm . . . I don't know, I have a feeling."

Carmen grinned. "You have a *feeling*?" This was incredibly weird, but also intriguing. She scooted closer to him and swiped his thigh with one hand. "That doesn't sound very mathematical."

"I know. It's the one thing in my life that makes me irrational and a little bit crazy, which is probably why I like it."

"Wait, you *like* this woo-woo premonition that you're going to suffer some horrible early death? That makes you feel good?"

Jobe paused and thought and then nodded vigorously. "Yeah, it really does," he said. And despite all her earlier resolutions, Carmen jumped up and slung one arm around Jobe, giving him the friendliest hug she knew how.

"That's actually kind of cool," she said into his hair. She didn't even mind when he slipped one arm around her and hugged her back.

After they'd finished unpacking, she and Jobe went into the vast kitchen and made a heaping plate of nachos with taco chips and slivered jalapeños and three different kinds of cheese. He heated them under the broiler—a complicated iron contraption that was separate from the oven—until their tops were crisp and brown and bubbling. Then he grabbed a container of sour cream and salsa from the refrigerator, along with two cans of lime-flavored seltzer water, and they snuck up one flight to his room.

Inside, it was like a laboratory, with a desk along one entire wall—long enough for three chairs set side by side—and shelves full of math and astronomy books. Jobe's bed was a single, but it was longer than regular ones by at least two feet.

"Geez, how do you find sheets for that thing?" Carmen asked, kicking the bed with one bright yellow high-top shoe.

Jobe looked puzzled. "Sheets?" he said faintly, as if he'd never heard of them.

"C'mon. I haven't eaten since, I don't know, yesterday some

time," Carmen said. And they sank to the floor, just as they had in Kensington Park.

Carmen had too much and destroyed her appetite for dinner, which she deeply regretted a few hours later, sitting at the massive dining room table next to Jobe. Across from them, his seventeen-year-old brother Nate—a Jobe lookalike who somehow managed to be more handsome and not so angular—ogled her from behind his water glass. Carmen looked down at her plate, the fat chicken breast that George (Mr. Garrett) had plunked onto it, and imagined her esophagus a tunnel that was closed for maintenance.

She'd gobbled way more than her share of the nachos, perhaps two-thirds, relieved the way one is when they've forgotten about food for twenty-four hours and suddenly remember—relieved, too, that she was with a man she could eat in front of. But while she was still digesting that heap of chips and peppers and gooey cheese, the act of putting one more bite in her mouth seemed impossible. Next to her, however, Jobe was methodically slicing and consuming everything on his plate.

"You're from Detroit, dear?" Olive asked. "Or is it Ann Arbor? They're close together. Is that right?"

Carmen nodded, happy to have an excuse to avoid her food. "I grew up in Detroit and I went to school in Ann Arbor." She'd already slipped into the past tense. College seemed more and more like a memory. "They're about forty-five minutes apart."

"And what are you studying?"

"Art history, with a minor in fine art. I mean, I know that sounds like the same thing, but it's really not. The fine art is actual application—you know, painting, drawing, sculpting—so I'll have a portfolio I can show people when I'm done."

"That sounds logical." George nodded. This was the first time Carmen had actually heard him speak. Jobe's father was a chemist who specialized in surface coatings, working mostly for the defense department and NASA. Jobe had whispered the last part as they sat side by side on his bedroom floor, as if revealing a secret, or a sin. And she'd laughed.

"My dad spent the last ten years making Suburbans, which are the biggest gas guzzlers in the universe. He's personally responsible for the problem with the ozone layer. You don't have to worry."

Now, thinking of that, she used her napkin—a square of gold cloth, smooth but as heavy as wool—to blot her pristine lips and hide the abrupt smile.

"I always loved the Romantic painters. Is that what you call them?" Olive picked up her wine glass but didn't drink, just held it in front of her, so Carmen saw her throat through thin crystal and clear, sun-colored juice. Jobe's mother had an ordinary, middle-aged face but a hooker's body—huge boobs and a twitchy little ass—that she hid in queen of England clothes. All the money, Jobe had told Carmen matter-of-factly, was hers.

"Rubens, for instance," Olive said. "I know you're supposed to like more modern things these days, those big splotch paintings and such. But I can't help it."

Carmen blinked. Suddenly, without reason, she loved this woman. "Baroque," she said softly. "Rubens was Baroque. He's one of my favorites. His Venus . . ." Then she picked up her silver and forced herself to take a few bites.

"When we were in Italy . . . remember, dear?" she asked George, who grunted and nodded. Olive speared a piece of chicken so small, Carmen wondered how it could be held by the tines of her fork. This woman would be better off with chopsticks. "There was that painting in the Uffizi, where Venus was standing in a shell. That was Rubens, wasn't it? I thought it was."

Carmen shook her head. This was the first time her degree had ever come in handy. "Botticelli. It's beautiful, with the Zephyrs. I can't believe you actually saw that, in person. I would *kill* to do that. But the school trip I was on didn't go to Italy this year and I couldn't afford to get there on my own." She looked around at the velvety textured wallpaper and mahogany sideboard the size of a small boat. Maybe she wasn't supposed to admit to having money concerns; it could be considered gauche. She tried to cover. "My mother died last year and my father hasn't been working as much . . . ." *At all.* The words echoed in her mind.

But Olive had stopped eating her microscopic bits of chicken and looked directly into Carmen's eyes. The woman was either slightly drunk or about to cry, Carmen thought. Perhaps both. "I'm so sorry, dear, I had no idea. That must have been absolutely terrible for you. For your whole family."

"It was." Suddenly, Carmen didn't care about hiding anymore: her family's financial troubles, or her loneliness. She just wanted to tell Olive the truth. "My dad worshipped her and he's been, well, kind of useless ever since she died. Europe was supposed to help me get over it but ever since I came back, things have really sucked."

There was silence around the table. Nate was looking at her bug-eyed, as if she'd just farted. Under the heavy cloth, Jobe put his hand on her thigh and she was grateful. She angled closer to him to let him know, and she felt a glow of happiness emanate off him. Finally, Olive spoke. "I'm sure you'll get to Italy one day, dear. It's not going anywhere." Then she stood briskly to collect the plates herself and never even mentioned that Carmen had barely touched her meal.

"I love your mom," Carmen said, as they drove through the damp, sultry streets. The outside thermometer read 82 degrees, though it was nearly ten o'clock. "She's not what I expected, at all."

"What did you expect?" Jobe signaled and turned left, using both hands on the wheel, just the way you were taught in driver's ed.

"I don't know, someone stuck-up I guess. Like, she grew up with all that money and I expected her to act like she was better than everyone."

A shower of streetlight lit up the car and Jobe, who looked genuinely puzzled. "Why would having money make her better?"

"I don't know. You're the one who told her my dad was some big shot at Ford. Wasn't that because they wouldn't want to associate with someone who came from a long line of grease monkeys?"

He turned into a parking place and centered the car, braking and turning off the key before he answered. "That's not why I told them that."

"Then why?" It was already getting hot in the car and Carmen didn't want to sweat. She'd showered after dinner and changed into one of only two dresses she'd brought, this one pale orange with ragged sleeves and an uneven hemline and ruffles around the waist. Jobe sat, not answering. "Well?"

"I just . . . I didn't want them to think you were interested in *me* for our money. That's all. I don't bring girls home all that often and I thought, if they knew about your situation, they might, you know, assume . . ."

"Oh." Carmen felt the prickles start under her arms. Fuck it. They were going to a dance club so she would be getting sweaty in any case. "Is that what you think? That I'm here because you're rich?"

"No."

"You don't sound very sure."

Jobe shrugged and turned toward her, his face bisected by a crooked shadow, more than half of it in darkness. "I honestly don't think money has anything to do with it. On the other hand, I'm not at all clear on why you're here. One minute you seem interested in me, the next you don't. And that's okay. But I will tell you straight out." She heard him breathe in and hold it for a few seconds then gently exhale. "I like you. I don't know why. You're too young for me, and a lot more prickly than I usually like. But I've heard these things happen sometimes and there you go. I'm just living proof of the way actual life doesn't make a lot of sense."

Carmen sat without answering. If she were honest, she would tell him now: *I'm sorry. I just don't feel that way about you.* It would hurt him and make things awkward; she might have to go home earlier than planned. But it was kinder than this, wasn't it? Letting him believe there was a chance things could develop when, really, she'd just wanted someone nice to take care of her for a few days.

She was about to speak, tell him the truth, when Jobe opened his door and got out, then leaned back down to stick his head into the car. "It's hot out here. Let's go in."

She breathed. It could wait. She'd formulate exactly how she wanted to tell him while they were on the dance floor. But once they entered the club, her heart started to thump in time with the music and she edged up close to Jobe's back, brushing his hand with her body twice, trying to stay with him in the throng. The air was thick with sweat and cologne, the space cavernous and dim; dust hovered in the pale rose and purple lights that lit up the open floor.

"You want a drink?" Jobe shouted into her ear.

"Yeah, better make it a seltzer." She was really thinking of her father but didn't want to say so. Instead, she held up her wrist with its neon yellow bracelet. "I'm tagged. Nine months 'til I'm twenty-one."

"Really?" He looked amused, that rusty smile glimmering through his beard. "That's unfortunate. Stay right here, okay? I'll be back."

She watched his head, above most everyone else's, as he bobbed away from her and toward the bar. He returned fifteen minutes later, sweat staining his shirt, holding four enormous plastic cups: two filled with clear liquid and two packed with ice and several inches of something brown.

"Here," he said, giving her one of each. "I told the bartender I didn't want to fight my way back through, so I was ordering twice. And I tipped him a twenty, which makes anything possible. It's a triple Glenlivet," he shouted, as she took a drink from the half-full cup and the smooth scorch started down her throat. "I figure if anyone comes up to us, you can just drop the Scotch and say you've been drinking the soda."

Carmen looked up at him. Talking was too hard and besides, it interfered with the insistent, sexual thrum. Her father was thousands of miles away, and she needed this. She took another long drink and started to go limp, weary from the day of travel, from the heat, from the rich food. Closing her eyes and edging a little closer to Jobe, she used his body like a post to lean on and he stayed perfectly stationary, though after a time—two inches of her drink later, perhaps—he put his left hand on her left shoulder, the bare one, so technically his arm was around her, but she didn't care because she was floating and it seemed necessary that someone, even this odd, loose-limbed scarecrow of a person, be there to hold her down.

"Do you want to dance?" he asked. His voice came to her out of the murk and swirl of cigarette smoke, his face lit with flashing lights. Maybe an hour had passed and her Scotch and half her seltzer water were gone. Jobe was still holding his cup and she glanced at it.

"Hey, you aren't even drinking!" She meant to sound accusing but the words came out like syrup.

"I'm driving," he yelled, mimicking with his full hands the act of steering. "I have to be careful."

"Okay, then." She giggled and grabbed his cup, taking a big swallow. "Fine, I'm ready."

He took the cup out of her hand and set it on a nearby shelf, a newly intense expression crossing his chronically worried-looking long face, and took one of her hands firmly in his. Once they were under the lights, Jobe dropped her hand and for one awful moment he stood; maybe he can't dance at all, she thought muddily, and he's going to try to fake it. Luckily, she was drunk enough to make the best of whatever happened. She took a step to the right, intending to circle him, and then he began to move.

Now it was Carmen who stopped, struck with wonder. Jobe had a robotic, perfectly syncopated way of dancing: his head moved by precise increments, his body dipped to the side, his feet made complicated diagrams on the floor. He was like a combination of David Byrne and Grizzly Adams. And precisely at that moment—as if the DJ wanted to highlight Jobe's odd, courtly dance—an old-fashioned silver ball dropped from the ceiling and its spangles bounced rhythmically across Carmen's world.

She couldn't have been more surprised if Jobe had pulled a boa constrictor from his pocket—her amazement due partly to the Scotch, no doubt—but eventually she found that if she made small movements mirroring his, he would pause just long enough to flash that gleaming smile.

For an hour, two, they lived on the dance floor and she watched him change with the shifting of the light. Her steps grew braver, more her own sinuous, bare-shouldered kind of moves, occupying the three square feet of floor space until Jobe reached forward to grasp her arm and reel her in—which she embraced, conforming her body to his side—and said hoarsely, "I need a drink," then led her back to the perimeter of the gyrating pack of people. Carmen had expected cheers and waves when they left the floor, but the crowd simply opened to allow them a path and closed again behind them. Jobe reached the bar and held out a ten-dollar bill. "Two glasses of ice water!" he called, and the bartender scowled until he looked up and saw the money.

"Coming right up," he said, filling cups with stuck-together ice clumps and shooting water in from his gun.

"Do you mind?" Jobe asked once they had the water and he'd turned over the ten, shaking his head in response to the bartender's gruff question about change. "I want to get outside."

They had their hands stamped at the door—in case they wanted to go back in later—then walked through a night that was, miraculously, no longer stifling but soft and warm and hazy. The nightclub was in a cluttered warehouse-filled area, the streets lined with low buildings and large vehicles. Both of them drank greedily, and the inside of Carmen's hot mouth turned cool as mint. When they came to the end of the block, Jobe tossed his plastic cup into a huge Dumpster. "Want me to throw yours away?" he asked, but Carmen said no, she was still eating ice. And quietly then, they walked back toward the car.

"Do you want?" Jobe looked out into the night, and for a moment Carmen thought the question would end there. *Did she want?* God, yes, she wanted the ease of her childhood and an answer about how she would pay for her last year of school and a plan for her, until recently, blessedly disorganized life. She wanted her mother back—or *a* mother, the truth being that it didn't have to be hers. She wanted to paint, to dance, to live somewhere other than inside her father's depressing, sinking house.

Jobe swallowed. "Do you want to take a ride?" he asked. "There's this place called Fell's Point."

"Sure." She swooned as she bent to open the door and climb into the car. Jobe got in and pushed a button to open the sky roof. Carmen gazed up and made a sound, feeling under her legs for the lever that would allow her to recline her seat and lie back. "Here, let me," Jobe said, and he reached underneath her—a strangely intimate feeling—to push on something that gave and suddenly she was prone.

Riding this way felt like levitating. She was rushing through the streets of Baltimore, feet first. She was sorry when he stopped the car but she said nothing. Jobe opened the windows and the faintly Japanese scent (Carmen had never been to Japan, she only imagined it smelled this way) of wet bark and cherry blossoms floated in.

They paused, with Jobe sitting looking straight ahead and Carmen lying back, peeking from time to time through slitted eyes at the charcoal sky that lay flat against the windshield pane.

"Do you?" he asked, and again he stopped so that Carmen began formulating answers to the truncated question. *Did she?* Well, yes. She did feel the lilt of alcohol still making her hopeful and heedless of the circumstances that had brought her out here, to this foreign place.

Jobe twisted in his seat, put one long hand on each of her arms, and asked, "Is this alright?" To which she murmured something that sounded like an assent but was nothing really. How could she have said what was alright? She had no clue. But everything felt as if it were happening according to some universal dictate. She was here in this unlikely place, utterly by chance, and had danced for hours with a boy she would have sworn might trip walking across an open field.

Then he was leaning down to kiss her, the Scotch on his breath identical to hers, his tongue hesitant at first but moving as his body had, with small darts that pleased her. She wasn't electrified by this, not at all; it wasn't the way she'd felt with the T.A., her body straining to mash itself against his. With Jobe, it was simply entertaining: the night, the breeze, the new sensation of this sinewy set of lines—torso, two arms, his long neck—making its strange narrow marks on her skin.

She did not participate as much as she could have. Her excuse could be drunkenness, she decided quite clearly through the woozy haze. But Jobe did not seem to mind: He had moved so he lay on top of her and rather than crushing her, as happened with the powerful, broad-shouldered men that she favored, this was like making out with a giraffe who was extended in all directions, all legs and hooves and neck and head. Imagining this, she giggled, and Jobe raised himself enough so he could angle his eyes down and look at her.

"What is it?" he said in a tone so plaintive, it actually hurt.

Not thinking of the consequences, only that he might be wounded forever—unlike her hot tea in the garden at Kensington, the careless derision she spilled on him might, she worried, genuinely emasculate him now—she said, "No, it's nothing, it just tickled for a minute," and pulled his head awkwardly toward her for a long, open-mouthed kiss.

After a few minutes he was panting and she pretended that she was, too. "I'm just too goddamn tall," he said.

"It's these German cars," she answered. "You should have bought American. A nice, long Chevy truck bed would come in handy. See?"

They both laughed then, which caused an aching sensation to begin in her bladder. She could *see* the large cup of water and picture herself drinking it, the splashing like a waterfall through her body's systems, down her throat and over the cliffs of her lungs.

"Uh, besides, I think I need a bathroom."

Jobe folded himself up, long limbs retracting and retreating to his side of the car. "Can you make it 'til we get home?" he asked. "It'll take about twenty minutes."

"Sure," said Carmen, relieved. She could make it for another hour if it meant the awkwardness was over. She'd done her duty, kissing her sweet but nerdy host so he would feel better about himself. Now she wanted nothing more than to go back to that purple bedroom and sleep until about noon.

She closed her eyes as Jobe drove deliberately through the [night, and when they arrived at the house, she rose unsteadily, having neglected to put the seat up before trying to get out of the car.

"You okay?" he asked as they entered through the door in the cavernous five-car garage.

"I'm fine." She nodded emphatically. "Just tired. You know."

She took a long time inside the little powder room off the kitchen, washing her hands twice and drying them with precision, staring into her own wide green eyes. Her hair was long and wavy, held back with a thick band that was woven on top of her head but just an elastic cord underneath her hair. The contraption was digging into her neck so she removed it and searched through the drawers for a brush but came up with nothing, so she raked her hands like claws several times against her scalp. One more look: Her face had grown older, somehow, in only the time she'd been here in Baltimore. It was more beautiful but also serious and more defined, as if crossing the threshold into this house she had skipped ahead several years, moving unintentionally from wild student to mature adult.

He was, of course, waiting for her when she emerged—sitting on a stool in the darkness of the kitchen. "Just like old times," he said.

"Yeah, only this is a lot nicer than that raunchy little WC in London. If you guys have so much money, how come you stayed in a place like that anyway?"

He shrugged; she saw the ghost of motion, his shoulders moving up and down. "I don't know. I guess maybe sometimes I get tired of . . . this."

Carmen leaned on the counter next to him. Apparently they were going to talk. She didn't want to be rude, but the Scotch had mostly worn off and she was so tired that parts of her, parts that she rarely noticed—her jaw, her ankles—had begun to ache. She closed her eyes for a few seconds and when she heard him stand and felt him reach for her, she wasn't really surprised. Maybe she wanted this, she told herself; maybe it wasn't just easier.

The stool turned out to be a convenient aid. Jobe backed up and sat again, drawing her with him, placing her between his knees. Now they were exactly on par, shoulders even. She could lace her arms around his neck and lean in and it was like being held or carried though her feet were still, technically, on the ground. Once she got used to the feel of his face, the bristling and hard bones, Carmen relaxed and began having fun. What the hell? He was a nice guy and he smelled good; so many of them didn't. She snapped at his mouth like a turtle and he responded by pulling her in tighter. It was amazing how perfectly okay this was, like spending the night eating popcorn and watching an old movie on TV if there was nothing better to do—it wasn't your first choice, but it was certainly good enough to fill the time.

Ten minutes went by this way and then, almost roughly, he rose and took her hand, leading her toward the stairs.

"Where are we going?" she asked.

"I've always regretted," he said, stopping and staring at his feet as if he were a small boy, confused. "That night when you offered . . . and I didn't. I wish that we could . . ."

And that's where they hung, in that space between what could have happened in London and his sweet, nearly pathetic longing now. Carmen was—she knew this about herself—not a good enough person, too quick to judge people according to their appearance or status. She had not showed her mother enough kindness at the end when she was burned and wan and bald. It was time that she, Carmen, become more generous, concerned about the feelings of others. And Jobe had been heartbreakingly honest with her earlier; he liked her, it was that simple. Now she just had to figure out the right thing to do.

They reached the broad second-story landing and stood for a

moment. Three hallways branched off it like half the rays of a star. They stood a few feet from the opening to Jobe's room and he raised his index finger to his lips. "My parents," he mouthed and pointed to the right.

She nodded and without even deciding, really, only sliding into this one harmless act that she saw as good and selfless, Carmen gave Jobe a little shove and followed him. They walked past the room where his parents slept and two more closed doors and an open bathroom whose fixtures and white tile glistened. Then across the threshold of the room at the very end of the hall and toward his extra-long, twin bed.

$\mathcal{J}$UNE 2007

A week ticked by and Carmen was split. If she let this thing go, this hard comet, it could take over her whole body and she might die. But the doctors at the breast clinic were strangely noncommittal: It was cancer—the biopsy clearly showed this—but what kind and how dangerous was up for endless debate. The only thing to do was to get inside her, cut it out, and look at it under a microscope, yet no one's schedule seemed to match up and she spent hours on the phone trying to arrange for an operating room, a surgeon, and a friend to take her to and from. It was tempting simply to give up and forget about the comet. Go on about her life.

But the emptiness of the days echoed. Without work, without Jobe to look after and fetch medications for, without the steady stream of people coming in to relieve and feed and console her, she was mostly alone. Siena was either working or curled up somewhere with Troy. Luca had a morning "jobs readiness" program this week. And then there was Michael, whom she was tempted to cling to and needed every ounce of her willpower to treat with motherly distance in order to let him return to feeling like a typical adolescent boy.

Technically Michael was the child she and Jobe never should

have had. If they had stopped at two, her family would be nearly raised by now, admittedly complicated by Luca's Down's but basically grown. There was no question Carmen would be freer. But even when she played the game where she erased Jobe and Luca and Siena—in her darkest moments, shuddering, but able to imagine such a thing—Michael was the one she couldn't bear to think about letting go.

He was the evolutionary throwback to Carmen's father, Antonio, and his father, Gus, a deli owner in Brooklyn. Like the sensuous working-class men in her family, Michael was doe-eyed and boisterous and at ease with his body. He played sports and collected friends like bottle caps. He didn't have Luca's sweetness or Siena's brains; but Michael alone emanated the robust normalcy that Carmen remembered from her youth.

Probably because he fit into the world so well, it was tempting for people to overlook Michael and assume that whatever happened he'd be fine. But what she had observed in the days after Jobe's funeral was a boy with no outlet for grief. Her younger son's job was to be happy and funny. Most of the time, this is what he did. But lately he'd begun, for the first time in his twelve years, to have trouble sleeping. He had terrible nightmares. Occasionally, despite the dust of mustache on his upper lip, he even came to her room at night.

She and the two older children—along with Troy, the fourth child she appeared to have inherited—had agreed not to tell Michael about her cancer until they knew more. So Carmen hid in her bedroom with the door closed, as secretive about these medical phone calls as she had once been about Danny. Finally, after calling the seventh name on her list of referrals, she found an oncologist willing to perform what everyone insisted on calling "the procedure." This was because, Carmen realized slowly as she sat on hold, they could not accurately name it prior to the doctor's cutting a hole in her. She would be trusting this man she'd never met to decide—while she herself was unconscious—whether to preserve her left breast or lop it off.

Sitting on her bed, clutching her cell phone with one shoulder, Carmen breathed in shallow sips. By the time the nurse returned from scheduling this event, Carmen was light-headed. Obediently, she wrote the woman's instructions on a half-used notebook abandoned by one of the kids on the last day of school.

"You'll need to make an appointment with your doctor for the day before the procedure," the nurse said. "Get a clean bill of health, other than the tumor, of course. And some Xanax. You'll need it."

This woman was completely insane. Last time Carmen had called to get an appointment for an annual physical it had taken a month and a half to get in. What were the odds she'd be able to pinpoint a day and demand a slot? But she scheduled the surgery anyway, because she had to start with something. "Your surgeon is Dr. Woo," the nurse informed Carmen crisply. "You're lucky. He's very good."

"That's great, thank you," Carmen said sweetly, though she wasn't feeling lucky. She might need this woman to do something for her in the future: slip her some Vicodin or put her out of her misery with a cleaver to her head. But this business about excellent surgeons was a lie; she'd found that out with Jobe. He'd had the best at Johns Hopkins; the university had insisted upon it, even pulling on medical school resources to dig up a specialist who had worked with precisely Jobe's type of non-Hodgkin's his entire career. This was the guy who set out the course of treatment that ultimately killed her husband. Eerily, that doctor had accomplished the terrible thing that she was secretly afraid she'd wanted bad enough to have caused. Since meeting Jana's Wiccan friends, Carmen wondered sometimes if she was some kind of inept witch, conjuring up evil unwittingly yet unable to fix Luca or make herself magically content with a perfectly nice yet tentative and periodically impotent man.

Carmen looked down at what she'd written on the page: TUESDAY, JUNE 12, 2 P.M. The symbols materialized like carvings in a headstone and her breath came sharply. This had been happening more and more; panic rose in mundane moments like a wild, bitter wind. But there was nowhere to go with it, no one to scream at or seek comfort with. Even Jana did not know the extent of her betrayal, the fact that she had—when Jobe's doctor's face had turned grave and he'd used the words *mortality rate* and *terminal*—rejoiced faintly in the privacy of her own head. It had been an unspeakable secret: Her own life sentence was being commuted by this freakish twist of fate. Abruptly, now, she recalled the day that Jobe, at twenty-five, had predicted it. He'd said he would die young. He'd informed her. It was the reason he could gather his nerve back then to take her dancing and coax her into his childhood bed. Did this, in some small way, let her off the hook?

She could not answer this. So, breathing slowly, she tried to work through the next conundrum. There were only two real possibilities, so far as Carmen was concerned: Either she was being punished for her sins against Jobe and had been sentenced to cancer by some judgmental deity, or there was something poisonous about this house, something lurking and ready to attach itself to the children, now that both the parents had been done in.

Clearly, she would prefer the first. At least then her children would be safe. But she would need to resign herself to the fact that her own life had been entirely misspent. It would not matter that she had stayed with the man and raised his children, showing the world a devoted wife and mother; what would come to roost, spreading its cancer throughout her chest, was her rancid, unloving heart.

But if the latter explanation were true, they were all in danger. She should be picking up the phone again, talking to someone who could come out and test the soil, the walls, the air quality . . . whatever it was that made human cells turn mutant. Only she had no idea whom to call.

Danny! She came to this as one finds the answer to a game show question: The moment she quit concentrating, it popped into her head. Danny did this for a living. He helped people figure out these answers. Now the next question was, did she call his cell phone number—which was programmed into hers—or go downstairs to look up the one for the information desk at the library? Fuck it, she didn't have time to worry about etiquette; besides, what if one of his colleagues answered? How, exactly, would she explain her situation to a stranger?

She pushed speed dial 3 and listened with growing irritation as the line rang and Danny's voice mail clicked on. "Listen, I know I've been out of touch. Sorry." She looked around the quiet room and realized that she was on her marriage bed, in the very spot where she'd been unwilling to talk to Danny before. "But I really need to talk to you. I have a few questions—professional. I need your help researching something. So, um, call me."

Carmen was calmer now, but ridiculously worn out from fear. She walked downstairs, her bare feet sticky against the wooden steps. Luca was in the living room. His bus must have pulled up while she was on the phone. He sat slumped on the sofa, eyes crossing slightly as he gazed down at a cushion; no one else was in sight.

"Hey, what's up?" she asked.

"Nothing." The word was not only thick but languid, and Carmen realized it was very literally true. In years past, she'd never worried about Luca's summers. Once he was released from school, Jobe, whose schedule freed him up around the same time, would take over. What they did together was a mystery, but movies reeled through her head of the two of them heading out the door—Jobe arcing over his older son like an oak—and metal doors creaking open then slamming, the soft revving of the car engine. Often, they would be gone all day.

She sat next to Luca, desperate to fill in for his father but feeling woefully inadequate. "Do you have anything planned for this afternoon?" she asked then instantly regretted it. What would he have planned? A date? A movie? A game of ultimate Frisbee? He could neither handle money nor drive.

Luca turned to her with lazy eyes, blinking. "No," he said.

The cell in Carmen's pocket rang and she reached for it. "Why don't you go shoot some baskets?" she said, stuck between wanting to care for her son and trying not to treat him like a child. It was a delicate balance under any circumstances, especially right now as she burned from shame. To have failed to calculate Jobe's loss in terms of Luca—and figure out how to mitigate it—this, even more than her other sins, was unforgivable. She'd been not only selfish but blind.

"We'll go out later, to a movie and dinner. We can take Michael and Jeffrey. Where are they, anyway?"

"CVS." Luca nodded. "Twizzlers," he said gravely, elongating the two z's, then rose. She answered her phone at the last possible second as Luca pushed the screen door aside, making a space just large enough for his body to slip through, and disappeared outside.

"Hello?"

"Hey, Car, you alright?" Danny asked. He sounded guilty, his tone a little strangled. It occurred to Carmen for the first time that he had never called to ask about her doctor visit.

"No, actually, I have cancer."

"Oh, Christ." Danny took a long breath and choked at the end. "Hold on. I gotta get out of here." She heard him mumbling in the distance—the phone no doubt held down by his hip, covered with one hand—and then there was the leaf-crunching sound of movement.

"Okay, I'm outside now," he said after this, his voice nearer now than it had been without the stone library walls to make it echo. "What's going on?"

Carmen glanced around. Still, the boys weren't back. But she'd have to be fast. "I went in for a mammogram on Wednesday. They saw something on the films and took me immediately for an MRI. Then a biopsy. And I got the official results on Monday." She counted on her fingers. This was Friday. Had it really been only four days since her future contracted and her entire post-Jobe life began wavering in front of her like a mirage?

"I'm going in for surgery next week. Tuesday." Less than two weeks from the mammogram to possibly losing a part of her body. Fourteen days if she counted back to Danny's actually detecting the cancer. She ran one finger along the rough wood grain of the table. She might have had an extra month or two of ignorance without him. Or maybe, if it hadn't been touched and examined and named, her comet might have dissolved, those deranged cells turning into brown powder she could simply cough out.

"Goddamn, I was afraid of that." Danny's voice brought her

back to reality. "Carmen, I'm . . ." He stopped and she heard the flare of a match. Looking outside, she saw that it was windless, everything preternaturally still: the best weather to be a smoker outside. "Listen," he said, and the change was complete: Here was her husky lover, certain and soothing. "I want to go with you. To the surgery, I mean. Have you called anyone else?"

She stopped moving her finger. "No. But how do we explain this?"

"If there's no one else there, we don't have to. The doctors aren't going to care. What do you think, the nurses are going to check my marital status? I've got about twenty personal days racked up so it shouldn't be a problem."

Carmen considered this. She imagined Danny sitting in a chair while she lay on a metal slab dressed in a backless shift and had a needle inserted into her arm. Then there would be that fog after, as she was coming out of the anesthesia acting not drunk but dumb. She would be sick and weak. Jobe had been stalwart about minor surgeries but twice she'd had to stop on the way home so he could lurch out and vomit by the side of the road. She had gotten out and run around the car, only to stand helplessly while he retched and the traffic whipped by. Then she'd hunched beside him to put one hand on his knee and ask, "Better now?" before helping him fold back into the passenger seat where he sprawled with a gray, dead-looking face.

She didn't want Danny to see her this way. That wasn't part of their deal.

"Where would you take me after?" she asked now. "It's not like you can show up here and blend in with the kids. They'd wonder who this guy was and why he was around all of a sudden. They'd ask questions."

"Tell them I'm a friend," Danny said. "They don't know all the people you do. They'd probably just go along."

"Not in this situation. Siena would know." Carmen saw her daughter's flashing, appraising eyes. Heard her words from that first night: *You seem glad that he's dead.*

"I suppose you're right." Was there a hitch of relief in these words? Disappointment? She couldn't tell. "So who are you going to get?"

"I'm thinking Jana. Though she'll have to get someone to fill in at the café. It's going to screw up her whole week."

"Yeah, I think she'll understand."

There was a pause. Time, she knew, for Danny to crush out his cigarette and head back inside. "The reason I called," Carmen said quickly. "I'm worried about the house: first Jobe's lymphoma, now this. I think maybe this place is contaminated somehow and I was hoping you could . . ." She waited, but Danny did not fill in the words. Clearly, he had no idea what she was hoping he could do. "Would you look this up, do some research, you know, help me figure out who to talk to, what kind of contractor can find out if we're living in Amityville?"

"Car?" Danny's voice was gentle. "Didn't you tell me once that your mother had breast cancer? That she"—he hesitated slightly before finishing—"died of it?"

Carmen stopped, shame filling and confusing her. Having the house checked out had seemed like such a reasonable, scientific path to follow—the sort of thing Jobe might have thought of—but it was only more voodoo, her trying to avoid the facts. "Yes," she said, her tone as grudging as the teenager's she'd been back when her mother was ill.

"Well, you know this disease runs in families, right?" Danny asked. "Any woman with a first-degree relative is twice as likely—"

"Jesus! Do you *memorize* all these statistics?"

"I can't help it. They stick in my head."

Carmen wandered in circles, scuffing her bare feet against floor and carpet in turn, feeling crazy. She'd always thought of Danny as the anti-Jobe. Now, here they were, having a conversation she could easily imagine having with her husband before he died.

"Forget about it," she said. Outside, she could hear the younger boys calling to Luca; then they were climbing up the porch steps, plastic bags full of candy rustling against their knees. "It was a stupid idea."

"No, no, I'll call someone today. It can't hurt. What are you thinking about, like chemicals, formaldehyde, asbestos, that kind of thing?"

"Sure." She hated being soothed. "Listen, I really have to . . ."

She was about to say *go*, but then Danny broke in, speaking in a continuous rush: "I'm worried about you . . . . I can't sleep . . . . Ever since that day, I've been wishing I could be there . . . . I think . . . I love you." Then there was a click.

Carmen turned off her cell phone and gazed at it lying in the palm of her hand. After so many furtive conversations it was almost as if this instrument contained her relationship with Danny. By folding it up and slipping it into her pocket, she could keep his words there.

She turned slowly as the door opened and the boys entered. In the background there was the rhythmic sound of Luca shooting baskets, a ball *thunk*ing against the garage, punctuated by the sound of his shouting—"Yes!" "That was a good one"—echoes of Jobe. Michael came toward her, extending his arm like a dance partner; but instead of taking her hand when she offered it, he deposited an enormous wad of chewed gum in her palm. Both he and Jeffrey laughed wildly and Carmen laughed, too, as she shook the gob into the wastebasket and scrubbed dramatically at her hand with a Kleenex.

"*Ratatouille* is here!" Jeffrey shouted in his underdeveloped voice. "Can we go?"

"It's a cartoon, a kids' movie," Michael sneered. "I don't want to see some stupid cartoon about a mouse."

"It's a rat." Luca stood in the doorway, sweat dripping from his square jaw, holding the basketball under one arm. "I want to see it."

"Me too," said Carmen. "You're outnumbered, three to one."

Michael flopped on the couch and stuck a long red licorice into his mouth. "Okay, fine," he said, grinning as he chewed. He had secretly wanted to see the cartoon movie all along, and for a moment Carmen's world felt right.

* * *

"Well, it's a brilliant strategy," Jana said as she switched her blinker on. "I'd have expected Danny to turn tail, but instead he's goobering all over you with this different-kind-of-love crap. It's like something out of a made-for-TV movie: *Our Special Love*. Maybe he's trying to turn you off with it, get *you* to leave *him*."

It was dawn and the sun, newly risen, glinted viciously in Carmen's eyes. She closed them, rather than squint. "It's really amazing that I asked you to come with me for comfort, don't you think?" She slouched in the bucket seat of Jana's little roadster, pleasantly buzzy from the Xanax she'd dry swallowed just before leaving home. "A real sign of faith on my part. No matter how big a bully you are, I just keep believing you want only the best for me."

"That," Jana said, turning into the hospital parking lot, "is because it happens to be true."

There were herds of them now, wherever Carmen went: women waiting for images of their breasts to be read and things extracted from them to be dissected and reported on. It was like becoming pregnant, when suddenly it had seemed as if everywhere she turned there was some other woman's huge, bulbous stomach; they'd all somehow swollen up simultaneously, according to some master plan. And now, she sat in the waiting room with seven others who were within—she was pretty certain—about ten years of her age. Other than this, however, there was no common theme. They were black and white and one was a regal Indian, with a red dot on her forehead under the paisley headscarf she wore with her candy-pink gown. Several came with men, assumedly husbands. One woman who dozed in a corner chair seemed to be alone.

"I hate pink." Carmen gazed down at the robe, the smooth, plastic hospital bracelet, the socklets, all variations on the same shade. "I'm not even two weeks into this and I already can't stand it. I can see the headline: *Cancer victim goes on rampage, strangles candy striper with pink rope*. Will you visit me in jail?"

"Only if you'll give me some of those drugs," Jana said. "You're toast." The Indian woman pursed her lips and angled her head away from them, burrowing more deeply into her husband's side.

Carmen felt a flicker of defiance followed by regret. The Xanax was making her experience every emotion more fully, as if it were a bath. Now, she was tearful that she'd offended this woman on such a difficult day. She wanted to apologize but her head was heavy and each word took real concentration, as if she had to locate it in a thick fog. So she settled for smiling and nodding, a carefully orchestrated gesture that she hoped didn't look like a leer.

They sat for more than an hour: The room was hot, the drug started wearing off. Both fatigue and fear had set in. Carmen dug through her purse to find the pill bottle and swallowed another, just seconds before her name was called. "You'll need to take those off," said the nurse—oddly male, in his pink shift—as he pointed to the rings on her left hand. "No jewelry allowed in the surgical suite. I can hold them for you."

"That's okay." Jana had come out of her own early morning stupor and risen to stand beside Carmen. "Give them to me. I'll hold on to them until you come out."

Carmen calculated what she'd had to eat the night before: Szechuan, brimming with MSG. *What the hell*, she'd thought when she ordered. *It's time to live like every day is my last.* Now, even without trying to remove the rings, her fingers felt like tight, inflated sausages. There was no way she would get them off.

"I'm not sure," she said, twisting the sapphire-and-diamond engagement ring she'd worn for twenty-two years and yanking it up to the knot her knuckle made. "They're kind of stuck on, I think."

"Here." The nurse produced a plastic bottle of hand lotion out of the pocket of his scrubs. Carmen found this so unlikely, she wanted to check inside to see what else he had (an Allen wrench? a plastic Papa Smurf?). Instead of handing her the bottle, he cradled her left hand in his and squirted some lotion on, using his right to slick the wetness up and down her finger until he could work the rings off. Carmen stared dumbly; this was weirdly intimate. And this man reminded her in some vague way of her older son. He didn't have

Down's, clearly, but he did have the solid stance, stubby limbs, and darting, green eyes. With a grunt, he finally worked the set up and over her knuckle, then free of her hand. He gave the rings to Jana, though he scrutinized her as he did. "Okay if your friend holds on to these?" he asked. "I could lock 'em up in the safe if you'd rather. They look pretty expensive."

You have no idea, Carmen almost said. *That's a million two you were slathering with Jergen's.* But she didn't. "Jana should keep them," she said then realized how that had sounded. Carmen hadn't meant keep them forever. There was, she found, a loss when they came off her finger that had nothing to do with their worth. She felt off-balance and unprotected somehow. She wanted to correct what she'd said, just in case there was some misunderstanding, but her head swam. That second pill was kicking in.

Thankfully, Jana understood. "They'll be here when you're done," she said, slipping the rings onto her own finger and holding it up for Carmen to see. "Look, a perfect fit. We're married now, it's my dream come true. Now get out of here and come back healed."

Carmen smiled and nodded, though she didn't feel like it. She was, in fact, terrified in a way she never had been before. She'd been stripped of everything: her clothes, her rings, her friend. Now she was being led by the portly nurse the way prisoners were walked to death. She wondered if this is how her mother felt, or Jobe—or if his mistaken belief that she was in the waiting room crazy with worry and praying for a miracle helped him in this moment. Carmen sniffled. She hoped it had.

"Hey, don't worry, this is going to be just fine." The nurse slipped his arm around Carmen's waist as if they were a couple, out strolling. And this is when she realized that she'd been crying. "You took a Xanax, didn't you?"

Two, Carmen almost blurted out, then—as her thoughts ground slowly through the mechanisms of caution—simply nodded.

"It has this effect, a lot of times. You get a little weepy. But we're going to take really good care of you. My name's Pete and I'm going to stay with you the entire way. We'll have you back to your lady friend in no time."

Carmen brightened at this. Had she been a little less stoned, she might have laughed. But the image of she and Jana—a happy couple the way she and Jobe had never been—brought her great pleasure. Perhaps, she thought woozily, she should suggest it afterward. Jana could move in and help her raise the children. Carmen tried to imagine taking off her friend's tie-dyed cap, striped cape, and cotton clothes and she stumbled. "Whoa, there. I think you better take my arm." Pete tucked her hand inside his elbow, as if they were walking together down the aisle of a church. "You don't look it but you're kind of a lightweight, aren't you?"

Carmen leaned gratefully. "Will they cut it off?" she asked. "What do you think? Does this doctor like to do that?"

Pete was unperturbed, clearly used to this question. "You signed, giving permission if the cells have spread?" he asked, and Carmen nodded. "Then the answer is yes, if there's any sign at all he'll perform a mastectomy. Dr. Woo is kind of a zero-tolerance guy where cancer is concerned. He thinks you just get rid of it. And he's right; his success rate is very high."

Pete led her through a doorway, into a room that looked not like a surgery but like a birthing suite, without the fancy linens. In the center was a normal hospital bed surrounded by equipment: monitors and masks and two IV stands. "Time to get in," Pete said, pulling back the white top sheet. "Doc's on a schedule. He should be here any minute."

She lay, stretched out like corpse, while Pete said, "You'll feel a pinch now," and slipped a needle under her skin. Of course, even if Danny were here, he would not have witnessed this humiliation. Like Jana, he'd have been in the room with the Indian husband and the lone woman in the corner—who had still, cruelly, been waiting when Carmen was called. Neither would he have been here to see her breathing speed up or the odd, utterly lonely feeling envelop her. Lying on this cot in the midst of shiny metal and white tile, she had become, suddenly, as small as an insect under glass. She could stop breathing as Jobe had that morning not long ago.

For the first time, Carmen felt not guilty but genuinely grieved. Tears ran down the sides of her face and into her ears. "What is this?" said the man who came into the room, scrubbed and masked, only his narrow eyes peering out over the blue. Oh, thank God, blue, Carmen thought as she wept. The doctor was not wearing pink. This was a very good sign.

Then there was haze and people moving above her: several masked, capped heads, the floating presence of a set of eyes that shone from the brightly lighted room as if it were darkness. Carmen blinked at them, only really it was just half a blink: she closed but neglected to open. There was a rubbery smell, like tires. And then she was gone.

Afterward, in the recovery room, she would remember nothing and have to be told about how she inhaled the anesthetic for three minutes before going easily to sleep. Jana had materialized beside her and the doctor was speaking to them earnestly. Without his mask, he had a shiny, round face and hands that fluttered and gestured. He had gotten the whole tumor, he said, making a scooping motion as if with ice cream. The margins, he told Carmen proudly as if she'd accomplished something, were clean. Here, he used his hands the way men do when they're outlining a woman, only the shape he made was of her comet and not humanlike. She was a lucky lady, he said, with very little to worry about. She should go home and wait for the path report. Eat well.

It wasn't until he said this that Carmen realized how nauseated she was. She lay back on the bed, which seemed—if it were possible for one hospital bed to be different from another—not the one that had been wheeled from her surgery into this cubicle. But Jana was bringing her clothes, pulling them out of a plastic bag and piling them at her feet. "Time to leave," she said. And though Carmen wanted to question this, asking for just a few more minutes the way she had when her mother awakened her for school, she sat up abruptly and the room began to turn.

"Here." Jana handed her a shirt. And Carmen, without any warning or noise, took it and was immediately sick all over it.

"Jesus!" Jana said, jumping back. "Now what the fuck do we do?"

She was gone for two or three minutes during which time Carmen sat with her eyes closed. "Can we give her a shower?" she heard Jana ask someone when she returned.

"Sorry." This voice was female, not Pete's. What happened to his promise to stay with her? This could be just a taste of the infidelity Carmen deserved—her life to come. "She's not in a room with shower privileges," the woman's voice floated in. "You're just going to have to clean her up with water and get her home."

"Fine." But Jana did not sound fine at all.

Carmen felt the washcloth on her arms, Jana's hesitant touch as she picked up Carmen's messy hands to clean between the fingers. It was soothing, nonetheless: Even a caregiver who was clearly disgusted could help. Suddenly, Carmen's eyes flew open. She looked at Jana, who was stone-faced and perspiring. But she was there, after all, lifting Carmen's hand to wipe under her wrist, Jobe's jewels glinting from her ring finger.

"They used to be in yellow gold," Carmen said, tapping the largest sapphire. "He had them reset in white gold because I wanted it. He wanted them to be mine."

"The man loved you." It wasn't a statement or an accusation, but somewhere in between. "Here, I think you're ready to have these back." Jana slipped the rings off and handed them to Carmen, then went to the sink and began washing her hands over and over, using big squirts of soap. "You're going to have to wear a hospital shirt home," she said over her shoulder. "They'll probably charge you for it but, whatever . . . ."

"Yeah, the one thing I have is money. Isn't that strange?" Carmen pulled on her jeans and leaned over—another woozy moment, but she managed to control herself—to slip on her shoes. "It doesn't help. Not at all."

"I've heard that about money," Jana said. "Of course, I've never had the opportunity to find out."

Siena watched from the front door as Carmen and Jana haltingly climbed the steps. They wore the same expressions she had whenever Jobe had come back from another surgery or treatment: part worry, part revulsion, part terror. This had always struck Carmen as precisely the right mix, and it still did now. She tried to smile at her daughter on the way past but succeeded only in straining her eyes. She closed them the moment Jana deposited her on the living room couch.

The next few hours went by in a slow-motion dream. Luca came by and ran his hand along the length of her arm, the way a little child might with a wall or banister. Then Michael, who'd been told only that his mother was sick, came behind him and did exactly the same thing. Carmen settled in then, feeling blessed, wondering if the boys had performed the same sacrament on Jobe. Despite the outcome in his case, she wished for this continuity. Their children's touch anointing both parents. Keeping them—even her—pure.

Carmen dozed while Jana had the kids help her make fajitas: Michael chopped vegetables under Siena's supervision while Luca grated cheese. When they finally sat at the table, Carmen was woozy but ravenous. She was sore under the bandage and found that using her left arm made this worse. Without asking, Siena assembled a fajita for her mother and handed it over with a pleading look that said, *Don't make a big deal.*

"Thanks, sweetie," Carmen said softly, remembering the dozens of times at the end when she'd had to cut Jobe's food and hold the fork up to his mouth.

By eight o'clock, Carmen was exhausted and she could see Jana was, too. There was a reason Jana hadn't had children; she didn't care for the dailiness of it or the mundane constancy of their requests. "I don't understand my math," Michael announced after the dishes had been cleared. "Can you help me?" It wasn't clear whom he was asking; his question went out to the room. But Carmen was dumb with pain and Vicodin, and Siena had gone off to call Troy, and Luca had never mastered anything beyond subtraction, which still sometimes confused him.

"Okay, why don't you bring it to the table?" Jana said so sweetly that Carmen knew—even through her haze—that her friend was nearly at the end. They worked through word problems while Carmen and Luca sat stumplike in their various places. It was as if an evil spell had been cast over their house. With Jobe gone, something had shifted and deadened; quiet as he'd been, he must have added some kinesis to the atmosphere.

At nine o'clock, Jana shooed the children off. "I've had my fill of you," she said, and they knew she meant it, so they went to their various rooms. Then she brought a bottle of white wine to the couch along with two juice glasses. "Here." She poured Carmen's all the way up to the brim. "I don't know how you do this every fucking day. It's enough to make me want to shoot myself in the head."

"Yeah, well, it wasn't going to be this way." Carmen lolled her head back, alcohol mixing with the drugs so she felt as if she were being pulled down by something heavy.

"How was it going to be?" Jana fell back into a huge easy chair. She was already nearly done with her glass.

Carmen squinted, as if she could see the answer in the air. And then she could: a series of days from two decades before. Young, smiling Jobe. Sunday dinners at his parents' house where Carmen now belonged. She could wander the estate at will and ride the two horses they kept at a close-by farm any time she chose. Often, when they arrived, Olive would kiss her cheek and tell her how beautiful she was, then mention they were having strawberry shortcake for dessert, because it was Carmen's favorite. Olive always smelled wonderful back then, not like an old woman but something almost magical— sandalwood or cedar. The time Carmen came bearing a picture of Esme's two big-eyed little boys Olive's face had changed, becoming nearly tearful.

"Aren't they miraculous?" she'd said, running one finger over the surface of the photograph. "You would have children like this, too."

But telling Jana about this—about how she'd gotten pregnant more for Olive than for Jobe—would make her sound stupid, like someone who deserved to get stuck in a loveless marriage. Jana would never make such a ridiculous mistake, so Carmen mentally edited the story to preserve her pride.

"I suppose," she said, "there were absolutely no money concerns. So it was like this huge barrier, the thing you said, you know, 'We'll start a family once we can buy a house,' or 'when we can start saving for college.' All that was removed in our case."

Jana nodded. This was making sense, so Carmen forged on. "I thought it would help, I guess. I thought it would make me grown up, and maybe I wanted to show my sister I could."

"Not a great reason to make a lifelong decision," Jana said, moving a pillow so she could recline sideways in the chair.

"No." Carmen poured herself more wine. The night felt unreal around her. Everything glowed. "God, I was young and stupid. It just kills me when I look back. But Esme was always telling me what a fuck-up I was; she had a husband and a little house of her own and two adorable babies. Then suddenly, out of nowhere, I found myself living in this *palace*. I married a man who was so brilliant . . ." She stopped for a moment and stared at nothing, feeling a wrench of pure pain. "Jobe was so good he got tenure the minute he stepped onto a college campus. But Esme, she told me once—way back—that she was afraid her husband was having an affair. That he might leave her. At least I knew Jobe would never cheat on me."

"Are you sure?" Carmen stopped and looked over at her friend, who was suddenly slit-eyed. "How do you know Jobe never cheated?"

"Because he just . . . wouldn't have. It wasn't in him." She swallowed, unwilling to disclose the real reason. Jobe didn't deserve to be humiliated that way, even in death. "Besides, he was socially withdrawn, and not very, you know, smooth."

"You know what?" Jana sat up. "Sometimes, I think you're a bigger bitch than this sister you're always talking about."

"Am I?"

"Are you what? A bitch?" Jana was getting ready to leave and Carmen didn't want things to end between them this way. But she felt anchored, suctioned to the couch.

"No, am I always talking about my sister?"

Jana stopped and thought. "Actually, you've only mentioned her a couple of times. That was an exaggeration. But I'm sorry, this whole thing just reeks of really bad karma. You get married to show up your sister, despite the fact that you don't even love this guy who would gladly throw himself under a truck for you. Doesn't hurt that he's obscenely rich, of course. And then you spend the next couple of decades living off his family and wishing him dead."

Wait, Carmen wanted to say. *Let's go back! I didn't tell you about Olive, about how much she wanted a daughter and a grandchild. A miracle, she said, and I wanted badly to make that come true. And there were moments I loved Jobe, even when he wouldn't touch me. He saved me in London. He brought me his T-shirt in the bathroom. Have I ever told you about the way he danced?*

It was too late; Jana wouldn't believe her selfless motives now. So she reclined instead and watched while Jana collected the knapsack she carried instead of a purse and slipped on her shoes.

"Listen, forget what I said, I'm just really tired." Jana kissed Carmen on the forehead. "I really hope the biopsy results are good. Let me know, okay? And just send the kids over to the café when they're hungry. I guess they do kind of grow on you. If I'd bludgeoned one of them earlier, I'd be really sorry by now."

Carmen had been planning to go back and see the doctor alone. But when Pete called to check on her and set up the consultation to go over the pathology results, there was something in his voice. "Who's coming to the appointment with you?" he asked, too brightly. And as on that day in the garden, she knew.

It was ten o'clock, a likely time for Olive to be out playing bridge or at her garden club. But she happened that morning to be home. Carmen told her first about the mammogram, leaving out the part about Danny, letting Olive think the comet was detected during her yearly screening. She heard Olive inhale sharply.

"The surgeon said he's sure he got everything," Carmen lied. "But they had to examine the, uh, tumor"—she hated that word— "so I'm going back today to get the results."

"What time?" Olive asked.

"Three," said Carmen. "And it's not necessary, but . . ."

"I'll be there at two-twenty," Olive said, and curtly hung up.

Her Mercedes glided up at precisely two-nineteen. *Greenwich calls Olive for the correct time*—that was always Jobe's joke. "Thanks for coming to get me," said Carmen, climbing into the car.

"How are you, dear?" Olive wore a pair of sunglasses with amber lenses and she drove intently, never more than fifty miles an hour.

"Pretty good, now that the drugs have worn off," Carmen said. "The nights have been a little strange." Of course, she didn't tell Olive about how she climbed into bed with Jana's disapproving voice ringing through her head, or about taking another pill simply to make the words recede. So many things needed to be hidden from this woman she adored. What did that say?

Even moving slower than the rest of the traffic, it took less time to get to the hospital than Carmen anticipated. This was some sort of trick of Olive's. They walked through the electric doors and found the surgeon's waiting room with ten minutes to spare. He was running late, the receptionist informed them. It would be more like three-thirty. So they chose adjoining chairs near the back of the room. Carmen picked up a soft, tattered magazine from two years before.

"I can't believe this," Olive said suddenly.

"What?" Carmen looked around.

"This! After everything else, Luca's difficulties and Jobe's illness." Olive never used the word *death*; Carmen was pretty sure she couldn't—at least not where Jobe was concerned. When George had died two years earlier, of a heart attack that struck him exactly like lightning on the golf course, when his nine-iron was raised, Olive had been resigned. Nearly businesslike. She'd planned a grand funeral and wafted through it dressed in widow's weeds. Even the drab black dress failed to conceal that at seventy-three her body was perfect. The woman had never lifted a barbell in her life, but she held up like Sophia Loren.

An idea dawned in Carmen's mind: Olive had never loved her husband, either. She had been far more vibrant than he, a brick shithouse of a lady who easily could have had men—gardeners, chauffeurs—on the side. George's death simply hadn't been something to mourn. She also had been waiting to be free, only her sentence was much longer than Carmen's: nearly fifty years. And it would follow then that she, too, might feel guilty, perhaps responsible for her son. Carmen shivered and took Olive's hand, which the older woman clearly interpreted as a sign of apprehension. "It will be fine, dear. I'm sure the surgeon took care of everything and there's only a little bit of tidying up to do."

Carmen giggled and gently squeezed her mother-in-law's fingers. No one else would refer to cancer treatment this way; she would have to remember to tell Danny, who always appreciated the stories about Olive and her dry way of assessing the world. They sat like this for some time before releasing each other to read their respective outdated magazines.

The receptionist knocked on her window. "Doctor is ready now," she said. Carmen rose feeling creaky, as if she'd been sitting for hours. Beside her, Olive popped up with no apparent problem. And together they went through the door.

"Carmen," the doctor said. Instead of shaking her hand, he took it in both of his and patted it for a few seconds. "I see you've brought your mother. I am Ernest Woo."

Olive smiled mildly and extended her hand. "Olive Garrett," she said, but nothing else.

"So sit, sit." The doctor appeared anxious, like the host at a party. "I have some things I want to talk to you about." Yet when he sat behind his desk, he folded his hands and stared at them. It appeared as if he were waiting for her to start.

Carmen was just about to ask what the pathology report had showed when he began to speak. "So we have completed the surgery and it went very well, yes?" He looked questioningly at Carmen and she nodded. *Oh, yes, she'd enjoyed that very much.* "The margins looked clean. I took five lymph nodes." He held up one hand with all the fingers splayed to demonstrate. "And they were all clean. Perfectly clean. This made me very happy."

Carmen was relaxing, melting into her chair a little. She still felt hung over from the anesthesia and now, also, from her relief. She'd been expecting the worst. So much for intuition. A little light radiation —maybe two months—that's what she'd read online about this kind of contained cancer. It was probably ductal, in situ, that's what she'd been hoping for. It was the breast cancer equivalent of having a mole removed. Thank God. It was time to go home.

"However . . ." Dr. Woo had shifted, his face becoming drawn and dark. He pulled a manila folder from the neat pile on his desk and opened it. "Then we received the lab results and I was not so happy." He had seemed to be addressing both of them, but now he turned to Olive. It was as if he thought they were having a private conversation and would decide later how to break the news to Carmen herself. "The pathology of this particular tumor is problematic in a patient of this age. It is what we call 'estrogen-receptor positive,' which means it tends to recur and grow in the presence of estrogen. And as you know, prior to menopause the female body produces large amounts of estrogen, each month, even when it is no longer necessary for childbearing."

Carmen blinked. Was she supposed to feel guilty about this? Her wild body with its naughty estrogen dance.

"We have found . . ." Finally, the doctor turned to her and his eyes looked weary, sad. "The best way to combat your kind of cancer is to shut down the body's hormone production completely." He made a motion with his hand, like closing a door. "I am a cautious man, so in order to be safe, here is what I recommend: three months of chemotherapy to eliminate any growth we may have missed, two months of radiation, and at the same time I'm going to give you a drug called tamoxifen. This will put you into menopause immediately. I think it's our very best chance."

Carmen was dumbstruck. Olive, thankfully, was not. "Is the chemotherapy really necessary?" she asked, and Carmen knew she was thinking of Jobe, the endless rounds of needles and X-rays that probably ended up killing him in the end. "You said you were able to take out the entire tumor, and I'm sure you did."

Dr. Woo nodded, an assent to her flattery. "That's a very good question, Mrs. Garrett. But the therapy is not intended for cancer cells I missed—though that is a remote possibility. It's intended for tumors that are growing elsewhere in the breast tissue, and according to your daughter's report it's very likely there are some. For whatever reason, her body is making a cancer that feeds directly off her hormones. Even right now, she is probably at a stage in her cycle where there is a wave of estrogen or progesterone." Both of them turned to look at Carmen, as if examining her for evidence. "I cannot be certain, of course, but my guess is that there are other tumors just beginning. We could cut off the supply of hormones tomorrow and hope that takes care of the problem." Dr. Woo shook his head. "But research shows that just isn't enough. It allows a growing cancer to get in under the wire, so to speak." He turned his hands up and shrugged. "As I said, I'm a cautious man. And you might want to seek a second opinion, but I would ask you not to wait too long."

Carmen put her head back. The room was stifling, or she was having a hot flash, or she was being corroded from the inside by some rampant cancer. Whatever it was, she needed badly to leave. "I don't want a second opinion, I believe you," she said, not to the doctor but to the air above her tightly closed eyes. "Let's get this on the books. Just tell me when I can start."

Because it was rush hour when they left, Olive took residential streets all the way back to Carmen's house, driving just as steadily as before, but the fancy, old-fashioned speedometer needle hovered at about twenty-seven miles per hour. It felt as if they could be in the car for hours.

"Do you mind?" Carmen asked and flipped on the air conditioner. She huddled in front of her vent and was nearly asleep when her cell phone made its text message sound. "How was ur appt?" Danny had keyed to her. She stared at the words for a moment then turned off her phone and threw it into her purse.

"Are you sure about this, dear?" Olive asked. She was staring ahead, her face like granite. She looked as she had that last night with Jobe. "Wouldn't you like to get a second opinion? I can make some calls, find out who's best at these things."

"Thank you." Carmen reached out to touch Olive's shoulder. "But I think we just *saw* who's best. Besides, I knew it would be like this. I had a feeling. In a way, that doctor was my second opinion. I was the first."

Jana would understand this line of thinking. But it was a risk to be talking about this with Olive, who might decide something devastating had happened to her daughter-in-law's brain as well. Carmen watched, curious, while Olive formulated her answer.

"I understand," she said and nodded. "George always teased me about my 'feelings.' He thought it was all nonsense. But if you know it, you just do."

Carmen nearly laughed. "Well, who'da thought we were both so psychically inclined?"

"Sometimes . . ." Olive gripped the steering wheel and looked straight ahead. "Sometimes, I think I can hear him speaking to me."

"George?" Carmen asked.

Olive chortled. "Good Lord, no. That man barely said seven words to me when he was alive. He couldn't be bothered to call me from an overseas trip. I'm sure he's not reaching out from the great beyond."

"So are you talking about Jobe?"

Olive hesitated, then nodded. "Once or twice, I could swear I've heard him. He was always the sweetest, the most devoted of my boys. Will was born with the drive to conquer and I think he forgets his family for months at a time. Nate is a lovely young man and I adore him. But Jobe. It's like he's still . . . watching. Because he knows how strange and lonely life can get. Oh, I know I sound crazy, don't I?"

Carmen was warm, lazing in the late afternoon sunshine that came in through the passenger window glass. It was almost possible to forget—momentarily, at least—about what the doctor had said. After all these years, she and Olive were coming to an understanding: They had more in common than most real mothers and daughters. Neither had loved her husband; both had experienced mysterious events. Putting these two things together, Olive probably *knew* how she, Carmen, had felt about Jobe. No longer would there need to be secrets between them.

"I don't think you're crazy," Carmen said, closing her eyes, feeling the car ride the way she had when she was a sleepy little girl. "There was one night, up in the attic. He, uh . . . appeared to me. Only he was huge, and sort of faint around the edges. Honestly, it could have been a dream. I don't know."

"I like to think not, dear." Olive reached out to pat Carmen's leg—while driving! This was as broad a gesture as it would be for some other women to sweep you up in their arms. "I've always hoped that there was more than this world. I hoped that for Jobe, and for myself, because wherever he is I'm going there soon."

And now for me, too, Carmen thought. But she didn't say it.

"It must have been hard living with George all those years." Carmen opened her eyes but stayed curled in the shower of sunlight, drunk on its golden shine. "Did you ever think of leaving?"

"Goodness, no." Olive made her signature hand wave—a regal dismissal—then clamped down on the wheel again. "He was a good man. We had three children. It was . . . my life."

"But didn't you ever wonder?"

"Wonder what, dear?"

"You know. What else you might have done. Who else you might have met. Didn't you ever play that game where you give yourself a completely different ending?"

Several seconds went by and Olive didn't answer. Finally, Carmen focused her eyes and looked. Her mother-in-law had slowed to around twenty miles an hour. Her lips were pursed, and her shoulders shook.

"Olive?" Carmen said.

"Are you telling me," the other woman whispered, "that you wished for something else? That you were playing this 'game' while you were married to my son?"

Carmen sat up as if jolted. She was confused, behind somehow. They had been sharing something, like mother and daughter, meeting on the same otherworldly plane. Now, in an instant, Olive was again Mrs. Garrett, the matriarch at the massive dining room table. And inside Carmen was a twist of bright fear.

"I thought that's what we were talking about." Her tone always became more certain, nearly condescending, when she was threatened. Carmen could hear it but was powerless to change it. Besides, the only option was to become mewling and needy, which would have been worse. "A good man, three children. Doing what needs to be done."

They were only four blocks from Carmen's house, yet Olive pulled the car over and turned the key to Off. The interior began immediately to grow stuffy, but Olive was shivering. She was at the stage of life where every temperature was some variation of cold.

She opened her mouth to speak twice before actually forming words. "I loved my husband, for all of his . . . quirks," she said finally, her gaze fastened on some point in the distance. "The question is: Did you love yours?"

Carmen sat. The heat of the sun had turned punishing in the closed, idle car. Snippets of the doctor's speech were running through her head: "three months of chemotherapy," "put you into menopause immediately." But these complaints seemed paltry, now, compared to the fierce cruelty she had unthinkingly inflicted on Olive. Carmen ached to take it back, for this single conversation to be the one decision in her life that she could re-script. She would gladly live again through the twenty-one years of a cool and confusing marriage rather than do this damage. Slowly, she forced herself to look at the old woman in the seat next to her, the Marilyn Monroe shape suddenly flaccid and hunched, like a plant midwither.

"Olive," she said, as gently as she was able. "I thought you knew."

There was a pause. The phrase "moment of silence" joined the others in Carmen's head. The heat was stultifying; she had to concentrate to breathe. Then Olive turned the key: Cool air rushed out of the vents, washing Carmen's skin in relief.

"I did," said Olive, nodding slowly. "I did know. But I hoped and prayed with everything in me that I was wrong."

May 1986

Carmen spent her twenty-first birthday in New York with Olive, in order to give Jobe time to finish his dissertation. They had a suite at the New York Palace. "I'm sure it's not as nice as if my son were here with you," Olive said as they stood on the deck, looking over the honking, moonlit city streets. "But I'm honored that you're willing to celebrate with me." She lifted a sizzling glass of champagne and clinked it with Carmen's, which she had already drunk half of. "Happy Birthday, dear."

The wind picked up and Carmen's dark hair—grown long and thick over winter—blew across her face. It still surprised her that she was here with this woman she hadn't even known on her last birthday, acting more like a daughter than she had with her own mom.

It was Olive who'd discovered her sneaking out of Jobe's room that drunken night nearly ten months ago. Carmen was afraid, smelling of sex and sweat and Scotch, holding her shoes and tights, peering down the labyrinthine hallways trying to remember which direction her room was in. She turned to look over the banister into the foyer, to reorient herself and recall the path she'd taken when she first entered the house, when Olive materialized on the marble tile wearing a long, dark robe, her cap of bobbed silver hair looking exactly as neat as it had at dinner. Carmen wondered, for one lazy second, if perhaps it was a wig.

In the next, she was struck with embarrassment: Mrs. Garrett surely knew. It was 4:00 a.m. and Carmen was standing outside of Jobe's still-open room. Reaching back, Carmen gently pulled the door closed then started down the stairs. Maybe she would be allowed to get a few hours' sleep before leaving. Or—she paused midway down—it was possible the woman might simply shove her out the front door.

Stoic, mouth twitching, Olive watched her descend. "You couldn't sleep either?" she asked when Carmen reached the bottom.

This was not what she'd been expecting. Carmen blinked and shook her head.

"Tell you what. I'll make us something to eat and put on some tea while you go in there and wash your face." Olive put her hands on Carmen's shoulders and gave her a little tap in the direction of the powder room off the foyer.

Carmen waited until she was inside to turn on the light. Then she faced the mirror. Her face was streaked with lavender shadow and black eyeliner; she looked like something out of a teenage horror movie, about to be bludgeoned. For just a moment, she imagined that's what Olive had in store.

But when she stepped into the kitchen—easy to find because it was at the back of the house and lit brilliantly—Olive was standing at the stove. "Grilled cheese sandwiches," she said. "How does that sound?"

Olive was glad to have company, Carmen realized that night. By the time they stood side by side on the rooftop deck at the New York Palace, she'd figured out one other thing: Olive had been secretly thrilled to see her coming out of Jobe's room. She'd always wished for a daughter; she told Carmen this one afternoon while they shopped for clothes. It wasn't that she didn't love the boys, of course. But it was hard living in a house full of men, all scientists and math geeks, who said little and wouldn't have noticed if she painted the walls bright orange.

Also, Jobe was her favorite and she so wanted him to have a nice girlfriend. "He's the most considerate of my boys," she'd said. "Even as a young child, he was the one who wanted to give away his allowance and bring poor people home to stay with us."

"Is that what I am?" Carmen asked, only half joking. She still questioned Jobe's family's offer to help her with her last year of school. "Just some poor girl he dragged home?"

"Of course not," Olive said, her hand fluttering. "*You* are like an extended family member."

But she was not yet, in any way, a family member. And this was exactly the point. Olive wanted her son to have what he wanted. And Jobe clearly wanted Carmen. So here she was.

"Have you thought about what you'll do after graduation?" Olive asked, settling into a padded deck chair so she was facing the setting sun. "It's nice that it coincides with Jobe's finishing up. George and I were thinking we might send you two on a trip."

"You've already sent me on a trip." Carmen turned toward the older woman and spread her arms. "We're here, in New York, staying in the nicest place I've ever seen—probably ever *will* see."

"Yes, of course, but this is for your *birthday*. And it's for me, too. A break, a girls' getaway weekend. That's all."

Carmen closed her eyes and leaned back. There was no real danger of falling: the terrace wall hit her a few inches above the waist. But she liked the dizzying possibility. It was a little like the way she'd felt with Rory the last time, when he ran his hand down the front of her T-shirt then leaned in to kiss the hollow at the base of her throat. She shivered now, simultaneously turned on and disgusted. Even thinking such things in front of Olive was a betrayal.

"You barely know me." Carmen's eyes were still shut and her voice soft, absorbed by the wind. "I don't think you should be doing all these things for me." To her embarrassment, she felt tears gathering in her throat and turned, sightless, in the direction of the setting sun. She would miss Olive terribly. It would be like losing a mother all over again, only this time someone she adored. And Olive, surely, would hate Carmen for the rest of her life.

"I know more than you might imagine." The wind had died down suddenly, and Olive's words cut neatly through the air.

Carmen shook her head, swiping at her eyes as she pushed the hair out of her face. Then she refilled her glass and held up the bottle. Olive raised one finger and downed her champagne. Swallowing and nodding, she said, "I'd love some, thank you."

Carmen poured and they sat, side by side, in their padded chairs. "What do you think you know?" she finally asked, hoping Olive would turn and say, *Everything. I know you only tolerate when my son touches you, that you went out the other night with a real estate agent and let him finger fuck you under the table in a dark bar.*

"I know that it's very difficult to figure out what you want at twenty-one." Olive—the real one, who had never said the word *fuck* in Carmen's presence and surely never used it as a verb in her life— squinted into the dying light. "I know that you've livened up my home and made my son very happy. I also know that there are certain things you need to just . . . believe."

Carmen groaned and frowned and drank. She wanted this, more than anything. But it wasn't working. She'd tried repeatedly to will herself into loving Jobe. But it hadn't worked. "Like what? Exactly what do I believe in?"

"Yourself." Olive had settled back in her chair as if to sleep. "You're a beautiful, warm, smart young woman, and if you really commit yourself to something, it will become—over time—what you want. What you need. I have faith in that."

That's such bullshit. Carmen almost said it, but she caught herself. Olive was looking satisfied and dreamy in her seat. The sun was a glowing orange ball, sinking behind the spires of Manhattan. There was champagne left to be drunk and dinner in a restaurant where Al Pacino was rumored to eat several times a month. It was Carmen's birthday and Olive had brought her here to celebrate. This was not the right time.

But four nights later, after she'd left Jobe on campus to teach his final discussion group of the semester and driven to the bar to meet Rory, Carmen decided that the time had come. At eight o'clock, she left a message with Nate saying that one of her girlfriends was having a crisis—her boyfriend had broken up with her, the friend had consumed an entire bottle of vodka, Carmen had to stay with her—and asking if someone else would pick up Jobe.

When she got back to the table, after using the pay phone, Rory was sitting wide-legged on his bar stool and he reeled her in so she was pressed against the V his lower body made. Carmen felt like she was shining and she wondered, again, at the whims of her senses. Like Jobe, Rory was tall and thin, dark haired, with hands so large he could wrap his fingers around her upper arms. But he was put together completely differently, his chest smooth and lean rather than hollow, his long legs graceful and not at all knobby. These small things mattered not at all, but they made such a difference. Carmen wished with all her heart that this were not true.

"Everything okay?" he asked her, his voice hoarse in her ear. And she nodded. He folded her head down against his shoulder and rocked her back and forth, humming into her hair. It was only their third date but Carmen knew this was what she'd been looking for. Rory's cologne mixed with the scents of beer and chips and lime. Her arm, delicate, twined with his in a Tantric sexual way. Every loose movement of his body seeming to suggest something, though he was only keeping time with Dire Straits.

Carmen drank a second vodka tonic, in honor of her imaginary friend. And she made a silent toast: This had to be done. It was not only time, the deed was well past due. She'd been unable to break up with Jobe any other way; several times, over winter break, she'd really tried.

They'd seen a movie then gone for dinner in a grotto restaurant that served a hot vegetarian curry. "Remember the masala in the park?" he'd asked, as he did every single time they encountered anything even remotely Thai, Tibetan, Pakistani, or Indian. And Carmen had said irritably, as she always did, "Of course I remember. It was less than a year ago."

When they sat she'd been prepared to blurt out everything, all the stock phrases she knew: *I just don't feel the way I should. You're like a brother to me. I want to be friends.* She'd known it would be the end of dinners at the club and of gifts from Olive, but it was the right thing to do. While she was gathering herself, however, Jobe started a long, complicated story about Bernhard Riemann.

He'd told her about the man before—exhaustively. But usually Jobe focused on the mathematical details: zeta function, complex manifold theory, dimensions higher than four. Carmen tuned this out the way she did when people talked about the stock market. Tonight, however, Jobe returned to a story about his hero that she remembered wisps of from that first night in Baltimore: a long-dead German mathematician's tragic death and lost work. The tale had a Gothic quality she liked. Their drinks arrived, along with chutney and spongy bread. Someone lowered the lights; tinkling music came from far away.

Riemann was just thirty-nine, Jobe said, gripping a beer bottle in his long-fingered hand. It was the year of the Austro-Prussian War and the mathematician had to leave his university and his town. But he was sick, something chronic—a fragile man, but brilliant. He left behind a sheet of paper that contained the proof of his hypothesis. And when he didn't return, his housekeeper threw it out along with all the rest of his things. No one else had been able to solve the problem since.

"But how does anyone know?" Carmen asked. Their curry arrived, steaming, flecked with bits of hot chili pepper. "If the only person to see it was the housekeeper, who's to say he proved anything? Was *she* some kind of mathematical genius?"

Jobe looked down at his plate, perplexed. He worked with strings of symbols so long they took up three blackboards. But her question seemed to stump him. "I don't know," he said, finally. "But I'm sure that it's true."

"Well, that's ridiculous!" She ate some of the food and it

warmed her. The little underground room was candlelit and flickery, like a dream. Dammit! This happened at the most inconvenient moments. Carmen would be with Jobe and realize that she actually was enjoying herself. "Look." She put her fork down. "There's something I need to . . ."

She looked up at Jobe then and saw that he was gazing into space, hearing nothing, pondering his weird thoughts. She sighed and watched as he tipped the bottle and drank what was left. "Maybe it's like a curse," he said before picking up his fork and taking his first bite. "It's some sort of universal rule: anyone who gets close to solving the problem has to die."

He chewed very slowly. It never seemed to bother Jobe when his food was cold—or, similarly, when his body was. Carmen had watched him just that morning walk out to the car in a T-shirt and jeans, ambling without so much as a shiver, as if the bitter wind stopped short of touching him.

"But at least no one will throw away my work," he continued, interrupting her vision of him slamming the car door and walking back to the house with the book he'd been searching for in one hand. "I know you would never let that happen."

This was such a simple sentence, it seemed utterly impossible to contradict. He hadn't made any grand pronouncements—hadn't asked her if she wanted to be with him, near his possessions and papers, at the hour of his death—he'd only absentmindedly assumed.

She'd failed to break up with him that night and every time she'd tried since. There was no *reason*; that was the problem. He was a decent, loving boyfriend with a great future. He came to her along with Olive, not to mention that glorious house, vacations, nice cars they could use whenever they chose. To walk away without cause seemed insane, whimsical, somehow childish. She imagined telling him she had to leave because she just didn't love him and having him stare at her uncomprehending. Or worse, cry.

The only way, she'd decided, was to sleep with someone else and then confess it. It was drastic but her problem would be solved: Jobe would break up with her. Carmen had been prepared to go out and find someone passable; any man who didn't repel her would do. But then she'd been lucky enough to meet Rory in a checkout line at Safeway, and her plan had changed. No longer was her goal only to get rid of one man; now she needed to have this other.

Rory was successful, only a year older than Jobe but eons more mature. Well dressed with a silky goatee that made him look vaguely Hispanic, though he'd told Carmen he was 100 percent Black Irish. He lived alone, in a condo, and carried an actual phone—a boxy, flesh-colored device—strapped to his belt. He groaned now and slid the thing to his hip so he could pull Carmen in closer. It occurred to her that he hadn't offered to let her use it when she said she needed to make a call. This was troubling. But she could feel him growing hard against her back and her plan was already underway.

"Want to go back to my place?" he asked.

She swallowed and nodded and he rose behind her, paying quickly for their drinks, keeping one arm around her shoulders as they walked through the bar and out into the warm spring night.

"Follow me." His voice was less guttural out here, more businesslike. "What are you driving?"

Carmen pointed to the BMW parked at the corner. Rory whistled down low. "Nice," he said.

This was the car Jobe had used to pick her up at the airport when she arrived in Baltimore the first time, and her only regret about tonight was that she would use it as one of her props. To involve Olive and George's BMW in her relationship with Rory struck Carmen as sordid, and she considered for a moment leaving it by the curb to be towed. Of course this would require her to disappear completely, never surfacing in the Garretts' lives ever again. And as suddenly as the idea popped into her mind, it made perfect sense! They would assume she'd been killed. Jobe and Olive would mourn her together. No one would be hurt.

"I'm really bad with direction," Carmen said, holding on to

Rory's arm. "And that last V and T hit me really hard. Why don't you drive us?"

Rory looked down at her, with the expression of a high school teacher hearing a tired excuse. She was losing him. She had to do something. So Carmen stood on her toes and kissed him, open mouthed, running her hand over the bulge in his pants at the same time. "Okay," he said, pulling her toward a dark Chevy her father would have loved.

The ride was blissfully short: Rory steering with one hand and letting the other play over her thighs; Pink Floyd pouring out of the speakers and echoing through her chest. Then they were in his apartment, a little smaller and danker than Carmen would have predicted but overlooking the water. Besides, her expectations probably had been thrown out of whack by Jobe's family's estate.

"You want something to drink?" Rory asked as he led her through dark rooms to the bedroom in the back.

"A glass of water," Carmen said.

"Coming up." He gave her a playful shove onto the bed and went into the adjoining bathroom to draw some water into a blue plastic cup, which he set on a table next to her head.

Carmen lay sprawled, her shoes still on. His windows were bare of curtains, framing a silver moon, and the room was eerily silent. "Hey, do you have any music? I was really digging *The Wall*."

"The lady has her demands." Rory pulled his shirt over his head and walked, hairless chest gleaming in moonlight, to the next room. Thirty seconds later she heard the opening chords. "Anything else?" he asked, coming back in.

"No." Carmen looked out the window at the lights swinging on their ropes and wires over the bay. "You."

He made a raw, animal sound that she could feel in her own throat. Then he was above her, hands moving: unbuttoning her shirt and laying it open, unzipping her jeans and peeling them down. Like a man skinning a fish, he stripped the clothes neatly from her raw skin and bones and hair. All the time, she was bathed in music and moonlight, her eyes wide open. This—Carmen thought as Rory crouched over her, sliding the head of his rock-hard cock up and down between her legs until she begged him to do it—*this* was exactly the way making love was supposed to feel. With Jobe there were always clumsy moments, small aborted movements that went nowhere, as if he'd started down a path to find her and run into an obstacle that caused him to back up and try a different direction. She usually ended up dry, pained by the friction, holding on to his shoulders and waiting for it to end.

Must stop thinking about that, she instructed herself and gave in then to Rory who was pumping into her rhythmically, making low yelps. She cleared her mind just in time to come at the same moment Rory did: a simultaneous arching and clawing that clearly meant something. They were joined in a way she and Jobe had never been.

Afterward, they lay panting, side by side. *Don't leave me now*, Roger Waters sang. Carmen edged closer but Rory did not fold her against his long body or take her hand. "That was great," he said, turning toward her. "You're really sexy."

"With you I am." Carmen said it before she'd thought through the implications.

"What do you mean, with me?" Rory popped up sideways and propped his head in one hand. "You're not sexy with other guys? I doubt that."

"There's just . . . this one guy. I mean, I don't really want to talk about that."

"What, are you shy all of a sudden?" Rory grinned. "After this? C'mon, it's okay. You can tell me about the other guys. It's not like I'm going to get all possessive on you."

"Really?" Carmen turned toward him and stretched, her nipples grazing his chest. "You wouldn't care at all if I went home to someone else?"

Rory laughed. "Oh, I get it, this must be the Beemer man!" He reached out to rub one of her breasts and though she'd been wanting him to do this—asking for it, really—now it stung. "Nope. You can go back to your boyfriend or your husband, or whatever you've got waiting for you at home. But next time you want to get laid by someone who knows where all the secret buttons are, you just give me a call. I'm always happy to help out a gorgeous woman in need."

The album had ended and after he said the last word, Rory's apartment was deadly quiet. Carmen sat up, reaching across him for the cup of water, and when he tried to touch her, she batted his hand away. This was irrational: She'd been using him to break up with Jobe and she shouldn't be angry. But she couldn't help it. Oddly, she was offended mostly on Jobe's behalf. However accurate he was, Rory had no right.

She went into the bathroom and stood for a long time, looking at her naked reflection in the mirror. Rory was accurate in this, too: She was gorgeous, her body sculpted, breasts high, waist small. "You're a beautiful, warm, smart young woman," she heard Olive say. When Carmen came out, Rory was lying on the bed with one arm slung over his eyes. She started getting dressed.

"Time to get you back to your car," he said but did not move.

"Don't worry about it," Carmen said. "I can find it myself."

He peeked out from behind an elbow. "Really? I mean, that would be awesome. I'm beat. But are you sure you know where to go?"

"I'll take a cab." Carmen shoved Rory aside and scrabbled for her underwear, which had become tangled in the sheets. "Money's not an issue."

"Whoa," he said sleepily. "You are like my dream come true."

Outside, the streets were damp. It had rained while she was in Rory's apartment and a fine mist continued, like cobwebs around her shoulders and in her hair. The night smelled faintly like motor grease—the way her dad often did when he came back from the plant. Carmen might have hailed a cab if she'd seen one. But her sense of direction had always been excellent and she figured out within a few blocks exactly where she was. The car was less than two miles from here and she deserved to walk.

"Help a guy out, miss?" A man suddenly blocked her way and Carmen shrank back until she saw what probably was his wife and baby huddled in a doorway nearby.

"Here." She opened her wallet and took out all the bills, about eighteen dollars, and handed it to him.

"God bless," he said, but Carmen only darted around him and walked on.

It was past three when she let herself into the house. Everything was quiet. Carmen placed her car keys in the bowl on the hall table, where she always did, and made her way up the wide stairs. As she neared the top, a voice came out of the darkness. "How's your friend doing?"

Carmen took the remaining steps and faced Jobe, who appeared more a darkening of the air than solid flesh. "She's better now. It was a bad night but I think she finally understands that she's better off without the guy."

His hand emerged from the dim to graze Carmen's shoulder. "Must be awful. I don't know what I'd do . . . without you."

He did not draw her forward, which is what Carmen had been expecting. Instead, they stood linked only by his fingers on her shoulder and the long bridge of his arm. After a couple of minutes, it was she who stepped in to find his actual body—checking to be sure he was real, not made only of shadow. And he was. She slipped her arms around him and put her forehead against the framework of his chest and he held her this way for a long time.

There was a week when Carmen thought she might not graduate.

She needed a photo ID to apply for her degree and somehow she'd lost her driver's license. She could not bear to explain this to Jobe, who had saved her from identity theft once before. Panicked, she looked everywhere. But just as she was about to confess the problem to Olive and beg her to bribe someone at the DMV, the card appeared as if by magic on the table beside Carmen's bed. It was a sign, she thought as she picked it up. If she could just quit being thoughtless and stupid—that girl who left her purse in the park with a stranger—everything would be fine.

There was a huge party planned to celebrate Carmen's and Jobe's graduations, hers with a B.A. in art history, his with a PhD in applied mathematics. This was like being an eighth grader feted alongside her older brother, the senior class valedictorian. But Olive ordered invitations inscribed with both sets of information and insisted that Carmen invite people. They resembled wedding invitations, only no one said so. And Jobe, as usual, seemed completely oblivious to the implications of what was going on.

He'd had offers from nine universities. Oxford wanted him back. Princeton had a postdoc they'd asked him to apply for. Johns Hopkins had offered him full professor status from day one. Meantime, Carmen was puzzled. She'd made some inquiries at museums and discovered that their curators—even junior staff—all had graduate degrees. Cincinnati offered her an unpaid internship but she would have to commit to a full year and move there at her own expense. For once, being an "adopted" Garrett was of no help. They had connections with arts organizations all over the East Coast, but no matter how Carmen hinted, Olive failed to make a single call.

It was unreasonable to ask for more, but these people had paid for Carmen's last year in school and given her a place to stay. Surely they wanted her to do something with her degree. Carmen was on the brink of coming right out and asking but she couldn't figure out how to start. "I need another favor" diminished the weight of what Olive had already done for her. But "You've already done so much" was too fawning. The rule, unspoken, was that they did not talk about money or influence. It was unacceptable; it created divisions between people. Only—and Carmen was more and more aware of this as the date of her graduation approached—natural, inevitable divisions remained.

Two days before the party that would mark the end of her childhood, first as her parents' daughter and then as an accidental beneficiary, Carmen wandered around the house with nothing to do. She'd searched for weeks to find the part of the city where she'd met Rory: a crumbly, trendy little cross-section where Jobe and his parents would never go. But she was avoiding that area now. And the only other place she'd found was the library, Enoch Pratt, where she sat paging through art books and watching the people. Beautiful young black girls in sequined high heels. Middle-aged women carting baskets full of romance novels. Homeless men wearing all their clothes, shirts layered over shirts, looking for a place to sleep.

Now, however, it was five o'clock on a Friday; the library was closing. George was out of town and Olive was away on a party-planning mission: talking to the caterer and hiring a couple of men from the country club to park cars. Carmen had made only a few friends in the year she'd been in Baltimore—her life was so remote from campus, and too difficult to explain. Plus, these girls were with their own families, celebrating the end of the school year. No one else, it seemed, was bored.

She was relieved—excited, even—when Jobe pulled up. He never seemed at a loss for what to do. One could work every day throughout an entire lifetime and still not understand the distribution of prime numbers, Jobe told her once. There was always something new to consider. Nothing stopped because the university was issuing his degree.

It was something to admire, Carmen thought, as she watched him emerge from the car. Jobe always moved into sunlight hesitantly, as if it were a force that bore down. Now he rose into the golden air of afternoon, gazing upward. Who could tell whether he was seeing the sun's rays, soaking them in, or contemplating how space expands? Carmen stood at the window in plain view, a fact he never registered as he neared the house. When he came through the door, she called out, "Hey," and he startled. Turning toward her, he stopped and fixed her with a puzzled look.

"I thought you'd be out tonight," he said. "Drinking to the end of college, all that."

Carmen shrugged. She couldn't admit, even to Jobe, that she had nothing to do. "Maybe I'm past all that," she said and checked for a reaction. He didn't even crack a smile. "I don't feel like it tonight, okay? How about a movie?"

"You mean, you and me?" Jobe took off his jacket, the one he wore though it was nearly 80 degrees. Underneath he had on a long-sleeved T-shirt. It was like he paid no attention to the elements, moving in his own separate, climate-controlled track through the world.

"Yes, you and me. A movie. It's not like a major operation." And yet, she was nervous.

Jobe squinted, which made him look even more bug-eyed than usual. Why was he being so difficult all of a sudden? Usually it was *he* who followed *her*, suggesting they do things. Take a walk, go shopping, eat at the little Indian place. Though since she arrived, last fall, they'd never been dancing again. They rarely stayed out past ten. They had made love perhaps a dozen times, when circumstances coalesced in just the right way: an evening when no one else was home and each had nothing else to do. Carmen could plot each encounter on a graph, not because the sex was memorable but by computing the factors that led directly to it. It was like being married, only without the security or social recognition. Perhaps Jobe, too, was finally tired of the tedium and ready to let her go.

She panicked but was careful not to show it, sauntering toward him. "Listen, this hot woman just asked you to go see a movie and you're not even answering. You know that's rude, don't you?"

Finally, Jobe relaxed and grinned. "What movie?" His hands twitched at his sides.

"*Top Gun.*" This was more like it. Standing just two feet from him, she could feel the way Jobe wanted her. It was confusing him, making him anxious, and she was glad.

"That sounds awful."

She grabbed his forearm, like a rebar inside his sleeve, and squeezed it. "Shut up. Tom Cruise and Val Kilmer. You're going to love it."

"No." Jobe's face twisted, monkeylike. "*You're* going to love it. I'm going to tolerate it."

"Well, all right then." Carmen let go and ran out of the room, climbing the stairs to get her purse and shoes. Turning, she called over her shoulder, "You're going to need money, because you're paying, too."

Jobe, at the bottom of the stairs, gazed up. "Not unless you buy me ice cream after," he said.

She stopped, looked down. His face was serious. This mattered. "It would be my privilege," she said and fake curtsied, then continued up.

It was a six-forty movie on a sparkling, warm Friday afternoon, so they had the theater nearly to themselves. They sat through the previews without any contact, Carmen in a ruffled miniskirt with her legs primly crossed. But in the dark—as the jets roared across the screen, their terrible engine noises rattling through the speakers, noses driving through the sky—Carmen felt something unexpected. She wanted him to touch her. It was an ache in her throat, almost like what she'd felt with Rory that first time.

Carmen edged closer, using the armrest more fully. She shifted as if uncomfortable and brushed his arm with the full right side of her breast. "Sorry," she whispered. And Jobe cleared his throat but said nothing. She let a few minutes go by. The planes twirled, rising up, trailing smoke. Then they landed and the scene quieted and she leaned in to rest her cheek on Jobe's shoulder. He was still but then—in a movement so slow and pained, she knew it cost him everything he had—he raised his arm and settled it around her. His deodorant smelled faintly of that night in the London hostel, and his hand reached all the way to her elbow. There was something primitive about this pose. Not sexual, but comforting. She was pleased that he didn't try to kiss her but allowed her to watch the movie in peace.

The sky was pale, dove white, when they stepped out of the theater. And a sudden breeze had sailed in from the west, stirring the branches and fallen flowers on the sidewalk. Carmen shivered and thought that Jobe was, after all, smarter for having worn long pants and sleeves. Her knees were freezing by the time they'd walked two blocks.

"Cold?" he asked. "You probably should have brought a coat."

She sighed and marched on. Nothing killed the mood faster than his pronouncements of the obvious. She was losing her desire to be with him, quickly. Time to pick up his ice cream and go home. She glanced at the bank clock as they passed—9:02—and sighed again. They were right on schedule.

Inside, the ice cream shop was tropical. Carmen leaned, relieved, against a huge freezer whose motor hummed and warmed her legs. The mirrors behind the long counters were streaked with steam, the scoopers in their billed hats sweating, people in line fanning themselves with discount coupons and cards. "Hot," Jobe said, and Carmen nodded. She watched, satisfied, as he pulled up his sleeves. They ordered: blueberry yogurt in a cup for her, a plain chocolate cone for him. Carmen paid and then they stood on the threshold—the border between warm air and cool wind—looking out.

There was an old-fashioned porch outside the shop with a few wooden tables and a hanging swing. The couple in the swing got up, leaving crumpled napkins and colored smears behind. "Let's grab it," Jobe said and covered the distance in four steps. Carmen walked over more slowly and stood.

"It's dirty," she said, pointing.

"Uh, yeah." Jobe considered this. "So you can sit on my lap. I don't care if my jeans get ice cream on them."

"But won't that make the swing lopsided?"

He eyed the seat for a moment, then turned and backed into it. "Not if we sit right in the middle, see?"

"The whole world is a math problem, isn't it?" she asked, but then she lowered herself onto his lap. It was like sitting on a wood fire that had not yet been lit: his legs and arms slender logs, his fingers and ribs sticks of kindling. The skin stretched over them seemed incidental.

He finished his cone but kept his hands off her, probably because they were sticky. Carmen grew tired of her yogurt and put the half-eaten cup aside. There was no reason to stay here now that they were done, but she wished they could. A gleaming sliver of moon had come out. People were talking all around them, creating a gentle buzz. And Jobe gave off more heat than one might imagine. By shifting so different parts of her were against him she was able to stay mostly warm.

Tomorrow her father would arrive and the following day there would be a party, and the day after that she was expected to know what to do with her life. Carmen could not conceive of what that would be. She pictured herself back in Detroit, picking up her father's socks and empty bottles and glasses, her sister stopping by periodically —babies hanging on her like monkeys—to nag Carmen. She'd fought so hard to get through college, even taking money from relative strangers, but what did it matter? She would still end up waiting tables or, at best, working in an art supply store.

"What are you thinking about?" Jobe's question startled her. "You look so serious all of a sudden." He had pushed back as far as he could against the swing, as if arching his body away from her. But this was Jobe. Carmen was almost certain he was only trying to get a better view of her face.

"Why do you even like me?" She hadn't planned to ask him this. She hadn't even been thinking it, consciously. But once the question was out of her mouth, Carmen was curious about the answer. She was moody and sometimes mean to Jobe. It wouldn't be exaggerating to say she wasn't even half as smart. Without his family, she had no home and no future. The only thing she had to recommend her was that she was pretty, but Jobe didn't seem like the kind of man who would be captivated by this—at least not for long.

"I mean it," she said, because Jobe had not answered. He was simply staring at her. "What is it that makes you want to be here? Now. With me."

He paused. "I don't know," he said, finally. Carmen glanced around to see if anyone was listening to their strange conversation, but the only other people on the porch were a group of raucous teenage kids who couldn't have cared less. "It's not logical. We're very different. But from the minute I met you in the park I felt like we were . . . connected somehow."

Carmen snorted and Jobe looked down abruptly. Guilty? Hurt? She touched his narrow neck, where his pulse was. "No. I'm sorry. I didn't mean to laugh. It's just that I burned you and then I got blood all over your sleeping bag." It still amazed her that she felt no embarrassment with Jobe, even about that. "Those didn't seem like real bonding moments."

"They were." Jobe was using two long fingers to stroke one of her cold knees and it felt good. Not sexy, but good. "Right away, I felt like I'd met this person I was supposed to find. Like I'd gone to London . . ." He blushed.

"What?"

"Okay, this is the least scientific thing you're ever going to hear me say. But it seemed like there was a reason I went to London with that dickhead, Tim. I was supposed to. I had to meet you, because we're going to be together for the rest of my life."

She would not realize until much later how oddly he'd phrased this. *His* life, not theirs. But right now, all she could think was that the time had certainly come. She needed to tell him about Rory; it could all be over. Or she could capitulate: fall into the warm ease he was offering her. His family, his life. There were only these two choices and she had to pick one.

There was a long quiet stretch. Even the teenagers were subdued. Then the wind swept in again, so hard it made Carmen's cheeks sting. She ducked her head, laying it against Jobe's shoulder, and his arm snaked around pulling her in tighter. Somehow, with this single movement, all of her was warm.

"Okay," she said. Gently, the swing rocked.

When her father walked off the plane with a travel bag slung over one shoulder, he looked to Carmen young and unformed. Despite the year and a half of heavy drinking and the job he'd finally found at a tire shop, which he'd told her had strained his back, Antonio had an easy, slouching gait. His color had come back; he must be eating better. Esme had told Carmen during one of their infrequent phone calls that their father had a girlfriend, but Carmen dismissed it: more of her sister's disapproval and fretting. Probably, their dad had given some woman a ride while her car was being worked on. Esme had overreacted.

But on the way to the hotel in the car, which he didn't even comment upon, he spoke twice of someone named Linda. He craned his head, looking around like a toddler in church. He'd left Detroit only a handful of times in the last twenty years, mostly to take his family on vacations to Florida. The East was unfamiliar. He found it cramped, he told Carmen, and toylike. All those narrow brick buildings and swinging signs and streets with barely enough room to park alongside the flow of traffic. It was hard to believe people really lived this way.

Antonio had never asked about her circumstances. This was good, actually, because they would have been difficult to explain. When Carmen had admitted back in August that she would not be completing school because her father had run out of money, Olive had waved her hand as if this were impossible. "It will be taken care of," she'd said, the tense confusing Carmen.

"*How* will it be taken care of?" she'd asked Jobe. "I don't understand."

"My mother will pay the tuition." He shrugged. "It's hard not to be crass about this, but what you owe is like spare change to her. We're talking about the U, right? Maybe four thousand to get you through the last year? That's less than she donates to the local humane society."

"Okay, I'm sorry, that did sound crass," Carmen teased him, all the while a weight lifting away from her chest.

She hadn't truly understood until late August, when Olive told her to "send for her things," that she would be staying on in the Garretts' house—like some sort of domestic exchange student—and using the BMW to commute.

Antonio had insisted on making his own hotel reservations, and Carmen was glad he still had that much pride. She turned into the parking lot of the Sheraton and got out, waiting for her father to retrieve his overnight bag from the back seat. He looked sober: steady and clear. Carmen wondered when he'd pulled himself together, and also why he hadn't called her up remorseful, apologizing for what had happened at the tail end of her college years and asking if he could make it up to her—perhaps by sending her to graduate school. But neither of them had ever mentioned his drinking or the tuition he hadn't paid or her lost senior year at Michigan. And it felt wrong to start now.

Earth movers grumbled and steel beams clanged in the distance. Baltimore was building a fancy new development on the Inner Harbor. What had been a slum with tent villages bordering the water was now becoming a baroque three-story restaurant complex with a nightclub and piano lounge. Jobe had promised to take her there the week it opened. Carmen pointed to a brand-new restaurant and told her father there was a life-size cherry-red Cadillac inside, hanging above the bar.

"So is he your boyfriend?" Antonio lit a cigarette and they hung outside the door of the hotel while he smoked it. "You don't talk about him that way, but it seems like you're going to marry him." Carmen instantly felt relieved. He acted more like an uncle or an old family friend, but Antonio was still her father. He understood her. He would help her figure out what to do about Jobe. She opened her mouth and started to form the words, *I need to . . .* , just as Antonio dropped the cigarette butt and stepped on it and said, "Well, let's get inside. I'm going to need a shower before I meet these future in-laws of yours."

She lay on one of the two double beds reading the Baltimore city guide from the bedside table while Antonio took his shower. He burst out of the bathroom, handsome in his uniform of black jeans and cowboy boots with a white towel over his bare, muscled shoulders, letting loose a wet cloud of steam. "Should I shave?" he called. "Is it that sort of dinner?"

Carmen thought about Jobe's full beard, Nate's messy attempt at one, George's ruddy cheeks. Her father stood in front of her, lean face shadowed, looking like some spaghetti Western movie actor—one of the sexy, filthy bad guys who would be dead by the end—and she felt an uncomfortable twinge of wishing for a man like this. Not *him*, of course. Though objectively she had to admit, sick as it was, she found her own father more attractive than she did Jobe.

"No," she said to him. "You don't need to shave. You look fine."

Yet when they arrived at the house, Carmen was sorry. They walked through the door and into the large foyer and when she turned, Antonio suddenly looked silly and shrunken next to her. A cartoon mouse, with a funny, twirling, Mexican-style mustache, standing on his hind legs in the opulent lair of a cat.

George, who had flown in earlier that day himself—taking a limo back from the airport though Carmen was there with one of his cars—entered the room with one large hand extended. "Good to meet you, Tony. Scotch?"

"Sounds fine," Carmen's father said hungrily. She watched as he took the glass and tried sending him a message with her eyes: *Don't bolt it*. Her thought rays were only moderately effective. By the time George turned around, shaking his own glass, making the ice cubes clink, Antonio had drunk at least half. His eyes were mellow and he'd begun to glow.

"For you, dear?" George asked and she shook her head.

"I'll just get some water." She backed out of the room and headed down the hall toward the kitchen. It was better not to watch.

"Is he here?" Olive asked, her back to Carmen as she slid a pan into the top oven. "Can you keep an eye on the Brussels sprouts while I go say hello?" She slipped her head out of the loop of her apron. "Just shout if anything starts to smoke."

Carmen drew her glass of water and walked the perimeter of the cavernous kitchen. There was a boxed cake on the counter, Olive's one concession: she was a great cook, she often said, but no baker.

Carmen circled again and this time she lifted the lid of the white bakery box. Inside, the cake was ice white and decorated with a combination of frosting roses and real ones in matching crimson. The calligraphy in the center said, CONGRATULATIONS CARMEN AND JOBE.

"I'm telling Mom," said a voice behind her and she turned to see Nate. He grinned—a softer, shorter, more graceful version of his brother—and swung up on the counter. "You don't want to snitch dessert before dinner. I did that one time when the 'rents were having these NASA guys over for dinner. Whoa! Talk about a bad decision. I was six years old and I still remember . . ."

"So what do you think this means?" Carmen interrupted. "Come here and look."

Nate slid down and came up behind Carmen to peer over her shoulder. "I think it means they're congratulating you."

"Yeah, I got that. But for what?" She turned and he was still so close she found herself inside his spread arms. The boy blushed, just as Jobe often did. Carmen had seen the way Nate watched her, his expression full of curiosity and pain every time she wore something tight or—especially—the one time he'd come home from baseball practice and found her coming out of Jobe's room. In fact, they hadn't been messing around that day; she'd gone in to look for a book she thought she'd left there. But Nate acted as if he'd caught the two of them humping on the dining room table.

"I dunno, you're graduating, I guess. Isn't that what this whole dinner is about?"

"Yeesss." Carmen wanted to believe this, but something was bothering her.

"How are those vegetables doing?" Olive asked, rushing in.

Carmen and Nate both jumped back from the box. "Oh, sorry, I forgot to check," Carmen said. "I hope they're not burned."

Olive scowled and opened the oven. "Nope, just perfect." Her face softened as she came toward Carmen and touched her cheek. "Your father is a lovely man but I think he's a little nervous. Who can blame him? He feels like a stranger in his own daughter's home. Why don't you go out and see if you can make him more comfortable? Nate will help me finish up in here."

When Carmen stepped back into the living room she saw immediately that her father was not uncomfortable, he was drunk. Sprawled on the couch, coat open, belt buckle jutting out, he was listing for George and Jobe—who had materialized when she wasn't looking— all his complaints about the manufacturing culture in Detroit.

"It's the goddamn unions," he said in a voice too loud for the room. "They mean well, but the rules have gotten so complicated you need a *book* just to know what's going on. Real people get lost in a system like that."

George was nodding in a fuddled way, Jobe staring down at his folded hands. When Antonio looked up and saw Carmen in the doorway he winked. "There's my beautiful girl. Come sit next to me. I was just getting to know your boyfriend here."

He gestured toward Jobe, who shot Carmen a guilty look, his sunken eyes large. She couldn't help feeling sympathy.

It was a painful few minutes until Nate called them to the dining room. Olive was already standing near her place at the foot of the table. Though she insisted on cooking company meals herself, she hired a woman to serve so she could eat with guests. Carmen had grown used to this but wished now that she'd thought to tell her father; he'd assume—she knew immediately—that there was a staff of ten working behind the scenes.

There was a bottle of wine already open on the table with the cork resting alongside. George picked it up and began pouring, his long arm allowing him to reach all the way to Olive though he remained sitting. He gave Carmen and Jobe each a glass, skipped Nate, then served Antonio and himself, emptying the bottle, going back to Antonio twice to add a little more. Carmen pressed her hands to her thighs with frustration. She could envision her father flopped in his seat and snoring by the end of the meal.

"Cheers," George said, raising his glass. And the rest of them followed suit. Even Carmen could taste how good this was: a dusty, rich red wine with an odor she could swear she remembered from France.

The server came out from the kitchen with plates. At least she wore jeans and a Maryland T-shirt, rather than a maid's uniform. Carmen hoped her father noticed. Then she glanced at the shapely woman whose nipples were visible, erect inside her bra, and hoped he didn't. She'd never seen him drunk in public; she had no idea how he would behave.

"We're keeping it simple tonight," Olive said as Miss Maryland set down the dishes. "Just roasted duck and vegetables, then the salad course, then dessert."

"Just the way I like it. I'm a meat and potatoes man," said Antonio, nodding.

Everyone ate in silence for a few beats. Then Olive cleared her throat and said, "Before our wine is gone, I think we should all toast Carmen and Jobe." She lifted her glass. "To their life together after graduation," she said.

But for once, Antonio did not rush to pick up his drink. Instead, he stared at Carmen with an abruptly sober question in his eyes. She wanted to answer it but could not imagine how. Even if they'd been alone, she didn't know what she would have said. She had acquiesced to something the other night, at the ice cream store, on the swing. Her deal was made. So she raised her own glass and turned from her father to smile brightly at Jobe.

$\mathcal{J}$ULY 2007

It seemed now that Carmen spent most of her time on the phone, talking to people who sounded either extremely urgent or bored by the whole breast cancer routine.

First, there was Dr. Woo's scheduling nurse who insisted chemotherapy should begin immediately. "You don't want to give anything a chance to grow," the woman said, as if there were a possibility that rhododendrons might sprout inside Carmen were she to waste too much time. "Doctor wants you to get in for treatment as soon as possible." Then she gave Carmen a number to call where she ended up on hold so long that she gave up twice—hanging up in frustration—before finally getting through.

Once she did, the voice on the other end of the phone was monotone, checking off details the way a weary carnival ride operator might announce, *Keep your hands inside the car at all times.* "We've got two slots for our three-hour people: seven to ten or one to four. Which one do you want?"

Carmen stopped to consider. Did she want to get up before dawn and have her body poisoned before lunch so she could spend the rest of the day swimming in chemical muck? Or would she prefer that flat, hottest part of afternoon—three hours of sitting idle in the middle of the day—then stepping out into rush hour with her organs freshly scalded and trying to fight her way home?

"Seven to ten," she said.

"Alright. We're going to need you here about thirty minutes early the first time, no less, so we can do a baseline blood draw," the voice droned on. "You probably don't want to eat breakfast that morning, but it's up to you. You'll get antinausea drugs in the cocktail, along with whatever your doctor ordered. Wear comfortable clothes and something to read or work on: knitting, crossword. No small children or pets."

Pets? Carmen imagined a clinic full of exotic animals, iguanas on leashes and brightly colored birds swooping through the room.

"Any questions?"

"My hair. When will I lose it?"

"Second treatment. Somewhere in the neighborhood of twenty-four to forty-eight hours after."

Carmen caught her breath. There'd been no wavering, no slim chance held out that she might respond differently than other women. "You're that certain?" she asked.

"It could take up to three days for everything to fall out," the voice revised. "But that's pretty much the limit. Most women shave it off before, to keep the drain at home from clogging up."

Carmen's third call was to a shop that had come highly recommended by the Breast Recovery Foundation for natural-looking human hair wigs. If she got in tomorrow to be photographed and measured, the woman on the phone told her, they might possibly be able to turn something around for her in four months. Six at the outside.

"But I'm going in for chemo next week," Carmen said.

"I sympathize," said the wigmaker automatically. "But we're very proud of our products and I assure you, they're worth the wait."

There was no trying to parse this logic. Carmen had more important things on her mind: She had to decide when and how to tell her children what was happening, and what to do about work.

She didn't need the money. Her paycheck was laughable compared to the money that came from other sources: Jobe's insurance,
and the trusts that George and Olive had set up for the kids. But she
did need the insurance coverage; Jobe's had lapsed the day he died
and Carmen had gladly let it go. Luca was covered under a Maryland
program for the disabled, but she and the other two children were on
her policy from the agency. And now Carmen was worried about the
myriad of other gruesome, unexpected illnesses that might come up.
What was it that long-ago ob-gyn had called it when Luca was born?
A mistimed collision. There seemed to be a lot of those going around.

Carmen called the HR director—who was also the agency's con-
troller; it was a small shop—to explain the situation. But when he
answered, this man she knew mostly as the guy who manned the grill
at their company picnics, she seized up. How did one go about telling
a relative stranger that so many calamities had been visited upon her
house? Surely he would judge her, understanding that she was guilty
of something even if he didn't know what.

"Do you have some time free tomorrow?" she asked casually.
"I'll be in around nine and could meet with you any time."

But once she was seated in his office, around two o'clock the
next afternoon, she realized she'd made yet another mistake. This
would have been so much easier over the phone rather than wedged
into his schedule, between the messy firing of a web site architect who
was downloading porn on his computer—the rumors had been flying
around all morning—and a meeting with the quarterly tax guy.

"You look wonderful, Carmen," said the HR man, picking up
his gold pen and holding it poised over a legal pad. The last time she'd
spoken to him he'd sounded distrustful, but he was all warmth and
Easter bunny goodness now. "Once again, my sincere condolences.
So"—he coughed, a kind of segue—"what's on your mind?"

"I have, um, cancer." She winced. It was a disgusting word, all
slippery and attractive on the surface, but rotted horror underneath.
"I'm going to have to start chemotherapy soon and I'm worried about
how this will affect my job performance. However . . ." The only way

to do this was to be honest; she'd come to this conclusion in the mid-dle of the night. "I need to maintain my insurance, for obvious rea-sons. I let go of the university policy when my husband died and this . . . " She held out her hands. "Is all I have."

"Oh, Carmen, I'm so sorry." The man was rising from his chair and circling the desk, coming toward her with his hands outstretched to grasp hers. "I don't know how you bear up under all this! Your poor husband and now *this*. You are a saint, I think. One of God's chosen."

"I thought those were the Jews," Carmen said, tugging her hands away discreetly.

"What I meant was . . ." He'd let go of her left hand but con-tinued to hold her right. "God knows who can handle tragedy and who can't. He must feel that you're very strong."

Carmen blinked. It was as if she'd never met this man before! Rather than the cheerful, red-faced man who forked over a bratwurst from inside a cloud of charcoal smoke, he was a lunatic. Some sort of hit-and-run preacher. Fury rose in Carmen's chest—feeding her can-cer no doubt. Everything would be better if she could gore this guy with his pen.

Instead Carmen pretended to cough and yanked her hand away, supposedly to cover her mouth. "Thanks," she said after she'd given a few convincing hacks. "But really, what I'm looking for is your pro-fessional advice. I wanted to come forward at the outset so this does-n't catch anyone off guard. But I'm going to have to plan my work schedule around," she plowed on as fast as she could, because it was the only way to say it, "chemotherapy. And I need to make sure that reducing my hours for a while won't affect coverage for me and the, uh, kids."

"Hmm. I need to . . ." The HR man perched on the edge of his desk. "I'm thinking, Carmen, that we should bring Fred in on this."

He left her to track down the agency owner and she was glad. As boring as it was sitting in this office, staring out through the enviable windows at the building next door, it was better than having to listen to him and confront someone else's suspicions that God had had a hand in her cancer. She already had enough suspicions of her own along those lines.

Ten minutes later when Fred Lang came in and took her hand, she reflexively presented her cheek. The last time she'd seen Fred was after Jobe's funeral when he had kissed her on his way out the door, his breath laced with garlic and hot mustard. Now he leaned down to press his cheek against hers—a more appropriate office greeting, Carmen understood—smelling of nothing but the faint midday sweat of someone who'd taken a walk at lunch.

"Carmen, I'm so, so sorry to hear this," Fred said. And like the HR director before him, Fred stood leaning on the edge of the desk. But this felt entirely different. Fatherly, almost. Carmen wondered why she and Fred had never been closer. She wondered, too, if he knew that she'd slept with an account executive a few weeks after starting her job. "We are 100 percent behind you. Whatever you need, we'll make it happen. All you need to worry about is getting well."

"Meaning . . . ?" The question drifted in from far away; Carmen turned. She'd nearly forgotten about the preacher. But he was inserting himself back into this conversation, questioning—Carmen was sure—whether she merited such wholehearted support.

"Meaning." Fred was smooth. Everyone knew this was why his firm succeeded in a field crowded with writers and designers who were no better than average (including, Carmen would have admitted ruefully, her). The owner alone was extraordinary: well dressed and charming. Also ruthless, though when he was negotiating, this trait never came out until the end. "If Carmen needs to work from home for a while, we'll set her up with a networked computer from there. And if not, we can adjust her schedule. How does that sound?"

Fred turned back to her and she paused, wanting more than anything for the man to sit down so she could crawl up on his lap. It was confusing, this feeling. She didn't know if she wanted him to continue being fatherly or rip off her clothes and take her on the desk. Whatever happened, she imagined that afterward they could plan in whispers how to vanquish the zealot forever so their cozy familial relationship could remain intact.

"That's very nice of you, Fred," she said, and cleared her throat. "I don't know yet what I'll need. I have my first treatment next week so I'll know more then about how it affects me." She took a shaky breath, picturing herself as that stork-thin, white, bald woman with a kerchief, sitting in her cube at work. There was no way this man, or any other, would want her then. "Can we put off planning until I know?"

"Of course, of course." Fred seemed lost in thought and entirely unhurried, which was part of his charm.

"There *is* another potential solution." The HR man moved forward, breaking into the bubble Carmen and Fred had created. They both swiveled in his direction. "I've been thinking . . . . You told me, Carmen, that you were concerned mostly about your insurance, that you'd let your husband's lapse. But according to federal law, you have ninety days to invoke COBRA after a spouse's death, and if I'm counting correctly, you're still within that window by a few days. If you're *not* able to work and you'd *rather* just focus on your health right now, you probably could go back to Jobe's department and fill out the paperwork. It's just a thought."

Carmen tensed and looked at the faces of both men. Had they talked about this, planned it as they walked through the halls to meet her? Fred appeared as surprised as she was, but he was a great actor. Everyone said that. It was another of the reasons for his success: He had the ability to appear riveted even by a client he loathed.

"Why . . . why would I do that?" she finally asked.

"Well." The man slid back behind his desk and started tapping on his computer, suddenly businesslike. "We're a small company, so we have certain limits on our policy. For instance, I believe there's a, yes, here it is, a one-million-dollar lifetime limit for you. Cancer treatment can *easily* run into the many millions. Especially if it"—at least he had the decency to avert his eyes when he said this—"recurs. But the university has thousands of employees and their pool is large, so they can afford a much larger cap. As I think you found out with Jobe."

"But wouldn't there be a deadline?" Poor choice of words. Carmen revised. "A time limit?"

The man nodded. "Eighteen months. Still, you might want to check into it. If the treatment is much better through their plan, it still might be worth it. Getting the very best medicine right up front is known to save lives in cases like this. And I'm not saying our insurer would scrimp. But there are certain economic realities. We're a small operation and, unfortunately, we can't afford to support a critically sick individual for very long."

The three of them sat in silence for a few seconds and Carmen listened hard to determine if she could hear her cancer cells clustering, moving, raising rabble, and threatening to overtake.

"It sounds like you have a lot to think about," Fred broke in. "No pressure from our side. You just let us know what your decision is. And you know, I hope, that we only want the best for you."

I do not know that! Not at all. Everything had changed, yet again. All images of her boss as father, lover, or protector had completely disappeared. Carmen rose. "Thank you," she said, holding out her hand, which he shook formally this time.

"I'd be happy to go over the two insurance plans with you, Carmen." The other man stood, too, but she was not going to give him the satisfaction of another heartfelt moment.

"Great," she said, gathering her purse. And without another word —about insurance or the two client projects she was late delivering— she turned and left.

Carmen was home by 4:15, which was just in time to call the benefits office at Hopkins. It turned out the preacher was right.

The man on the phone looked up Jobe's employment history with a series of tapping keys that Carmen could hear and said, "Yup, died April seventeen. I show you've got eight more days. And the lifetime benefit limit is five million. Should I send you the paperwork?"

"Sure," Carmen said. It was already past pick-up time today so the form would go out in tomorrow's mail. Then she'd have seven days. She could leave this dilemma up to the U.S. Postal Service. If the envelope reached her in time to complete the transaction, she would take the five million over eighteen months. If not, she'd stay on at work and keep her paltry million-dollar coverage for the duration. Heads or tails.

"That is so totally not like you," said Jana when Carmen told her. "Come on, Car. You see what's going on here, don't you? I mean, you're not stupid. You've been paying premiums for how many years, and now your company wants to drop you on the spot because you've got cancer? It's not right."

Carmen shrugged. They were sitting on the porch in the sun, drinking margaritas. If she was going to start chemo in a week, Carmen had decided she would eat and drink everything she wanted for the next seven days. Plump up and enjoy things while she could, before the metallic taste and ceaseless nausea set in.

"I don't know." Carmen, in a rocker, leaned back and closed her eyes. Why was it that dying sunlight felt better than any other kind? "Do you know why we took my insurance in the first place? Because Jobe was sick and we knew it. He'd gone into remission after the first bout and we thought it was a good idea to have double protection. So *we* were trying to game the system; and now the system is trying to game us . . . me . . . back."

"Why do you work?" Jana leaned forward, picked up the pitcher, and refilled them both. "You never talk about your job. You certainly don't get your identity from it, which, by the way, I love. But you don't even act like you *like* the work. It's something you tolerate, a place where you kill eight hours a day. For Christ's sake, you guys are loaded. It's not like you need the money. Even the insurance. Couldn't you get by without?"

Carmen shook her head, eyes still tightly closed. "You'd think. But having money almost makes it worse. We have millions, cancer costs *tens* of millions—or more. It can wipe out fortunes, depending on how long you live." She paused. How many times had they calculated Jobe's chances, the potential costs and number of days he had left? Now the people she'd worked alongside for three years were doing this with her. Maybe everyone came down to this in the end: inherent value versus liability. Jobe wasn't the only one.

"Anyway. Change of subject. I asked Siena to come down."

"You think it's time for your sexually active teenager to start drinking with us?"

"Sure." Carmen half opened her eyes. "I'd be all for it if it meant she'd mellow out and lose her death grip on Troy."

Jana snorted. "That's literally what it is, you know."

Abruptly, Carmen sat up. "Do you realize what would happen to her if I were to die? Or get to the point where I'm just lying in bed, useless?" She pictured Jobe, that last month, his waxy skin and fetid breath, his motionless body able to do nothing but need. Were she to reach this point, who would tend to her? Jana had the café, Danny wouldn't dare. Now that Olive knew how Carmen had betrayed her son, surely she would refuse. That left Siena. Carmen could see her daughter trapped in this house with a disabled young man, a terrified younger brother, a dying mother. "I owe it to her to shoot myself if I start to get really sick. Or crawl away somewhere by myself to die."

"Yeah?" Jana sounded either fascinated or horror-stricken. There was a fine line. "Where would you go?"

"I don't know. The woods? Some hotel? That's where the money would come in handy." Carmen's voice trailed off as the screen door hinge creaked.

Siena stepped out onto the porch, balletlike, in bare feet with her long hair hanging like a cape around her narrow shoulders and back. "What's up?" she asked. It was impossible for Carmen to tell how much her daughter had heard.

"Sit down," Jana said. She scooted over and made twice as much room as Siena needed on the cushions of the rattan loveseat.

"Sweetheart," Carmen said. "I think we need to . . ." She

stopped and Jana and Siena sat quietly, staring, like an audience waiting to be informed or entertained.

"I'm trying to make some plans for the next few weeks."

"Your mom is worried she'll be sick, the way her mother was,"
Jana interrupted. "She's concerned that you might end up the way she
did as a kid: lonely and resentful because you're responsible for too
much."

Carmen looked at Jana, amazed. They had never discussed this
specifically; Carmen didn't think she'd even *thought* it clearly. But
Jana had just located the exact center of the problem. Siena could become just another version Carmen, with all that entailed.

"I feel awful," Carmen started again. "Not that there's anything
I can do about it, but you just don't need this on top of the thing with
your father. And I'd like to make sure we have plans in place so you
don't end up feeling responsible."

"Me, I can be a plan." Jana drained her glass, cross-eyed,
appearing less than ever like a viable plan. Still, Carmen warmed. She
could see Jana coming over with pot and getting them all high—Carmen
to ease her through the crushing nausea and pain, Siena to help her forget her burdens—then feeding everyone through their munchies.

"Your grandmother is here for you, too. Nate and Jessica. You
can call your Aunt Esme if things get really bad."

Siena made a disgusted face and Carmen laughed. It shouldn't
have made her happy that all three of her children found Esme irri-
tating and frumpy. But it did.

"There's Troy," Siena said, gazing down at her own toes. "He'll
help me. And his mom. She's really cool."

Carmen felt a stab of jealousy for this cool mom—no doubt
married to her soul mate and cancer-free—who would be supporting
Siena. She struggled to put that aside and concentrate instead on what
damage could come, how history might repeat.

"I understand you feel that way now," Carmen said slowly. "But
I think there's a danger in your relying too much on Troy and his family. Especially if things are bad here. If I'm . . ."—she swallowed and

made the decision to go ahead and say it; shocking Siena might actually help—"dying. It will make you vulnerable in a strange sort of way. And you could, if you're not careful, get, uh, stuck."

"Stuck how?" Siena was eyeing her warily. Suddenly, Jana was, too.

"You know: indebted. You could start to feel like you owe Troy and his mom. Like you need to give them something back. You could end up sort of attached to these people for life, if you're not careful. Because they helped you through a hard time and suddenly you feel like there's no way out."

"Is that what happened to you?" Siena gaped at her. "You felt like you owed Dad so you married him?"

There was a moment of silence. Carmen looked at Jana, wild for help but there was none there. *You got yourself into this. . . .* Jana's expression seemed to say as she settled back against the cushions like a bear.

There had to be a reason she was doing this, Carmen thought. First Olive, now Siena. It had to be intentional, on some subconscious level. She was finally telling the truth. And it was possible that there would never be another chance.

"Yes, in a way, that's what happened to me. I was like you, sort of. I'd lost both of my parents in a different way: my mother had died, my father was an alcoholic." Carmen glanced at her salt-and-tequila-smeared glass. "But I was responsible only for myself. I didn't have brothers. . . ." She waved at the upper story of the house, though neither of the boys was there. "I didn't have all the things that might fall to you."

Siena paused. She'd brought a bottle of Diet Coke out to the porch with her and she lifted it now, tipping her head back in the sunlight to drink and looking to Carmen like some carefree girl in a commercial. Again, there was a flicker of jealousy, but it was dimmer than before. Carmen stretched her arms up and saw that they were slightly leathery. She became middle-aged anyway. Staying in the wrong marriage, sacrificing herself to a dying husband, didn't erase the years. Justice didn't apply. Her skin aged. Her breasts not only hung lower, they'd started behaving badly. There was—no matter how she lived—a finite period of time left.

"Are you telling me you're going to die?" Siena asked. And as on the night she'd first learned about Carmen's cancer, she sounded angry. This hostility was fear! Carmen not only recognized it, she remembered it. Sunlight glinted between the gaps of the tall trees standing like sentries at their property line. And right in front of Carmen's eyes Siena shifted into and out of her younger self: young Carmen in the mirror with makeup streaking her cheeks; a slightly older version in a hotel room in Richmond, Virginia; Carmen in a sheath dress on her wedding day.

"No, I'm not going to die. Not now, anyway." The trees rustled and bowed in a sudden breeze, and Carmen let her head loll back in a reverse prayer posture. Still, she was praying that this was true. "I'll be really sick for a while and it might seem like I'm going to die. I won't be much use. Your brothers will be frightened. You will be lonely." She raised her head and locked eyes with her daughter. "But you don't have to find someone else to take care of you. I'll be back."

Siena cracked a weak smile. "I'll be back," she mimicked in a low, raspy voice. "You sound like the Terminator."

"How do you know about *The Terminator*? That movie came out when I was about your age."

"Everyone knows about the Terminator, Mom. It's on TNT, like, every other weekend. I've only seen it, like, nine times." Siena pulled her feet up onto the seat and propped her chin on her knees. "How do you know you won't die? Daddy did. He didn't want to, either."

"No, he didn't *want* to but that's different from knowing. From the time he was a teenager, Jobe said he knew he would die young. It was only a question of when." She paused, then when no one else said anything, Carmen went on. "I don't feel that way. This all feels more like a . . . test, or something. Not the end."

A darkened patch of sky slid across the sun, plunging them into dusk, and at the same time everything quieted. The scent of barbecue from a far-off neighbor's grill drifted over the porch. Carmen lifted her nose to inhale the plum-colored, crackling fat air and began actually believing what she'd told her daughter. Eventually she would be fine, weathered but alive.

"Oh God! You have gone entirely off the deep end, Mother." At first Carmen didn't even recognize the words as Siena's. They came so abruptly, interrupting her calm. Besides, in twenty years of parenting Carmen had never been "Mother," only Mom.

"I'm not crazy, Siena." It was difficult to say this with conviction while actively questioning it herself. "It's just that I think there are things in this world we don't understand. Your father dealt in such things, mathematically. It makes sense that he might . . ." She was rambling, totally confused by what she herself was saying, not believing a word of it. No one interrupted her, but Carmen quit speaking anyway and closed her eyes.

"I'm not Michael, you know," Siena finally said, her tone withering now. The girl was a remarkable change artist, from angry to sympathetic to disapproving in three minutes flat. "You don't have to make shit up. I'm not Luca. I don't think I 'see' the ghost of my dead father appearing to me in the middle of the night."

"Wait. Jobe's been appearing to Luca at night?" Jana asked.

"He said so and *she*"—Siena tilted her head toward Carmen— "agreed with him that that's what was happening." Overhead, the darkness passed; the sun returned, only paler. "I thought," Siena went on, looking at Carmen, "that you were only trying to make him feel better. But now you sound like some kind of freak, going on about Daddy having these 'premonitions' before he died."

"He did." Carmen could hear how stiff she sounded. This was unfair; it wasn't she who had claimed to know the future. Jobe should be here to help back up her story. "Back when we were dating, when he was in graduate school, he told me he would die young. Just the way . . ." She looked at Siena—her open, disbelieving face—at Jana, who was leaning forward, grinning, obviously filled with delight at this turn of conversation. "The way Riemann had," Carmen finished, though she was only handing her daughter more ammunition. *My mom got cancer and now she's, like, a total wacko*, Carmen imagined Siena telling her friends, her teachers. *She thinks she has visions.* Carmen could see exactly how Siena would roll her eyes, the sympathetic looks from adults, the hugs of solidarity from other girls.

Instead Siena pivoted to face Jana and report, "Luca actually believes he talks to Daddy now. In his dreams. It's totally freaking Michael out. And *she's* been part of the problem. Sometimes I think she believes it herself." The girl shook her head sadly and in that moment everyone's role shifted. Jana and Siena became the two rational parents on the couch, while Carmen—youthful, confused, gullible—faced them apprehensively from her chair.

There was a moment of silence, a visible deepening of the plummy night sky.

"Mom." At least Siena was back to calling her that. "I can't understand why you're doing this. Frankly, you never seemed all that crazy about him when he was alive. What is all this stuff about talking to Daddy now that he's dead?"

It was not, though Carmen desperately wanted it to be, an impertinent question. Siena was measured, honest, genuinely asking. And Jana—the only person in the world qualified to answer the question other than Carmen herself—sat quietly between them. She said nothing but gave Carmen a quick sympathetic look.

"There are things between a husband a wife that you don't see," Carmen started. She stared into two skeptical faces. "And it's true that I didn't, in these last years, spend much time just talking to your father. Because . . ." She searched her brain for the last time they'd sat over coffee, touched spontaneously, or laughed. But she couldn't recall. "He was sick. And before that, we'd gotten sort of weirdly estranged in a way that married people . . ." She stopped. "I'm kind of sorry now. I wish I'd spent more time talking to him. I think he was an interesting guy, and I like the idea that maybe my chances aren't completely gone."

It was another lame attempt to appease her daughter, but it was also truer than anything else she had said. Carmen leaned back in the gathering dusk and felt her body, still hers, cells both whole and diseased clinging together in the web they'd devised. Siena sighed. She gathered her Diet Coke and rose. "I need to call Troy," she said. Carmen met Jana's gaze and something like humor passed between them. They both knew what the topic of the conversation would be, and the tone.

"Say hi for me," said Carmen, and Jana winked at her.

After Siena left, they sat for a time in the growing dark. "Do you really wish you could talk to Jobe, or were you just making a point?"

"Sometimes." Carmen rocked. "It seems like he's the only one who would understand. I wouldn't mind."

"Huh."

"I always kind of liked him, you know, as a person. I just never should have tried having sex with him." With voices disembodied in the dark, Carmen thought, they could have been teenagers, or a couple of octogenarians sitting together in the old folks' home.

"Well if he's a ghost, sex shouldn't be a problem anymore."

"Yeah, you'd think."

Before Jobe died, Carmen had imagined that she and Danny would meet more frequently after—or at least more spontaneously—but in fact, just the opposite was true. She'd never realized how often Jobe was with the boys, at ball games or eating dinner with Olive, when she was lying in various hotels around town.

Michael was slowly coming out of the bewildered funk of losing his father and beginning—tentatively—to act like a near-teenage kid. Once, she saw him laugh at something Jeffrey said then cover his mouth, as if he were embarrassed; but lately, he seemed to be struggling to balance the two realities. His father was dead; his own life would continue. Carmen watched her youngest more and more vigilantly as the week before her treatments dissipated. She still had not told him about her cancer. A coward, she'd been waiting to see if either Siena or Luca would break the pact and talk to their brother. So far, neither one had.

Under these circumstances, the idea of leaving her twelve-year-old to meet her lover felt obscene. It was only when Danny called with the name and number of a house inspector and asked for the dozenth time if he could see her that Carmen relented.

"I'll get the room," he said. "You don't have to worry about anything except being there." He texted the name and address a few hours later: the very same hotel, now tired and outdated, where her father had stayed when he came to Baltimore for her graduation—the last time he'd visited before Jobe's funeral.

Carmen mused about this the following afternoon, as she left the boys—plus Jeffrey, of course—with a pot of chili and a pile of videos to drive the exact same route she had taken to retrieve her dad twenty-one years before. She was watching the road, sort of, but also seeing images of her father over the years. Thinking about how strangely durable he was. Despite the decades of heavy drinking, Antonio had aged well. He had that dapper, elastic look that skinny, older Italian men often had, a little like Sinatra without the voice. He'd cut back in the past few years from six Scotch-and-waters a night to three on his doctor's advice. Mornings, he played thirty-six holes of golf. There was—she pulled into the parking lot, wincing as her arm brushed her own sore breast—no deterioration in sight.

"Hey," Danny said softly, opening the door even before she could knock. He must have been waiting, listening for the particular sound of her keys. Pulling her inside a little roughly, he faced her and looked intently—as only he could, sized perfectly to match—into her eyes. "How are you?"

"I'm, um, okay. Scared actually. And kind of mad at the world. But okay."

"What can I do?" A pleading question.

Carmen turned away and made a project out of settling her enormous purse on the floor. If this was the way it was going to be, she might have to leave.

"That guy." Her voice was sharp and she could see that

Danny was hurt, so she stopped and gathered her breath, softening it. "You know. . . . Tell me about the inspector you talked to."

Holding her hand as if they were two children on a playground, Danny led her to the bed and sat. "Basically, he said he'll charge you about nine thousand dolars to come out and run all his tests on the place, everything from radon to lead paint to toxic mold." Danny shivered, breathing out, and she could smell the four or five cigarettes he'd smoked in a row that afternoon, probably downstairs on the hotel steps. "It's amazing how many dangerous things can live in a house."

Carmen did not react. This was a side of Danny she'd never seen and she couldn't decide whether she liked it or not. He was cocky, the kind of man who would bring his wife over to his mistress's dinner table and introduce the two with a smirk. He'd never taken anything very seriously. Or at least, that's what she'd thought. It was possible, however, that she wasn't the best judge of character. Bad or good.

"Anyway, that's basically it. The price is for testing only; it doesn't include any mitigation. That can cost up to a couple hundred grand. And the guy said he usually doesn't find much: maybe one or two levels that are on the high side of normal, but nothing he can really *point* to."

"That was surprisingly up front for a man who could make nine thousand dollars just by sweeping his special detectors around my house."

"Yeah, well, I told him this was for close friends of mine. The husband had already died of cancer; the wife was just diagnosed. He got a lot more sympathetic after that."

Carmen looked down and grinned at their locked hands as an odd, alien warmth spread through her. She relaxed, possibly for the first time since the biopsy. She liked it when Danny lied. Also, there was something about the idea of him being a close friend of Jobe's that made her amused and hopeful. She closed her eyes and the image she'd seen before—that floating series of golden rings, moving gently through her mind—appeared again.

Now there was the soft feeling of his face against hers, hands like wings on her jaw, the gentle working of his lips and tongue against her mouth. Carmen lay back slowly but without strain; it was as if something were supporting her all the way down. When her back touched the pillows, Danny moved his hands to the front of her shirt. This was the first time they'd been together since the day he found the comet, which was now gone. He had unbuttoned her and was leaning down to kiss her collarbone.

Abruptly Carmen sat up, nearly clocking him, and pulled her shirt around her.

"What? What's wrong?" He sat back, hands up, like a suspect.

"My . . . I can't." First there had been the gash in her chest, oozing blood-tinged pus into gauze. Then the bruise that spread like ink under her skin. It was fainter now, green and lavender instead of that dark death color. But the ugliest part was the concave pocket Dr. Woo had left in her breast, with skin folded and stitched unevenly. He'd been pleased when he saw how it was healing and Carmen inferred that she looked the way she was supposed to a couple of weeks after surgery. But it made no sense. What was all this excitement about "saving the breast," if it was going to end up mangled and purpled and green?

"Does it hurt?" Danny asked, still sitting some distance away.

"Not." She breathed out like a dragon. This was humiliating. "Not anymore. But it doesn't feel *good* anymore either."

"You've tried?"

"You mean?" She swallowed, disgusted by the idea. "No. I haven't."

"So. Let me." He seemed to be growing as he sat there. Carmen blinked. This was a strange illusion: Danny, whose compact size and flippancy she'd relied upon, becoming suddenly grave and large.

"Let you what?"

"Let me . . ." He reached out slowly, as if she were a skittish dog, and peeled her fingers from the shirt she was holding closed. "Try."

This time, when Danny lowered her it was he who held her on the way down. "The lights," she muttered. "Can we?"

"Don't move," he said and got up to pull the curtains shut—including the heavy ones designed to block light during the day—and turn off the room's two lamps. The room was murky, brighter than night, lit from the edges of the windows and the crack under the door. When Danny came back to the bed he stood over her for a moment, looking down. Then he pulled his own shirt over his head without unbuttoning it. "Take your clothes off for me."

Even his voice seemed deeper than before and she obeyed, first sliding out of her jeans by arching her back and moving her hips from side to side. Then she removed her socks and finally sloughed off the shirt she'd been holding tight around her.

Danny stood another few beats, simply looking at her, and Carmen felt herself growing warm. Slick with desire. Her body seemed not to understand the circumstances. "Take off your pants," she said in imitation of him, and he laughed but did what she said.

He climbed on top of her, carefully, and perched on his knees so their pelvic bones matched. He was hard inside his boxer shorts and the fabric between them made her breathless, the way she had been once when he bound her wrists over her head with the tie from a hotel bathrobe then fucked her agonizingly slowly, stopping and starting again, until she begged him to make her come.

"This feels good, doesn't it?" he said, voice floating to her through the room's haze and she nodded, closing her eyes.

Danny bent over her; she could smell tobacco and coffee as he neared her face. At some point, he must have taken his hair out of its customary ponytail because it fell on all sides of her, tickling her ribs and making a dark tent around her head and shoulders and neck. He reached under her and unhooked her bra, drawing it off, letting it fall to the floor. Carmen kept her eyes shut. They'd adjusted to the darkness—even in middle age, her vision was perfect—and she didn't want to see his face.

"Does this hurt?" he asked, circling the nipple of her right breast with his finger.

She shook her head. That was the side that was still whole and healthy, at least so far as she knew. Dr. Woo had given her the sense that cancer might be lurking anywhere, ready to latch on with its sharp, rotten teeth.

"And this?" Danny had moved laterally to the left now; she could feel the shift in his body. But there was no sensation on her skin. It felt dead, like a layer of plastic had been inserted between her nerve endings and the rest of the world.

"It doesn't hurt." She tried to keep the frustration out of her voice. She could no longer feel his cock between her legs, either. He must have gone soft just looking at her. "But it's like I'm numb. Maybe you should just . . ."

"Quiet!" She opened her eyes and met Danny's in the gloom. He smiled, a kindly librarian. "Just be quiet and let me take care of things."

"Okay," she said, feeling suddenly, inexplicably, sleepy. She shut her eyes again and lay without struggling, giving in. Then something started, like music so low it's barely audible. There was a weak signal from her left side, a tiny fork of lightning. She made a sound and moved against the sheets; Danny brought himself down more fully along her body and she felt him rock hard against her leg.

Shifting, using her hands to pull him back into position, she used him shamelessly, humping his still-covered penis until she was on the edge of orgasm. "Stop!" she said, and realized that he had been sucking on her nipples, each in turn, and the left was now working nearly as well as the right. It was a fainter feeling—like a voice coming from downstairs instead of the next room—but it was there.

"Now," she ordered. It was so easy to take over, become the instructor. And Danny seemed not to mind.

He stood, leaving her uncovered and briefly cool, to pull off his underwear. Then he straddled her again, his cock extended like a flag. "I don't want to hurt you," he whispered, and somehow the words twisted brightly in her head to become exciting.

"Please," she said, not knowing if she meant "Please do hurt me" or "Please don't," but not caring, either, because there was only sensation and that was better than deadness and it felt like nothing she'd ever experienced before: loud and strange and foreign but wonderful. Like a teenage boy, she came within minutes and he then speeded up, determined. A few hard thrusts and he let out a long, strangled groan.

He rolled off her and they were side by side on the bed, breathing raggedly. It was growing later and the light seeping in around the curtains had begun to blend with the tenor of the room. "Did that work?" he asked after they were quiet again.

"Yeah, that worked," she said. For the first time she could ever remember, she reached out and held his hand.

For once, instead of disappearing each in their own direction, they stayed together, side by side in the narrow hotel bed, talking in a desultory, nearly married manner about Carmen's home inspection, Danny's attempts to get Mega into credit counseling, the insurance dilemma, and finally—for the first time—her kids.

"Michael doesn't have Jobe to talk to anymore, and his older brother has Down's so he can't be of much help." Carmen decided to skip the part about Luca's already being in conversation with his dead father. "Jobe's brother, Nate, is terrific. He loves my kids and spends time with Michael when he can. But Nate's got his own life. A wife, a job, two kids of his own."

Danny shifted and found a more comfortable spot but didn't let go of her fingers. This closeness—and the talking—was new; she was surprised how much she liked it. "Now he's going to watch his mother get . . ." She stopped. There was no point describing to Danny how ugly she was bound to become. Soon enough, he'd see.

"I could try," Danny said. "Talking to him."

She turned toward him; he remained on his back. There was no way to tell what he'd meant. This was the first time they'd even discussed the children. Danny had never wanted children and made it clear from the beginning he wasn't interested in the day-to-day. Surely he wasn't offering to step in and become that out-of-the-blue uncle figure for her son. "What are you saying?"

"I mean, I could take him to a baseball game or something. You know, do guy stuff every once in a while."

"Why?"

"What do you mean 'why'?"

"I mean, that's not what we do. We don't get entangled. No commitments, remember? Don't look at me like that. It was your rule."

"So?" Danny let go of her hand and got out of bed. "I wasn't talking about that. This isn't a fucking marriage proposal, it was an offer to help you out in a tough situation. But forget it." The last three words came out muffled as he bent to pick up his boxers.

"Of course it's not a marriage proposal. You're already married."

Danny had pulled his jeans on over his shorts, but he paused now, the zipper and button still undone. He targeted her with his eyes. "Yes, I'm married. And you're not anymore. Is that what this is about? You want me to *marry* you now?"

Carmen lit up with rage. But a tiny part of her was still quiet, still measured. How had this happened so fast? One minute they were in bed together, close in a way they'd never been before, and now . . .

"No, I don't want you to marry me. For Christ's sake, I've never wanted to be married to anyone! I was so anxious to be single I actually *wished* for my own husband—who never did a single bad thing in his whole life—to die." She was breathing hard again, and sobbing. "That's how desperately I wanted to be single. That's how awful I am. So just." She huddled, her knees drawn up with the sheet over them, head bowed so she could see the tangled ends of her hair. "Go."

They were silent for a time. Out in the hall, doors creaked open and thudded closed. People ran and laughed and got ice. The darkness deepened. Carmen waited for Danny to walk out, for their door to slam shut.

Instead he walked forward and put his hand on her head,

atop the long, curly mass of hair that would soon be gone. "I'm not leaving," he said.

Carmen raised her head, exerting pressure against his palm. She felt about six years old. "Why do you even like me?" she asked.

There was a faint memory, something she couldn't place. A cool night, a sugary smell, the movement of a swing. Then it disappeared.

Danny sighed. "I don't know, Car. Sometimes I really don't." He paused, and she thought that was all there was. "But I think it has something to do with your fierceness. You take care of everyone— even Jobe, the guy you say you never loved. At the end when you were cleaning the shit from his sheets. I kind of liked that. Jesus, you're kind of a bully but . . ." His hand dropped away and he sat on the bed next to her. "For some reason, I just sort of. Love you for it."

Carmen nodded. There were glimmers of that long-ago ice cream shop appearing in her memory like a house behind a thick stand of pines. She rested her head on Danny's shoulder and they stayed that way, silent, until he had to leave and go home.

Olive arrived at dawn dressed in a smart yellow suit—the kind one might wear to an afternoon luncheon—and pushed her way through the screen door onto the sun porch where her son had died. Carmen stood watching from her spot in the kitchen. It was approximately where she'd been when Jobe stopped breathing, and this time, too, she was holding a cup in her hand. But—because she was leaving to be stuck with needles, poisoned and instantly nauseated—rather than coffee, she was drinking weak tea.

"Hello, dear." Olive crossed the porch and set her purse down on the kitchen counter. "Are you ready?"

Never! Carmen shivered. "Just about," she said. "Can I get you something?"

"I'm fine." Olive fingered the brooch at her throat. It looked like rhinestones but Carmen knew it was not. "I stopped for a little breakfast on the way here."

"Okay." Carmen gulped the last inch of her tea and put the cup in the sink, feeling irrationally irritable and rushed. "I'll just grab my stuff and we can go."

They had been like this—formal and stilted—since that disastrous talk in Olive's car, the day of the meeting with Dr. Woo. Olive had phoned the following evening to ask when Carmen's first chemotherapy session was scheduled and inform her that she, Olive, would be accompanying her. There was an unnaturally hard edge to her voice. Carmen wondered for one frantic moment if her mother-in-law simply wanted a front seat to her suffering—to watch the shrew, who hadn't loved her son well, writhe and retch and die.

But when she climbed into the front seat of Olive's Mercedes, Carmen had to hoist herself over a pile of supplies on the floor: bottles of sparkling water, brand-new magazines, a bag of hard ginger candies. "I was remembering Jobe's treatments," Olive said curtly. "I thought those things might help."

"Thanks." Carmen slumped, which was due to the early hour but also, probably, to the way she was dressed. She'd been warned to make herself "comfortable" over and over, as if you *could* be comfortable while someone was pumping toxins into your blood. Grudgingly, she'd put on her sweat suit, fuzzy white socks, and tennis shoes. Her hair was unbrushed and wild, which she liked. The more present it could be, the better.

"I have a favor to ask," she said. As if this weren't favor enough. But Olive didn't seem perturbed.

"What can I do?"

"I need to tell Michael, today. I just haven't had the . . . I know I should have. But he's so young, and he's still really upset about Jobe. I thought it might be easier on him if you were there."

"Of course." Two words, perfectly even. Suddenly, Carmen was irritated with Olive. With this whole *uncomfortable* situation. It was a puzzle whether she had a right to be, but she was too anxious to figure it out.

"I still don't know what to do about my job," she volunteered after a few miles. Here was a nice, neutral topic. "I got the paperwork yesterday and reinstated Jobe's insurance, just in case. But I don't know if I want to let go of mine . . . stop working." Carmen looked out the window. It was early enough, there were only a few cars on the road—mostly people drinking coffee out of enormous white paper cups.

"Do you *like* your job?" Olive asked. "It's always been hard to tell."

Carmen narrowed her eyes. Olive's voice was pleasant. But this could be code, a clever way of circling back to the subject of Carmen's fickle nature. Finally, she shrugged. "I don't love it, I don't hate it. It was . . ." What? A way to bide time, to get out of the house, to provide an easy excuse for her afternoons with Danny? "No, I guess I don't really like the work much. I just always thought I should."

"Should what, dear?"

"Should have a career, something that made me of use, beyond being just a wife and mother."

"You've been of use," Olive said starchily, turning into the parking lot. They'd arrived. The torture was about to start. Carmen got out of the car as slowly as she could, then reached down to get the gifts Olive had brought her. "No matter what you might think," Olive said, as they walked up the concrete path. "You were necessary."

It was such a strange comment, Carmen remained distracted during the battery of invasive questions and tests that followed. A lab tech dressed in jeans and a Hawaiian shirt had Carmen leave a urine sample, drew her blood, and inserted a needle with a short, floppy tube into the back of her hand. Then he led her into a barnlike room whose walls were lined with chairs that looked like they'd come from a dental office—with padded headrests and feet that could be raised. Each one had an IV stand next to it, a small metal table, an emesis basin. Two patients were lying back already with bright amber fluid flowing into them.

"You're early," he said. "Pick your spot."

"You mean?" She stopped. This was worse than anything that had happened so far. Jobe's treatments had taken place in a small, private cubicle at Johns Hopkins; now she understood that it had been a favor to someone in his department. "We're all in this room together? Isn't there anywhere else?"

At precisely that moment, one of the two patients already receiving treatment lurched forward and vomited with a noisy slosh into his basin; he paused then repeated with a deep, rumbling throat-clearing sound. Then he lay back in his chair and closed his eyes, as if nothing had happened.

The tech seemed not to have noticed. "Nope, this is it. Better for the nurses, you know. They can keep an eye on all of you at the same time."

Carmen walked forward into this new nightmare. She chose a chair as far from the other two people as she could get, and the tech gamely went to retrieve a folding chair for Olive. But just as Carmen was getting settled in, her feet up and head back, a bald woman with a pinched face, penciled-on eyebrows, and a bag of knitting in her hand came and took the chair immediately to their right.

"I just want to get this over with," Carmen said to Olive. But they sat for nearly fifteen minutes in tense silence, waiting. A nurse came out with a bag she was holding by the ends and tipping from side to side, but she went directly to the stand behind the bald patient and hung it there, fussing as she attached the tubing to the woman's IV. "But we were here first!" Carmen cried, loud enough for the woman in the adjoining chair to hear and turn.

It's no honor, her small eyes seemed to say. *Just you wait.*

Then another nurse appeared—the twin of the first—with her bag, an even brighter, more luridly orange concoction, and hung it above Carmen's head. Reaching for the end of the tube that snaked down, she uncapped it without a word and clipped it neatly into the needle in Carmen's hand. Both she and Olive looked down as the first of the poison entered her body. *I can't believe I'm doing this.* Carmen put her head back. *This is insane.* But she didn't object. Rather, as in the MRI machine, she lay perfectly still.

"Does it hurt you, dear?"

Carmen looked up and Olive's face was twisted. Clearly she was in pain, and love for her mother-in-law swelled in Carmen. "No," she said, reaching out with her free hand to brush the sunny yellow sleeve of Olive's suit. It was the one bright spot in this barren room, Carmen realized. Like a daisy in the desert. "It's just, I think about Jobe." She watched Olive flinch inside her clothes, but it was a small movement and she covered it well. "After watching him go through this, the treatments. You know they killed him—maybe slower than the cancer would have. I don't know. But doing this . . ." She glanced at the glowing bag above her head. "It feels like an invitation. Like I'm just inviting death in."

Olive shook her head. "You're wrong. This will help you. I saw it in a dream." She blinked, as if she was appalled at what she'd just said. "Or at least, I think it was a dream. Jobe was there."

Carmen stared at the ceiling—beige acoustic tiles with tiny holes—and wondered if perhaps *she* was the one who was sleeping. Or crazy. Or dead already. None of this seemed real, not the chemicals coursing into her arm or the old woman sitting beside her, talking about clairvoyant dreams. She closed her eyes and then recalled something.

"Luca talks about this, too, getting messages from Jobe." Now Carmen was floating, the hum of other voices in the room comforting rather than intrusive, her legs heavy in the chair. "I didn't believe him." *Was this true?*

"Believe him," came Olive's voice through the haze. "And believe Jobe when he comes to you."

Carmen shook her head, side to side on the padded cushion of the chair. "I don't know what you're talking about."

"Yes, you do."

Carmen peeked. The room was full now, lit with fluorescents, but thankfully cool. Some people had covered themselves with quilts. "What in Christ's name are you talking about?"

"I'm talking about my son, how he loved you. And how you . . ." She stopped and examined the back of one liver-spotted hand. "Loved him."

"Olive, I . . ." Carmen's stomach twisted. Was it the chemo, already making her sick? She waited, reminding herself to vomit on the side of the chair where Olive wasn't sitting, to avoid spattering the brilliant yellow suit. But the twinge passed. "I'm sorry about that. I thought . . ."

"No, no." Olive held up her hand. "If anyone's sorry, it should be me. Believe me, Jobe let me know that."

"You mean from the great beyond?" Carmen struggled to keep the derision out of her voice and failed.

"No." Olive laughed and sat up even straighter, knees crossed. Damn, the woman had Tina Turner legs. Carmen could easily imagine her mother-in-law on stage. "I mean when he was alive. We talked about it, a couple times, just before he died. He was pretty upset about the way we—I—railroaded you. He said I did it like I was acquiring a small company. Or snaring you in my web." She flashed a grin. "He started calling me the Black Widow, after George died."

The smile faded, slowly, until Olive's expression was smooth and serious again. "I told myself over the years that it was the right thing, that you were too young to understand your own feelings. My son was such a wonderful man, so intelligent and fine, I was sure you'd grow to love him over time." Tears gathered in Olive's eyes and she blinked. Her training was ingrained. She would never, under any circumstances, weep in public. "Before your wedding, I told him the same thing."

"I did love him." Oddly, when Carmen said this, it actually felt like the truth.

"Yes, you did, but not the way . . ." Olive looked into the distance, as if watching something unrelated to the twenty sick and dying people in the room. "Not the way you should have."

Carmen was silent.

"When you had Michael after all those years had passed, I told myself it had happened. You'd fallen for Jobe, just the way I planned. The way couples do in an arranged marriage. Then he got sick and you stayed, you took care of him. When he died I thought—no, I convinced myself; I was sure—you were mourning the love of your life. You seemed so remote, so inconsolable. . . ."

Next to them, a stick-thin man called for his nurse. He had to go to the bathroom, immediately. There was a scuffle, but they didn't reach him in time. Urine leaked onto the floor in an acrid, yellow stream.

Remote, inconsolable. The words echoed through Carmen's head. It was not an inaccurate description of the way she had felt.

There was an odor. She looked down and saw that the trail of urine had snaked its way over. "Here, your shoes will get ruined." Carmen nudged Olive. "Pick up your feet. Put them on the end of my chair."

Olive did so. And they sat watching the clean-up team come in with mops and buckets, their feet clustered together, close enough to touch.

July 1986

There was no real reason to rush the wedding. Carmen wasn't pregnant; Jobe wasn't shipping out to some foreign war. It simply made sense, Olive explained to nearly everyone they encountered that summer. Carmen heard the argument so many times, it echoed through her head every time she thought about the ceremony that would be held during the most oppressive days of summer.

Olive and George were giving the couple a honeymoon trip to Italy as a wedding present—one of several gifts, actually, but this went unmentioned—and it would be better for them to travel then. It would be warm there, too, Olive would concede; but the purpose, mostly, was for their darling new daughter-in-law to tour museums and study great art. Also, Jobe had taken a post at Johns Hopkins that would begin in the fall and they needed time to settle in before he began work.

Carmen sat in the plush dressing room of a bridal shop so exclusive, it did not have a street-facing entrance, listening as Olive went through her spiel for the sales clerk. "Perfectly understandable," the woman said. Everything in this place was soft and rich, including the clerk's voice and hair—a cloud of silky blond floss she had pulled back with a wide jeweled scarf.

"We need a dress that's formal but not heavy to wear. It could be ninety degrees. We don't want the bride fainting from heat." Olive laughed. "I was hoping you could help us find something pretty—and appropriate—but cool."

Carmen sat on a huge, pale pink toadstool holding a glass of white wine. She sipped and made a face. This place might be fancier than any dress shop she'd ever seen, but their wine was cheap. A year's worth of meals at the Garretts had taught her what to look for. This one had no structure at all.

"I think I know *exactly* what you're looking for," said the woman in a breathy, lackluster Marilyn Monroe voice. She turned to Carmen, who was busy trying to set her wine glass down. But the carpet was too deep, everything in this place was pillowy. There wasn't a firm surface in sight. "Would you stand up for me, hon?"

Carmen rose grudgingly. She felt trapped and this stranger had become her enemy, one of her captors. *Hon?* What a simp! She probably spent her time guzzling Coors at sports bars when she wasn't hawking trillion-dollar gowns.

"You're what, maybe a four?"

"More like a six." Carmen sighed. There was no way the sales clerk had made a mistake; she could probably guess a woman's weight to within an ounce. Carmen hated being falsely flattered and condescended to this way.

"Excellent. That's our standard size!" She looked as pleased as if she'd spun all the dresses herself out of hay. "You wait here and I'll be back with some things for you to try on."

She left and Carmen was relieved. There were a few minutes of silence. She sat again, leaning back, and drank more wine. But when she straightened and looked at Olive, Carmen felt a quiver of fear. The older woman's face was dark, her eyes gleaming—this was precisely the look Carmen had been expecting when she was caught, last summer, coming out of Jobe's room.

"Is something wrong?" she asked.

"I'm . . . surprised," Olive said. She hesitated then went on. "It is important, in my view, to treat service people with respect. Having money doesn't give us the right to be rude. Nor, frankly"—she paused again, considering, eventually deciding to go on—"nor do I understand why anyone would *want* to."

Carmen's face burned. She recalled her own mother, pale with a smooth scarf-covered head, insisting that she was well enough to shop for prom dresses. How she had nearly expired after only two stores and Carmen had had to abandon the search in order to call her dad. She wished now that Olive had been there that day, too—not only to take charge, but to put Carmen in her place and demand that she be kind.

Just then, the clerk came bustling in with an armful of dresses so bulky, it was a mystery how she carried them. One by one, she hung them on the rack that lined one wall. "I think you'll find something you love here," she said over her shoulder as she clinked the hangers onto the rod. "But if you don't, no worries. We'll just keep going until you fall head over heels."

"These are just lovely. Thank you, dear." Olive smiled at the woman and gestured at one of the dressing room's three cushioned chairs. "Do you have time to sit with us and help us decide? It would be so nice to have your professional opinion."

"I'm yours for the duration, ladies," the woman said and sank gratefully into a chair. She and Olive both turned to Carmen, like audience members.

"Should I, just . . ." Carmen turned her hands so her fingers pointed loosely toward her body. "Change right here?"

"Do you mind?" Olive asked. "We could step out if you'd prefer, but then it will take an awfully long time."

"No, no. That's okay." Again, Carmen looked for a place to put her glass but the room hadn't changed. She drained the last of the wine and propped the empty glass on the floor, tipped against the wall. She slid her skirt off and placed it on the toadstool. Then she began unbuttoning her shirt.

It made no sense that she felt reluctant. As a freshman at Michigan, Carmen had been that girl who walked around shirtless in her dorm room, not even caring when the door swung open and girls from her hall streamed in and out. She liked the feeling of air on her breasts, and while she wasn't exactly attracted to women—at least not in the hot, powerful way she was to men—it was a turn-on to show off her bare, rounded shape, especially when it was obvious they were watching and assessing, comparing themselves to her, often falling short.

But undressing in front of this woman and Jobe's mother was strange. It could be, Carmen decided, because this was the first time Olive would see what her son panted for and groped and stabbed with his hard penis at night. It could also be that for once, Carmen was faced with a woman—thirty years older—whose body was probably better than hers.

Working at it with studied diligence, she managed to talk herself through. Off came the shirt and silky camisole she wore underneath. Now Carmen stood in her bikinis and lacy bra and the sales woman jumped up, as if they were about to dance. The woman took the first gown from its hanger and expertly opened it. Like a small child, Carmen ducked, held up her arms, and dove upward into a frothy dress that the clerk then tugged and fastened around her.

"Oops, we're never going to get this one buttoned up," she said from behind Carmen's back. "You're a deceptive one, aren't you? I'd have thought you'd just slide into a six but you're quite a bit bigger in the chest than you look. What cup size do you wear, hon?"

"C," Carmen said sheepishly and looked at Olive, who was impassive. She seemed not to find this at all strange.

"Well, most of our ladies in your size are about a B, so we're going to have to alter whatever you buy."

"That won't be a problem," Olive said. "As long as you can have it done fast. Remember, the wedding is in just a few weeks."

Carmen could have sworn the woman glanced at her midsection, looking for signs that this rush to marry had a baby behind it. But this was the one place the dress fit perfectly.

"But that's not the one," Olive continued. "It's adorable, but not quite right for Carmen. Too much tulle."

They went through two thirds of the gowns on the rack and though she was getting used to the process, Carmen was bewildered by the fact that it felt like so much *work*. "I'm sorry. I'm starting to sweat a little," she confided at one point. As if the woman to whom she'd been lifting her arms was unaware.

"Happens," the clerk said. "Don't worry about it, hon. These are just our testers and you're all sweet and clean. You'd be amazed what other girls get on them: lipstick, wine, God knows. I've found stains I can't figure out and don't even want to touch." She wrinkled her nose like a rabbit and Carmen laughed. In the background, Olive did, too. Suddenly, the room righted. Everything was better. The next dress, a sheath, slipped over Carmen's jackknifed body like Cinderella's shoe.

"Mmm," Olive said. And Carmen knew, even before she turned to look in the mirror, that they had found it. "Isn't that just beautiful?"

Carmen revolved and saw that it was. Also that she looked like someone she had never met. The pink streaks in her hair were gone, and where she used to shave her head, soft, long curls had grown out. She'd begun seeing Olive's stylist, who cut the longer pieces at a slant so they came to a point at her chin. In this dress, with its wide neckline, tight-fitting bodice, three-quarter-length skirt and soft scatter of pearls on satin, Carmen appeared in the mirror like a woman who'd stepped forward from the 1920s. A passenger on an ocean liner, a mistress to Hemingway or Picasso. She twisted her body from side to side and watched the material shimmer in the dressing room's soft light.

"We have the same problem here." The woman continued to fuss at Carmen's back, straining to pull the dress closed. "I could zip it up all the way if I really had to, but you probably wouldn't be able to breathe. So I'm just going to hold it so you can get a better idea of . . ."

"Oh, no need," Olive said. "This is the one. That is." She stepped forward and reached out to touch the fabric over Carmen's heart, her voice dreamy. "If you like it, dear. What do you think? Would you like to try on a few more?"

"No," Carmen said. "This is perfect."

All she wanted was to be the woman in the mirror. Beautiful, sophisticated, mysterious. The only problem was she couldn't imagine someone like that spending a lifetime with Jobe.

At home, there was remarkably little to do. A pile of invitations sat stacked in a box on the dining room table and Carmen had brought out her calligraphy set from senior seminar. She sat on Saturday addressing envelopes for a couple of hours, but then her back and neck grew stiff and the quiet started to feel heavy around her. She wandered through the rooms. There was something Poelike about the weird stillness: dust motes floating above the staircase, furniture lurking in unexpected corners, portraits on the walls hanging straighter than she remembered.

Nate had left for a summer program in California and would be back just days before the wedding. George was either working or out on the golf course. Olive had her coterie of women friends. And Jobe, Carmen's soon-to-be husband? Ever since the night of their formal engagement—when he'd given her the sapphire-and-diamond ring that once belonged to his grandmother—he'd been fading like a dream, only the idea of which remained. She rarely saw him. And in only a month he'd gone from geeky to professorial. His beard was thickening and he was absentminded in a way that Carmen suspected might be partly put on.

The previous night, for instance, he'd acted completely blindsided when she came out of her room dressed in a frilly summer dress that Olive had insisted on picking up for her while they were wedding gown shopping. "Going somewhere?" he'd asked. And though she felt like running back into her room and stripping the stupid thing off, she'd answered, "The Science Center benefit. Remember? Your mother gave us the tickets last week?"

"Oh," he said, looking perplexed, though Carmen distinctly recalled a long conversation with Olive about how Jobe should start showing up at events like this one, his role as a professor important to the local scientific and academic community. Carmen was to be the ingratiating beauty on Jobe's arm, she understood. Now she waited— carefully coiffed and made up—while he rooted through his closet to find a jacket that didn't need ironing.

Once there, they'd been the youngest people in the room by about twenty years. Carmen talked to only three people all night, ate the sauce-smothered chicken, and sat next to Jobe without touching or speaking. At one point she'd felt his hand brush her inner thigh under the tablecloth and she'd actually fantasized for a moment that he would stroke her, sliding his fingers under her dress and into the space between her legs, as Rory had. She'd promised herself to Jobe and was doggedly trying to spark some excitement between the two of them. It could be done; Olive had said as much. *If both of you tried, it would be possible to grow love.* But he'd apologized and withdrawn, acting as if he'd touched her only by accident. Were there reasons for his hand to be lurking under the table, in the vicinity of her clitoris, *other* than to get her off during dessert?

She had no desire to repeat the uncomfortable quality of that night, but she was bored. All her friends had left town already, or they were working in post-college jobs and internships. They had new lives that did not include command appearances at benefits or stiff fiancés. And Carmen could have that, too. She could walk out of this house right now—at least she assumed she could; it was possible it would suck her back in or crumble upon her—but then what would she do? A year ago, she'd been able to book a trip to Europe and simply take off. But this felt like a lost skill; it had been replaced by something else. She had sold her youth for the opportunity to live here in comfort and now she was permanently, eerily stuck.

Her hand was on the wooden banister, which was smooth and cool and curved. She stood contemplating then made a decision. Marching up the stairs, she tried to adopt her old Detroit ways.

"Jobe," she called. "Where are you? Jobe? I'm coming to get you and we're going out."

He wasn't anywhere. She checked his room and the kitchen. Where he went every day was a mystery: He had an office at the university but there was nothing going on there at this time of year. She looked at the clock: 5:43. She would wait until seven, Carmen decided, and if Jobe didn't call her or come home, she would pack her things and leave. No note, no explanation. She'd just walk out the door and let him figure it out. Just thinking about this made her feel better. Flipping through the *TV Guide*, she found a channel with a program she could tolerate that ran from six to seven. Perfect. She would watch and when it was over, she would be done as well.

It was rerun time, when the local station ran shows from the previous year, but she'd never seen this episode of *Cagney & Lacey* before. By the quarter-hour commercial, she was hooked. Here were role models who could help her, especially the smart-mouthed blonde one. She was pretty, too. Living in New York, working as a police detective. This wasn't a good possibility for Carmen but it demonstrated that there *were* possibilities. A smart, attractive, free-thinking woman could strike out and live somewhere on her own.

At the precise moment Jobe opened the front door, the episode's cliffhanger was about to be resolved. This presented a dilemma. Should Carmen stand up and leave the television, go find her future husband, and tell him they needed to talk? Or should she take a chance he'd stick around for the next ten minutes and watch the rest of the show?

She heard him go into the kitchen and open the refrigerator. Option two, then. If Jobe was going to eat, he'd be around long enough for her to finish and find out who'd murdered the prostitute. The ending was not as satisfying as she'd hoped—the killer was exactly the person she thought it would be. She switched off the TV and rose, going into the kitchen. Jobe sat at the table with a plate of unrelated foods in front of him: crackers, carrots, a leftover cookie, a slice of deli turkey spread with mustard. She looked away.

"Hey, what are you doing tonight?" She tried to keep her voice casual, but there was a high note of something in it. Fury, panic. Why after a year of hovering had he suddenly proposed, then withdrawn? She wanted to shake him and ask this question.

"Nothing that I know of," he said. "Why? Is there something you'd like to do?"

"I'd like to do something," she said. That sounded dumb.

Jobe must have thought so, too. He had his puzzled I'm-trying-to-be-helpful look. "Okay, let's do something. What?"

"Something crazy. I want to do something totally off the wall."

"Such as?" He was trying in his way, placating her, and Carmen felt as if she might cry. This was it: the ultimate test. If Jobe could not come up with an idea that surprised her, she should walk. Maybe, just maybe, this would be the moment he would burst out of his mathematician suit and become the gangling puppet he'd been that night when they danced.

"I want . . . I want, like a road trip or a night where we do something new—something neither of us has ever done before."

He removed his jacket, revealing a faded black T-shirt with sweat stains under the arms. This was a tiny bit of progress and she seized it, grabbing his arm. "Come *on*. We have plenty of money, which most people don't. We've got a Saturday night. There is nothing stopping us from doing anything we want to do."

"That's true," he said. "You're absolutely right. I just don't know what it is. If you just *tell* me where you want to go, I swear I'll take you. Wherever it is."

He'd caught it, some of her frantic feeling. She could hear it in his voice and see it in his eyes. Jobe was frightened. Carmen was nearly sure of it. And that was at least a start.

"A road trip," she said.

"Where?"

"I don't know. What's close? But not too close."

"New York?"

Carmen shook her head. "Nope, I was there with your mom a

couple months ago. I mean some place different. Somewhere neither of us has ever been."

"Philadelphia?"

"Maybe." He was being weirdly accommodating, which took some of the fun out of this. But the idea of getting in a car and escaping still had its appeal. "What's south?"

"Virginia."

"Perfect! I've never been to Virginia. I've never even *thought* about Virginia. What's the best city?"

"I'm not sure." Jobe rose carefully from his half-eaten plate, like an old man. She couldn't figure out whether this was an affectation or he'd suddenly aged four decades when he was handed his degree. He went into the den, a leathery book-lined room that always made Carmen think of the game Clue: Colonel Mustard in the library with a candlestick. Jobe took an atlas from a shelf and flipped through its oversized pages. "Richmond," he said. "Or Greensboro, but that's in North Carolina and it's a ways."

"How far is Richmond?"

Jobe used his thumb and index finger to measure the distance, then squinted at the key. "Two and a half hours, maybe three," he said. "Greensboro is . . ." Again, pincerlike, he gauged the distance with his long, skinny digits. "Another three, plus. So a total of maybe six, by the time we've stopped for restrooms and snacks and such."

Carmen was nearly reclining against the doorframe. "How do you manage to make a spontaneous trip sound like a science project?"

Jobe looked up quickly and for one awful moment, Carmen actually thought he was going to cry. But he didn't. He stood in place, swaying, with a twisted expression as if he were deciding something. And then he spoke. "Maybe we should just forget all this," he said.

Carmen's chest filled with something, blood probably. Her heart picked up speed and there was a rushing in her ears. "Do you mean going to Richmond?" she asked. "Or do you mean something else?"

"I mean everything." He sounded not angry but tired and

Carmen took a step forward but stopped, no longer supported by the doorframe, facing him, computing the various outcomes of this moment. There were so many; Jobe surely was better at this.

"It's all so fast," he continued. "You come to visit and then you move in here and next thing you know, we're getting married. No one really stopped to think."

"Think about what?" This was it. A door was opening. Jobe was opening it for her. And all she had to do was walk right through. It was that easy.

"About whether or not this is the right thing to do."

"Can we sit?" Carmen asked gently, head inclined toward the couch. They went to it together, Jobe still holding the atlas. She felt nervous; there was no telling what would happen. She could leave this room a free woman, and without having to betray Olive or break Jobe's heart. It was he who was breaking up with her, for absolutely no reason. She hadn't, technically, done anything wrong.

"Are you saying you don't want to marry me?" It was strange how much she cared about the answer.

Fear crossed his face, the look of a small animal about to be clubbed. Instinctively, Carmen inched closer and slid one arm behind his spiny back. "I do. . . ." He fell silent and she let the surprising relief this brought her seep down. Her hand on his back was making small motions, touching his bones and the spaces in between. "But I'm not sure it's right. I'm not . . . I don't think you'll stay."

"What?" Carmen sat up abruptly and withdrew her hand. "You still think I'm just some gold digger? I'm going to stick around long enough to get some money then run off?"

"No." Jobe shook his head and looked down at his lap, bowed thighs in khaki pants. "I don't think that at all. I think you'll get tired of me, of road trips that get planned down to the last Cheeto."

She laughed, a sound like a hiccup. "I wouldn't complain about that, believe me. I love Cheetos!"

He grinned and the handsome Jobe appeared, like a scarecrow whose head had been switched for one less grim. "Me, too."

"You're kidding. You never told me that! *Why* don't we ever eat Cheetos?"

"My mother." He grimaced. "She'd, you know, have a stroke. They turn your fingers orange. It's not refined."

"Fuck refined." Carmen swore his eyes shone when she said it. To test this, she moved closer and whispered in his hairy ear. "Fuck all of this. Take me to Richmond, buy me Cheetos. Fuck me."

It was an experiment—that was all. She sat back and watched, curious to see what would happen. Jobe placed the atlas on the table next to the couch and turned to her, his face grave. "Are you sure?"

The door was still open. Carmen sat for a moment, thinking about walking through it. She could collect her things and leave, call a cab, and go . . . where? Back to Detroit, to explain to her father and sister why she hadn't married the kind, exceedingly wealthy mathematician? Olive would understand and she might make an effort to stay in touch. Jobe, however, would probably never speak to her again. He would sink into his teaching, his research, and diligently forget her. Eventually, he'd find a girl who would love him—some homely, brilliant, professorial type—and she, not Carmen, would wear the beautiful pearl-studded dress.

"Let's go," Carmen said. And despite his mustard-and-deli-meat breath, she kissed Jobe roughly, prying his lips apart with her tongue.

It would be that easy, she told herself as she threw a pair of jeans, a bathing suit, and a T-shirt into a cloth string bag. All she needed to do was bring Jobe her way, loosen him up. That's what he'd said he wanted, in the beginning. She could make this marriage work out— make her whole life work out—if only she kept coaxing him. There was no need to give up Olive and Baltimore and everything they'd planned.

Carmen sailed out of her room with the bag slung over her shoulder and headed down the stairs. Jobe was waiting for her at the bottom, in the foyer. His face was wary; he'd put his jacket back on. "We're stopping at the store on the way out of town," she said, purposely bumping him as she walked toward the door. "We need Cheetos and beer."

The dress was perfect. Carmen hardly recognized herself. Behind her, a woman hired by Olive was arranging Carmen's hair, making it like a soft, silken crown, weaving tiny pearls that matched the bodice of the dress throughout.

From across the room Esme sat watching. Carmen's sister wore a lavender dress—a color Carmen only vaguely remembered choosing—and matching shoes. Esme probably hated her for this, Carmen thought as the woman pinned something to the top of her head. Though, really, her sister had very little to complain about. Olive had insisted on picking up the costs for both bridesmaids, Esme and Carmen's childhood friend, Tina, saying young girls shouldn't have to foot the bill for dresses they would, no matter what anyone said, never wear again.

"I thiiinnkk," the hairdresser breathed out, "we're just about done. What do you say, matron of honor?"

"Awesome," Esme said. Her head held straight so she wouldn't dislodge any of the woman's careful work, Carmen couldn't tell if her sister was being serious or sarcastic. There was such a fine line. Besides, she was out of practice. The Garretts didn't talk to one another the way she was used to; there was no irony, it wasn't part of their lexicon. She might have bantered with Nate, once or twice. But it had occurred to Carmen since Esme and Tina arrived that all the acid-tongued cynicism she knew from back in Detroit was lost on her new family. No wonder she so often felt as if she had nothing to say.

There was a flurry as Olive was called to approve—she came in, smiled and nodded, then rushed back out—and the woman picked up her box of tools and left. Then they were alone, the two sisters, staring at each other in the mirror.

"It does look really nice, Car," Esme said finally.

"Thanks." So she'd been serious! Baltimore must have this effect on people. "Um, how are the kids?"

Esme beamed. "They're amazing. I love being a mom. You'll see."

"I don't know. Maybe."

"You two haven't discussed it? Having children?"

Carmen concentrated. Had they? It was ridiculous to have gotten this far and have no idea. She could call Jobe now, only—she checked the clock—they were supposed to be getting married in twelve minutes. It was probably too late.

"Oh, sure. It's just . . . you never know how things are going to work out."

"No, you don't. Anyway, I was pretty surprised to hear you were getting married. I mean, you're not exactly the type."

"What's 'the type?' " Carmen felt like a talking doll, perched on her seat, using only her mouth so the rest of her would stay arranged.

Esme shrugged. "Me," she said. Then: "Jobe wasn't what I was expecting."

Suddenly the room felt chilly. Someone must have turned the air conditioning up. "What *were* you expecting?"

Again Esme shrugged in the mirror, her plump shoulders moving up and down, shifting the neckline of her purple gown. "I don't know. One of your usual boyfriends: jocky, flirty, mean. This guy's really . . ."

Carmen waited. It seemed in this moment that Esme's pronouncement might help steer things, give her a clue.

"Nice," her sister finished.

But there was no answer in that. "So where's Tina?" Carmen asked.

It had been a little embarrassing to call, out of the blue, and ask her best friend from high school to be her second bridesmaid. But it was necessary because Jobe had two brothers. Will—a charismatic computer mogul who looked thrillingly wolflike—had flown in from San Francisco to be Jobe's best man. He was walking with Esme; that left it to Carmen to find a partner for Nate. But she had left her college friends abruptly in Ann Arbor, too ashamed to tell them why she was dropping out. And when she'd called her former roommate, the girl had acted as if she couldn't believe Carmen was getting married to some professor in faraway Maryland. Plus, Tina had seemed happy to do it when Carmen offered to pay for the ticket and a hotel room. She'd even asked if her boyfriend could come, at his own expense, of course.

"Tina's with Brad." Esme used one finger to edge her mascara, open mouthed, in order to elongate her face. She had dark, veiny eye circles under her makeup. Marriage had aged her sister, Carmen observed. Fast. "Those two are just horny little bunny rabbits. Did you notice?"

Carmen stared at her beautiful self in the mirror. How could she have missed Tina and Brad? They had that lusty, magnetic thing going on. When Tina walked by, Brad—a tanned, blond computer technician who wore dock shoes and sunglasses on a leather string around his neck—would stare, hungrily, after her ass.

"We went to Richmond a couple weeks ago, Jobe and I." Carmen knew, the moment she spoke, that this was an odd thing to say. Like when a small child will suddenly announce what he had for lunch. But she couldn't seem to stop. "It was fun. I mean, he loosened up and we just hung out. . . ." She stopped to remember what, exactly, they had done. There were Cheetos in the car, their late-night drive to a low-roofed, no-name motel that made her feel risky and wild. She'd changed—putting on the mask of an actress she saw in a movie once—the moment Jobe opened the door. Pulling the grimy key from the lock, she had pushed him inside and talked low.

"Do you want me?" she asked, running orange-tinted fingers up the front of his shirt and then down to rest on his belt. "C'mon. Tell me. Tell me what you want to do to me."

Jobe stood, as if he were being held up, just inside the room. It smelled musty. She wanted to open a window but couldn't figure out how to make it fit into her vamp routine. "I want to, uh . . ." Even in the darkness, she could see his face turn red with blood. "I want . . ."

"Do you want to fuck me?" She had to force herself to say it; with Jobe, especially, it felt out of character. But that was the point, wasn't it? And she genuinely wanted to help him.

"Yes." It came out like the sound of an animal in a trap. Sexual excitement or profound discomfort? Carmen couldn't tell.

She was lost, too, she wanted to tell him. She was only twenty-one goddamn years old! He was supposed to be the older man. He should be taking her by the arm, leading her to the bed, then holding her wrist over her head—maybe even capturing both of them in one hand—so all she could do was writhe while he ripped her clothes off with his other hand.

Instead, she was cradling his sweaty hand in both of hers and pulling. "Show me," she said. "Let's just do it."

But then they'd gotten into the bed and, for the first time since she'd met him, Jobe couldn't. The huge erection he hadn't been able to get rid of the first time she'd laid with him in London was entirely gone. She couldn't tell her sister this. Nor could she admit that since that night in Richmond, her fiancé hadn't touched her once. Not once. Not so much as a kiss.

Again, she checked the clock. Four minutes until the wedding began, until her father—who was here with Linda—was due to knock on the door. Maybe he'd get wasted and forget to come for her, Carmen thought. Or keel over on the pathway through Olive's garden that was serving as an aisle. These were things that could save her. Because it simply was not possible to stand up at her own wedding and say she couldn't marry today because she appeared, literally, to emasculate her groom.

There was no way she was going to call off the engagement after Jobe couldn't get it up. She could never be that cruel. Instead she'd told him she understood and gotten out of the bed to throw open a window, which helped only a little. The room still reeked of old water and fungus. She had tried to sleep next to Jobe but done a poor job of it, napping instead in the car on the way home. And once they were back in Baltimore neither of them mentioned it; they simply went ahead with their plans as before.

There was a loud knock on the door. "The father of the bride is here," Antonio bellowed and Carmen swallowed hard. Damn Linda!

She seemed to have cleaned their father up to the point where he was more reliable even than he had been back when their mother was alive.

Carmen stood, slowly, and her eyes met her sister's in the mirror. "Ready," Esme said. But Carmen couldn't tell if it was a question or a statement, so she simply nodded. "Ready." And together, they went out the door.

Their wedding night took place in a hotel that Carmen had never even known existed. Blank on the outside, the building could have been a brownstone where a wealthy lawyer lived. But next to the red-painted front door there was a small gold plaque. ALEXANDER HOUSE, it read. There was a button to push for the bell and they were admitted by a tall, pale man dressed like a funeral director. Carmen half expected him to poke his head out and check, furtively, in each direction, before shutting the door.

It was like stepping into a different place, a different season. There was a fire roaring in one corner and though they'd just walked through an afternoon so sticky that Carmen had felt as if she were swimming, she shivered. This lobby existed perpetually as if it were late fall, with vents piping out cool air, and filled with dark, foresty furnishings: brocade couches, tasseled cushions, and warm, gold lighting. And it was silent. Other than the two of them and Lurch, behind the desk, they were alone.

"Mr. and Mrs. Garrett?" he said.

"No, we're . . ." Carmen began, then stopped.

"Yes," said Jobe. He handed the man a credit card, one Carmen did not recognize. She stood next to this man, her husband of—she checked the clock—three hours, and watched. This was her prerogative now. When Jobe took the card back, she read the name and saw the Johns Hopkins logo. He was paying for the hotel himself. Their first married sex would not be underwritten by Olive. Moving a step closer she put a hand on his forearm and he paused, looking from the paperwork to her face.

"Do you need to see the room first?" he asked.

"No. Why . . . ?"

"Oh, I thought you were trying to stop me." He pointed with the pen to the form he'd filled out with everything but his signature.

"No, that's not . . ." Carmen removed her hand from Jobe and backed up. Suddenly she was so tired, all she wanted to do was curl up on the couch in front of the fire. "Go ahead. I'll let you finish."

There were a couple of simple exchanges: Jobe's signed promise to pay ($420! Carmen had read while she stood at his elbow), then an old-fashioned gold key on a ribbon and directions to a room on the second floor.

"You go ahead. We'll bring your luggage," Lurch said. Carmen looked at the two overnight bags, so small that she herself could have hoisted them easily up the stairs. Back at the Garretts'—home, she reminded herself now—they had eight suitcases of various sizes packed and piled up. But tonight, all she'd packed was a toothbrush, some makeup, a change of clothes, and a T-shirt for sleeping in. She'd debated over the last item, it seemed wrong. But she and Jobe had never, in all of their encounters, slept together nude.

Their room was like something out of "Sleeping Beauty," a bed with four posts and draping whirled around them, so high that there was a stool provided for guests to climb in. A wardrobe hid a TV, as well as a drawer and a minibar full of snacks.

"No Cheetos," Carmen said, pawing through. "There's just stuff like paté and summer sausage and those biscuits you're supposed to eat with wine."

"Are you hungry?" Jobe looked at the clock and Carmen followed his eyes. It was 7:15.

"Not really. There was so much to eat at the wedding. I'm actually kind of . . ." She checked her stomach. "Sick."

He looked startled. "Are you okay? Is there anything I need to do?"

"No." She kicked her shoes off and climbed the stool—a complicated maneuver in the sheath dress, which did not allow her to bend at the hips—then lay on the bed. "It was just the heat, all that champagne, the day. You know."

"Oh." Jobe slumped into a chair. And after a few minutes. "I am kind of hungry. You mind if I get something?"

Carmen propped herself up on her elbows. "You mean, you want to go out?" Instantly, the idea appealed to her. He would leave. She could turn on some HBO movie and crack open one of the little whiskey bottles she'd seen in the cupboard, mix it with 7-Up, and drink while she lay on the bed.

"Nooo." He looked again at the clock. 7:21. "I don't want to go without you, so I'll just get some food from the minibar."

Frustration rose inside her. Jobe didn't like TV—he thought of it as a mindless source of noise—so with the two of them in a single room, she was stuck. It was as quiet as a library. No, a tomb.

It didn't help that Jobe was opening the package of summer sausage as she thought this. Their two helpless bodies lying on the bed as life outside flew by without them. Only the odor of warm meat and garlic floating through their room.

Carmen groaned and turned on her side. There was a tall, narrow window, a view of the city, the sun shining with a near midday brilliance. The evening seemed endless and blank, a symbol of the rest of her life.

She must have fallen asleep, because the next time she stirred, Jobe was turning out lights and the room was muddy. Carmen sat up, the taste of stale champagne in her mouth. "Where's my toothbrush?" she asked. She hadn't meant to bark, but Jobe simply pointed to the set of bags now sitting inside the door.

She took hers into the bathroom—an enormous marble space with a tub large enough for four people—urinated, brushed her teeth, battled her way out of the formfitting dress that clung to her ribs, and slipped into the oversized T-shirt she'd brought with a sigh of real joy. Minty-mouthed and comfortable, this was the best she'd felt in days.

But she had to leave this room. With a feeling of dread she

turned the knob and entered the room where Jobe was lying on top of the bed, next to the very spot where she'd been sleeping. Carmen thought back to Rory's apartment, the thrilling pull of his bed, the beat of the music, the way she'd felt lost in something dark and velvety and deep. Right now everything was flat, static, still. For just a second, she panicked. She thought she might actually begin to scream.

"Are you coming to bed?" he asked from the grayness.

She listened hard but could not hear longing. "Yes," she said as matter-of-factly as she could muster. And she made herself cross the room, climb the stool. Because he was on the near side, she had to climb over him, and she did this awkwardly, almost kneeing him in the stomach by mistake. *Take my hand,* she willed him. *Turn over and kiss me. Please. Just do something.*

But he didn't. Jobe lay as still as a corpse and stared at the ceiling. Carmen would have made a little nest for herself and drifted off, but the nap earlier had left her wide awake. Finally, she couldn't stand it.

"It's our wedding night," she said.

"Yes."

"Do you even care?"

"I care very much." His tone was maddeningly professorial.

"So why don't you even touch me?"

There was a gap, filled with nothing. Then he said, "Because I'm never sure you want me to. Sometimes, when we start, you seem so" —he swallowed—"disgusted. It makes it hard for me to, you know. . ."

"So this is the answer? We're going to have a celibate marriage?"

"I don't know the answer, Carmen. That's what I'm trying to figure out."

Loneliness enveloped her then, a kind she'd never experienced before. It seemed that the rest of the world had simply vanished once they promised their lives to each other and this was her sentence: Decades of life lived in silence with a man made of wood and stone. Her mind raced. She could leave this room and wander out into the street in a T-shirt and no underwear to flag down a cab. Carmen envisioned lifting her arm, the shirt rising to expose her, the feel of the cracked vinyl seat under her bare bottom, the smell of gasoline and old fast food. It was a comforting vision. The only problem was she couldn't fathom where she would go.

Eventually Jobe fell asleep, his hands clasped to his chest, and she reached out to take them once. They were cold. She thought about waking him and encouraging him to get under the covers with her, where it was warm. But in the end, she didn't. She watched the clock turn from midnight to one, then two, then three a.m. And sometime after that, though she couldn't remember feeling tired, Carmen slept.

They made love, finally, on the second night—which came a surreal thirty-nine hours after the first, given their ten-hour flight into Florence.

Being in first class helped; the meal on china plates, the plump pillows, and the series of movies showing on a screen just two rows up. By the time they got to their hotel room—a square block nearly filled with a bed, unlike the luxurious suite where they'd not even touched—Carmen and Jobe fell into the bed, prickling with exhaustion, and rolled together without preamble. There was a good amount of fumbling and grunting and a workmanlike effort from Jobe. He got stiff immediately and worked himself into her the way you might wedge a matchbook into a window frame to keep it from rattling. Carmen lay under him, relieved and feeling the sort of mild pleasure she did when scratching a mosquito bite. Jobe shuddered for a long time after he came, as if the experience had hurt him and she stroked his chest—marveling at the hard bumps of bone—until he stopped.

That was the only time while they were in Florence. There were two full days at the Uffizi, but after the first morning, Jobe sat mostly on a bench reading a book while Carmen wandered. Their dinners were sedate. Surrounded by the florid sounds of shouted Italian, they ate mostly without speaking. They'd been together all day, what was there to discuss? And at night, in their room, he sat working at the desk while she read American magazines. Sometimes they shared a bottle of wine. On the third day, Jobe rented a car and they left the stinking, hot, teeming city for the seaside. Briefly, as they approached from the east, Carmen felt a glimmer of hope.

Riomaggiore was a town of colorful buildings, varied and stacked like a child's blocks, against the side of a jagged hill. Behind it, the Mediterranean sparkled. She and Jobe bumped along brick roads so increasingly narrow, Carmen held her breath each time they were about to pass another car.

Jobe parked precariously at the top of a ridge, in a sliver of a spot perched between the roadway and the drop-off into town. Carmen got out carefully. The rental office was tiny, occupied by three small, swarthy men. "You follow me," one of them said, after they'd each handed over their passports. And they did: down the winding path to a sidewalk lined with markets and trinket stores, past a building painted fuchsia, then up a dank set of stairs that turned three times. "Left at the lion," the man said, thumping his hand against a metal lion's head that protruded from a crumbling pillar. "Now right, when you see Coca-Cola," he said at the next turn, pointing to the overhead billboard with the familiar white and red.

Jobe and Carmen were panting by the time they reached the door marked 7. The man, easily forty-five, looked as placid as if he'd been sitting in a rocking chair. He placed the key on a dresser and left, and once again the newlyweds were alone.

"I suppose I should get the luggage," Jobe said.

"Ugh, carrying it all the way up here? That sounds brutal." Carmen thought for a moment. "How about we grab just what we need for tonight and leave the rest in the car?"

"Sure." He nearly smiled, and she realized it was the first time since their trip began that she'd actually seen his teeth—or remembered how they lit up his face. *I need to make this more fun*, Carmen thought as they descended. *Get him to laugh*.

They retrieved from their suitcases an odd assortment of toiletries, underwear, hiking shoes, and books, threw this into the emptiest of the six suitcases, and started off—Carmen in the lead, Jobe bumping along with the little stewardess-style case on wheels behind him.

"You follow me," Carmen said, twitching her hips at her new husband then looking back to be sure he'd noticed. He had. "Left at the lion." She slapped the cat's face too hard. "Ow!" she cried, pulling her hand back, and she actually heard Jobe chuckle. "I think he bit me," she said, even though this was going so far into cute territory, her inner voice was saying, *Oh, Christ.*

It was nearly evening now and for the first time since they'd arrived, a cool breeze washed over them. Carmen stopped on the stairs, in sight of the Coca-Cola sign, and tipped her head back as if to drink. "Mmm. That feels good."

"Should we walk a ways along the Cinque Terre?" Jobe asked. For this is why they had come; Olive and George had visited Liguria on their honeymoon and trekked the five cities (which Carmen found hard to imagine: stoic, red-faced George skipping like some goat herder's assistant down the rubbly path). It was Olive's dearest memory, however.

"Might as well. Then we can tell your mom next time we call home. It'll make her whole day."

Carmen had been referring to Olive only as "Jobe's mother" since the wedding, despite the complete reversal Olive had done, telling Carmen that morning that she should start using her first name. It had been a year of "Mrs. Garrett," no matter how close they'd become. She felt as if she were producing something unnatural when trying to make the word *Olive* come out of her mouth—like the character in a book she'd just read who was put under a spell by evil witches that made her spit out feathers and pins.

"Olive," Carmen said under her breath while lacing up her shoes. It helped, she found, to think about the food—green and black orbs in a dish—rather than the woman to whom the name applied.

"Ready?" Jobe was standing with the door open, looking out worriedly. "It looks like it may rain."

Carmen shrugged. They'd had a large lunch at two, as was the custom, so she was ready for a good, vigorous walk. "Who cares? So we'll get wet?" And she darted ahead of him out the door.

Once down on the main thoroughfare, it wasn't hard to find the way. A sign with an arrow pointing left directed them through a tunnel and once they'd reached the other side, they were on the path. The first leg of the journey was easy, a nursery school stroll. It was called *Via Dell'Amore* or The Love Walk another sign told them—no doubt, Carmen thought, because this was such a cliché of a honeymoon spot. But she and Jobe walked the distance more like an old married couple, without speaking. They came to the town of Manarola, passed through, and trudged on, listening to the Mediterranean's gentle waves.

Right before Corniglia, the next town, began a series of staircases that stretched up as far as Carmen could see. "There are 377 steps, thirty-three separate flights," Jobe said, reading from a sign at the foot. "What do you want to do?"

She faced him squarely. "What do *you* want to do?"

Go back to the room and take your clothes off, lick your sweaty body all over while you listen to the water. She stared. That had been her imagination. "Let's go," Jobe actually said.

They started climbing, sprinting up the first half dozen staircases then slowing down. By the midpoint they were both breathing heavily, but Carmen was still managing to keep up with Jobe, whose legs were easily five inches longer. Toward the top, both were red faced and it had begun to drizzle. By the time they reached the center of Corniglia—a tilted little storybook town—the rain was steady.

"We should probably head back," Jobe said, looking around as if this wetness were something foreign and completely unexpected. Possibly dangerous.

Carmen hesitated. It was exhausting trying to draw him out, make him laugh. She dreaded having the entire evening ahead: dinner in one of Riomaggiore's cramped little cafés, then hours in their room with nothing to talk about and nowhere to go. That endless dance they did where she waited for him to touch her, both wishing he would and hoping he wouldn't. "C'mon, let's do one more," she said. "We can make it four-fifths of the way, to Vernazza. Besides, I love that name. Ver-naaa-zaaa. It'll be fun."

It was not fun. Jobe never objected, but less than half an hour passed before Carmen said, "I'm sorry, I think you were right. Maybe we should turn around now." The drizzle had turned to a steady, drenching rain, not cold but unusually thick. And the dark was settling around them. Carefully, as if they were in danger of losing their place, Carmen and Jobe pivoted in the dirt and started walking back.

Whereas they had started out in a pack of tourists, the two were now utterly—permanently, it felt to Carmen—alone. Both the storm and the night deepened. They had to slow their pace, peering at their own feet simply to find the path. "Do you want to stop, try to get some shelter under there?" Jobe asked her, pointing at a bent tree.

Carmen shook her head then realized he probably couldn't see her. She was crying but it didn't matter; the rain kept washing her tears away. "Let's just keep going," she said. "We can find a place to stop in Corniglia and wait this out." But as they inched on, she recalled the closed-looking little town and wondered what they'd find. An old church, perhaps? A pub with a one-eyed bartender? The cottage of some *strega* who would punish her further by making her eat feathers and pins?

Time passed. It seemed like hours and Carmen would have sworn that night had intensified beyond any degree of darkness she'd ever experienced before. She no longer tried to hide the fact that she was sobbing and bumped up against Jobe, hoping he would put his arm around her, say something comforting, even just take her hand. "Are you okay?" he asked, speaking loudly because it was somehow harder to hear in the gloom.

"How much farther do you think?" she asked.

"I don't know. Let me look." Jobe stepped away, two long

strides, and climbed onto a rock at the edge of the path. He raised one hand to clear the rainwater from his eyes. "I think I see . . ."

Carmen saw him begin to fall, like a tree that had been sawed through. His feet went out from under him on the slippery surface and Jobe tipped forward, one hand reaching back in the air to grasp nothing, pitching headfirst toward the black water below. It was a long way, maybe a quarter of a mile. Or half. Who was she to say?

In a flash, Carmen saw the bed in which they'd laid the night of their wedding. She felt again the terrible loneliness of being trapped there. She recalled her dread at going back to their room in Riomaggiore, her dread that all of life would feel exactly like this. And she saw how easy the answer was: All of that misery could be averted if Jobe were to fall.

She didn't have time to consider her part in things, whether there were actions that were right and others that were wrong. These were only facts that came to her. A situation had presented itself—miraculously—that would solve all the problems she faced, and without her having to make her feelings clear.

It couldn't have lasted more than a second, but Carmen had a feeling of prescience and certainty unlike anything she'd ever experienced before. Surely this was no coincidence. It was being shown to her, presented with everything but voice-over, and she now knew the truth: Jobe would have to die for this awful mistake to be undone.

She saw it all unfold in her mind, scene by scene. At the same exact time she leapt forward and grabbed his outstretched hand.

AUGUST 2007

Carmen stared as the nurse, a hefty middle-aged black woman, slid the little weight left and left and left again on the beam of the scale.

"One twenty-five," she said.

Carmen stepped off the platform and reminded herself to breathe evenly. It helped with the vertigo. "Finally, after all these years, my driver's license is right."

"Sounds good to me. I'd kill to be 125." The woman flipped through her records. "Where did you start?" She scanned, pretty brown eyes darting all over the page. "Okay, I guess that's not so good: eleven pounds in two weeks. Are you really sick? Lots of puking?"

Carmen shook her head. "Only twice. But everything tastes terrible—dead, kind of—and I'm just incredibly . . ." They were still standing in the hallway; she glanced around to see who was listening. "Constipated. It's been something like eight days since I, you know, went."

"Yeah, lots of women have that." The nurse sighed as if to say it's not the dying that's so bad, it's the not being able to shit. "That's because of the anti-emetics. They stop everything coming out, doesn't matter which end."

"Makes it hard to eat," Carmen confided. "You think about everything just sitting there. In your stomach. Rotting. Like garbage." *Like cancer*. She didn't say that part, but the thought hung there.

The exam room was chilly. Once the nurse had taken her blood pressure and temperature and left with a promise that Dr. Woo would be in soon, Carmen got up to look in the mirror over the sink. She hadn't weighed 125 since the year she met Jobe. She remembered her body back then, how sleek and limber it had felt. Now her abdomen was rock-hard and stuffed; she was so tired she sometimes slept entire days away. But when she raised her arms in the sleeveless top she wore, they looked youthful and slender. Her collarbones were prominent—on display like some finely crafted musical instrument—the skin over her cheekbones hauntingly thin and blue. Her hair, cruelly, had never looked better. It was plush and full around her lean face. So far cancer had given her back five years, at least to the naked eye.

Perhaps, she consoled herself, this is why Michael had barely reacted to the news. She and Olive had been waiting for him when he came home from school a couple of days before, sitting around the table in the kitchen, trying to pretend they were simply meeting over coffee.

"Have a seat," Olive said the moment his backpack hit the floor. "It's been ages since I've heard about school."

Carmen had fixed Michael a snack while they talked—a self-consciously ornate arrangement of crackers and cheese on a plate—then sat and picked up her cold prop of a cup. "There's something I need to tell you," she'd begun. "I went to the doctor the other day . . ." Then she'd watched his swarthy man-child face closely as she said the word *cancer*. Across the table, Carmen could feel Olive tightening, as if girding herself. But there had been no great tsunami of grief.

"Are you going to the hospital?" Michael had asked. "Will I have to stay with Grandma?" He'd chewed, eating the cheese and the crackers separately. Only at the end, after his food was gone and Olive had risen to get him some juice, did Michael look at Carmen closely. He peered at her in a way that reminded her of Antonio, when he suddenly focused his attention after a long spate of work or drunkenness.

"Are you alright, Mom?" he'd asked in an eerily old voice. Behind him, there was a shimmer: tall like a weather front, darkness filled with stars. Then it was gone, and Olive was on her way back to the table with a bright red glass of Cran-Apple juice. Carmen swallowed, caught between the truth and the right answer.

"I'm okay," she'd finally said.

Now there was a knock and almost simultaneously the door began to open. "Everything all set in here?" Dr. Woo called. Carmen dropped her arms and jumped away from the mirror, hopping up on the exam table where she belonged. This was the promptest doctor she had ever met.

He shook her hand, sat on his stool, put his hands on his thighs, and frowned. "How's the tummy?" he asked.

"Bearable," she said.

"Good, good." Woo smiled broadly. "For twenty years, I heard more about nausea than about cancer. It was the worst part. Now . . ." He held up his hands like a magician who'd just performed a trick. "In most cases. Gone."

"I'm, uh." She looked down at her swinging feet. "Really constipated."

"I see that." For a moment, Carmen thought he meant he could tell by looking at her. Then she glanced up and saw him reading her chart. "A little milk of magnesia might help with that."

"Seriously? I should just pick it up at the CVS? That's it?"

The doctor shrugged. "As cancer patients go, Mrs. Garrett, you're a dream. No excessive vomiting. No signs of anemia. Healthy in every other way. With you, I don't worry so much about tolerating the chemo. Though keep in mind, you're still in the honeymoon stage."

"*This* is my honeymoon?"

"Recovery tends to get harder with each successive treatment. There are more minor symptoms. Heartburn, hair loss. I want you to call me immediately if you become very dizzy or light-headed. We'll get you in here for a blood test. Otherwise, everything looks very good."

He stood. That was it? He was done advising her, leaving her to fight through the thicket of cancer and life and work and kids all by herself? She needed to ask something, find out something more. "You said with me you don't worry so much about the chemo. What do you worry about?"

Woo was standing, readying himself to go. He was a regal-looking man from this angle, Carmen thought. Small but sober. A little warriorlike in his white coat. "Youth, Mrs. Garrett. It's our greatest challenge here." He looked at the door—a little longingly, she thought—but sat back down. "Studies show the number of years between recurrence grows increasingly larger with age. This has nothing to do with you in particular, of course, but on average a woman in her early forties, like yourself, is more likely to present with another tumor within five years than, say, a woman of sixty-five. It's not a perfect predictor, and there are other factors."

He leaned back, resigned to staying now. "Years ago, I had a forty-five-year-old patient with only one, single breast cancer event." He held up his forefinger. One. It was the only integer, Jobe had once told her, that was neither prime nor not prime. "She's nearing sixty now and her biggest health concern seems to be arthritis. But in most cases, youth makes me cautious. The body is still fast; it grows things well. Hair, nails. New skin where it is cut or burned." The doctor wiggled his fingers, the way someone might simulate sprouting plants. "Fetuses—whole living human beings—in a woman so young as yourself."

Carmen saw again her own image: rosy, unlined cheeks and thick, long hair. The phantom baby that could be but was not—thank God—growing inside her.

"Mathematically, I would prefer your chances if you were ten years older, which is why I insist on pursuing every treatment. At the same time, you should not feel burdened by statistics. I as your doctor must take them into account. You, however . . ." He shook his head.

"Remember. *Groups* are consistent; individuals are random. You are but one point in a set of millions. Your course is not determined."

He rose to leave again, but more slowly this time. "Have I answered your question?"

"Yes, thank you," Carmen said quietly.

After he was gone, she gathered her things and let herself out. There were people in the halls of the clinic but they floated past Carmen, like faces in a dream. "One point in a set of millions." Through the dark concrete parking ramp and as she drove out into the glinting sun, the phrase echoed like a far-off but persistent series of bells in her head.

Carmen was pawing through a box of papers when Danny showed up early, looking as nervous as if he were there to take her daughter out on a date.

"Prompt today, aren't we?" she said, as she let him in. "Where's the guy who used to keep me waiting twenty minutes in a hotel room?"

He blinked rapidly, looking as if he didn't know whether to storm out or laugh. "I thought it was important. Kid just lost his father, his world keeps getting turned around. Showing up on time seemed like the least I could do."

"That's sweet." She moved in and put her cheek briefly against his neck. It was warm. "I'm sorry. It was a stupid thing to say. This just feels a little strange, you know, you being here."

"It feels strange to me too." She backed away, in case Michael heard them and came out. Danny looked around him. "This isn't what I imagined."

"But, wait . . ." Carmen pictured the cockier version of Danny, standing across this very room, chatting with Jobe's brother Will. "You've been here before. After the funeral."

"I suppose." Danny stared soberly, as if he were just now mourning Jobe. "But it seems different now. Or, I don't know. Maybe I wasn't paying attention back then."

There was a pause. "So," Carmen broke in, "what did you imagine?"

"Something haughtier, I guess. More . . ."

"Expensive looking?" He nodded and she laughed. "That would be my mother-in-law's house, plenty of ancient Chinese vases and Persian rugs. I'll have to wangle a dinner invitation for you." She stopped to consider Danny and Olive together at a table. She couldn't picture them in the dining room but could see them together in the kitchen— at the table where she and Olive had eaten grilled cheese sandwiches on Carmen's first night in Baltimore—using their fingers to pluck bites from the same roasted chicken.

"Hello?" Danny's voice and questioning tone interrupted her fantasy.

Carmen turned and there was Luca, planted in the doorway, watching Danny. "Hey, sweetheart." She cleared her throat. This was ridiculously awkward. "You remember Danny, from the funeral?"

Luca didn't respond one way or another but continued to stare, slit-eyed, exactly the way she'd taught him not to when he was a child. It didn't seem right to correct him now that he was an adult; that would be humiliating. But why did Luca have to backslide in front of Danny, whom she'd tried to keep separate from every messy, imperfect detail in her life?

"Luca. Hi. It's good to see you." Danny stepped forward, crossing between Carmen and her son, to extend his hand.

Please shake his hand, Carmen willed Luca silently. Whether in response to this or not, he did.

"Are you here for dinner?" Luca raised his nose as if to sniff the air. No, there was nothing cooking.

"I'm here to take your brother to a ballgame, actually," Danny said.

"Grandma and I are . . ." Carmen jumped in to reassure Luca that she and Olive were taking him out, as well. Forever trying to make up for his disability with movies and treats.

"Michael's afraid," Luca told Danny, interrupting Carmen. "He cries all night." Luca made two fists and twisted them in front of his eyes in a comic book demonstration.

Danny was silent for a moment, looking Luca over. Once again, as she had in the chapel, Carmen saw how similar they were in size. These two men looked each other straight in the eyes.

"What do you think he needs?" She'd never heard Danny's voice so gentle, certainly not with her. "What should I do for your brother?"

"Did you know our dad?" Luca asked.

Danny shook his head. "I'm sorry, I didn't. I think I would have liked him."

"He was very *smart*." *Thmaart*. Luca said this word reverently, which pained Carmen to the point that she almost missed what came next. "It's like God died."

It was a simile. This was the first thing Carmen noted. Once, a rather dim, young speech therapist had listed for her the things Luca could and could not learn to do. She would be able to help Luca eliminate the thickness from his pronunciation, the woman said, but he was incapable of grasping higher-level language skills, such as metaphor and simile. Carmen grinned. The woman had been wrong on both points.

Then, she heard the actual words her son had used. *It's like God died.* For a moment, the world around her felt turned inside-out in the way of a reversed glove that looks right except for the seam. Then it flipped back.

She blinked and glanced at Danny who wore a questioning expression, as if asking her, *What do I say now?* Carmen shrugged. But she stepped forward and put her arm around Luca, drawing in his warmth. "Why don't you go find your brother, then get ready for dinner?" she said. "Grandma will be here soon."

"Okay." Luca turned to go, then seemed to remember something. He turned and stuck his hand out again. "It was nice to meet you." Words that long-ago speech therapist had taught him. She had—despite her prejudices—done a few things right.

"You, too," Danny answered. "And I'm really sorry about your dad."

After Luca left, everything was different. Her world had intruded completely and Carmen knew that she and Danny could never go back to the thrilling, secretive relationship they'd had before. So she might as well go for broke. "Got a couple minutes before you have to go?" she asked. "I'd like to show you something, get your opinion."

Danny checked his watch. "Sure. I did leave the house way too early. Mega was . . ." He caught himself, still trying to adhere to the old rules. "Anyway, I've got time. What is it?"

"Come." Carmen led him down the hall and into the dining room, where she'd already spread two boxes' worth of papers across the surface of the table. "I'm trying to organize these. Figure out what's important. But it's like trying to glue together a bowl after it's been shattered. Every piece looks similar. At least to me."

Danny raised his reading glasses and picked up the sheet nearest his hand, squinting at the tiny penciled numbers. He put it down and picked up another, circling the table. After repeating this a half dozen times, he looked up at Carmen and pulled off his spectacles, letting them drop to his chest. "Maybe he really was God."

Michael must have heard their voices. He edged into the room, shy, dressed in jeans and a Baltimore Orioles shirt and hat.

"Hey, sweetheart." Carmen worked to sound casual. "This is Danny, your escort for the evening." *That was a stupid old mom thing to say*, she thought immediately. Danny probably was looking at her now as a doddering, inane housewife. But there was no way she could think of to sex up her image now, in front of her son.

Thank God they'd given up on their plan to stage an accidental getting-to-know-you breakfast. Originally, they'd been going to meet at Sunrise Deli, pretending to bump into each other while she was out on a Sunday morning with Michael. But Mega had seemed to catch on and suddenly she needed Danny to help her plant some rosebushes that weekend; she'd never, in their eight years of marriage, cultivated a single other thing, Danny swore.

It was fine, Carmen told him. She'd guessed wrong about Michael at every turn, assuming he'd crumble when she disclosed her cancer only to sit down with him and Olive and have him take the news with prosaic calm. *Yes, parents do this; they get cancer.* It was just another outlandish thing about them, like the way they insisted you clean your room every week even though no one was going to see it but you.

"I'd made such a big deal of it, asking Olive to be there with me." Carmen laughed, re-creating the conversation for Danny so it was absurdly light. "But Michael was just like, 'That's a bummer. Can I get back to MySpace now?' "

"Maybe this baseball game was a stupid idea." Danny had already bought the tickets from a coworker and Carmen thought she could hear disappointment in his voice. "He seems to be coping just fine."

Why did she do this? In order to preserve her stupid pride, she'd made Michael sound heartless.

"No," she said, serious now and telling the absolute truth. "He's coping just fine with my being sick but he's still heartbroken over Jobe. Michael is *like* me, but he was much closer to his father." She paused for a beat. "All the kids were."

"Michael," Danny said now and walked around the dining room table. "I'm Danny. Good to meet you."

For the second time that afternoon, Carmen watched her lover reach out to press his fingers and palm against the hand of one of Jobe's sons. Dust hung in the air, light shifting—raising shadows—between her and the two dark-haired forms. She remembered the night at the restaurant more than a year ago, Jobe's hand stretching out across the table, touching Danny's.

And again there was that image. The golden circles appearing, sinking, and dissolving, like ripples in a pond. Carmen felt buoyant, the room around her an aquarium in which her body bobbed.

"Paired prime ideals occur more often in commutative rings," Michael said, pronouncing each syllable with exaggerated care,

Carmen was jolted. "Excuse me?"

"Right there, it says that." Michael pointed to a random paper lying cockeyed on the table, where it was written complete with a question mark. "I think Dad did it."

She remembered Jobe's voice now, a reedy tenor. She'd always longed for him to be low and husky, more muscular sounding. Yet now, she found the memory of his oboe-hued words as soothing as a lullaby.

"Order is everywhere in mathematics," Jobe had told her. It was nighttime and they were sitting somewhere in moonlight—on a porch or under a blank black sky waiting for fireworks to begin. "It's the rule, the basic structure. But even within that ordered universe, there are random occurrences. Sparks." His hands had flickered in space when he said this, dancing. "Just like in life."

She was back at the dining room table, hunched over the piles of papers again, when Olive walked in.

Carmen craned her head to peer at the clock on the kitchen wall. "You're late! That's so unlike you. And just this afternoon, someone who's always running behind . . ." Carmen trailed off then, unable even to talk about Danny—the man for whom she'd once waited for an hour in a Super 8 Motel, checking her watch every few minutes, only to discover later he'd been waylaid by a surprise visit from his wife's parents—despite the fact that he was rapidly turning into a benign family friend.

"I know. I was, well, sleeping." Olive sat. Her hair, for the first time in Carmen's experience, was ruffled. And there was a pillow crease, thick and red among the wrinkles on Olive's cheek. "I'm sorry, dear. I don't know what came over me this afternoon. I was so tired I couldn't take another step, so I thought I'd lie down for a few moments. But when I woke up, hours had passed." She gazed at Carmen wonderingly, glassy-eyed. "And such dreams! It took me some time to get free of them."

"Are you alright?" Carmen asked, trying to keep the panic out of her voice. This of all things had never occurred to her, that Olive might become frail or sick. It was ridiculous that it hadn't; the woman was seventy-three. She'd been through the deaths of her husband and her son. "Here, you sit. Let me get you a glass of water. Or some wine?"

"Actually, dear, if you wouldn't mind. A little scotch over ice wouldn't hurt."

Carmen grinned. "No problem. I think I'll join you. Unemployment has its perks. Though we may have to call a cab to get to the restaurant."

Olive waved her hand—that gesture she seemed to have been born making. "What the hell?" she said, and Carmen gaped. Had her mother-in-law opened her mouth and begun barking it couldn't have come as more of a surprise. Then she laughed.

"You *are* in a strange mood."

"Yes." Olive pulled a compact and a hairbrush out of her purse and began straightening her silver curls. "You may as well bring the bottle."

It took Carmen several minutes to get everything together. Someone—Siena and Troy, no doubt—had emptied all the ice trays and stuck them back in the freezer without refilling them. So Carmen was left to chip shards out of the automatic icemaker they'd given up using because it created a discolored glaciery block. Finally, Carmen returned to the dining room carrying two glasses filled with yellowish ice and the Glenlivet from Jobe's study. It was as if she and Olive had simply switched places; now the older woman was bent over the papers that Carmen had been studying, shaking her head and muttering to herself as she leafed through.

"Oh, thank God," Olive said when she saw Carmen. "I'm going to need to drink if I want to understand any of this."

"Believe me, there isn't enough scotch in all of Edinburgh." Carmen set the glasses down and poured a couple inches into each. "I've been going through these all day. I had this friend of mine . . ." She grew warm, but handed Olive her drink and went on. "He's a librarian and used to deciphering things, but he couldn't understand any of this. He said from what he's read, Jobe was working in an area no one else understands."

"No offense intended to your friend, dear, but I think it might be better to have a mathematician go through them."

Carmen's cheeks burned in earnest. She turned to the sideboard to refill her drink. "I thought of that," she said, facing the mirror on the wall. Her eyes were huge in her face, her hair lustrous and longer than it had been in years. She looked—for this brief moment—the way she had during that trip to New York with Olive more than twenty years before. "But what's to stop that person from saying there's nothing here, then taking all the work Jobe did and stealing it?" Swiveling, she tipped the bottle over Olive's glass. "Maybe I've just watched too much *Law & Order*, but it seems like a risk. Besides, I was looking for something math geeks wouldn't necessarily pick up on."

"That being?" Olive tilted back in her chair, looking uncharacteristically off-balance. What was happening to the people in Carmen's life? Danny becoming responsible, Olive giddy and disheveled.

"It was something the doctor said to me today about general patterns and randomness. Jobe spent his life on this problem: trying to prove that prime numbers get *generally* farther apart as the numbers go up, but there are exceptions—points where the primes contract—that are impossible to predict."

There was a beat of pure silence. "I had no idea you knew so much about Jobe's work," Olive said. She sounded either young or tearful or drunken. Maybe all three.

"Neither did I, to be honest." Carmen put her glass to her cheeks, one and then the other. Something had happened to her. She was pulsing with heat. "I thought it was all beyond me. I talked to him about it but only, you know, that way you do when you're married. Listening because it was his life. Never really trying to decipher anything. Now, I wish I'd paid more attention."

"What did the doctor say?"

Carmen shook her head. The scotch was in her mouth, reminding her of a night—another lifetime—back when everything had been truly random. Nothing was yet determined. Everything could change.

"Nothing, really. The chemo is going to get harder. I'm going to lose all my hair, get sicker, possibly anemic." Carmen took another drink, the whisky's resinous flavor almost erasing the aluminum she'd been tasting nonstop for weeks. "He's doing this because I'm young and statistics show women under fifty have more recurrences. But I should-n't give up hope, because I'm an individual. A unique point." She held up her forefinger, just as Dr. Woo had done, and stared at it, willing away the tears that rose. "I know, I know. I'm grasping at straws."

"No, dear. I don't believe you are," came Olive's prim voice. Carmen blinked. Her mother-in-law, too, had morphed back into that neat, patrician wedding planner from 1986. What was happening to the two of them? It was like time travel. "All signs tell me you're grasping for exactly the right things."

"What *signs*?"

"Luca!"

Carmen thought at first this was an answer. But Olive's voice was full of the heedless warmth she reserved only for her grandchil-dren. Carmen turned to see Luca walking in to greet his grandmother. On the way, he swept his hand—the right, which he had used last to grasp Danny's—along the rounded line of Carmen's cheek.

Yes, signs, pay attention, Mom, he seemed to say with his chor-tle. Then he bent to hug Olive who raised her arms and seemed to levitate up, out of her chair.

An image rose in Carmen's head and for once she didn't run away from it. Rather, she moved in and watched her earlier self half-reclining in a hospital bed on a winter day twenty-one years before. Pallid and spent, awash with shame and a sense of failure, young Car-men extended a blunt-faced infant to Olive. And her mother-in-law took an involuntary step back.

It was only a single moment, and Olive had recovered quickly. Then she'd taken Luca carefully in her hands and up into her arms. "Poor baby," she'd said, swinging him gently, her grip on him ap-pearing to grow stronger as she swayed from side to side. "Poor, poor baby." But Luca had only stared and yawned at her, as if bored.

Then Jobe had walked into the room. So young! Carmen could see that now. Olive's own least beautiful child, and secretly her favorite. "You'll find a way to make this child happy," Olive said to him. It was an order, more than a prediction. Jobe had nodded vigorously as if to say, "Of course," though Carmen could see tears gathering in his eyes. And she'd wished, for one fleeting speck of time, that he was standing close enough for her to take his hand.

"I had this very strange dream today," Olive said, once they were seated in the little Turkish restaurant that was Luca's favorite. Lamps swung around them, twinkling light reflecting off the high cherry wood booths like stars in a forest.

"Was it about Dad?" Luca asked. The menu sat unopened under his folded hands. He had it memorized; there was no need to struggle through the printed words. "Did he tell you?"

"Yes, in fact, he did, dear," Olive said. "So what do you feel like eating tonight?"

Carmen looked from one to the other, their faces—both—like cherubim in the rosy glow.

"Tell you what?" Carmen demanded. She didn't believe any of this, yet she was panicked. If Jobe were watching, if he knew about Danny, if he were able to communicate with Olive and her children, there was no end to the damage that would be done. "What did Dad tell you?"

"He solved the puzzle." Luca rested his chin flatly in the palm of his hand.

"What puzzle?" They were looking at her as if she was missing something obvious. "You mean Riemann? That puzzle?"

Both heads bobbed up and down—Luca's and Olive's—moving in and out of the light.

"I suspect it's somewhere in those papers you were looking at earlier," Olive said as she studied the menu. "I was so delighted when I got to the house and saw you already had them. Though Jobe seemed sure you'd take care of it somehow." Then she turned to Luca. "Will you eat some spanakopita if I get it? The piece they serve is always too big for me."

Carmen was envisioning herself stirring Jobe's documents, holding glasses full of liquid precariously over them, dropping the page that held his one, crucial, victorious formula and letting it slide under the table. She saw herself walking through the dining room later, spotting the dirty, walked-on piece of paper, bending and crumpling it. Throwing it away.

She blinked rapidly. Clearly, the spirit of Riemann's cleaning woman was haunting her. Carmen wondered what retribution had been like in the 1860s. Had that woman been mutilated and pumped full of poisons for her sins, too?

A waitress in a long white apron and pinned-on scrap of veil hat appeared. "Can I get you something to start?" she asked.

Carmen had never noticed before how two hundred years ago this place was. Looking around at the dark tables, chained lanterns, and hunched diners' backs, she counted forward: thirty-eight hours until her next chemo session. Time expanded and contracted. Centuries of research, twenty-one years of marriage, four meals, another drink. She'd paused too long since the question; everyone was staring.

"Give us a flask of the house red and some stuffed grape leaves," she said too brusquely, but Olive nodded. "Luca, how about you?"

"Seltzer," he said, struggling visibly to form first the t and then the z.

Once the waitress had gone, Carmen turned back to her son. "So your dad came to you in a dream and told you he'd solved Riemann? And to you, too?" She glanced at Olive, a well-dressed, upright woman gazing into the distance. What was happening? Her mother-in-law had turned into a less crone-y version of Nancy Reagan. She herself was having some kind of Ebenezer Scrooge moment, seeing ghosts of mathematicians past. Her son was talking to his dead father. Siena was right. Their entire family had gone nuts.

"He didn't *tell* me," Luca said. "He *showed* me."

"So could you solve it now if I gave you a paper and pen?" She actually began reaching for her purse, but Luca simply rolled his eyes.

"It's not like that, Mom."

"How is it, then?" she asked gently.

Luca fell silent—this was more than he usually spoke in two days—and looked at Olive, whose eyes were shining like a child's.

"I thought . . ." Olive began, then stopped and started again. "You know me, dear. I'm not like this. Some guilt-ridden old woman so destroyed by her son's death she begins imagining things. That's what I told myself at first."

"Guilt-ridden?"

Olive breathed deeply through her nose and scanned Luca from his shoes to the top of his head. It was as if she was doing an inventory, and when she was done, she turned full-on to Carmen. "For lying to my son and pushing your marriage forward, even after that young man came to the door with your driver's license. That very handsome"—Olive shifted her eyes but only slightly, so she was gazing at an empty spot in the air—"very . . . confident young man."

Carmen felt squirmy inside, and as cornered as she had that night long ago when Olive caught her coming out of Jobe's room. No, more. She looked pointedly at Luca, wondering what had made Olive decide to have this conversation now, in this place, in front of him. But Olive ignored her.

"What was his name?" she asked, not unpleasantly but with the air of an old lady simply trying to grasp a memory. "Robert? Oren . . . ?"

Carmen relented. "Rory," she said. And as she did, she could see him standing on the Garretts' wide brick porch, holding the little, plastic card, smiling down at the well-formed middle-aged woman who answered the door. Carmen wouldn't have been surprised if Rory had made a pass at Olive. At the very least, he'd have turned on the charm, made her understand what kind of man he was.

"So he returned my driver's license, and you put it on my bedside table without saying a thing. Why?" Carmen stared directly at her mother-in-law now. It was time. To her right, Luca seemed to preside —a benevolent presence neither disturbed by the conversation, nor judgmental about it. Only witnessing.

"Because." Slowly, Olive refocused and held up her end of the stare. "I didn't want to know anything. Oh, not that I would have said so at the time. I think, back then, I just convinced myself that it was nothing. That what the boy said was true."

"Which was? What did he say?"

"That you'd stopped in to his office to talk about rental properties. He was checking your credit. You'd left it behind." Olive's voice was robotic.

"So?" Carmen challenged her, senselessly. Suddenly, without knowing why, she'd switched sides. "You thought I was trying to leave Jobe and move out on my own. Get an apartment without him."

"Yes, I thought you were considering it. Or rather . . ." There was a flash of pain on Olive's face and Carmen felt remorse. But before she could reach out, Luca's hand crept somehow more quickly than hers to touch his grandmother's hand. "I told myself this was what had happened: You were uncertain—scared—that you thought briefly about leaving then realized how much you loved my son. Only . . . there was a part of me . . ." She shook her head. "That Rory was a very handsome young man," she repeated after several seconds had passed. "Exactly the sort of boy I could imagine you dating, going to parties with, dancing with. . . ." Here, thankfully, she stopped. But the next logical item on the list hung silently in the air.

Olive fixed her eyes on Carmen now, but gently. She was asking.

"I need to go to the bathroom," Luca muttered and rose, stumbling a little in his haste to get away from the table. It was exactly the sort of self-conscious thing any young man would do if his mother and grandmother began discussing an old affair. And Carmen had never loved him more than she did at this very moment.

"Did you?" Olive asked once Luca was out of earshot.

"Did I what? Date him? I don't think you could call it that.

Dance with him? Not that I recall. Sleep with him? Yes, once." She was looking down at the table. Some time during her response the waitress had come, set down the drinks and grape leaves, then departed again without taking their dinner order. Carmen didn't care. As far as she was concerned, the entire restaurant could hear. The only thing that mattered was what Olive thought. And—if he was truly eavesdropping on them from some dust beam—Jobe, as well.

"Then why did you marry my son?" Olive's voice was stiff and cold, exactly as Carmen had been afraid it would be on the day she found out the truth. "Why didn't you just fornicate with the cute, young real estate agent and leave Jobe alone?"

It was like being slapped. But Carmen deserved it; she'd deserved it for more than two decades. "Because Rory wasn't nice to me," she said softly. "Jobe was."

"Even though he knew."

Luca had emerged from the men's room and was making his way across the restaurant. Carmen didn't have much time. "What do you mean by that?" She picked up the wine flask and filled their glasses, leaning closer to hiss at Olive. "Are you saying Jobe knew about Rory?"

Olive nodded regally. "He told me you were seeing someone else, that you didn't love him, and I . . ." She picked up her glass and stared at it, Carmen watching and recalling the night they first met: this woman holding a glass of wine while ambivalence, like two opposing weather fronts, rose inside her. She had been living perpetually with this feeling, Carmen noted, ever since that day.

"I lied," Olive continued without taking a drink. "I told my son that he was wrong. I knew what it was like to be a young woman in love, and the things you were doing were normal. Your affection for him would grow as you became more confident. I told him"—Luca was, at most, two tables away now—"to be patient, believe in himself, go ahead with the marriage. Because he deserved a wife like you."

Luca pulled out his chair, sat, picked up a grape leaf.

"We always want what's best for our children," Olive said. Her tone had changed, becoming airy for Luca's sake. "We're just not always clear on what the best thing is."

The next day, Carmen walked into a discount salon and asked for a haircut. She had never been in one before: It was bright white with colored curtains hanging between the chairs. Packed with people. She had to wait twenty-five minutes before someone called her name, but at least here the magazines were plentiful and up to date.

"I'm Lori," said the girl who led her back across a floor strewn with hair clippings in every color. "So what are you thinking about today?"

"I want it all cut off," Carmen said. She put her purse on the floor and settled into the chair, her increasingly bony backside painful even against the cushioned seat. "Leave about a quarter-inch all the way around."

"Are you sure?" The girl squinted in the mirror. She was about twenty-three, with bright butterfly tattoos peaking out of her cleavage. So, some women put needles into their breasts on purpose. What a luxury to have that choice. "I mean, you have really nice hair and it's flattering with your face shape." The girl began using the edge of a comb and her long fingernails alternately, trying different arrangements, causing Carmen's scalp to tingle. "I could just layer it a little, give you a whole new look, without—"

"I have cancer," Carmen interrupted. The man in the adjoining chair turned to look at her. She hadn't considered how communal this place was. It had just seemed ridiculous to pay seventy-five dollars for someone to hack off her hair. Ridiculous to pay anything at all. "I'm going to lose it all anyway."

Abruptly the girl stopped what she'd been doing and raised her hands a couple of inches. "Oh, God, I'm really sorry," she said.

Then go back to doing what you were doing, Carmen wanted to tell her. But she didn't, of course. One more sensation lost—it hadn't occurred to Carmen previously. Without hair to run one's fingers through, a scalp massage was no good.

The hairdresser was all business now. She pulled a ruler out of her drawer, grasped Carmen's hair at the end and pulled it out long, then measured and squinted like a carpenter preparing to saw a length of wood. "Another inch and a half and I could give you the cut for free," she said. "Locks of Love. We'd donate it. But it has to be ten inches." With that she stuck the ruler back in her drawer, pulled a pair of scissors out of its blue disinfecting bath, and cut off a hank that dropped to the floor.

Carmen winced. "What's Locks of Love?" she asked.

"A benefit for kids with cancer, I think," the woman said, and her face reddened in the mirror. "They make wigs out of it. You know."

"Yes, I do know." The right half of Carmen's hair had been shorn off to the ear; her left still had long, puppy-tail curls. "I tried to get a wig made out of human hair. They said it would be six months and a thousand bucks."

The girl paused and shrugged. "I guess sick little kids get a better deal than sick grown-ups," she said simply.

"Yeah . . ." Carmen watched in the mirror as the girl circled her and began on the left. "I really hope they do."

Slender and shorn, Carmen looked like a punk teenager, or a war-protesting rock star. She compensated for this youthful appearance by draping herself in long shawls and scarves that she wound around her head. It was a hot summer, hotter even than the one when she'd arrived, but Carmen felt perpetually cool. Icy, almost.

"You're lucky," the woman in the adjoining chair told her at her next chemo session. She pulled out knitting needles with exactly half a flossy baby sweater—the breast panel and back, plus a single arm like a tiny elephant's trunk—and spread it neatly over a fleshy lap. "Chemo is like divorce: some women lose weight, others gain." She shook her head. "I'm a gainer and when you're fat, your head's really the only place you release heat—no way I was covering it up. Plus, there was the tamoxifen. Whoo, boy! Instant menopause. Hot flashes that just scorch you up inside."

Under any other circumstances, Carmen might have wished she could get away. But the woman's chatter distracted her while a young, dreadlocked nurse prepped her hand and slipped the needle in, then hung the amber bag.

"This is my third time through." Her knitting needles clicked and flashed in the overhead lights. "First time I was just forty-four, lost the right breast. That was seventeen years ago and I went through treatment *without* the anti-emetics. Now, there's a party. Spend so much time in the bathroom, you get to know every tile. But I *still* managed to gain about ten pounds. How?" The woman shook her head vigorously. "I have no f-ing idea. But there it was. Size eighteen when I was finished. Can you believe it? They say chemo does that to some of us really unlucky ones. Talk about adding insult."

Carmen waited, uncertain if the woman's monologue was done. Sure enough, she took a breath and swept in again. "I didn't do that breast reconstruction they talked to me about. I don't know why—too expensive, I was tired of doctors. It took a while to feel normal walking around all tilted to one side. I mean, really, I never really *did* get to feeling normal. But I got used to it. Then, a couple years later, howdy do. There's a big honkin' rock in the other breast and all I could think was, Okay, at least now I can get this body evened out."

The woman rested for a moment and actually closed her eyes. Carmen breathed. Maybe she was done.

"But you know what?" *Nope.* The woman's stream of words just kept flowing on. Carmen worked hard not to sigh. "My husband, Glen, he just never seemed to mind. Fat, de-formed." She pronounced it as if it were two words. "Barfing all day. He's not a man who does much, mind you: It wasn't like he was bringing me tea or checkin' the drains after my surgery. He went to work, like always. And then . . ." Her needles stopped moving and the woman looked at Carmen, more slowly than she had done anything else to this point. Her eyes were beautiful, socketed in a pouchy face but deep blue—the color of midnight stars. "He came home." She resumed her knitting, but slowly, concentrating on picking up each individual stitch. "I was going to these support groups with other women my age. Mind, this was back—remember?—I wasn't even forty-five. And there were all these young women there, pretty like you. One of 'em, her name was Sarah, I think. She told us her husband wouldn't touch her anymore."

Carmen could relate. Perhaps if she'd had this disease twenty years ago, she could have gone somewhere to talk about her problems with Jobe. *He won't make love to me. . . . Of course, I don't want him to.* It was a problem like a Möbius strip, with no beginning, no end, and no way out.

"She tried everything, Sarah did," the woman continued. "She had the reconstruction and let them stuff her with corpse parts." Now, Glen's beloved wife shuddered and stuck out her tongue. Even it, Carmen noted, was fat. "That's how they did it back then. For all I know, still do. They take those dead bodies that get donated to hospitals and pull off the skin, then sew it together into a fake boob. So Sarah, she's walking around with old parts of someone else inside her all so's her husband can pretend she's real, but you know what? It's not good enough for him. He wants a nipple. That's what she tells us. He doesn't like seeing her naked because she's got a scar where the nipple oughta be. And she told him she could get one tattooed but he doesn't like that either because it would be flat—you know, just like painted on. Wasn't good enough."

This time, when the woman closed her eyes Carmen waited anxiously for her to open them and begin speaking again. But she didn't. She continued reclining, hands holding the needles loosely but not moving.

"So what happened?" Carmen asked.

"What do you mean?" She lay like a heap of used clothing in the reclining chair, eyes still shut. Carmen missed the starlit blue.

"To Sarah?"

The woman shrugged. "He left her. Around Thanksgiving, if I remember right. She stopped coming after a while. Odds-wise, she's probably here." The woman looked around the room and Carmen actually believed, for a moment, that she might spot Sarah, with her cadaver-filled breast. "Or dead, I suppose."

Carmen flinched and the woman watched her coolly. "Sometimes," she admitted, "it's hard for me to work up a lot of love for people like you and Sarah. Been gorgeous all your life. Everything came easy. So something like this happens and you know how the rest of us feel." The woman adjusted herself in the chair. "But I'm sorry. That's not very Christian, is it?" There was an awkward pause. "You got a husband?" she asked.

"He died," Carmen said. "A few months ago. Cancer."

"You're shitting me." The woman's eyes opened wide; unfortunately, this eliminated their appeal. "Just goes to show, I don't know what I'm talking about. I guess you've suffered your share."

Not really, Carmen considered saying. *I didn't suffer nearly enough*. Every situation was a new opportunity to lie or tell the truth. "It was complicated," she said, finally. "We had some problems before he got sick, too. It wasn't . . . perfect."

The woman snorted. "I been married thirty-eight years, never is." The knitting went back into a bag and a can of Coke came out. She fished in and pulled out another one. "Want some?" she asked, and though Carmen couldn't remember the last time she'd drunk a soda, she nodded and was handed a warm can. Holding it away from her to open it, she got only a little spray of the sugary stuff.

"You stayed with him, 'til the end?"

Carmen nodded. This felt oddly intimate. She wasn't even sure she liked the woman and it was too late to ask her name.

"Counts for a lot in my book," Glen's wife said, leaning over to pull a shapeless, gray, acrylic sweater out of her endless bag and put it on. Apparently, her knitting was for other people. "I gotta get some sleep now, okay?" the woman said and turned away, as if it was Carmen who had been chattering away, asking questions and preventing her from getting her rest.

Time moved weirdly on the ward: so slow all morning that it seemed like a purgatory, everyone's sentence stretching infinitely on. But then there was always a flurry at the end, with people being disconnected in their turn, standing and testing their bodies for new symptoms, gathering their things. This was the treatment, Carmen had been told, that would change things: cause her hair to fall out, make her nauseated and anemic and weak. She had maybe—she checked her watch—twenty-seven golden hours left before the drugs kicked in.

"Carmen?" came a soft voice from above. She shifted and tried to focus. She hadn't been sleeping, exactly, just floating. Now she felt a broad hand first on her cheek, then her arm. "Since when do you drink Coke?" asked Danny, as he removed the sticky can from the grip of her hand.

"I, um . . ." Carmen's eyes darted over to the woman who slept curled in the chair like a homeless woman on the library steps. "I don't. Really. Someone just gave it to me."

Danny sat in the empty folding chair at her side, eyes wide. He looked around at the rising specters: one old man tottering out of his chemo chair and nearly crumpling, reaching out for a passing nurse who caught him just barely in time. Then Danny shifted his gaze back to her and looked at her as if she were a stranger, or a painting. "I meant to get here sooner. I thought I could sit with you."

She examined his face. Was this true? "It's okay. I told Olive to stay home this time. It turns out it's not during the chemo that I need . . ." She paused, unable to go on. "The hard part seems to be a couple days after."

"Good. That's good, I guess." Danny nodded. A blank-faced nurse was approaching. Any moment she'd be pulling a needle from Carmen's hand and reciting a list of instructions that included what to do in case of nosebleeds or explosive diarrhea. "So, I have some answers for you. I mean, potential answers. Some people we can consult to find out—you know—if Jobe was right."

"You're not making much sense. Are you talking about Rie-mann?" Carmen held her arm out straight as the nurse compressed the bag to drizzle the last few drops of poison down the clear tube, then slid the needle from her hand.

"Uh-huh." Moisture made Danny's face shiny at the hairline and along his cheeks. She had never before seen him sweat, other than during sex. "Did you know there's a math conference?"

"There are hundreds of them. Jobe used to fly all over, present-ing papers." As if prompted by these words, the nurse handed Carmen a sheet of instructions and moved on to wake the woman in the rum-pled sweater and pull out her IV.

"Yeah, but I mean . . ." He stopped and swallowed then changed course completely. "Car, I didn't even recognize you when I came in. You look so different, I was standing at the door for about ten min-utes trying to figure out if it was really you."

Carmen ran her hand over her bristly head, then down past the collarbones jutting out in points beneath her chin. What had felt sleek just hours before now seemed only sad. "Cancer will do that. It's going to get worse, you know."

But Danny went on, as if he hadn't heard her. "You look ethe-real, like . . . Tinkerbell."

"Tinkerbell?" She laughed, too loudly. No one else in the place was laughing. "Are you serious? Like, you're going to ask people to clap if they see me and my light will get stronger?"

Danny grinned and looked like himself for the first time since he'd arrived. "Something like that," he said.

All around them people were bending to retrieve their pouches and purses and bags full of drugs, shuffling toward the door. It was a death march. Standing, Carmen imagined them color-coded, the ones who would live and the ones who would die. Rose would be the indication of life, brown—the hue of curled, desiccated leaves— the mark of those for whom chemotherapy was pointless. She raised her own left hand. It was white, nearly translucent, fingers so slender she had to grip to hold onto her rings.

"Hey, Car, you ready to go?" Danny was behind her, touching her lightly at the waist.

"I need to get my medications from someone," Carmen said. Antinauseants, heartburn tabs, laxatives. Everything she did was focused on moving food from the top of her body through to the bottom.

"You wait here," Danny said. "I'll get them." And he walked off, leaving her with her hand still held up to the light.

Glen's wife was up, too. She stared at Carmen openly while she removed the fabric slippers she'd been wearing and wedged her feet into a pair of blocky brogans. Once she was done, she took the three steps over, wincing with each one. The shoes seemed to hurt her. Standing, she came up to Carmen's neck.

"So you stayed with the husband." The woman's breath was stale. "But you had a little bit on the side."

Carmen nodded.

The woman looked her over, piercing blue eyes moving from Carmen's face to her knees and back up in a loop. "Now, it looks like this man's gonna stick by you," she said with what could have been a sneer. "It all comes around." Then she nodded, picked up her bag, and was gone without another word.

Carmen felt like weeping. She turned her hand slowly, so instead of staring at the back, now she faced the palm. It was completely unlined, which she was sure had not been the case before. The back—where her knuckles lined up—felt cradled in midair.

"I've got them, Car." Danny was back, holding up a white, waxed bag that could, in another place and time, have contained a jam-filled croissant. "It's time."

"I know," she said. Then blinking, she took one more look. There were now creases and networks in her palm, like the seams of a stuffed bear, and from the fleshy part a hue. It was faint but distinct, like the light before dawn. A pale rosy glow.

* * *

"You okay to go for coffee or something?" Danny asked once they were outside the building.

It was 11:30 a.m., yet Carmen felt as if days had passed while she lay inside. She blinked in the hard sunshine and pulled her shawl tighter as if to block the rays. "I'm fine." She swallowed once to check. The metallic taste had not yet appeared; she probably should drink a cappuccino today. Enjoy it.

"Are *you* okay to go for coffee?" Carmen asked. "I mean, we never have."

Danny shifted. "Yeah, somehow that just doesn't seem like a big deal anymore. Things have changed."

"What exactly?" She faced him, this person whose body had been inside hers dozens of times, and understood even before he answered. It was not that Danny was different, or that his feelings were. It was she who had transformed. She'd shed her hair, a section of her left breast, and a percentage of her corporeal self. But in losing all this, she'd become someone new.

"For one thing." He pulled a pair of sunglasses out of his pocket. "I've decided I kind of like your husband."

"It's a little late for that." Carmen felt the glow intensify, a weird, pulsing calm.

"I'm not so sure." Danny threw his long hair over one shoulder and slipped the sunglasses on. "We're taking my car." He put one hand on Carmen's back and steered her toward the curb. "Don't worry. I'll bring you back for yours."

She thought of Rory, the long, shame-filled walk back to Olive's BMW. Her young self, still damp with sex and regret. Then Jobe's arms, bent like cricket wings, folding her in when she arrived home. That was the other Carmen. This one was unfamiliar but clean. She walked side by side with Danny—matching his steps exactly—and, for the first time in their relationship, climbed into the passenger side of his car.

"Kind of fancy for coffee, isn't it?" She peered up through the windshield as Danny parked outside a little bistro she'd never before seen. There were wrought-iron chairs on a patio made of wooden slats and a weathered sign that said, DOMAINE THÉRÈSE.

"You need to eat," Danny said.

"People keep doing this," Carmen murmured, mostly to herself. "It makes me feel like I'm dying."

"People keep doing what? Feeding you? Taking care of you? It doesn't mean you're dying. You're just stubborn and not used to letting anyone else be in charge." Danny turned and raised his sunglasses. "C'mon. We'll have a nice lunch and I'll tell you about this nice, young math wizard I've been corresponding with. Althea."

Carmen leaned back, lolling in her soft leather seat. The temperature in the car had risen since Danny stopped it—his face was turning umber in the heat—but to Carmen it was delicious, the trapped fire feeding her, seeping in through her skin. "Althea? Hmm. Yes, I do think I need to hear about her."

At least the hostess led them to a table on the patio. It had an umbrella but Carmen moved her chair so she was out of the shade and directly under the brilliant midday sun. In order to keep her scalp from burning, she wrapped a scarf around her head.

"I feel like I'm having lunch with a bedouin," Danny said, grinning. "Or Audrey Hepburn, traveling incognito after she helped the mobster in *Breakfast at Tiffany's*."

The food came and was light, inoffensive but bland, or perhaps this was due only to Carmen's hijacked senses. Her hunger was for none of the usual things—wine, food, sex—but for light, heat, music, and wind. She longed to go home and plunder Jobe's CD collection, to find a piece that was meandering and waterlike, filled with cellos and bassoons.

"Two cappuccinos," Danny said when the waiter came to clear their dishes. "I promised you coffee," he said to Carmen after the man was gone. "And, I promised you this." Leaning down, Danny drew from his briefcase a thin sheaf of papers. He handed the top sheet to Carmen. *Geometry of Riemann Surfaces: A Conference to Celebrate the Man*, it said. Below was a list of participants and Danny had circled two names: Althea Markos and Jobe Garrett.

"Did you know about this?" he asked. "It was held in Greece, earlier this summer. About two and a half months after Jobe died."

Carmen shook her head. "I didn't. But I wouldn't, necessarily. He went to these things. Sometimes he told me what they were about, other times all I knew were the dates he'd be gone."

"That's odd. Because he'd been planning to take you."

Carmen read the notice again, taking note of the location. "Anogia? I've never heard of it."

"It's on the island of Crete, mountainous, supposedly the birth-place of Zeus."

She shook her head, cheeks disappearing alternately into the fab-ric of her scarf. "You librarians know the most amazing facts."

"Don't give me so much credit. I looked it up on Wikipedia." Danny paused as the waiter set two bowl-sized cups in front of them. The sweet coffee-and-milk steam rose to Carmen's nose. This. She was hungry for this, too. "Jobe had booked a room for both of you, and a place for you at the dinner the first night of the conference."

"How do you know?" She held the cup with both hands and inhaled. This was possibly the very best smell she'd ever encountered in her life.

"I talked to the organizer."

"In Crete?" She imagined, for some reason, a crackling late-night call on an old-fashioned phone. Something from decades before that would cost three dollars a minute.

"Nope, Brooklyn," Danny said. Not even a different time zone. "He said Jobe was expected to present something very exciting at this conference." Danny grinned. "That was his word. I don't think I've ever used the word *exciting* to describe math."

"You have no idea. It was like a religion. When someone solved a proof there was always this Our Lady of Lourdes moment. Jobe would get completely awestruck." She flushed, warmth emanating from inside her for the first time all day, as she remembered her husband earnest and wild-eyed as he explained the Poincaré Conjecture, which one of his colleagues was close to solving. "I miss that. It was like, for just a minute, I could see this amazing, different world."

Danny went quiet and she wondered if she'd hurt his feelings. This was so tricky, reminiscing about her husband with her lover—who might, for that matter, no longer be her lover. In *this* different world of sparkling light and chemotherapy and public lunches she couldn't be sure.

"Althea says Jobe was very close to solving Riemann," Danny finally said. "I mean, she sent me an email that said that. *She's* in Greece. A grad student who was working with Jobe somehow—I haven't quite figured out the connection. But between work and Mega, I couldn't quite swing a phone conversation."

"Luca said that, too."

"What, that my wife won't let me make an overseas call?"

"No, about Riemann. Only, he said Jobe actually did solve it. He had a dream, Luca did. Olive, too."

The sun had shifted and Danny had put his sunglasses back on, so Carmen couldn't read his face. "They had dreams." His voice was deadpan. "Are you serious?"

"They were, dead serious," she answered. "So to speak. They're absolutely positive Jobe has been visiting them at night, speaking through their dreams. And they both say the solution to Riemann is somewhere in those cardboard boxes from his office."

"For Christ's sake, Carmen."

She stared into her empty cup. The dregs of her cappuccino—grounds and crusted foamed milk and bits of cinnamon—clung in a pattern she could not decipher. "I know. It's insane, and I've been trying to talk to Luca about—"

"Why didn't you tell me?" Danny had removed his glasses and was leaning forward intently. "I've been digging through what's in the public domain, talking to people who knew Jobe mostly by reputation. If you have the actual papers and the solution, that's easy. All we need to do is fax a copy of everything in those boxes to Greece!"

"Excuse me?"

"Okay, I'm not crazy. I don't believe your dead husband is appearing to his mother and your son. I mean, sure, it's a remote possibility."

"It is?"

He stopped and considered, his narrow eyes flickering as if he was silently counting something off. "Maybe. I don't know. I don't fuckin' know much of anything. But if there's even a chance that Jobe solved that problem and his work is just sitting in one of those boxes, we need to do something about it."

"You mean, we owe it to him?"

Danny sighed. "Maybe. We owe it to someone. Don't you think?"

She was finally thoroughly warm, which seemed backward. The wind had picked up. There was a thunderstorm coming. And the sun was fainter now, glimmering from behind a long, dark cloud.

Carmen loosened her scarf and removed it slowly from her head, setting it around her shoulders like a stole. "Yes," she said, sounding to her own ears like Olive, which pleased her. "Yes, I believe we do."

FEBRUARY 1987

Jobe moved into his office at Johns Hopkins three days after they returned from their honeymoon in Italy.

He was teaching three courses and starting a research project; so often, Jobe would be gone for twelve hours. And though she was relieved for the perpetual closeness of their honeymoon to be over, Carmen was at a loss. They had more than enough money; she didn't have to work. She'd already established there were no jobs for art history majors. If she were single, she'd probably be waitressing somewhere, looking at graduate schools, or joining one of those do-gooder organizations like the Peace Corps.

Olive had found them a home while they were gone: a rented brownstone in Charles Village that she said would be a perfect place to start out, while they looked for houses they might want to buy. She gave the couple veto power, of course.

"If you don't like it, just say so," Olive said, after giving Carmen and Jobe a tour while the rental agent looked helplessly on. "I have six or seven others on my list."

But what was not to like? It was a cozy, compact, wood-lined two-bedroom in a neighborhood filled with other faculty, interesting little shops, and an old-fashioned drugstore with a lunch counter on the corner. Olive and George were giving them a year's rent as a post-wedding gift. Carmen could spend some time furnishing the place, Olive said; it would be fun. And it was, for a couple of days. Carmen bought a twelve-piece sectional couch in forest green—paying a breathtaking $3,700 in cash, plus $250 for delivery—as well as a four-poster bed, a long teak dining table, and several brightly colored floor pillows.

But when Olive came over the first time and walked through, nodding too enthusiastically, Carmen very abruptly saw the apartment from a different point of view. It was hasty and unsophisticated—a mishmash of different styles and colors and tastes. She was ashamed, and confused. How was it that she, who had studied art and was able to deconstruct the elements of a great painting, was unable to synthesize a home? This could be an innate deficit, a sign that she was destined never to be a real part of any household but rather an outsider, poised to flee as she had been the entire time she stayed with the Garretts. The brownstone was one more mistake that she would have to leave behind she decided, as she followed her mother-in-law back down the winding stairs to the kitchen.

But once there, Olive looked around at the random dishes Carmen had picked up at yard sales and antique stores. "Oh, I *miss* this." She sighed and then laughed. "That just-starting-out phase where things aren't set yet and you get to try on anything and everything you like."

Now it was Carmen who nodded like some bobbing animal toy, because she didn't know what else to do. Tears came into her eyes as she turned toward the stove to heat water for tea. This was unlike her—to cry for absolutely no reason—but she felt desolate and confused. It was completely unclear whether Olive was humoring her or genuinely liked the strange, eclectic way Carmen had furnished the place. It was also unclear to her, under the circumstances, whose home it was, exactly.

No matter what the answer, the tasks of filling up the tiny place were quickly done and Carmen was left with an endless stretch of empty days before her. She went to the library one day, pretending to be that tattered and unencumbered recent college graduate who moved along a parallel track in some other continuum. Keeping her left hand jammed in the pocket of her jeans so he wouldn't see her sapphire and two-carat diamond ring, she asked the earnest, long-haired young man who sat behind the desk to help her research volunteer options. He did so, quietly but with an eagerness that let her know he was interested. Here she was, wearing a skimpy T-shirt over breasts that seemed to have grown larger overnight, a selfless person who wanted to help others.

She had never dreamed there were so many ways. Not only the Peace Corps but programs that would take her to Benin to work as a nurse's aide, or to the Bronx where she could tutor ten-year-olds who didn't yet know how to read. She could teach fine art in Japan any time she chose: There was a three-page list of postings for young American teachers in that country alone. There was a boat shipping out to Antarctica looking for hardy young people volunteering to tag penguins for an environmental study; the trip would take four months all told, the ad warned, and for most of that time participants would be unreachable by phone and completely out of touch.

Carmen sat at a table surrounded by the materials the young librarian had given her, bewildered by the fact that she had never thought of this before. Had she spent last spring signing up to mentor inner-city kids or save endangered animals, rather than cheating with Rory and looking halfheartedly for jobs, no one would have objected. George and Olive might have felt stung, but would have had to admit that the money they spent educating her was being put to good, philanthropic use. Jobe undoubtedly would have understood.

She sat, staring at the materials for most of the afternoon, finally rising—fifteen minutes before the library was to close—to ask if she could get some Xerox copies. There was a frumpy woman behind the desk now and she fussed irritably, glancing at the clock, sighing, and demanding that Carmen give her fifteen cents for each page. But as she waited for her copies, the male librarian returned. He was fine boned and blond with a sparse, jazzy little goatee.

"Hey, did you find everything you were looking for?" he asked, returning to his chair but not sitting. "I have a friend I could ask about the Peace Corps for you. She . . ."

He paused, staring down. Carmen followed his gaze. She had grown sloppy and stood with her left hand resting on the boxy computer top: the heavy white-gold band, sapphires like two deep eyes, and glittering diamond with its million of tiny facets sending off sparks of light in between. By the time she looked back up, however, the man had readjusted. "My name is Brant," he said almost formally. "You can ask for me if you call."

Once back at the brownstone, Carmen sat at her own sturdy oak table, again examining the smeary copies. Antarctica would mean four months away, no contact with anyone. It was extreme but feasible. She could drive to the airport in some other city, such as Philadelphia, leave her car at the airport, and board a flight bound for Buenos Aires. She had access to enough cash for the ticket; their wedding had brought in nearly $30,000 from Olive's and George's friends, most of which still sat in a joint savings account.

Even if Jobe and his parents succeeded in finding out where she'd flown, there would be no way to guess her final destination. Antarctica was the most remote, unlikely place she could imagine. According to the flyer, once she flew the rest of the way to Ushuaia ("the world's southernmost city"), she would board a boat owned by an environmental group that she had never heard of. She would be virtually impossible to trace.

Of course, it could be a scam. This could be nothing more than a pipeline to white slavery: young women just out of college shipped off from the bottom of the globe to markets where they would be sold to rich, fat sultans. Then she'd be in the same position, only far worse off—with a brutal owner instead of a meek, pale husband who came home at seven o'clock each night, apologizing for the fact that he'd forgotten about the time, pulling off his long, black socks and massaging his veiny feet while he asked if she would like to go out to eat.

She weighed the risks again the following morning, sitting with her coffee, wearing only the long T-shirt in which she'd slept. When she stood to get another cup, her breasts grazed the table's edge. They were suddenly enormous—plump and round and tingling. The current became more intense when her nipples made contact with the hard wood. Carmen was puzzled; she'd been a solid C cup since high school. And though men took notice of her breasts on a near daily basis, she'd never given them much thought. Now, however, they seemed to be growing and alive. It was as if they were trying to tell her something she couldn't decipher. *Stay. Go.* It was impossible to tell.

But it wasn't until a week later, when she pulled out her calendar to schedule a dentist's appointment, that Carmen realized how late she was. She'd never been very good about keeping track, but she distinctly remembered the last time her period had come: It was about three weeks before the wedding, she'd gone out tasting cakes with Olive and eaten too much because inside her gut was that sucking, achy feeling that only food could soothe.

"It's like wine tasting, dear," Olive said at one point. "You don't *eat* so much as analyze, just a smidge so you'll have room for the next."

"I thought you spit when you tasted wine," Carmen said, through a hefty bite of white cake with icing of lavender essence.

"That," said Olive, "is a ghastly practice dreamed up by Californians."

And this, now, was the phrase that wound through Carmen's head. *A ghastly practice dreamed up by Californians.* It seemed to have some hidden application to her current state, about which she had no doubt. But she had nothing to do that afternoon, anyway. So after the receptionist had confirmed her appointment time and Jobe's as well (she was trying to be the kind of wife who would protect her husband's teeth), Carmen drove to the drugstore and picked up a pregnancy test.

It said to wait until morning, indicating that only the "first day's catch" of urine contained enough hormone to trigger a result. Carmen paid no attention. She went into the bathroom immediately and sat on the toilet, catching some pee in a cup, splashing her fingers in the process, dipping the little paper strip in before even washing her hands. It was positive: rudely, brightly so with its two parallel blue stripes.

Carmen threw the strip, box, and urine cup into the trash can out back, so Jobe wouldn't run across them before she was ready to talk to him. But she ended up blurting out the news anyway, the moment he came home. He was barely in the door, bike-messenger-style briefcase still slung over his shoulder, and he looked bug-eyed and terrified for a moment. They stood on opposite ends of their rented living room, staring at each other in horror. But somewhere inside Carmen there was a tiny, interested voice. Jobe was frightened, too—he wasn't ready for this. For all she knew, he was off at work every day looking for opportunities to teach in far-off universities and one day he'd simply disappear on a South American flight of his own. It made her braver, this thought.

"Are you upset?" she asked. "Do you want me to look into . . . ending it?" It struck her then that despite her own horror at discovering she was pregnant, this was the first time the possibility had ever even entered her mind. "If you do, I should probably see someone fast. I'm pretty sure this happened in Italy."

"Jesus, no!" Jobe came forward three full strides, then stopped. He had cut the distance between them in half and there it stayed. "I don't want that at all! I'm just . . ." He stopped midway.

What are you? Carmen wanted to ask. *Surprised? Scared? Completely fucking blindsided?* But standing in this unfamiliar place that was supposed to be their home, she felt as if she couldn't. She missed the buffer of Olive and Nate. Or even George, whose absentminded bumbling through a room could somehow bridge the murky pool of space between her and Jobe.

The topic of abortion never came up again. In fact, Carmen made sure. Every time she'd tried to leave Jobe over the past year and a half something had happened to prevent her, each event more dramatic than the last. She didn't want to know what would come after this: a crippling accident, maybe. Carmen had never been superstitious before but she remembered her mother's avoidance of the color yellow, aversion to crows, and perpetual four-touch signing of the cross.

Besides, it was easy enough to carry this baby; pregnancy turned out to be like a playground slide—once you started down it, there was only one natural way off. Carmen ran and biked well into her seventh month. Because she was not quite twenty-two and very healthy, Carmen's doctor had been completely neutral on the topic of prenatal screening. "Chances of anything going wrong for you are incalculably small," he'd said. "There's no need for an amniocentesis unless you want to be 100 percent sure."

Carmen shivered and signed the waiver saying she declined. She didn't want anyone sticking a long needle into her bulging middle! It might pop like a balloon.

Privately, she marveled at this baby's very existence, stemming from one of only two times she and Jobe had made love on their three-week honeymoon. She hadn't even thought it was the right point in her cycle. And it seemed significant that she should have blossomed into pregnancy immediately after marriage when they were even *less* sexually active than before. Sometimes she wondered if Olive really *did* have some kind of witchy power: She could stand in front of the fireplace inside her big house on the hill, tap her feet and wave her arms, recite incantations, and—poof!—there would be the grandchild she wanted tucked inside Carmen's womb.

There were a number of more logical explanations, of course: the best being that Carmen had gone off the pill after Rory. She didn't want to be tempted to stray by the ease of built-in birth control. But she hadn't mentioned the change to Jobe. Instead, she'd been fitted for a diaphragm, and if he thought it was strange that she excused herself and went to the bathroom for a long time whenever he got amorous, he never said. Likely, it never occurred to him. He would lie back on his pillow and dream about equations, perhaps even forgetting what he was waiting for. But when she returned, full of sticky, clear spermicidal gel, they would resume awkwardly. Sometimes he would go soft and roll away from her but at least half the times they were able to finish, in some manner of speaking. Then Jobe would fall asleep and Carmen would lie staring at the ceiling and feeling the loss of something she couldn't name.

Now that she was pregnant, however, she was turned on all the time; even the seat of her bike sometimes rubbed her effectively enough that she rode crazily, weaving in and around traffic while the waves coming from her clitoris built in a series of expanding arcs. It was a comical problem she would have liked to share with someone. But for some reason, she couldn't even admit to Jobe that she wanted sex. Instead she complained of being hot at night and took off her T-shirt, turning toward him, bumping him with the little rounded belly. He complied more often than before, growing hard silently and turning her—especially once she got into the third trimester—so he could slip into her from behind. Facing away, Carmen was braver. She would pick up one of Jobe's long hands and place it between her legs, sometimes moving his fingers to the spot he never seemed to find on his own.

During the day, they never mentioned these things. Jobe worked and Carmen filled her days shopping for the baby. She had failed when they first moved in to put together a grown-up home, but things were changing now that she was going to be a mother. There was money in the bank—she thought of it as her Buenos Aires fund, though that seemed a ridiculous fantasy now—so she used it to buy a three-wheeled stroller with shock absorbers, a matching changing table and crib in regal cherry wood, and a glider-rocker for night feedings. Still, the supply of baby-related items was endless. Tiny T-shirts and diaper covers, receiving blankets, socks with built-in rattles, stimulating mobiles, nursing bras.

She bought several sets of stencils as well and began on the nursery wall, outlining Humpty Dumpty, Sleeping Beauty, Little Red Riding Hood, various elves. Stepping back one pale late afternoon in

April, she saw that she had accomplished the job perfectly. There were even a few artistic flourishes: on the wolf that peered from around a tree, for instance—she had given him sly, lit-up eyes and erect ears, making him far more menacing than he appeared on the package. Was this good for a baby? She wasn't certain. But it was, at least, a place where she could see her mark.

If Carmen were in a movie about her own life—she paced now, blowing on a milky cup of coffee—she would drop the grade school arts supplies and bravely begin sketching out something of her own. She could picture herself doing this. But the truth was she'd never been quite good enough. Carmen knew that if she were to put aside the stencils and start on the wall freehand, with a tracing pencil and paints, she would create an embarrassing mess.

It was late. She gathered up her supplies and stacked them on the second level of the changing table. It was time to make dinner, something else she wasn't terribly good at. Though Jobe did like her mother's goulash and it was a cool, rainy evening. If she got started immediately, she could be pulling the casserole out of the oven right around the time he got home. She had a doctor's appointment in the morning, where—while she had her legs spread and he had his large warm hands stuck inside her—the avuncular man would ask what she'd been eating. Better to tell him about this homemade meal than the cheese popcorn and Diet Coke she'd had for lunch.

More important, warm, spicy food would fill the evening and soften the gap between them. The smell of her mother's cooking made Carmen feel a little less lonely. She hurried downstairs through a clash of gloom and bright silver rain to begin thawing the meat.

Over goulash and salad and dark beer (his alone—Carmen drank milk) Jobe asked, abruptly, how the baby was doing.

"You make it sound like I can just check in with it and say, 'What's up, baby?' " Carmen lifted a forkful of noodles to her mouth and closed her eyes as she popped it in. Food had never tasted so good in her life. "I don't have some secret pipeline, you know. It's not like I hear things you don't."

This was almost, but not quite, a bald lie. Tomorrow, it would be. On her last visit, the week before, Carmen's doctor had recommended an ultrasound.

"Nothing to worry about," he'd said, patting her bare foot in the stirrup. "But you're eight months along and you've only gained fourteen pounds. I think it might be time to check in on your bambino and measure."

"Could I find out the sex?" Carmen asked. She'd gotten used to talking to this man with her legs spread out, up in the air.

"Depends on the way the baby's turned." He rose to wash his hands and she watched. He had wonderful hands, wide and strong, not at all like Jobe's. "But chances are good."

She hadn't told anyone about the ultrasound. Jobe already knew so much compared to her. This was something she planned to keep, this tiny bit of knowledge. From now until the delivery, only Carmen would be able to picture this baby and understand him. Or her. She would be able to think more carefully about names. She could finish the wall painting in the nursery, looking at that wolf from her baby's point of view.

The next morning, she drank her milk and coffee then three full glasses of water. With her bladder pinching and rippling, she drove to the doctor's office and waited twenty frustrating minutes to be called.

"You better hurry," she said when he came in. "Or I'm going to pee all over your examining table."

"Patience, patience." He glopped some clear gel onto her hard stomach and smeared it with a blunt instrument that resembled a dildo with a flattened head. "I guess that's easy for me to say, right?"

There was the sound of a heartbeat, but she'd heard this before during every exam since her fourth month. The machine's little screen was turned away from Carmen and she craned her head. "Can you tell?" she asked. "What is it, a boy or a girl?"

The doctor was squinting, moving the wand by millimeters, back and forth. "Uh, I can't see yet." His face was slightly red and he looked embarrassed, this man who had stared directly into the space between her open legs. "I need a better view. Could you turn just a little to your left?"

Carmen shifted and a couple teaspoons of urine leaked out, wetting her thighs. "I'm serious, I really need a bathroom," she said. But when she looked over her right shoulder, the doctor's face was like thunder.

"What's wrong?" Her pulsing bladder faded into the background, a faint but persistent ache. Now the thing Carmen felt most vividly was the icy fist inside her chest. The certainty that something terrible had happened without her knowing. A wild loneliness for her mother, or Olive, or even Jobe.

"Don't move," he said sharply. Then, more kindly: "Relax. I'm just having trouble getting the picture I need."

But Carmen knew this wasn't true. After she had been allowed to rise, clenching her bladder as if she were carrying it, to use the toilet and dress, Carmen sat alone in the doctor's office, waiting. She had never been in here before. It was a stately room containing a heavy oak desk, two easy chairs, and bookcases lined with fat textbooks. She wondered if they were real or only for show.

As if to answer her question, the doctor came in at precisely that moment, white coat flapping, and pulled a book from the shelf. He stood flipping through the pages. Again, he was squinting. Then he replaced the book and walked around the desk to sit behind it, facing her. *Don't talk to me*, she almost said. *I don't want to know.*

What he'd seen on the screen—which he had never turned toward her, she realized now; nor had he given her a little black-and-white picture of her baby, the way obstetricians did on TV—was a small pool of fluid on her baby's neck. There was, in addition, a strange brightness to the bowel. And he had measured the baby's nose; it was unusually small.

The doctor paused and Carmen's brain worked frantically, trying to add up these things. Surely someone smarter than her could see the sum of them. But nothing appeared to her. And then there was something: a wide, gold, fat zero in her mind, like an angel's halo that had grown.

"Our next logical step . . ." he had grown so *formal*, this doctor who once told jokes while sliding his lubed fingers in and out of her, "is an amniocentesis. There's a four percent chance it will cause preterm labor, which probably would result in bed rest for the remainder of your pregnancy. Our other option is simply to . . . wait."

"For?"

"Do you think you should call your husband, Mrs. Garrett?" he asked.

Coward! He couldn't bear to answer her question. He wanted another man in the room, someone to calm her. "No," she said. "He's working. I don't want to bother him."

"I'm sure he wouldn't mind."

"No." Carmen straightened. She was glad now that she hadn't wiped herself off carefully with water. It was good that she was leaving urine streaks on this man's expensive upholstered chair. "What are we waiting for?"

The man sighed and looked at the ceiling. He felt caught; Carmen had seen this expression before. "Your baby has several of the markers for Down's syndrome." It was as if he was reciting some sentence out of his book. "I can't be certain, not from looking. A very small percentage of normal fetuses also have these features."

Carmen folded her hands over her midriff and squeezed in. She didn't want to hurt the baby, just mold it into normal shape.

"We elected not to do fetal testing because of your age." The doctor had opened a drawer and was riffling through some files. "I have the document right here."

"I know I signed it." Her voice was flat, suddenly old; she could hear it. "You don't have to show me. I'm not going to sue you."

He cleared his throat and reluctantly shut the drawer. "It's too late to terminate your pregnancy here, in the state of Maryland," he said. "By law, there would have to be some risk to your life.

And you're one of the youngest, healthiest patients I have." He raised his hands in the air as if, once again, his point had been made. "However." He cleared his throat. "There are a few places where you could . . ."

Carmen let this hang in the air. She envisioned the procedure, like the gutting of the wolf at the end of "Little Red Riding Hood." Her belly would be slit open with a knife and a whole human pulled out. But then what?

They sat without speaking for a time. Then the doctor shifted in his big chair. "I'm sorry, I have other appointments," he said softly. He did sound genuinely sorry.

Carmen stood easily. She'd never gotten awkward, the way a pregnant woman was supposed to. Obviously she had been doing something wrong. "Go ahead," she said, then lied: "I'm fine."

He put his hand on her shoulder. "It's, ah, a boy. Did I tell you that?"

He hadn't, but Carmen nodded anyway.

Later, she would not remember driving home, parking, going inside, or making lunch. But she found herself there, in the empty brownstone, staring at half a sandwich (had there been another half originally? had she eaten it?) and leafing through her folder of brochures. Africa, Japan, Antarctica. She'd done this so often they were soft with wear, the paper like cotton.

There are a few places where you could . . . The doctor's voice escaped the privacy of Carmen's head and echoed in the air around her.

It was possible, still, to take that flight to Buenos Aires. For all she knew, it was one of those places where a baby could be erased. And if she were lucky, no one would be able to track her; they would never have to know what she'd done. Over time, Jobe and Olive—even the baby himself—would grow faint.

Carmen rose and went to the entryway where a small black-framed mirror hung. This was one of Olive's only contributions to the décor: She'd said it would open up the small foyer. Carmen stood in front of it and stared directly into her own eyes. They were not the same as the ones she'd seen on her wedding day, less than a year before. Her face was leaner even despite the pregnancy, with large eyes and hard planes. It was—the thought popped up, like the ghost that burst out of a Halloween pumpkin toy when she pressed a button, which she'd had long ago—more like her husband's. She was carrying his child, a deformed boy who would probably never look like either of them, and somehow absorbing Jobe through the baby's genes.

The front door opened, catching her at the elbow. She moved to the side and Jobe suddenly appeared next to her. This was not like the pumpkin at all. In childhood, the surprise had been the same each time.

Carmen backed up, her tailbone touching the wall. She remained held in the mirror and watched as her face receded; she saw his both real and reflected, furrowing and dark.

"What are you doing here?" she asked. Anyone watching would have thought she was frightened of him, that he was an intruder in her home.

"There's something wrong," he said.

"Yes." She continued to watch herself. There were tears running down her cheeks that she could see but not feel.

He turned and took a step, and she was dizzy for a moment as the actual Jobe moved toward her but the flat image of his back in the mirror moved away. It was as if he were separating, becoming two people. Then he was inches from her, smelling of fear and opening his arms. She bumbled in, placing her cheek against the soft fleece of his JHU sweatshirt, and gratefully closed her eyes.

"Maybe the doctor was wrong," she said.

Time had contracted and it was evening, a fresh, rose-and-lavender spring dusk that could not help but fill her with hope. That, and the full glass of white wine she'd drunk after a completely alcohol- free seven months.

"He said he saw a. . ." She strained to remember, her head blissfully light and fuzzy. "I don't know. A short nose. A bright bowel?" She nearly laughed. Could he really have said that? "And fluid on the"—she touched her own, without thinking—"neck." She looked longingly at the open bottle but one glass was already too much, especially given what she was proposing. "He never said he was *sure*. We'd need an amniocentesis for that. I could do it tomorrow." Her voice spiked, too shrill.

"Isn't that the test with the long needle?" Jobe's face was long and sad. He wasn't going to let her hope and she knew very soon she might hate him for that. "I don't think you should. I mean, I don't think there's any point. The doctor isn't wrong."

Fury rolled in Carmen. She felt like slapping him but balled her hands so she wouldn't. "How can you know that?" Slowly, the impulse ebbed.

Jobe shrugged and stared at the fireplace in which there was no fire. "I just do."

"The same way you know you're going to die?" She was taunting him, but also considering. If both things were true, what else did Jobe know and how much of it did he control? Why was she alone tumbling through life without information, making all the wrong choices?

"Not really," Jobe cut in. "That's more of a . . ." He stopped and kneaded his head. "That's a feeling; I've had it for years—practically as long as I can remember. But this is a fear. It just started a few days ago. I told myself it was irrational."

How's the baby doing? she remembered him asking. Was that just last night?

"But," he continued. "When I saw you today, I thought . . ."

She waited. "You thought what?"

"I was sure." He put his hand out and covered her belly with it, long fingers draping over in a melting way. "But I also thought it was . . ." He paused again. This was, Carmen noted, the first time Jobe had reached for her in weeks. "Necessary."

"Necessary for *what*?"

The doorbell rang then and Carmen heard it echo from a distance inside her head. "Just a minute," Jobe said, and extracting his hand slowly, as if it had been suckered to her stomach, he got up. "I ordered dinner," he announced when he returned holding two brown paper bags. "Chinese. I didn't know what you'd want so I just . . ." He dragged the coffee table over and started unloading the bags. Little white cartons piled up like toy soldiers. "Got a lot."

Carmen lay against the couch and mused while he went to the kitchen for plates and one fork. Jobe would use chopsticks, but she never could quite master them and didn't have the patience tonight. "It's handy, isn't it?" she asked when he came back, napkins fluttering like birds on top of the stack he was carrying. "You never, ever have to stop and question. Do I have enough money? Should I order dinner? Can I pay for this? You just go ahead and do whatever you feel like."

"Yes."

He'd agreed with her, but his one-word answer seemed inadequate. It made her angry, even as she piled her plate with Mongolian beef and moo shu pork. "I mean, you do get that the rest of us don't live that way, right? We can't just do or buy anything we want. It's harder than that."

Jobe stared at her. He hadn't even begun filling his plate. It was as if he was doing this deliberately, further separating them. Making her eat alone. He didn't speak but she heard his answer anyway: *But it's not harder for you, Carmen. You're like me now.* She looked around at the ornate, expensive furniture she'd purchased on a whim. She had spent more than a year's salary for the average art history major on outfitting their apartment and still, they sat on the floor.

"Okay," she conceded, though Jobe had not yet said a word. And finally he began spooning out food for himself. "It's just weird that having all these options can make you feel so . . . trapped."

"Yeah, tell me about it," he said, as Carmen sat up. He'd sounded, during those five words, like the person she met in Kensington Park. She ached for that day, for the gangly, sweet boy whose grin had flashed so unexpectedly. "All my life, whatever I've wanted, it's been there. Money to travel, the schools I want. You." He was concentrating on the inside of a carton of fried noodles. "It's too easy, too much. There are no rules. There's no, you know." Jobe raised his head and locked eyes with her. If she were encountering this brash, free-speaking man every day, she might not be collecting travel brochures. "Order."

"And this"—Carmen gestured at her body, the part that looked like a snake's belly after he'd swallowed a baby giraffe—"gives you order."

"It does." Jobe lay back and dangled the noodles into his mouth. Truly, she had never even met this guy before. He was like a slightly older version of that strange, brave boy from London, and so much more interesting than the man she'd awakened next to fourteen hours before. "It gives *us* order. Hell, I think it probably gives the whole world order. Seemingly random events provide the structure in any complex system, mathematical or otherwise. It sounds backward, but I really believe it's true."

"You believe?"

"Yeah, that's actually the basis of my research project." He'd already had a couple of beers but now he emptied the wine bottle into his glass and drank, eyes glinting. Carmen moved a tiny bit closer to where this different new Jobe lay sprawled on the rug.

"I didn't know that," she said. "You never told me."

"I never thought you'd find it interesting. People don't."

"I'm not people, I'm your wife." The word felt strange and antiquated in her mouth, like a dusty thimble.

Jobe snorted, bull-like, which made her smile. It didn't fit him at all. "I guess. Whatever that means."

She liked him so much more this way: coarse, confident, almost rude. "It means, we have to decide what to do about this baby."

"Yup. The ugly genius and his pretty little wife are going to have a retarded baby. Did you ever hear that joke about George Bernard Shaw?" Carmen was leaning in, one hand gathering to stroke his chest, anticipating the narrow lines of it. Her stomach was pleasantly full. The baby was sloshing around in its private place. The spot between her legs was warm and wet. "He met this beautiful woman at a party and she told him they should have a child together because it would have her looks and his brains. So he said to her, *But what if the baby has my looks and your brains?*"

Carmen pulled herself up straight and didn't breathe. The room around her expanded, darkness unfolding in all directions. There was a moment's pause so loud she thought it might make this whole conversation moot because her inadequate brain would simply explode.

Jobe eyed her from where he lay then sat up hurriedly, gathering his long legs in his hands and folding them. "Carmen, I didn't mean that the way it sounded."

"Really?" She ached to go back in time and make this true. But there was no way, ever, to erase what Jobe had said. And how it sounded. Woozy, she rose slowly, her hips sore. Her mind felt even more battered: squeezed and dented, like a car's engine that had been crushed. Maybe Jobe was right: She had grown dumb in addition to everything else. That would explain how she'd walked straight into the wrong life.

"Please, Carmen. I'm worried about the baby and I drank . . ." He nudged the bottle and it careened demonstratively across the wood floor. "It's just. No, don't leave." He caught her hand, his Venus fly-trap of a hand closing over hers, but she shook him off and backed toward the stairs. *Sleep*, that would make all this go away. "I'm just worried. About the baby. About you."

"You're worried that I'm just too stupid for a genius like you?" It made sense now that she considered it from his point of view. He was not in her league looks-wise. She was not in his when it came to brains. The joke about . . . who was it? George somebody—she didn't even recognize the name, which only proved Jobe's point—was mostly true.

He was staring at the floor. "No, I'm worried you'll leave."

Carmen stood, hands fisted at her sides, thinking but not saying a dozen cruel things. Everything tilted nightmarishly. It felt as if she were on some lifelong carnival ride, strapped in to her seat no matter how desperately she wanted to get off.

"I know you don't love me." Jobe still sat with his head bowed, talking to the floor. "I've always known. Marrying you was the worst, really, the most idiotic thing I ever did in my life but I convinced myself that we were fated. . . . I thought over time, we'd have a baby together and make a home and eventually, you'd feel connected to me." Jobe rolled to a stop and sighed drunkenly. "But I don't know if that can happen now."

"Because?" Carmen's whole body was twitching, she was so tired.

"Because, honestly, I'm not sure you can fall in love with anyone who isn't beautiful. It wasn't you who was dumb about this, it was me. I was the one who expected this baby to have your looks and my brains. I was, in fact." He hiccupped loudly and Carmen almost laughed. "Counting on it," he finished. And the moment for laughter passed.

"So what happened to random events providing structure?"

"I believe that. But you . . ."

"I can't really understand?" She waited, silently willing Jobe to rise and move toward her. Even if she were going to reject him—and she didn't know if she would—Carmen was rooting for him to try. "Is that what you're trying to say? Or that I don't have it in me to love a retarded child? What?"

As if the baby heard, he kicked at precisely that moment and Carmen closed her hand over one tiny heel, holding on. "I'm sorry," Jobe said, though what specifically he was referring to was not clear. Carmen thought about asking, sitting down next to him and touching his bony shoulder. But the thought of it—after all of this—remained unappetizing. It was the only word she could think of and again she nearly let loose a frantic, inappropriate laugh. Touching her own husband was like eating soggy eggplant; it was something she had to muster her will to do.

"I really need to go to bed," Carmen said and meant it. Her legs were growing numb and she was in danger of toppling forward. She turned without another word, groped her way up the dark staircase, and got under the covers without removing her clothes or brushing her teeth. Hours later, she awoke in total darkness and a sense of being anchored. She had to pee, desperately, but something was pinning her. Bad thoughts she could not quite remember were swimming in her head.

She moved like a fish, thrashing. And Jobe made a sound. He was lying on top of the quilt, as far from her as he could on the queen-size bed. She recalled in a gauzy, vague montage leaving him in the living room. He'd been on the floor. Why? she wondered, as she lurched toward the bathroom. Her mouth tasted of wine, which was odd as well.

Sitting on the toilet, hunched over her body, her meeting with the doctor replayed and hit her with full force. Their baby: He had Down's. She remembered that now. Weeping, she leaned even farther forward. There was no way out, no escape from this. She had made terrible mistakes and now both she and this baby would have to pay.

"Carmen? Are you alright?" Jobe appeared in relief against the murky bedroom, his body outlined like an Indonesian shadow puppet —all long neck and jointed torso and arms. She had been in such a hurry to reach the bathroom that she'd forgotten to shut the door.

There had been another bathroom door, in London, firmly shut. She thought of this now. What if she had never opened that door but had crawled out a window instead? Was there even a window in that long-ago WC?

Jobe hunched down and put one hand on her knee. This was the benefit of being married to someone you weren't attracted to, Carmen told herself with a strange, internal motherly voice: You didn't mind his finding you squatting and urinating because there was nothing to lose.

"Are you in pain?" he asked, and she saw that the real Jobe was back. Not the one from last night whom she could picture, fuzzily, lolling on his back. This Jobe was upright and taciturn. Almost mournful, though she couldn't recollect exactly about what.

"I'm fine." She stood sniffling, dribbling everywhere. Pulled up her underpants without even wiping. It was like she was trying every way she could to turn off her husband. "I need to brush my teeth."

"Okay," he said. "I'll be waiting." As if this, after the past few moments, was private. She took a long time with her toothbrush, reapplying the paste twice and scrubbing out every remnant of white wine. She was appalled that she could be so irresponsible, no matter what the doctor had said. This was her baby, as much as it was Jobe's. And she needed to protect him.

"Better now?" Jobe helped her as she lowered herself backward into their bed.

She didn't know the answer. Was she better now, or worse? But she simply said, "Yes."

$\mathscr{S}$EPTEMBER 2007

The descent was abrupt. Twenty-six hours after Carmen's lunch with Danny at Domaine Thérèse she was huddled in bed, damp with fever, vomiting into a metal bowl.

For days, various people appeared at her side—Olive, Siena, Luca, Jana—each holding a glass of water. Their only mission, it seemed, was to get her to take a sip. Once she did so, whoever it was would fade backward, as if dematerializing in the air, and Carmen would be left alone until the next person arrived with a straw to insert into her scorched, tired mouth.

Twice she got up to use the bathroom and had to be helped. Luca could support her alone; he was four inches shorter than her but deceptively strong and as stable as a three-legged stool. The second time it was Olive who took her and they tilted against each other in a rickety way. Carmen tried not to lean but nearly fell on the way back and Olive had to catch her by the arms. For one perilous second, they stood locked together and swaying. It was Carmen's only flash of real clarity: She saw her mother-in-law's face, determined and beading with sweat. Both women mustered what force they had and somehow righted each other. After she had tucked Car-

men back into bed, Olive slumped in the chair alongside it, breathing in short gasps.

"I think," she said between inhalations, "next time I may ask
for help."

But there was no next time. Because Carmen descended even further, into a soup of memories and dreams, tingling nerves, aching
bones, and swimming head. Her body felt fragmented in the bed. She
wouldn't have been surprised to discover one of her arms lay separate
from the rest of her. Her feet seemed miles and miles away.

There were flashes of her childhood: the smell of pot roast when
she walked in the door from Girl Scouts, learning to drive her father's
enormous New Yorker, sleeping with her sister in some hotel room—
where? she did not know—and feeling the soft curve of her leg.

Then Jobe appeared by her bed and sat straight in the chair, lit
as if from a spotlight from below. It was night, that darkest part of it.
His hands were enormous, moving and glowing like starfish. They
were floating luminous above the arms.

She couldn't keep her eyes away from them.

"You came," she said. Or didn't. It was hard to tell whether the
words were spoken aloud or appearing like subtitles inside her head.
"Did you solve it? Riemann? Is the answer in the box?"

It doesn't matter. These words clearly did not come from him
—the man, or the ghost, or whatever he was—but unfurled in the
space between her ears, which was very confusing. How was Carmen
to know who had spoken, whether it was her dead husband or she
herself?

"Of course it matters." She was angry, and this was cleansing.
A wash of pure emotion that dulled her nauseating pain. "Tell me."

The answer is there. You will find it. You will understand.
His hands were on her head now, cradling its hot, egglike shape
and soothing it, like a cap made of cool water that stilled the fires in
her skull.

"But I never understood," Carmen said petulantly. "That was
the problem."

Remember? The golden Jobe leaned forward, but like a doll—all at once, tilting rather than hinging. *Seemingly random events provide the structure in any complex system. . . .* He was beginning to fade away.

"But why?" There was a question bubbling around on her brain, like something in boiling water that kept moving, rising, going under again. "Why did you?" She concentrated, hard, still watching his hovering, translucent spaceship hands. Finally, she grasped the idea by its tail. "Why *didn't* you tell someone? Althea—that woman in Greece. You had time. You could have sent her the solution." Jobe was disappearing, growing smaller and darker, disappearing the way a television screen used to into one center spot. "No, wait. Tell me why."

Because the solution is yours. It's up to you. He was collapsing, contracting, becoming as tiny as Alice when she fell down the rabbit hole then smaller still. Carmen sobbed and reached out as her husband vanished. Then she, too, was falling, tumbling backward into a dark space.

Shutter glimpses appeared to her. Dr. Woo and an endless trail of zeros rising and falling like golden doughnuts behind him. Olive holding a wine glass and looking at the sky. Jana wearing Carmen's rings, turning her hand to make the diamonds flash in the light. Siena and Troy walking with Michael as if they were his parents. Luca contemplating her room from the doorway (was this real?). Young Carmen lying on the table while the doctor ran his ultrasound wand over her belly. Pictures flashing from an unseen screen.

Carmen and Jobe, so young, sitting in a restaurant with scarves like billowing sails between the booths.

"At least no one will ever throw away my work," he said. "I know you would never let that happen."

"The same way you know you're doing to die?" she asked.

"I was wrong," he answered.

"No, you weren't. You're already dead."

He placed his elbows on the table and leaned forward, looking her straight in the eyes as he spoke. "Seemingly random events provide the structure in any complex system, mathematical or otherwise."

"You've said that before. Or no. Wait." She struggled. The plate before her was steaming with the strong scent of curry. "You'll say that in the future."

"Life isn't a single path, Carmen. That's only an illusion. I've proved it."

And then there was nothing for a very long time.

She awoke in a tangled nest of bedclothes, her mind wiped free of dreams, thinking only of her thirst.

"Mom?" It was Michael next to her, his voice deeper than she remembered. He stood and put his hand—cool, long fingers—on her forehead, as if checking for fever. "Are you okay?"

She looked into his face and saw that he was frightened, then down at the pillow that was covered with fuzzy bits of hair.

"You're bald," Michael said.

"Totally?" Carmen reached up with two careful fingers and ran them across the moonlike bumps of her skull. She shivered. "This is not a great way to wake up," she said and grinned at him. Michael made a sound in his throat and took a step back. Carmen focused and straightened and looked into the mirror opposite the bed; she was a wraith, white with stretched-looking skin and a jack-o'-lantern smile.

"Get me that," she said, pointing, and Michael brought her the scarf that lay on a chair in the corner. Moving slowly—her muscles ached as if she had run a marathon—she wound it around her head. "How long have I been in here?" she asked. Judging from the weight she'd lost, it had to be a month.

"Four days," he said, squinting. He was trying to compute her new face. "Grandma said one more day and you had to go to the hospital. Do you need to go to the hospital now?"

There was a hopeful lilt to his voice. What teenager needed

another parent lying around the house, waiting to die? Carmen hesitated then spoke gently. "Not right now," she said. "But if I get sick again, I think I will."

"Alright." Michael sat back down. He was examining her in short stints, as if dipping himself into cold water, getting used to the temperature. "That guy was here. The one from the baseball game."

Carmen blinked. There had been no baseball game in her dreams. She shifted—it was an effort—to review the actual time before her last chemotherapy session, before her lunch with . . .

"Danny!"

"Yeah, that guy. He came a couple days ago and talked to Grandma."

"Really?" Carmen worked to contain her curiosity. Danny was just a family friend, right? Someone who had come out of concern, who took fatherless boys to baseball games and called housing inspectors and researched mathematical formulas in his spare time. "What did they talk about?"

"Math experts, mostly," Olive answered as she appeared behind Michael, tired-looking but proper in a zippered velour warm-up suit and Keds. "Also, his hair. It's quite lovely but too long, I think, on an adult man."

Carmen looked at the hair on her pillow then back in the mirror, where her alien self stared back: white, cratered head propped on the stalk of a neck. "Which math experts?" she asked faintly, as Michael slipped from the room.

"How do you feel, dear?" Olive stood over her, lips pursed. She was twitching, as if trying not to laugh. Or cry. "We came very close to calling for an ambulance last night. Though Mr. Woo said . . ."

"Doctor," Carmen interrupted.

"Oh, yes, how strange. I suppose I was thinking about that old movie with Lon Chaney."

"Funny, I always think about that song by Steely Dan." And she sang in a warbling, cracked voice: "Katy tried / I was halfway crucified / I was on the other side / Of no tomorrow."

"Dear me, how frightening." Olive sat in Michael's chair. It felt to Carmen as if she was holding court: Each of her subjects came in, one by one, to be heard. "I was worried *you* were going to the other side of no tomorrow. But Dr. Woo said he thought this was the worst of it. The second treatment often is—they have no idea why—and unless you ran a very high fever or became dehydrated, there was nothing they could do for you that we couldn't do. . . ." She held her hand out, swept it around Carmen and Jobe's bedroom. "Here."

"I remember. You were all giving me water."

"Yes. You should be very proud. Siena and Luca each took their shifts. Three hours apiece. They are good young people. You raised them well."

Carmen sighed, spying Jobe's bathrobe—still hanging on its hook in the open closet—out of the corner of her eye. "*We* raised them well. Which is a miracle." She paused. "Speaking of miracles, I saw. Or rather, I dreamed. Jobe was, um, here."

"I'm sure he was, dear," said Olive, rising. "I wouldn't be surprised if he did his three hours as well."

Carmen's head buzzed with frustration, or possibly confusion. "Why are you acting so *unmoved* by all of this? It's like I never even knew you. Were you running séances in your living room all these years and just not letting on?"

Olive had been heading for the door but now she stopped and turned. "No," she said.

"Then what changed all of a sudden? How come you just accept that your dead son is floating around talking to people?"

Soberly, Olive assessed Carmen. "I suppose," she began. Then confused, she paused. "There have been so many awful things. Jobe's"—she struggled to say the word—"death. And now, your illness." She checked the hall before continuing, quietly. "Luca, his problems. You know I love him even more than the others, in a way. But I wish for him so many things that will never be."

Carmen shrugged, an effort that made her breathless. She lay back on the pillows regarding her mother-in-law. "But that's life. It's always been that way."

"Not *my* life." Olive smiled but it was shaky. "Up until I was about forty, nothing ever really went wrong. I was born wealthy. When I was a little girl, we vacationed every year in France. I married someone who loved me. We had friends. My boys were born healthy, smart."

"What happened?" Carmen had been doing the math: Jobe was only sixteen when Olive was forty.

"One day I got an inkling that life wouldn't be quite so easy for my child. Oh, Will did fine. He was very popular, good in school, a tennis player. And Nate has always had this . . . way about him. He's happy no matter what. But Jobe was so lonely. Lost. He was always on the outside. He never had a girlfriend—during all of high school. My heart ached for him. It was the first time in my life having money and the right family did no good."

Carmen snorted. "It's hardly tragic, you know. Being an outcast in high school." Though she had to admit that as a young woman she wouldn't have felt that way at all.

"No, but it was the beginning. And I did what I knew to do. I waited until you came along and I used what means I had to fix things. To make sure you stayed here with us, married him, had a nice home. But then Luca was born and Jobe got sick."

"And even you couldn't fix them."

"No." Olive shook her head. "Even I. This did not fit into my worldview. It was incomprehensible, really." She paused. "Then Jobe died and I realized what I'd done, that you had both in some sense been unhappy for all those years. My mixing into things, arranging them, had actually"—she swallowed—"caused my son and his son—and you—pain. There were a few very bad nights . . ." Olive looked at Carmen with wide, old eyes. "Then Jobe came to speak to me."

"What did he say?" Carmen asked softly.

"He said I should stop trying to control everything. That things happen, you know . . ."

"Randomly?"

"Yes. I believe that's even the word he used. Jobe told me I couldn't see it yet, but there was an order to life. Your illness, your . . ." She blushed but went on. "Your romances. He said. I can't express it but somehow I understood."

She gazed at Carmen, suddenly regal again. All traces of sorrow and guilt were gone. Olive was back. "I'm going to make you some lunch now. Really, it's high time you ate something. You're like a pile of sticks in that bed."

"But wait, you never answered my question!" Carmen called as Olive began turning to leave for the second time. "Which math experts?"

"There's this young lady from Greece. Althea something, I think your friend said. He thinks she might . . ."

"Yes, we need to bring her here. The money. I have the insurance money. I can buy her a ticket and get her a place to stay." The words were pouring out of Carmen so fast, they sounded connected—like one long idea. "We can pay her whatever she needs to leave her position for a while. Bring her husband if she has one. We need her to come look at Jobe's papers and see if the solution is there. It's very important."

Olive paused in the doorway, looking at Carmen. She smiled, very slowly, but it was like the sun breaking out. "Yes, dear. I was thinking the same thing. But no need to fret so; you just lie back while I get your lunch. It's already been done."

Carmen was bored. Only six hours had passed since she awoke with Michael in the chair at her side. Luca and Siena and even Troy had all come to speak to her, and Carmen had been shy at first. But Luca had acted as if nothing was different about her, casually answering her questions while gazing straight into her eyes. Troy, on the other hand, stared at his feet the whole time he was in the room. And Siena reacted in a way Carmen never would have predicted.

"Oh, Jesus," she said, examining Carmen. "You look terrible, Mom. I want you to lie here in this bed until you gain at least five pounds. And we need to shave your head." Then she ran her hand over Carmen's skull lovingly, like a mother. "You have bird fuzz."

Troy, next to her, looked embarrassed. But Carmen laughed. "I promise I'm going to eat and get myself better soon. Because it sounds like you've been hanging out with Jana *waaayyyy* too much."

And the morning then was pleasant. Carmen had eaten twice: a bagel with jam that Olive brought her and a cup of strong coffee she'd drizzled with heavy cream. Then an omelet stuffed with sausage and spinach and cheese that Luca brought her, which she insisted on sharing with him—trading the fork back and forth—until she had quelled the aching emptiness inside her gut.

"Food hasn't tasted so good to me since I was pregnant with you," she told him. But Luca only gave her a long look that could have been deep and wise or could have signaled he was unable to fathom what pregnant was exactly and how he ever could have lived tucked inside her. She started to clarify but couldn't think of a way to do it that wouldn't be demeaning so she stopped and simply let the moment pass.

By noon she was stuffed and warm, far too full to eat again for several hours. Troy had offered to pull a TV into her bedroom but the thought of lying back and watching daytime talk shows or soap operas only depressed her. She had seen all the movies in the house. She hadn't started a new book since Jobe died, so her bedside table was bare. Carmen itched and shifted, as the afternoon marched on insistently sunny and empty, petulant and restless as a small child.

Finally, when she couldn't stand the tedium any longer, she rose despite Siena's admonishment and crept down the stairs. The children were nowhere to be found. It was early September and they were in school! Carmen realized they had been staying home to care for her, or in case she died. But now they were gone. Olive was lying on the living room couch, her shoes still on, legs angled crookedly so her feet were off the cushions, eyes closed. Carmen envied her mother-in-law the satisfying fatigue of hard work. She wandered into the kitchen. Never had her home seemed less her own: Olive, or someone, had purchased groceries with unfamiliar brand names; they could have come from France or New Zealand, for all Carmen knew.

She went into the dining room. The table gleamed. Had Olive taken time to polish it in the midst of ministering to Carmen and taking care of all three kids? That made no sense. But as she neared the table she saw her own reflection appearing—a dark, wavering sepia image, as if she were looking into a river of chocolate—and smelled the oil and lemon. Jobe's boxes were stacked against the wall under the thermostat. But Carmen didn't like seeing them there. It was too risky. Someone could mistake them for Goodwill offerings, or outdated tax documents, and toss them out.

She tried lifting one. It contained only papers but it was immovable. She must have been severely weakened by the past week. Giving up on that task, Carmen opened the box and began fishing pages out. She took them to the table but reconsidered when she got within a couple of feet of that smell. The oil would stain them, might even bleed through and smudge the pen marks. Carmen stood for a few seconds, considering. She turned and went upstairs to the linen closet, then came down again on the creaking wooden stairs, peering over the banister every few steps to see if she was disturbing Olive, carrying an old sheet that flowed behind her like a veil.

It was thick muslin, vintage linen that she'd bought out of romantic desire when she was first married. But one after another the children had stained it with various body fluids, liquid acetaminophen, and popsicle juice. Now they used it for picnics, or to soften the edges of furniture when it was being moved. Carmen flung the sheet high over the table—breathless with effort—and let it drift down. At the same time she saw an image of the white drape settling down over Jobe's coffin. It fluttered similarly at the edges. Carmen caught her breath, feeling a moment of fear. But the picture in her mind was replaced by that trail of golden zeros and she felt, rather than heard, his voice say, *Don't worry, you will be fine in the end.*

Once the table was covered, Carmen withdrew a sheaf of papers and sat down to make some sort of arrangement. She sorted the first three sheets into separate piles but couldn't discern the reason why, when she looked carefully at them. Moving the pages closer, she scanned each one and looked for anything she could use to help categorize. Strands of Jobe's dinnertime conversation from throughout the years floated back to her: *Restricting the range of prime numbers . . . An analytic continuation of the zeta function . . . What hasn't been proven yet is the distribution of zeros . . . Real part must always be one-half.* These words cleared up nothing, even as she stared at the figures he'd written in long, sentencelike strings.

But over the next hour, a few patterns emerged. There were papers containing only one or two formulas with cryptic, slantwise notes in the margins; others looked like dictionary pages with solid paragraphs of math. Carmen recognized one symbol again and again: the zeta, which looked like an elegant, unfinished uppercase E. Jobe drew this almost like a Chinese figure, with calligraphic flourishes of his pen. She put all of these documents into a separate pile.

There was a soft scuffle in the other room: a door opening and feet, first clipping across the floor then muffled by carpet. Olive must be up. Carmen continued dealing the papers out like playing cards; now that she'd developed a system, it was satisfying to do this. Though she couldn't have said what function it might possibly serve.

"What are you doing?" The voice was not what she expected and Carmen jumped then had a fierce desire to hide. Danny stood in the doorway, looking at her. She pulled her bathrobe even tighter but this was a mistake. She was wasted, with hardly any real body against which to pull the fabric. It had never bothered her to be naked in front of Danny but now she felt ugly and exposed, drowning in her own clothes.

"I'm just . . ." She reached up and felt her head, which was rough and patchy. When she drew her hand away, there was a fine down of hair covering the palm. "What are *you* doing? It's the middle of the day."

"It's Tuesday," he said. "My—you know, our—afternoon off."

"Oh." She backed up, feeling cornered. Had he meant to be hostile?

"I thought I'd just come over to see how you are." He was wearing his sunglasses and a black shirt, sexy faded jeans, his waist-length hair loose. An affront.

"I'm fine," Carmen said stiffly. *No, I'm not. I'm ugly. I'm bony and bald and disgusting. You'll never want to sleep with me again.*

"What are you doing?" he asked, gesturing at the papers in front of her. "Your, uh, Olive talked about bringing Althea Markos here to look at those."

"I know. She told me." Carmen paused, awkward. "Have you seen her, Olive?"

"Yeah, she's asleep on the couch. She looks really beat." He peeled off his sunglasses as he said this.

Carmen stepped forward. "And I look horrible."

"You look sick."

They stood facing each other, cold space between them. Finally, Carmen spoke. "We should get out of here if we're going to talk. The children will be home any minute." Actually, she had no idea if this was true: Michael could very well go to Jeffrey's, Siena to Troy's or to work, and Luca was enrolled in a new program this year. She couldn't remember what the schedule was.

But Danny nodded and then Carmen was stuck. She led him up the stairs and stopped in front of her bedroom door but remembered, suddenly, the night she'd considered bringing Danny here. She'd decided then never to bring him to Jobe's bedroom. And she wasn't ready to acknowledge that things had changed, becoming benign since her conversion into a crone, so sitting on a mattress with him would be as innocent as if she were his grandmother.

So she bypassed the door on the other side of which her unmade bed lay rumpled, as unromantic as a balled-up dishrag, and continued up the stairs to the attic. Carmen hadn't been up here in months. There was a CD player and an empty glass on the floor in front of the sectional; a fleece blanket was draped over the back of the couch.

"This is so weird," Danny said. "It's exactly like my mother's living room when I went home from college the first time. She'd just redone it and—"

"How old *are* you?" she asked.

"Thirty-six," he said. "Why?"

She laughed. It was a relief finally to know. "I guess I never had the nerve to . . ." Carmen looked at her wedding ring, heavy and loose, circling her finger. She and Jobe had been married for three years by the time Danny went away to college. "Nothing, it doesn't matter. Anyway." She sat.

"Carmen." He sank down on the cushion next to her and took her hand. So formal. She half expected him to drop to one knee. "Are you okay? Should I be worried?"

"Well, I have cancer."

"That's not funny."

She sighed. "No, I'm sorry, it's not." She drew herself up and resolved to be dignified. "The truth is, I'm not terribly comfortable being here with you right now."

"I know," Danny said, nodding.

He knew? He was uncomfortable, too, seeing her like this. Uncomfortable in the way one is when they pass a hunched street person and throw a dollar into their hat. If it were possible for a person to shrivel, that's what Carmen was doing. Overnight, she'd become haggard. Pitiful.

"I honestly never thought I'd feel guilty," Danny went on. "I didn't even think it was in me, frankly. But the more I get to know your kids . . . And Olive . . ." He looked down at his lap. *Who was this man?* He was acting as contrite as some character out of some old Frank Capra movie. "The strange thing is I even feel bad about Mega."

Carmen took a sharp breath. Here it was. "I understand. So you're saying you want to be done?" *Of course he wants to be done! What man could see a woman this way and want to touch her ever again?*

"No," he said, sounding miserable. "I'm not saying that. But I'm confused."

Carmen stared. "You're confused? C'mon. Just admit it: You don't want this." She pointed to herself, toward the spot between her own legs, which was now—perhaps permanently—papery and dry. "You can be honest, you know. Not that that was ever a part of the deal, but it might be time to start. I know what men like about me." She swallowed. "What men *used to* like about me, I mean."

"You are so full of shit." The voice was scornful, and not Danny's. "Jobe would have loved you if you had burn scars and a glass eye." They both turned to see Jana in the doorway. "Hey, sorry to interrupt. This sounds real intense. But I could hear every word from the second floor and frankly, Carmen, you were being a real ball breaker." Jana came farther into the room and extended one hand. "Danny, right?"

He gave Carmen a questioning look. "She knows?"

"Jana's the only one, okay? I mean, I had to tell someone. And the only other person I confide in is Olive, but she didn't seem to be the best choice."

There was a pause, then Jana let out a loud braying laugh. Even Danny smiled. "Hey," he said, shaking Jana's hand. "Nice to meet you."

She squinted, as if looking directly into the sun. "I can't believe I'm actually saying this, but it's nice to meet you, too."

Twilight descended, deepening at least an hour's worth of shades, and still the three continued to talk.

Downstairs, Carmen could hear the noise of her children arriving home from wherever they'd been, their grandmother calling out to ask how school was and if she could make them something to eat. Carmen was tucked under the blanket on a corner piece of the huge sectional between Danny and Jana. It was the oddest configuration she could imagine. Jana had scuffed off her shoes and tucked her feet under her denim skirt; Danny sat upright, almost primly—like a librarian, Carmen thought and chuckled to herself.

A contented warmth spread inside her, the words she'd spat at Danny mellowing in her mind the way things did after a drink or two. She knew this was only a reprieve but it was one she was glad to take advantage of, listening quietly while the other two talked. But after they'd spent an hour trading information—speaking with equal authority about Olive and comparing notes on what they'd observed over the past several days—Jana turned to Carmen.

"So. Should I get out of here and let you two continue your, uh, conversation?"

Her tone was mocking and now the room was divided again, the easy conviviality all but gone. It was Danny and Carmen—or Danny *versus* Carmen—with Jana looking on. Once Carmen's advocate, now suddenly an impartial referee.

Carmen shrugged. "I don't think there's any . . ."

At the same moment Danny half rose and said, "I really should be . . ."

"Oh, for Christ's sake, sit down," Jana barked, glaring. Danny obeyed—lowering himself slowly back onto his seat—and Carmen laughed.

"Like magic, isn't it?" she asked Danny, her voice conspiratorial. "I don't know how she does it, but it works with the kids, too."

Jana swiveled to face Carmen. "Yeah, the only one it doesn't work with is you."

There was a beat during which the three readjusted. This was, Carmen thought, like those endless shifting alliances you made in high school. Relationships were hard enough when there were just two, but exponentially more difficult when a third party joined the pair.

"Look, I don't want to play life coach here," said Jana. "It's too late in the day and, besides, no one's paying me. But just because you're sick doesn't mean you get to spout total crap. I happen to know that *he*"—she pointed at Danny, as if there were other people in the room to whom the pronoun might apply—"was here over the weekend, checking in, even though you weren't exactly your sex goddess self. And if your husband were still alive . . ."

"What? What if Jobe were alive?" It felt wrong doing this in front of Danny. But it was, after all, Carmen who'd imagined the two men were connected when they met at the restaurant in Federal Hill. Maybe this—her deconstruction of one man in front of the other—was fate. The inevitable outcome of her warped fantasy.

"Why do you think Jobe got involved with me in the first place? Did you ever ask yourself that? I was an impoverished art student with very little talent and a screwed-up family. He was brilliant, he had money, he had parents who"—Carmen swallowed, recalling the way she had lusted after Olive as a girl—"loved him more than anything in the world. There was only one thing I was good for. One. But even that, I didn't do quite right."

"What do you mean?" Jana asked.

Carmen stared into her fleece-covered lap. Which of the two unsaid truths could she finally admit? Which would do the least amount of damage? It was more wrong, she ultimately decided, to trot out Jobe's sexual problems for her lover. "I guess," she said, apologizing silently to her son, "I felt guilty. I was supposed to be the perfect young wife, produce these adorable little babies. And then we ended up . . ."

"With Luca," Jana said.

Carmen nodded but did not look up.

"I always wondered if it bothered you," Danny said after a few seconds of silence. His voice was husky and warm, and finally Carmen raised her head. "But you never talked about Luca. And then when I met him, he just seemed so kind of . . ." Danny, never at a loss for words, paused. "I don't know. Essential."

For the first time Carmen felt simple affection for Danny, along with a pleasant tug of hunger. Whatever had overtaken her was done, she knew; she would be well now, at least until her next treatment. The idea of walking back into that chemo barn—as she'd begun to think of it—terrified her. But that was more than a week away. For now, the three of them were unified again and the attic was cozy and warm.

"When Luca was about three," she said musingly, "this television show came on on Sunday nights about a family with a Down's syndrome son. Remember that?"

Both Jana and Danny shook their heads. "Heartwarming. Not my style," said Jana. "And I'm betting he"—she pointed at Danny—"was way too young."

Carmen grimaced. "Anyway, it was lovely. This really sweet story about a boy who lived above his parents' garage in an apartment. I think he even got married at the end of the show. I can't tell you how many times I've thought: If only that program had been on when we found out. We might have watched it together. It's amazing how much of a difference something like that makes in terms of making you feel normal. As it was, we were just . . . terrified."

They sat for a few seconds in silence. "I'm starving," Jana said. "What's for dinner?"

"How strange! I was about to ask you that," Carmen said.

"Really? You're hungry?"

Carmen nodded.

"Well, hallelujah. Let me go downstairs and see what I can pull together." She stood in a jangling of bracelets and necklace pendants, like the sound of coins tossed in a soft, leather sack. "But don't get used to this. I swear, next time I come over *you're* cooking for me." She bent to kiss Carmen's cheek and into her ear whispered, "Don't break his balls. I think he's really trying."

"I am trying, Car," Danny said the moment Jana was gone. "But I'm in this situation where . . ." He paused and looked in the direction of the window, as if he wanted more than anything to run. "There's no way to do the right thing. I know. I put myself here. I get that. But doing the right thing by you means wrecking my marriage, and I've been such a shitty husband already. I have no clue why I even married Mega in the first place."

"Because she's a knockout?" Carmen tried to make her voice nonaccusing but failed.

"Yeah, probably. I was this geeky Indian guy who hung out with old-lady librarians. Having a hot wife helped my reputation. A lot." He shook his head. "I don't love her, never have. But the way I've gone about this is just wrong. So I'm trying to figure out, you know, what would Jobe—"

"If you say, what would Jobe do," she cut in, "I will murder you on the spot."

He grinned. "Okay. But tempting as it is to play the hero, I don't really have the résumé for that role. And I'm honestly not sure, if we did . . ." He stopped, considered, then went on. "I don't know if, in the end, I'd do the right thing by you, either. Maybe I'm just not built that way."

What a cop-out, Carmen wanted to say. But for once, she didn't. Instead, she looked toward the window that Danny had been focusing on earlier and let her eyes go lazy. Everything blurred, the shadows and lights outside becoming like the streaming, watery scenes outside a moving train. At the edge of her field of vision, Danny rose—a flash of black: black hair, black clothes, black shoes—and approached her. He bent as if to kiss her, the way Jana had, but didn't, only resting his cheek like a grandfather upon her patchy head.

Then he left quietly and Carmen sat still staring through the glass, until Jana shouted up the stairs to say she should come down, the food was done.

Carmen had slept—however fitfully—through more than four days of her between-treatment break, so the third chemo session came upon her before she was ready. But would she ever really be ready?

In the week that she felt strong enough to dress herself, to drive, to attend Michael's beginning-of-the-year open house, Carmen had prepared herself as well as a person possibly could.

She ate her oatmeal each morning with fruit and heavy cream then spent long afternoons sitting in bakeries, sketching idly while she conducted the real business of filling her body with calories: éclairs, prune kolache, napoleons spackled with lemon icing. Jana had shaved Carmen's head the night Danny left—neither of them mentioning him—then given her a neck and shoulder massage so languid that Carmen wondered briefly what it would be like to be Jana's lover instead of her friend. Dr. Woo had told her that hair often was changed when it grew back: curly or gray or pure white. Perhaps some women's sexual preference came back changed as well. *Now that would qualify as a seemingly random event, don't you think?* she had asked Jobe inside her head.

This was happening a lot lately. She spoke to Jobe as easily as if he were an ever-present old friend. And though he never responded —nor had he appeared to her again after that last chemo-laced dream—she felt comforted. As if he were listening. Standing in front of the mirror each morning, she debated her choice of scarves and wrapped her head carefully. She had gotten good at this, making a knot that she tucked into the turban in back. *Ready now?* she would say to her own reflection. And from somewhere the answer would come, *Of course.*

Yet these were lonely days, too. Olive stayed until the end of the first week but announced one morning that she was no longer necessary, missed her own bed, and was going home. The children were absorbed in school. They seemed to have forgotten their mother's brush with death, which Carmen knew was good. But so soon? Michael was involved in two fall sports, which meant he was rarely home for dinner. Luca had his first real job—a stocking position at a suburban Safeway that Olive and his social worker had arranged; afternoons, a bus picked him up for this three-hour shift, and after riding back through rush-hour traffic he, too, often arrived home after seven. Siena was on the yearbook committee, working, and connected to Troy every other minute. Carmen joked to Olive that the two had begun to share a bloodstream. What she did not tell her mother-in-law was that twice she'd come home to a preternaturally silent house, only to find Siena's door closed and little mouse rustles and cries coming from within.

Would a good mother stop her daughter from having sex in the house, and what would be her reasoning? Was it better to chase them outside to get it on in cars and fields and friends' houses, the way Carmen's parents had done? The answer was complicated by an ugly truth: Carmen was jealous. Her fundamental objection—which she admitted only to herself and the Jobe in her mind—was that her daughter had the privilege of feeling things that she, the mother, might never experience again. Heat, wetness, orgasm. It was weird and distasteful to compare their sex lives this way. Carmen wished she wasn't doing it. But there was no getting around the fact that Siena had something she wanted. And not only was Carmen's body like something made of popsicle sticks, but Danny seemed to be gone.

He had not contacted her since the night he walked out of the attic. And to be fair, she had not contacted him. Instead she concentrated her energy on eating, reading, drawing, and sitting with the kids during the odd hours when they ended up at home. The first thing that she allowed to break her routine was the email she received the afternoon before her third chemo session was scheduled to take place.

"Plane from Athens does arrive 3 p.m. tomorrow at BWI airport. Will you be picking up?" It was signed with the initials AM.

She called Olive first. "I'm assuming AM is Althea Markos. Did you arrange this?"

"No, dear. I gave your friend my credit card number and told him to charge a flight. I'm assuming he did. Why don't you ask him?"

Why didn't she? Because despite crow's-feet and cancer she was still, essentially, sixteen years old. And this broke basic rules: calling the boyfriend who'd dumped her. She could not bear to give him the satisfaction.

After saying good-bye to Olive, Carmen sat for a few minutes. *Be a grown-up*, she told herself and solicited support from Jobe. But he was maddeningly silent. Finally, Carmen dialed Danny's number, barely breathing. She pictured him holding his cell phone and watching her name pop up on the screen, shaking his head and pressing End.

"Hello?" She was so surprised to hear him answer, she forgot what she'd been intending to say. "Car, what's wrong? Are you okay?"

"I'm fine. I'm just . . . I got this email today, from that woman, the Greek." This was so jerky and cryptic. Why didn't communicating with men get easier as you aged? "I'm calling because Olive said. She thought you were the one who arranged this and we should . . . talk."

"Yeah, I did. Listen"—he dropped his voice—"can I call you back?"

"Sure," she said, and the line went dead.

Hours passed and she had finally reconciled herself to the fact that Danny wouldn't call back (that he would never, in fact, call again) when her phone rang.

"Sorry. Jesus. I hate this. But I told Mega everything and things are, well, worse." Danny broke off and Carmen reached for something to say, but nothing came. "I've only got a couple minutes," he went on, and she felt a stab of righteous anger—she'd given him hours at a time back when she was still married, even while her husband lay dying—but held herself in check. "I'm sorry. I completely forgot about sending that ticket, what with everything else. But yeah, I talked to her, Althea, and she said she'd come look through Jobe's papers. The interesting thing was, she seemed to know what I was talking about even before I said it. I mean, she wasn't surprised to hear the solution to Riemann might be there."

He'd sounded like the old Danny for a minute, the one who breathed into the phone and talked about licking her until she came. Carmen was caught by this, briefly hopeful. "So what's the plan? I'd be happy to pick her up but I have chemo tomorrow morning, and given what happened last time—"

Danny cut in: "Christ." There was a long dead pause and Carmen wondered if he'd hung up.

"You still there?"

"Yeah, I'm just . . ." His voice was low, furtive. "I'm thinking. I'm supposed to be at an all-day off-site, and I've already missed so much work." Again, there was silence. "Okay, how about we do this? If you can, you pick her up. And if you absolutely can't, call me. Or have someone else call me—Olive. I'll make some excuse."

This was not satisfying. It felt transactional, like a patched-together carpool arrangement made between distant coworkers. Carmen waited but he said nothing else. "Alright," she said. "And Danny?"

"What?"

She filled her lungs with air, with pride. "I hope everything works out." Even she had no idea what she meant by that. *Works out for whom?* But it made her feel better to say it.

When Danny answered, however, she knew this, too, had been a mistake. His tone was even more questioning and miserable, packing infinite discontent into a single word. "Thanks," he said.

When she arrived at the clinic for chemo the following morning, Carmen was, for the first time, showed into a private spot.

"Your doctor's office phoned ahead to say you had a severe reaction to the last treatment," said the nurse as she ushered Carmen and Jana into a stall with a curtain, if no door. "So we're going to keep an extra little eye on you today."

If anything, privacy prolonged the treatment. Carmen waited more than half an hour for someone to come in and insert her IV—and this only after Jana stepped out to remind the staff. "So very sorry, ma'am, I forgot you were in here," said the lovely Jamaican girl who had tamped the needle into Carmen's hand. Her skin was the color of dark chocolate, her lips full as ripe peaches, her hair streaked with gold. When she left, the girl was all Jana could talk about.

"Stunning," she said for the third time. "But I couldn't get good radar on her. What do you think? Straight? Bi?"

Carmen was oddly hurt yet amused by her own reaction. *I really do think I'm the center of the universe, don't I?* she commented to her internal Jobe.

For the first hour, she lay back and pretended to sleep while Jana paged through a magazine and opened the curtain periodically to check for the lush figure of the Jamaican girl. Carmen waited, expecting the poisons to roil inside her and rise up suddenly, causing her to have a heart attack or begin retching blood. But nothing had happened for more than a day last time, she reminded herself. And eventually she gave in, not relaxing so much as resigning herself. Another round of severe dehydration could put her in real danger, Dr. Woo had said at their appointment yesterday. She was to call him the moment something happened. She touched the cell phone at her hip in which she'd programmed his pager number. That was all that could be done.

"So what's up with you and Danny?" Jana asked suddenly.

Carmen peeked out from under her eyelids. "Absolutely nothing, why?"

"I don't know. I just thought you were getting into a pretty deep conversation that night. I guess I kind of wondered what happened, why he left so fast."

Carmen wished that one of them was a knitter. It had been so much easier talking to Glen's wife while her eyes were on her yarn. "He dumped me," Carmen said, holding her face as still as plaster so Jana wouldn't see even a twitch of pain. "Okay, it wasn't exactly like that. There was a lot of stuff about his marriage and how he's trying to do the right thing. But basically, that's the gist. He's gone."

"And you're okay with this?" Jana's eyes narrowed in. She saw. It didn't matter how blasé Carmen tried to be.

She sighed and let go of the last of her false indifference. It was a relief, as with Danny when she had allowed her blouse to slip down and her scar to show. "No, of course I'm not okay with it. But I keep telling myself this is exactly what I deserve. It's like you said a couple months ago: I was supposed to be the good-time girl. No complications, just sex. But then my husband died, I got sick. And to top it all off, I got ugly. Skinny and bald. I suppose that's what I deserve, taking up with a younger guy. I probably look like his"—she gulped before saying a word so terrible—"mother."

For once Jana was hesitant, her words thought out. "I'll admit, you do look different." She glanced at Carmen, checking for a reaction. "Beat up and strung out and not so much old as, well, a little like an alien."

Carmen's neck burned from shame. She poured a glass of water from the plastic pitcher at her side and took small sips.

"But." Jana raised one warning finger. The Rastafarian schoolmarm. "I think you're selling the guy short. I don't get the feeling this is about your hair or your . . ." She motioned up and down Carmen's half-reclining form. "You know, the way you are."

"Excuse me?" Carmen struggled to appear powerful and indignant, which was hard while she was tethered like a trapped animal. "This is a guy with a blow-up doll for a wife. Besides, wasn't it you who predicted he would run for the hills the minute I was diagnosed?"

"Yeah, well, I hadn't met him yet. I was wrong."

I was wrong. It echoed in Carmen's mind. Twice in the past few weeks someone had told her this, when for decades she'd assumed that it was she alone who kept doing things wrong.

"Look at it this way." Jana parted the curtain and peered out for a couple of seconds then snapped back. "Blow-up dolls are only good for one thing. Maybe Danny can't get a jones on for his gorgeous wife."

Carmen had closed her eyes again and the chair felt airborne. Like dying, but in a good way. "Funny," she murmured. "That would be the one thing Mega and I have in common." The next second, everything came horribly sharp and clear. *Had she really said that out loud?* Dammit. She hadn't meant to. "Anyway," she said, opening her eyes, desperate to move on. "How do you know Danny doesn't . . . ?"

"Wait a minute. What did you mean by that?" Jana was staring. "Are you talking about you and Jobe?"

Inside, Carmen was apologizing as if she was praying. Despite Rory and Danny, all those clandestine meetings, this felt like an unforgivable betrayal—even though Jobe had been dead for nearly half a year. She weighed her answer carefully. "My own husband," Carmen finally said, "wasn't able to." She swallowed. "I mean, there were times when it worked. But for the most part Jobe just didn't seem, uh, turned on by me. In the slightest. He couldn't . . ."

"Are you telling me he had erectile dysfunction?" Jana cried, and Carmen imagined the question slipping out under the curtain, bouncing around the room full of dying people. She grinned briefly, then sobered and nodded. "Eight times out of ten. We barely ever. You know. It's a miracle we had three kids."

"Christ, it must be absolute hell to be a man." Jana knotted her forehead, concentrating. "You know what I think? I think Jobe loved you completely—enough to leave you the goddamn key to the mathematical kingdom—and the whole sex thing . . . Well." Jana looked up at the ceiling. "You were pretty attractive in your heyday but let's face it, you were also kind of a narcissistic twit."

Carmen stared. "This is supposed to be helping build my self-esteem, right? It's really hard to tell."

Jana laughed and leaned down to hug Carmen roughly. "See? That's why I keep you around no matter how big a twit you can be."

They settled back into their respective spots, like actors returning to their places onstage. Several minutes went by before Carmen broke the silence.

"I've always wondered," she said, then caught herself in the lie. "No, that's not true. I've only just now thought: It's possible I would have grown to love Jobe, exactly the way Olive said I would, if we'd just kept at it."

Jana cocked an eyebrow.

"Stop it. I didn't mean it that way." Carmen looked down at the crook of her arm, delicate skin bruised purple and green. "Or maybe I did. But the way we were with each other, it became like a habit. And I wonder if somehow we'd have found a way to *touch* each other, you know—literally. Instead of always being so distant and formal."

Carmen thought back to the night of her flu, Jobe's long hand stroking her hair. And a third path unfolded in her imagination: an alternate world in which she moved toward him and he slid his arms around her. Where she was held in the space just under his chin, not just on that long-ago winter night but for years afterward and even now.

"I think—and please don't tell me it's too late, because I know that—but I really think I could have." She paused, startled. There was something at the back of her head, an inexplicable softness cupping her raw and fragile skull. "Fallen in love with him," she finished in a low tone.

Jana eyed Carmen in a challenging way. "Maybe it's not too late," she said. Then she tilted her chair onto its back legs and sat precariously tipped against the wall with her arms crossed.

By the time the nurse finally came to remove Carmen's IV— sadly, for Jana, not the Jamaican but a fretful gray-haired woman— nothing had happened. Carmen considered each part of herself but felt no more light-headed or ill than she had walking through the door. "You call the minute there's a problem," the nurse said, looking at Carmen with dour eyes. Even this did not faze her.

"I think I'm fine." Carmen turned her face to the sun as they walked out of the building. "You can drop me off at home and go back to the café. I know you need to. I'll pick up Althea myself."

"Are you sure? Maybe I should go. Maybe"—she turned to Carmen, leering—"Althea is some hot Greek lesbian. Did you ever think of that?"

"No. I never did," Carmen said. "Tell you what, assuming I don't die in the next couple days, I'll invite you over for dinner. You can figure it out for yourself."

Jana stood on the curb, suddenly serious, assessing Carmen. "Are you sure? I mean, you look fine now. . . ."

"As fine as an alien can."

"Exactly. But something could happen. This afternoon. Will you call me?"

"Yes." Carmen took Jana's arm, like old ladies do, to cross the street. And Jana let her. "I will call if I need you," she said.

As they crossed to the metered spot Jana had run out three times to fill, Carmen tightened her grip. For the first time in her life, the idea of someday becoming that doddering old widow who clutched at her friend's elbow didn't seem so bad.

Carmen waited outside the airport terminal in almost the exact same spot where Jobe had sat in his BMW on that scorching day that she first arrived.

The big difference was that unlike Jobe, she had no idea what to look for. Danny had described Althea as young, a graduate student. But beyond that, Carmen had nothing to go on. She kept looking for lone women, dark ones, emerging goddesses, when there was a knock on her window. Carmen turned sharply, expecting to see a police officer who would order her to pick up her party or drive on. Instead, she looked directly into the face of what appeared to be an Iowa farm girl: plump and rosy-cheeked with wild red hair caught back in a cloth scrunchie—the kind that American women had abandoned fifteen years before. It was only upon noticing this that Carmen realized she'd forgotten to do anything about her own head.

Carmen pressed the button to lower her window and watched the girl's face drain of color. "Apparently, no one told you I've been sick," Carmen said as levelly as she could. "Don't worry. Get in. I feel better than I look." She yanked down the sun shield, lifted her sunglasses, and glanced in the mirror. The woman who peered back at her had a pointy, hairless, ratlike appearance. "Much better, actually."

Althea clumped slowly to the back of the car and lifted the

hatch, shoving two huge bags inside. *Was she planning to stay for a month?* Carmen wondered. She'd forgotten to ask Danny this, too.

They were mostly silent on the drive through rush hour back to Carmen's house. Once, she asked Althea how the trip had been and the girl shrugged then said, "It is okay," in an accent so exotic that Carmen looked directly toward the passenger seat, then remembered she was driving and turned back just in time to brake behind a bus.

"You're not from Greece?"

Again the girl shrugged. "Romania," she said in the voice of a fairy-tale spirit, with the vowels broken in unexpected places and a soft whisper underneath the R and the N. "My mother is Greek, my father Romanian."

It seemed unbelievable to Carmen that this simple person would be able to decipher Jobe's work. She had a twinge of fatigue and wondered, too, if the chemotherapy was closing in and about to make her wretchedly ill.

Thankfully, they had reached the edge of Carmen's neighborhood. "I'm afraid I haven't done much in terms of dinner. I've been out all day. . . ." She stopped, not ready to discuss it with this person. "You'll be staying with my mother-in-law. But she had a commitment for tonight." *Because my former lover made the arrangements to fly you in and communication between him and the mother of the man I cheated on with him has been a little difficult.*

Carmen almost laughed but caught herself. She took a long breath and the cloud of weariness abated. "Anyway, I hope you don't mind takeout."

"I like Wok and Roll." Althea grinned, as proud as a third grader, and her wholesome face lit up, becoming as beautiful as any Greek goddess Carmen could imagine.

"How do you know Wok and Roll?" Carmen turned onto their street.

"From when I live here before," the girl answered, but said nothing else.

They left the suitcases in the car, though Althea removed a small mesh bag from one that Carmen could see contained female supplies: mascara, lip gloss, tampons. She ached briefly to be a woman who needed only those things to freshen herself. Then she followed Althea inside.

Luca was there, waiting in the living room as if he'd known the precise moment they were due. Carmen introduced the two and watched carefully as Althea warmly shook her son's hand with both of hers. There was none of the shock in her face that Carmen's appearance had provoked. Althea must have known about Luca; Jobe must have told her. But Carmen could not imagine a circumstance in which her taciturn husband would be moved to do such a thing.

Siena was out with Troy, and Michael was in his room, playing Halo. It was not quite five o'clock, which felt too early for dinner, so Carmen offered Althea a cold drink and showed her around the main floor, purposely ending her tour in the dining room where Jobe's papers lay in three neat stacks on the table. Althea recognized them instantly and stood as if in supplication. Carmen hung back and barely breathed; she wouldn't have been surprised to see Althea bow or genuflect. "Would you like to look?" Carmen asked.

And despite what must have been a fourteen-hour flight, Althea nodded reverently. She walked toward the table slowly, as if she were approaching something living. Carmen could have sworn there was a glow emanating from the girl.

She left to fetch soda water and took her time preparing two glasses with ice and cutting limes. "Would you like one?" she asked Luca when he wandered into the kitchen.

"Yeth," he said. He stood watching as Carmen filled a third glass and garnished it with two lime wedges. Then, as she handed it to him, he spoke. "I like her."

This was uncharacteristic. Luca rarely offered his opinion, unless asked, and tended not to judge people—good or bad. Still, Carmen had noticed he had an uncanny sense: He had always steered away from Fred Lang, for instance, despite the fact that her boss had oozed interest in Luca's direction. "Why?" Carmen asked, almost fiercely. "Why do you like her?"

Carmen was desperate for guidance. It was imperative that she know whether she could trust Althea, but the girl left her conflicted. One moment Carmen wanted to confide in her, the next she felt something surreptitious. But if Luca liked Althea, that might mean Carmen was imagining the latter. Perhaps chemotherapy had interfered with her ability to read people, the way it had altered her senses of taste and smell.

Luca stared at his feet for a moment then shook his head, like a cow lowing. "Ah don't know," he said. "Ah just do."

Carmen was growing more tired by the second. She had to muster all her will to go into the other room. When she did, she saw that Althea had in that short time completely rearranged the pages, taking some from each pile and arranging them in a circle. The rest she had laid out at various intervals. She raised her head when Carmen came in. "Do you have, ah . . ." She made a pushing gesture with her thumb. "Tape?"

"Of course." Carmen crouched to put Althea's glass on the floor, away from the papers, and was swept with vertigo as she rose. She tilted, spilling half of the other glass she'd been carrying. And suddenly Althea was there, holding her, supporting her with strong farm-worker arms against a soft, generous chest.

"You sit?" she asked, her mouth as close to Carmen's ear as a lover's. Carmen nodded, and together the two propelled toward the large, armed dining room chair at the table's end. Althea lowered Carmen into it, settling her gently. "Here, I take," she said, prying the half-full glass from Carmen's hand.

Once Carmen was settled, her pointy body slumped in the vast chair, Althea left the room and Carmen could hear her talking to someone rapidly. Surely it was Luca, and she was speaking English. But the distance and Althea's accent combined to make it sound as if the words were in a foreign language, some mystical combination of Romanian, Greek, and math symbols. Carmen shook her head, trying to clear it. But now that she was seated, she did not feel dizzy so much as sunk into a thick, golden haze.

Althea came back with a roll of paper towels and squatted, efficiently mopping up the puddle on the floor. She also, Carmen was amused to note, had the Scotch tape in her hand. Either she'd consulted Luca or she'd simply pawed through the kitchen drawers until she found it. Once she'd dried her hands thoroughly, Althea started anchoring down each page with two strips of tape.

"Is it there, the solution to Riemann?" Carmen asked weakly from her chair. "Have you had enough time to look?"

"Of course, it is here." Althea moved around the table and frowned, jumping one paper over another before securing them both down. "But it always is here. We are waiting only for you."

Carmen squinted, having trouble making sense of this. "What are you saying?"

But Althea didn't answer. Instead, she pulled out her cell phone and began taking pictures of the design she'd made.

"I have a digital camera," Carmen said. She had made her decision: Althea was to be trusted with Jobe's work. Whatever clandestine thing she sensed, it had nothing to do with this. "Go into my room. Top of the stairs, to the right. The camera is on top of my dresser. You're welcome to use it."

Althea stood for a moment, hesitating. Then she said, "Thank you," and strode toward the stairs. No one would know she'd been awake for more than a day; or perhaps she was one of those calm, robust people who can sleep on planes.

Carmen pondered the possibilities, and when Althea returned, with the sleek silver camera in her hand, Carmen asked the question that kept blossoming in her head. "Have we met?"

"Yes." Althea hardly responded, and just started clicking pictures. "It is maybe eighteen month."

"Jobe was in remission." Carmen saw a look of confusion and struggled to clarify. "The cancer was . . . on vacation. He was not sick."

"Yes." *Click, click, click.*

"Were you one of his graduate students?" For the first time, Carmen saw Althea wince. But she recovered quickly.

"I am on . . . ex-change." The word clearly was hard for her to pronounce. "For one semester. To work on Riemann." This she pronounced like a song. European names, Carmen mused, always sounded better in the mouths of those from the Continent. It had been that way in Italy, too. *Giovanni. Parmigiana. Ferrari.*

She straightened. Again, she'd been drifting. Now she looked intently at the girl who stood in front of her, dangling the camera by a strap. The truth dawned on her slowly, not coming through the voice that had been speaking since that day in the MRI machine but coming, rather, from her own heart and mind.

"You were in love with him."

It was a ridiculous thing to say. Carmen half expected it to bring a laugh, derision. She was the failing, envious widow, making up stories. On the other hand, if it were true, Althea might tearfully confess. But rather than react in any of these ways, Althea said nothing. She only stood, eyes level. They were, Carmen noticed, an ordinary hazel but glinting with tiny sparks of gold. Also tired.

And in them was some measure of assent, so Carmen went on.

"You were involved with my husband, but he wouldn't . . ." she stopped, not out of propriety but because she couldn't think of a word that Althea would understand. *Consummate? Commit adultery?* "He wouldn't go to bed with you." It was nearly triumphant; Carmen expected perhaps fury, for the girl to storm from the house.

Instead, Althea slowly shifted her eyes down toward the floor and Carmen grew completely still. "He did?" Her hands and feet felt very far away, as if they were floating in space.

Althea nodded and finally, a tear rolled down her cheek. This, Carmen could see, was due more to the fact that the girl had been awake for more than a day and was exhausted. Without thinking it through, she used her foot to push a chair away from the table. "Here," she said gruffly. "Sit."

"We were. Once." Althea knotted and undid and reknotted her hands in her lap. "He know that you have . . . lovers. That you do not like the marriage. We work so late." She was really crying now, and

Carmen, rather than angry, simply felt uncomfortable. Also relieved that someone wept so for Jobe.

"It is spring." Her accent was even harder to understand through the guttural sound of tears. Carmen leaned in, to hear. "We are so . . . close. To Riemann. He think he has the solution. It is." Althea lifted her face to the heavens, as if giving thanks. "And we kiss." She checked quickly. Would Carmen strike her, order her out? "Then we go to my room. . . ." Althea made a strange motion with her fingers, like the children when they acted out itsy-bitsy spider.

Did this bother her? Carmen stopped to check and was genuinely surprised by the answer, which was yes. And it was not only her pride that was hurt. Because inside her, deep down somewhere, was a stinging, regret-filled pain. She put one hand on her stomach as if she could calm it, and strangely this did some good.

"But then, three days later," Althea went on, holding up her thumb and first two fingers, "he come to me and say we cannot. Anymore. He is not presenting Riemann." Althea shook her head.

"Why?"

"Because." She drew a ragged sob. "He say you take care of him, always. You love him. He say it is all his fault. He is too afraid to love you in, ah"—Althea gestured, as if trying to pick words from the air—"many right ways."

And despite Althea's broken English, Carmen could almost hear the echo of Jobe. It was the night they'd bumped into Danny and his wife at the Federal Hill restaurant. After she and Jobe had made love, just as she was falling asleep, he had whispered something in her ear. *What was it?* She concentrated but his voice in her memory was like wind.

She had been exhausted that night, and satisfied. Not as she would have been with Danny—there were no shuddering aftershocks, no ragged breathing—but in the quiet way of a late-night swim. Talking might have ruined it, so she'd curled like a possum and pressed her head against the wiry hair of his chest. All she knew was that he had apologized for something, pulling her ever closer.

"It's okay," Carmen remembered muttering in response. But she had wanted nothing more than to sleep and would have done anything to get him to stop talking, even if that meant letting him wrap his long arms around her and lying snugly inside as if he were holding her in a cocoon. Without thinking about what she was doing, Carmen crossed her own arms around her narrow chest and held herself now.

"So, you left?" she asked Althea, imagining the scene between her husband and his assistant that had followed that night.

The girl shrugged. This was, Carmen realized, a universal symbol of disavowal, one Althea used often. "He will not publish," she said. And this, it was suddenly, luminously clear, was the central issue. Not whether he would divorce his wife and move in with Althea, not whether he loved her. "I leave. He say *you* must decide about Riemann"—she pointed at Carmen—"once he is gone. He will publish only for you."

"Jobe once told me . . ." Carmen's nose wrinkled with the haunting scent of curry. "At least he knew I wouldn't throw out his papers after he died, the way Bernhard Riemann's housekeeper did. I think he was, kind of, *testing* me."

"But see? It is alright. You do not." Althea stood and opened her arm wide, pointing toward the table like a girl on a game show. "The solution, it is here."

"So what do we do with it now?" Carmen reached for the half-full glass Althea had taken from her but before she could grasp it, the girl picked it up and handed it to her.

"There is a . . ." Althea stood, thinking, an exasperated expression on her face. "Prize!" she finally said triumphantly. "The Clay In . . . Insti—"

"Institute?"

Althea nodded. "It is in Boston."

"What kind of prize?" Carmen asked.

"It is one million dollar." The girl's pale eyes shone.

"Would Jobe's name go on the solution? And yours, of course. Could you write it? You can certainly have the prize money."

"Oh, no!" Althea looked horrified, hair coming loose from her scrunchie and electric around her head. "I am tiny part, should have only a few dollar."

"Mom?" Something had just ended on TV and Luca was calling from the other room, no doubt starving.

"We'll deal with that later," Carmen said, rising. She grabbed the table for support but didn't need it. Her legs felt skinny but strong. "You need to eat and get some rest. But can you start on this in the morning?"

Althea nodded. And on the way to the kitchen where she would place an enormous order with Wok and Roll, Carmen reached out to take the girl's arm. "Don't worry. My mother-in-law will be here soon. Jobe's mother. You'll like her. She'll take very good care of you while you work."

April 2008

They flew out on a Wednesday, skimming through the rose-colored sunset, retrieving their suitcases, and emerging from Logan Airport into a windy moonlit night.

Carmen shivered and commented to Jobe that she could feel it, the difference. What was it about location—movement just four hundred miles along the shore of a shared ocean—that made everything seem completely foreign? She closed her eyes and breathed in the diesel fumes from trucks growling along distant highways. This was the smell of her youth, of Detroit, only in Boston it was mixed with magnolia and salt air.

You should be here, she thought fleetingly. *But you are here*, she answered herself.

They were all a bit ragged and weary. The flight had been delayed nearly three hours, during which they had eaten a meal too late to be lunch and far too early for dinner in a crowded restaurant on the main concourse, and Siena pointed out they could have driven half the distance in the time they sat. The food was heavily salted but otherwise tasteless. Yet Carmen ate diligently as she did these days, still trying to pad her body the way a sculptor adds wet clay, one layer at a time, to make a rounder, more voluptuous shape. The room buzzed with an uneven noise. When they finally boarded the plane, Carmen felt the sort of relief one did leaving the dentist's office and entering a quiet car.

Then Siena slept—or pretended to—while Luca stared out the window, riveted by the rushing, darkening sky. Olive ordered a martini that she somehow made last for the entire flight. And Michael, using the laptop Carmen had given him for Christmas, watched half a movie that involved both martial arts and cross-dressing, actually complaining when the plane touched down because he had to turn it off.

Now, standing at the curb, Carmen was suddenly bleary. Her shoulder stung where the strap of her purse cut into it. And getting a taxi to Cambridge large enough for five people and nine bags was turning out to be more difficult than she had anticipated. One after another, the drivers turned them down, pointing to their signs that said, MAXIMUM CAPACITY: 4. And they stood in a clump on the curb, perplexed, until Luca finally said, "Can't we just take two?"

"I am so not the traveler I used to be," Carmen said, hugging her older son. "Thank God you're here."

By the time they reached the hotel it was nearly midnight. Carmen paid for three rooms, handed the key cards all around, trying to keep track of who was rooming with whom and failing (there would be an exchange later), accepted with a weak smile the strapping, elderly bellhop's offer of assistance, and followed him toward the room she'd taken for herself. She was aware, at moments like these, of the now blade-thin division between simply tired and beaten. Once she'd crossed the line, there was only a short time before she was gone.

Her room was small and square. The light coming in through the window was just enough to illuminate its outlines: a low, dark dresser, the angled open door to a tiny bathroom, and a bed that was taller than any she'd ever seen. The bellhop placed her suitcase on the floor and reached for the cord of a lamp, but Carmen put out her hand to stop him and then handed him a twenty-dollar bill. "Ma'am, this is too . . ." he began, but she shook her head and nudged him bodily toward the door. It was like they were dancing and, too tired to speak, she caught his eye. The man chuckled. "Alright, ma'am. My name's Joe. You just let me know if you need anything else."

Once he was gone Carmen shrugged off her purse and sighed with relief. There was a footstool at the side of the bed and she climbed it then sat, dangling her feet off the edge of the bed, leaning over to unzip her black leather boots and letting them fall, each with a soft, carpety *clunk*, to the rug below.

She lowered herself back onto the mattress and groaned. This was like entering another country: something from a fairy tale, a magical, tufted sanctuary enveloping her in pillows and a feather-stuffed duvet. Scrabbling among the softness, Carmen tugged her dress over her head and peeled off her tights and bra. She threw these things over the side, imagining they would waft down and down and down for miles, then slipped naked under the covers and lay curled to the left, stroking her right hip with a feathery touch.

The room was all shifting shadows, its objects hazy as she let her gaze go loose. Only her top arm moved; the rest of her was perfectly still. And the hand she used seemed to draw its energy from some other source, traveling the length of her thigh, crossing the knee, returning up the inner side and finding that place that was, once again, damply warm after months of feeling barren and numb. The fingers moving there, gently circling, felt not like her own.

Sometimes exhaustion helped. It took only minutes to coax waves from her body and they rippled into the first velvety layer of a dream. She could have sworn she heard Jobe—for the first time in so long. *Thank you, Carmen.* Her body lay anchored to the bed, but she strained toward him elsewhere: a place hidden between her heart, her eyes, and her brain. He pushed her back with one golden hand then slipped it under to cradle her sleeping head. *Rest now*, he said. *Tomorrow, you will be fine.*

* * *

The next morning was sharp and deliciously cool.

Carmen awoke all at once and tested her limbs under the comforter, like a creature swimming. Everything, as the voice predicted, had been healed by sleep. She lay considering, remembering. It was a dream. That was the only explanation, really. But she couldn't deny the existence of something left inside her—an iota of light or sound—that hadn't been there before. Mulishly, she spent a few moments insisting to herself that she must stop this nonsense . . . or at least go to an expert (a psychiatrist? a psychic? she could never quite decide) to figure it out.

But after a time, Carmen gave in and lay calm. *You will never quit telling me what to do, will you?* she asked the space above her. *Even if you're only in my head.*

She rose then to put on her robe and made coffee in the little pot that the hotel provided, pouring a cup and taking it to the balcony, a small platform with a waist-high fence around it jutting out over the street. Her coffee balanced on the wide rail, Carmen watched the college town's rush hour traffic—the cars generally smaller and more worn than those in downtown Boston, but just as fervid—dart and angle busily below.

A breeze came up and she shivered, retreating back into her room. This was the longest she'd gone without speaking to another human being since that four-day stretch when she was unconscious. Since that time, the children and Jana and Olive had been hovering close. But now, bathed in silence, Carmen dropped her robe and stood in front of the mirror gazing at herself.

She had gained back more than half of the weight she'd lost last fall but retained a fragile, sparrow-boned look. Her eyes were huge and looked darker than before because her hair had come back in not only curly but a thick, snowy white. It was just long enough now that she wore it in the same style she had when she married: the 1920s bob cut short in the back and angled down toward her chin. Whether she should dye it had been a topic of some discussion; Jana had offered to do rainbow colors. But turning her head from one side to the other in the hotel mirror, Carmen decided that for now she would leave it. She was different and it was right that this would be reflected. Perhaps her body knew what it was doing, even if she did not.

Other things had changed, too. Danny, for instance, had vanished for a time in the fall then appeared at the clinic during the third hour of her final chemotherapy treatment. Olive had accompanied her but must have stepped out while Carmen was dozing, because she had opened her eyes and there he was, materialized at her feet with six miniature roses on a ridiculously large cloud of baby's breath and a tired, worried face.

He had offered Mega her freedom and the house, Danny told Carmen that day. But she had said no. Mega liked being married, the security of it, and to dissolve what they had would mean impoverishing them both. As long as he could behave himself and avoid getting anyone pregnant or falling in love, he was free to do as he liked. But there would be no divorce; he had made a promise and she was holding him to it.

"We could just go back to the way we were," Danny had said.

Carmen, then wracked and sinewy, still bald, with veins standing out at her temples and on her arms, had turned away in disgust. "No, we most certainly cannot," she had answered, and meant it. But when he sat down next to her and took her hand, she let him tuck it into his and together they waited until the poisoning was done.

Later that month Siena had, without preamble, suddenly loosened her clinch on Troy. It took him several weeks to come to terms with this fact, and Carmen spent half a dozen afternoons between Thanksgiving and Christmas counseling Troy after she found him skulking around the outside of the house. He was puppy-sad and bewildered. But once Siena was done with something, apparently, that was that. There was no other boy, Carmen told Troy truthfully. Siena seemed to have turned away from all that completely; she was intent upon finishing her senior year and applying to colleges. She planned to earn a degree in particle physics, hopefully to use her father's work in her own research. Siena, Carmen said gently, had moved on and was planning her own life. Troy must do the same.

Then there was the evening in late January—a low, early, and freakishly balmy dusk—when Dr. Woo had called to tell her that her the latest scans were entirely clean. "No evidence of disease," were the words he used. After thanking the doctor and hanging up, Carmen had turned, dazed, to open the door and walk out into the flat, gray, ever-expanding world. Standing in the yard in front of their house she had faced west, barely registering the forty-degree temperature though her skin was still stretched tight and thin over her bones.

Is it over? she'd asked. *Do you know?* There was no answer, but as she stared into the smudgy sky, a shower of light began cascading in the distance. Carmen blinked, as if to clear something from her eyes, but the continuous twinkling remained. Fireworks, she thought at first, then realized it could not be. There were no hollow booms. Only a low, whispering sound that swirled around her like mist.

Now, looking intently at the woman she had become, Carmen touched the scar that shone like a comet's tail across the top of her left breast.

Later, after she had taken a hot shower and dressed, Carmen assembled everyone for a late breakfast and together—like schoolchildren on a field trip—they trooped through Harvard Square. The day had turned sharp and clear, green grass and brilliant sky. Carmen lagged behind the others as they walked through the yard.

There was a pretzel stand and another stand with kosher hot-dogs, the sweet, greasy scent of the meat filling the air. All around her, college students were clustered. Some sat in circles, discussing intently things from their notepads and books.

In the distance, Carmen spotted two long, denim-clad legs: a tall, bearded young man lying in the grass. She stopped and squinted. She'd forgotten to bring sunglasses and the day was dazzling, the yard like a tableau under the gleaming blue sky. Carmen took a step toward the bearded man and nearly tripped over someone's backpack. "Watch out," Luca said thickly and reached up to grab her arm. And she let him stop her. Luca was right, she thought as she took one last glance at the lone reclining boy. She did not want to go toward him. She did not want to find out if he was real.

Besides, she had promised the children a sightseeing tour before the ceremony, so they went to the Old North Church, Boston Garden, and Faneuil Hall. Michael, always hungry, plowed through a paper boat filled with nachos while they watched jugglers in the square outside. Then he went back into the building and returned with four fat pastries stuffed in a waxed, white paper bag.

"I can't believe you're going to eat that," Siena said as he plucked out his third, a raspberry Danish. "That is so gross."

"Mmm." Michael rubbed his stomach with a circular motion and opened his mouth to show his sister the masticated dough and jam inside.

Luca laughed, then Olive and Carmen did, too. But suddenly she noticed the sun sliding at an odd angle and looked at her watch. "Okay, enough of this," Carmen said. "We have to get back. And you"—she reached up and poked Michael in his ribs, as narrow and rock hard as his father's—"better lay off so you can fit into your suit."

"Not to worry," he said, starting on the fourth pastry.

Indeed, when they showed up in the lobby dressed for dinner, Carmen was startled to see her children so grown-up: the boys in dark jackets with festive red ties (knotted by Olive, no doubt) and Siena with her hair wound regally around her head. Carmen wore a black sheath and golden shawl with her high-heeled boots. She had long ago removed her many rings and now had only her wedding set on one slender hand. When Michael approached, he put out one arm like a sheltering branch and pulled her to his side. She walked with him through the padded skyway and into the banquet room as if down the aisle of a church.

Althea was already there, sheathed in emerald green, a strapless taffeta dress that seemed to Carmen to belie the young woman's status as one of the world's top mathematical minds. But maybe that was the point. When Althea saw them, she hurried over. It had been months since she left their home and she approached Carmen questioningly, her eyes widening. "You look . . . so nice," she said shyly.

Carmen hugged the girl, feeling the strong little back under her fingers. "You, too, honey. Congratulations."

The ceremony was exactly as dry as Carmen had feared, only much longer. It began with an extended cocktail hour with hors d'oeuvres set out on a long table, next to the plastic-encased nametags they were supposed to wear.

"I am *not* pinning this ugly thing to my chest," Siena said at first. But after noticing the postscript beneath her name—DAUGHTER OF JOBE GARRETT, WINNER OF THE MILLENNIUM PRIZE—she changed her mind.

When, after a dinner of lukewarm pot roast and overdone vegetables, the director of the Clay Institute finally announced the prize and said Jobe's name, Carmen heard Olive take a ragged breath and reached down to grab her mother-in-law's hand under the table. It was impetuous; had she thought about it, Carmen never would have done such a thing. But the old woman's fingers closed hard over Carmen's and she held on until the director made his closing comments and sat down.

There were then fully two hours of speeches about Jobe's and Althea's solution. It had been examined literally hundreds of times in the preceding months by mathematicians from dozens of different countries, and proven beyond any doubt. But still there were nuances to discuss—myriad branches of analysis. One after another, men and women rose to talk about the finding's effect on science, on space travel, on the understanding of infinity. And just when Carmen was praying the speeches were finally done, she was asked, without warning, to say a few words.

Rising from her seat, she pulled the golden shawl more closely around her and walked slowly to the stage. Lowering the microphone, she faced the room full of mathematicians, reporters, university officials, and family members. Siena was sitting, as she had at Jobe's funeral, in precisely Olive's straight-backed and refined manner. Michael, Carmen noticed, was gazing at Althea and her cleavage-baring dress with lust in his eyes, and this so surprised her that she nearly laughed. But the impulse faded quickly as she searched her mind for what she would say.

There followed a pause—hundreds of people in front of her shifting like the bits in a kaleidoscope not yet settled—and suddenly Carmen felt herself tumbling into a vast and endless absence. It was as cold as midnight yet bright with sun. She saw Jobe lying on the day bed, no longer breathing. And the pain that struck her was so piercing and new, Carmen thought for one instant that she had cried out. Then, from that podium on the stage of the silent auditorium, she was transported back to that warm January night when she had stood in darkness under a glittering shower of stars.

Carmen blinked and searched the faces until finally her gaze found Luca's—pure and wide open—and she locked on this, drawing from him something she needed, like water or air.

"Seemingly random events provide the structure in any complex system, mathematical or otherwise," she began.

Ann Bauer is the author of a novel, *A Wild Ride Up the Cupboards* (named a best book of 2005 by the *Minneapolis Star Tribune* and *The Providence Journal*), and coauthor of a culinary memoir, *Damn Good Food*. Her essays have appeared in *The New York Times, The Washington Post, Elle, Redbook,* and *The Sun*. From 2006 to 2010, she was a regular contributor to Salon. She lives in Minneapolis.

AnnBauer.com
TheForeverMarriage.com

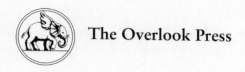

The Overlook Press

The Forever Marriage
Ann Bauer

Readers Group Guide

Discussion Questions

1. Carmen openly wishes for Jobe to die. How does this make you feel? Can you understand the situation, or does it make you dislike her? Does your feeling for Carmen change by the end of the book?

2. The children, Luca, Siena and Michael, are each affected very differently by Jobe's death. Why is this?

3. Danny, Carmen's lover, is both reliable and unreliable. Is he worthy of her—or anyone's—trust?

4. Many people in *The Forever Marriage* are unfaithful to their spouses. Do their reasons seem valid? Are there circumstances in which infidelity is an understandable response?

5. Olive causes a great deal of pain and misery with her well-intentioned meddling. Do you see her as a heroine or a villain in this story? How do your feelings for Olive change throughout the book?

6. Do you believe events such as Carmen and Jobe's marriage, and Luca's birth, were "meant" to happen? Could they have been changed?

7. How do Jobe's mathematical theories affect the characters' understanding of their lives? How, if at all, do they affect yours?

8. After he dies, Carmen, Olive and Luca all dream about or see visions of Jobe. Why did the author include this more spiritual storyline? What does it add to the book?

9. The voice in *The Forever Marriage* is "close-third," meaning it is told from Carmen's perspective and she is present in every scene. Is there any other character whose thoughts you wanted to hear?

10. What is the purpose of Luca's Down Syndrome? How does it add to the novel? Do parents of children like Luca often feel guilty, and how does this affect a marriage?

11. Many other books have focused on the entrapment of a bad marriage, including *Jane Eyre* and *Rabbit, Run*. What's different about this one?

12. Does Carmen fall in love with Jobe at the end? And if so, is this enough? Does the author imply that Jobe's spirit is still around to love her back?